COLD
HEART
CREEK

BOOKS BY LISA REGAN

COLD HEART CREEK

LISA REGAN

bookouture

Published by Bookouture in 2019

An imprint of Storyfire Ltd.
Carmelite House
50 Victoria Embankment
London EC4Y 0DZ

www.bookouture.com

ISBN: 978-1-83888-014-9
eBook ISBN: 978-1-83888-013-2

For Jessie Mae Kanagie

We're blazing new paths on this journey through motherhood.

I love you.

CHAPTER ONE

Josie wriggled beneath her mother's weight, the cold of the tile floor seeping through her thin nightgown. The knife in Lila's hand flashed in the overhead light of the trailer kitchen, and fear stopped Josie's heart for a long second and then snapped it back into a gallop.

"Mommy, no!" Josie choked out.

Lila's blue eyes flashed, and Josie knew at once that her mother was past the point of reason, past the point where Josie's screams could reach her. When she got angry like this, there was no stopping her. She was a storm, and there was nowhere for Josie to hide.

Lila used her free hand to press the left side of Josie's face into the floor. The knife came closer.

"Mommmmmeeeee," Josie wailed. Her limbs shook. She felt a loosening in her lower body, like she might wet herself.

"Shut up," Lila snarled.

From the corner of her eye, Josie watched the silver tip of the blade puncture the skin where her ear met her cheek. Then, with steady pressure, Lila sliced downward. Searing pain shot all the way down Josie's jawline to her chin. She blinked the hot blood from her right eye and screamed, "Mommmmmmeee nooooo! Stop! Stop!"

But Lila didn't stop. She never stopped.

"Your daddy thinks you're so damn special," Lila said, taking the knife away to admire her handiwork. A satisfied smile curved her lips. "You ain't so special. You bleed just like everyone else. He thinks he can just leave me? He thinks he can take you with him and just dump me? Leave me behind? He thinks you're *more* important?"

"Mommy, please stop," Josie whimpered. "Please."

Lila brought the knife closer, touching it to the bottom of Josie's chin where she had left off. "I'll show him. We'll see how special he thinks you are after I destroy this pretty little face of yours."

A hand clamped down on Josie's arm.

"Josie," said a man's voice.

As Lila began to slice again, Josie drew in a deep breath and howled in pain. Suddenly, Lila was gone, and everything went pitch black. A new terror took hold. She blinked but the darkness was complete. Nothing penetrated it. Squirming, Josie felt the scratchy carpet of the closet floor against her bloodied face. "No!" she cried. "Not the closet. You promised, Mommy! Not the closet!"

The man's voice came again. "Josie!"

She stood and pounded against the closet door. "I'm here! I'm in here. Please let me out!"

But the door didn't open. It never opened. Not until Lila said so.

Salty tears streamed down Josie's face, stinging the place where Lila had sliced her. "Please," she begged. "Please let me out."

"Josie. Josie, wake up!"

She shot straight up to a sitting position, arms and legs flailing. Punching and kicking the air around her. Terror tore from her lungs. Her entire body was slick with sweat, wicking her nightshirt to her skin. As her surroundings came into focus, she realized she wasn't in the trailer. She wasn't six anymore. This was her bedroom. She was a grown woman. Lila was in prison, and Josie's boyfriend, Noah, was beside her in bed, reaching tentatively for her.

Josie fought the urge to slap his hand away as the last vestiges of the nightmare left her gasping for breath. It's just Noah, she reminded herself. She blinked rapidly and looked around the room. Noah had turned on the light on his nightstand, and it cast a soft glow across their king-sized bed. The covers lay twisted at the bottom of the bed. Josie's pillow lay on the floor. Noah sat next to her, bare-chested, his brown hair in disarray and his hazel eyes dark with worry.

Josie reached up and traced the thin scar that ran down the right side of her face. It had been a nightmare, but also a memory. One of the worst from her childhood with Lila Jensen. She closed her eyes, trying to slow her breathing. Noah stroked her back.

"What was it?" he asked softly.

Without opening her eyes, she shook her head. He already knew the story. She didn't want to talk about it. "Just a bad dream," she said.

Noah chuckled softly. "Yeah, I figured that part out."

She opened her eyes and looked at him again, disarmed by his smile. She was safe, she reminded herself. That particular horror was in her past.

Noah said, "What can I do?"

"Nothing," Josie said. "I'm going to shower. I'm soaked."

He sighed, put his hands behind his head, and laid back on his own pillow. The clock on his bedside stand read three thirty-two a.m.

In the bathroom, she peeled off her damp nightshirt and underwear and dropped them in the hamper. She ran the water in the shower and studied her pale face in the mirror while it warmed up. It wasn't fair, she thought. She had had to live through Lila Jensen's abuse once; she should not have to revisit it over and over again. But ever since the calls, and Lila's impending—

"No," she said to the woman in the mirror. She wasn't going there. Not now.

But her mind went there anyway because the moment you told your brain not to think of something, that was precisely what it conjured. Josie needed to forget. To lose herself. To give her brain something else to wrap around. Something that would leave little room for bad memories and future worries.

Back in the bedroom, Noah was still awake, staring at the ceiling. He sat up abruptly when he saw her standing naked in the doorway.

"Actually, there's something you *can* do for me," she told him.

He didn't hesitate. In two steps she was wrapped in his arms, every conscious thought subdued by his deep kiss.

CHAPTER TWO

Coffee dripped from the kitchen ceiling. Josie swore under her breath, tore some paper towels from the dispenser over the sink and started mopping up the floor first, then the cabinets, and finally the counter. Then she pulled a chair over and climbed on top of it, trying to reach the ceiling.

Noah's voice startled her, and she nearly toppled off the chair. "Did you say something about the 'damn toaster oven'?" he asked.

She glared at him. "I did. I told you we don't need a toaster oven. We have a toaster, that's good enough."

He stepped further into the kitchen, and she noted his T-shirt and boxer shorts. "You're not even ready," she pointed out.

He motioned toward the brown spots on her white ceiling. "What's going on here?"

Josie got down from the chair and tossed the wad of paper towels into the trash bin. Looking down at her clothes, she decided she could get through the day just fine. Luckily the coffee had only splashed onto her shoes and the bottoms of her khaki pants. No one would be looking at her feet anyway.

"What's going on," she answered him, "is that I made myself a cup of coffee, and then I turned away from the counter and my wrist bumped that unnecessarily huge toaster oven you insisted on bringing, my mug broke, and coffee went everywhere. Literally everywhere. We're going to have to paint the ceiling."

She saw his smile and pointed a finger at him. "Don't you dare laugh."

He covered his mouth with one hand.

She stomped past him, out to the foyer. "I'll get coffee at Komor-rah's on the way in. Now go get ready. I don't want to be late for work on our first day back from vacation."

Noah stood at the bottom of the steps. "You could shower with me. We could have a repeat of last night. It will make you feel better."

He was right, sex would make her feel better, but they didn't have time. "The Chief will be all over both our asses if we're late," she said. "That's the last thing I need today."

The two of them worked for the city of Denton, Pennsylvania's police department—Josie as a detective and Noah as a lieutenant. Their small team did its best to cover roughly twenty-five square miles across the untamed mountains of central Pennsylvania with one-lane winding roads, dense woods, and rural residences spread out like carelessly thrown confetti. The population was edging over thirty thousand—even more than that when Denton University was in Fall or Spring session—just a large enough population to keep their department consistently busy. Josie and Noah had been dating for about a year and a half and had only moved in together a month earlier. It had been more of an adjustment than Josie had thought it would be. She had lived alone for several years now and although she regularly entertained friends and family, living with Noah on a permanent basis required more compromise than she had anticipated.

Ten minutes later, Noah slid into the passenger's seat of Josie's vehicle, the sight of his still-damp, tousled brown hair softening her mood. For a moment, her mind flashed back to the hours they'd spent in bed on vacation—every bit as passionate as last night's activities—and she wished they were back at the beach. With a sigh, she backed the car out of her driveway as Noah buttoned up his Denton PD polo shirt and said, "You know, a toaster oven does a lot more than just a regular toaster."

Josie groaned. "It's too big. It takes up so much counter space."

"Counter space you use for what? All the cooking you do?" He was being sarcastic but not malicious. Josie swatted his shoulder with the back of her right hand.

"Touché," she said.

"I lost the bed argument. You have to give me the toaster oven."

Josie shot him a raised-brow look. "It wasn't an argument. My bed is bigger and newer than yours. It just made sense to keep it and get rid of yours."

They pulled up in front of Kommorah's Koffee and Noah opened his door. "I'll get the coffee," he said. "Then you'll forgive me and agree to keep the toaster oven."

Josie laughed. "Get Gretchen some pecan croissants while you're in there, and I'll think about letting you keep the ginormous toaster oven that does not fit into my kitchen."

"*Our* kitchen," Noah said as he shut the door and jogged into the café.

Ten minutes later, Josie deposited a brown paper bag filled with pecan croissants in front of Detective Gretchen Palmer, who sat at her desk in the Denton PD's bullpen—a collection of desks in the center of the large room on the second floor where officers did paperwork, made calls, and conducted research. Josie, Noah, Detective Gretchen Palmer and their newest Detective, Finn Mettner, had permanent desks, whereas the other desks were shared by the rest of the officers. The receiver of Gretchen's desk phone was pressed to her ear. Her face lit up at the sight of the Komorrah's bag. To the person on the phone, she said, "Can you hold on just a second?"

She pressed the hold button. As she looked up, Josie noticed the deep circles under her eyes. Josie said, "Have you guys been busy?"

Gretchen nodded. "I think this August heat is making everyone crazy. Lots of domestics, a few bar brawls, and some stolen cars. What I've got on the phone is a lot more complicated. You guys want it?"

Noah took a seat at his desk which faced Gretchen's diagonally. "What is it?"

"Couple of bodies in the woods," Gretchen replied.

"We'll take it," Josie said.

Noah laughed. "Not so fast, Quinn. Let's hear more."

Josie said, "Gretchen's been here all night. If she takes it, she'll be here all day too."

"I know," Noah said. "I was joking. Have some more coffee and let's hear the rundown."

Gretchen nodded toward her phone. "The game commission officers have been out inspecting the woods in anticipation of hunting season which starts soon."

Josie said, "State gameland is to the south of us, though. That's Lenore County, not Alcott."

"Right," Gretchen said. "Initially, the wildlife officer assumed it was Lenore County jurisdiction but when he called the Lenore sheriff's office out to the scene, they said it's Alcott County. Guy says where they found the bodies is actually part of Denton."

Josie felt her phone vibrate in the pocket of her jeans. She ignored it, letting it go to voicemail as Gretchen turned her computer monitor so both Josie and Noah could view it. She pointed to a thin ribbon of road snaking through miles of forest marked as State Route 9227. It was a largely rural route that skirted the edge of Denton proper, running north to south through the city into Lenore County below.

Gretchen said, "He says it's right here, a couple of miles from where this route intersects with…" Gretchen put her reading glasses on and leaned closer to the screen. "Otto Road."

"Not sure about the jurisdiction there, but we can figure that out once we see where the actual scene is located," said Josie.

"Homicide?" Noah asked.

Gretchen shook her head. "They're not sure. That's why they want someone to go down there and have a look. I'm on the phone now with the sheriff's deputy from Lenore County. His name's Josh Moore. He says it looks like a couple were camping out in the woods and passed away. He said it's an unusual scene but wouldn't elaborate."

"Hmm," Josie said, studying the screen as the vibration in her pocket started up again.

Behind her, Noah said, "I think your phone is ringing."

Josie pulled out her cell just as the call ended. Her stomach rolled. She knew what number she would see when she brought the notification up. Two missed calls from State Correctional Institute, Muncy. The state's women's prison.

"You okay?" Noah asked as Josie clutched the phone to her chest so he wouldn't see.

"Fine," she said. She pointed to Gretchen's desk phone where one of the buttons blinked orange, indicating that Deputy Moore was still on hold. "Give him my cell phone number. Tell him we'll meet him where Route 9227 meets Otto Road. Then he can walk us out to the scene. Noah, grab some handheld GPS units. We're going to need them to navigate that deep in the woods."

CHAPTER THREE

Josie picked her way around the edges of the small campsite, Noah in tow. Behind him, Lenore sheriff's deputy Josh Moore stood watching. She stopped next to a large red maple tree and wiped the sweat from her brow. Insects crowded her face and she waved them away. Glancing back at Moore, she was surprised to see he wasn't sweating nearly as much as she and Noah were. He was in his mid-forties, Josie guessed, tall and thick like a tree trunk, but obviously fit since he hadn't had any trouble leading them nearly two miles through the forest to this small campsite.

Noah fiddled with the buttons on his handheld GPS device, attempting to zoom out. The device took several seconds to power on and load. Noah grunted in frustration and said, "How far are we from the county line?"

Moore shrugged. "Hard to say. Maybe a half mile. I do believe this is Denton, though."

Josie's GPS unit worked more quickly. She studied the screen and agreed, "It is, technically. We're maybe a quarter mile from the county line. This is our jurisdiction. You were right to call."

Moore said, "Great. I'll be on my way then."

Noah said, "You have something more pressing than two dead bodies?"

Moore gave a humorless laugh. "This isn't my jurisdiction."

Noah pointed toward the other side of the campsite. "You heard Detective Quinn. A quarter mile in that direction is your jurisdiction."

"But the bodies are here. In Denton."

Josie said, "Deputy Moore, I know you have to return to your duties in Lenore County, but could you just give us a few minutes to assess what's happened here in case we need your assistance?"

He gave a slight eye-roll. Noah opened his mouth to speak, but Josie stopped him with a look. "A few minutes," she said to them both and turned back toward the site.

From the treeline, Josie studied the scene. A small blue tent had been erected to her right. One of its flaps had been tied open. From where Josie stood, it looked unoccupied. Several feet away from it, directly across from her, lay the remnants of a campfire: a ring of stones with smoldering wood and ash inside it. Against one of the opposite trees lay a rolled sleeping bag. All around the clearing lay various camping supplies, as though someone had walked around the site with their backpack hanging open, spilling items haphazardly, most of which appeared to be clothing. She could see a pair of bodies in the dirt, a man and a woman, positioned so their feet were near the campfire. Josie took a step closer, her heart taking a couple of uneven beats in her chest.

Walking up beside her, Noah murmured, "They almost look like they're sleeping."

The bodies lay side by side on their backs, their hands clasped together. Josie saw a chunky gold band on the man's wedding finger. They were young, probably not thirty yet. Both were dressed in khaki shorts. The man wore a blue T-shirt with the Nike swoosh logo emblazoned across it and the woman a tight-fitting purple tank top. Their lithe frames and well-worn hiking boots indicated they spent a lot of time outdoors. They hadn't been dead long. Out in the middle of the Pennsylvania woods in the thick August heat, they would have started to smell a lot worse if they had been.

Josie snapped on a pair of gloves and stepped closer to the bodies, kneeling beside the woman's head. She pointed to the woman's mouth. "You can see signs of cyanosis—their lips are blue—and it looks like dried froth on their chins."

Moore took a tentative step from the trees into the campsite. "How long do you think they've been dead?"

"Not long," Josie said. "They haven't even started to bloat yet. In this heat, decomposition would be fast." Gently, she prodded the woman's arm. It was stiff and unyielding. "They're still in rigor mortis." She looked over toward the man and pointed to a blister on his cheek. "Maybe three to six hours?"

Noah looked at his watch. "It's eight fifteen now. So they died early this morning."

Josie sighed and stood up, panning the campsite again. "I'm thinking maybe they ingested something. I don't see any signs of violence. No cuts, scrapes, or bruises. No stab or bullet wounds. No torn clothing."

Noah motioned toward the trail of clothing and toiletries. "What about that?"

"Not sure it indicates a struggle. It could have been one of them looking for something."

Moore's voice came from the trees behind the tent. "Looks like we've got something over here."

Josie and Noah followed the sound of his voice several feet into the woods. Moore covered his nose and mouth with one hand, his eyes fixed on something on the ground. As the smell of vomit reached her, Josie identified several large piles of it scattered among the trees.

Noah said, "Looks like whatever they ingested made them pretty damn sick before it killed them."

Josie looked at Moore. "Can you take another look around the campsite, see if you find any more of this?"

Moore raised a brow. "I shouldn't even be here. I've got work to do in my own county."

Josie smiled tightly. "How about you search below the Lenore County line then? Will that work?"

With a heavy sigh, Moore trudged off into the woods. Josie and Noah went back to the campers.

"If they were sick," Noah asked, "why didn't they just go for help?"

Josie said, "It's at least a two-mile walk from here to any sign of civilization. Maybe they were too ill to move far." She took out her cell phone and tapped in her passcode to bring up the home screen only to see another voicemail notification. She didn't need to listen to it to know it was from Muncy. A flash of her nightmare from the night before rushed at her. She didn't realize she was swaying until she heard Noah's voice.

"You okay?"

Josie looked up to see him staring at her with a quizzical look. She braced herself against a nearby tree and willed her mind and body to obey. This was work. She needed to focus.

"Fine." She held her phone up in the air. "I've only got one bar. Cell service isn't great out here."

"You think maybe they tried to call for help, but their phones didn't work?"

She nodded.

Noah stepped toward the tent, leaning over and peering inside. "We should try to find their phones."

"Wait," Josie told him. "I want to call Hummel and have the Evidence Response Team come out before we start moving things around."

He turned back toward her. "You think this is a homicide?"

"I think it's suspicious."

Noah looked back toward the bodies. "If they were that sick, they would have gone into the tent, not laid down on the ground to die." He hooked a thumb back toward the tent. "I saw one of those portable ceiling fans for tents in there. It probably would have been more comfortable for them in there, as sick as they were."

"That's what I'm thinking," Josie said. She pushed off the tree, testing her own steadiness.

"Maybe it was some kind of suicide pact," Noah suggested.

"Maybe. Or maybe someone poisoned them and staged their bodies like this."

Noah frowned. "Not sure I'm sold on that, but we don't know enough to make that determination."

"Exactly," Josie said. Phone still in hand, she punched in Hummel's cell phone number. He picked up on the fourth ring and she briefed him as quickly as she could, then gave him the approximate location. "Noah will go back out to the road and wait for you," she told him. "I don't have great service out here so call the medical examiner before you leave."

She looked back toward the couple. Noah stood at their feet like a sentry. His face was flushed, a sheen of sweat covering his skin. Josie knew that the forecast called for a ninety-degree day. Very soon, the bodies would enter a more advanced stage of decomposition and it would not be pretty. "I want to get these people out of the woods as soon as possible," she added.

CHAPTER FOUR

It took a half hour for Hummel and the ERT to arrive. Noah walked behind them. Thick clouds rolled overhead from what they could see through the canopy of trees, but the heat only increased. Each person who arrived sported sweat stains on their clothes. "I put an officer out by the road until Dr. Feist gets here. She's right behind me," Hummel told Josie. "She's trying to get two ambulances so we can get both bodies out of the woods at the same time."

Josie glanced over at the dead couple whose skin had started to expand and turn a light shade of green. The smell of putrefaction grew stronger by the minute. "That's a good idea," she said.

Hummel and his team went to work photographing and processing the scene while Josie and Noah waited on the fringe.

"Moore hasn't come back?" he asked.

She shook her head.

"You think he took off? How long does it take to look for vomit?"

"Apparently, a long time," she said.

"What an asshole," Noah groused.

Ignoring him, Josie looked around again. "This is kind of deep in the woods for camping," she said.

Noah pulled out his GPS unit again. "Yeah," he said. "It's weird that they chose this spot." He zoomed out from the red pin only to see miles and miles of green forest around them. "Well, I guess if they wanted to get far from civilization, this is a good spot."

Hummel emerged from the small tent with a backpack in each hand. "I think I've got IDs," he said.

Josie and Noah put gloves back on and walked over to where Hummel stood. He handed Noah one of the bags while he riffled through the other, finally coming up with a man's wallet which he handed to Josie. She flipped it open, found the driver's license and read off the name. "Tyler Yates, age twenty-seven. Lives in Fox Mill."

"Fox Mill?" Noah said. "That's near Philadelphia."

"At least two hours from here," Josie agreed.

"Well, we are on the Lenore County line, and they've got a lot of state gameland. A lot of people hike and camp there," Hummel pointed out. "It's the only thing Lenore County has to offer tourists."

"True," Josie said. She took out her phone and snapped a photo of the driver's license before placing it back in the wallet.

Noah searched through the other bag until he came up with a large woman's wallet. After thumbing through several credit cards, he found another driver's license. "Valerie Yates, twenty-nine," he said. "Same address. Maybe a murder-suicide? Maybe the husband poisoned the wife, then after she passed, he poisoned himself and when he was ready to go, he laid down next to her and held her hand?"

"It's possible," Josie conceded. "We'll dig into their backgrounds when we get back to the station." She snapped a photo of Valerie's license before handing it back to Noah. Then she swiped back and forth between the photos, studying their young, vital, smiling faces. Sadness stabbed at her. They weren't much younger than her and Noah. She wondered how long they'd been married, and if this camping trip had been some kind of romantic getaway. Josie wouldn't have chosen camping herself, but it was cheap and in an area as remote as the woods in which they now stood, it would be ideal for a couple to have some alone time.

"Let me see that bag," Josie said to Hummel. He handed it to her, and she took a quick look through it, finding nothing more than a pair of shorts, two pairs of men's underwear, some deodorant, a lighter, a phone, and phone charger. "We'll need the phone," she said and then handed the bag back to Hummel.

Valerie's bag had considerably more stuff in it—a couple of sports bras, several pairs of shorts, a half dozen T-shirts, underwear, socks, feminine hygiene products, a brush, hair ties, some makeup, a paperback book, and just like her husband's pack: deodorant, a phone and phone charger.

"What are you thinking?" Noah asked.

Josie addressed Hummel before answering Noah. "How did you find these? Were they open or zipped up?"

"Open," Hummel responded. "Just like you see them now."

She looked at Noah. "Maybe they left these bags open, but I'm wondering if someone went through them. Look around. There's no food. No water. No actual camping supplies. No flashlights, no battery packs, no pots and pans, water bottles. No mosquito repellant or sunblock. No first aid kit. No soap or towels or wash-cloths—nothing to wash up with. You don't go camping with a couple of outfits and some deodorant."

Josie handed the pack to Noah and looked behind her at the trail of items discarded around the campsite. More clothing. A couple of toothbrushes. Josie ducked inside the tent and looked around. A small cooler sat just inside. Josie lifted its lid, but it was empty. In fact, the tent held nothing at all save the cooler and two sleeping bags side by side.

"Shit," she said, turning and moving out of the tent. She looked from Hummel to Noah. "We have a problem."

They stared at her, puzzled. She pointed to the sleeping bag rolled up against the tree. "There are three sleeping bags, but only two dead bodies."

CHAPTER FIVE

"We need more units," Josie said, taking her cell phone out. "And search and rescue dogs." She had to walk to the outer edge of the campsite to get a bar to show up on her cell so she could call dispatch again, asking them to send more Denton units and to call the Alcott County sheriff's office and ask for their K-9 unit to come to the campsite as soon as possible. Once she finished, she pocketed her phone and turned to go back into the campsite. The fine hairs along her arms and nape of her neck prickled. The sense of being watched was like cold fingers tracing slowly along her spine. In spite of the oppressive heat, she shivered. Trying to keep her body still, she swiveled her head from side to side, studying her surroundings. There was nothing to indicate another person was nearby, other than her team, of course. Nothing in the woods moved.

Hummel's voice startled her. "Boss?"

She turned and stepped back into the small camping area, tossing her head as if to shake off the strange feeling. Was it sleep deprivation? Leftover anxiety from her nightmare and the phone calls? Or was there someone out there? Someone watching them? It couldn't be Moore. He had walked off in the opposite direction and likely returned to his cruiser to head back to the Lenore sheriff's station. He'd been frustrating but she hadn't felt threatened by him. The other camper, maybe? Or something worse?

She studied the bodies again. Some clinical part of her brain, driven only by evidence she could see, identify, and quantify, told her that there was nothing here to indicate violence. But the deeper, more instinctual part of her brain told her not to dismiss her body's reaction so quickly. Her hand reached for the reassuring weight of the Glock at her hip. The team would find out if there was anyone in the woods soon enough.

"How many guys have you got out here with you?" she asked Hummel.

"Five."

"Send four of them out to search the woods," she instructed. "While you and one other person keep working. This camper could be sick and dying out there. As soon as the other units arrive, we'll send them out to search as well—and we'll need to make sure they've all got their GPS units with them. I want everyone on alert. We don't actually know what's going on here, and I don't want anyone getting hurt. When the K-9 unit gets here, see if they can use the sleeping bag to scent the third camper."

Hummel nodded and then started barking commands to the officers on his Evidence Response team. All but one of them walked off into the woods. Josie said, "Also, look inside the sleeping bag and see if there's anything we can use to identify the missing camper."

"You got it, boss," Hummel replied.

Beads of sweat rolled from the nape of Josie's neck down her spine. Her polo shirt clung to her skin. The August heat was getting thicker by the minute. Overhead, the clouds had turned a deep gray, plump and oppressive. Storms were rolling in. That wasn't good news for their crime scene. She took out her phone again and walked around outside the scene until two bars appeared on its screen. She dialed Deputy Moore's number.

"Where are you?" she asked without preamble.

He sounded annoyed. "I'm in the damn woods looking for puke like you asked."

She wasn't sure she believed him, but it didn't matter now. There was work to be done. She explained what they had found, let him know she'd called more units as well as a K-9 unit, and asked, "Have you had any reports of anyone acting suspiciously in or around the woods this morning?"

Moore said, "Not that I'm aware of, but I can call dispatch to see if they've heard anything and also have someone call the nearest hospital. That's pretty far from here, though."

"That would be really helpful," Josie said.

"I'll head back to my cruiser then and make some calls."

"Some of my people are likely going to be searching for this third camper within the Lenore County line."

She could visualize his shrug of indifference. "Do what you have to do, I guess."

She hung up before she said something unprofessional and then made a call to dispatch, asking them to check for reports of suspicious behavior as well as anyone admitted to the hospital for poisoning on the Alcott County side. She waited on the edge of the scene while Hummel and his colleague continued working. Noah stood beside her. The additional units arrived, and Josie dispatched them to search a wider area for the missing camper.

"The K-9 unit is at least two hours out," Noah said, after making some calls of his own. "But we're due for some pretty bad storms and it's not safe for them to work if there's lightning, so it may have to wait till tomorrow."

"Damn," Josie said. "Yeah, we can't have people out here if there are storms rolling in. Will that destroy the scent trail for the dogs?"

Noah shook his head. "Nope. They said the dogs will still be able to find it, most likely. Water doesn't destroy a person's scent, apparently. The lady also said that time isn't a factor either. They could come tomorrow or two months from now, and the dog should still be able to find and follow a scent."

"We don't have two months. What if this third camper is dying?" Josie complained.

"Two months was just an example. They'll be here in a couple of hours and as long as the weather permits, they'll work. In the meantime, we'll do grid searches. We can get more units and some of the fire department out to search as well."

"That sounds good," Josie acquiesced. She didn't say that they couldn't have grid searches in bad weather either. Her team was doing the best they could, but the last thing she needed was a searcher getting struck by lightning or crushed by a tree branch.

"I found some boot prints," Hummel called from the camping area. "I'm gonna try to get casts of them before the rain washes them away."

"Thanks, Hummel," Josie said.

The Alcott County Medical Examiner, Dr. Anya Feist, arrived, picking her way carefully through the woods. Her silver-blonde hair was tied back in a ponytail. A fine sheen of sweat glistened on her pale skin. Behind her were four paramedics, carrying two scoop stretchers which they leaned up against nearby tree trunks. They hung back, waiting while Dr. Feist got to work. Josie checked the GPS unit, on which she could monitor the other members of the Denton PD as they searched for the third camper. The radios were quiet which meant no one had found anything yet. She looked back toward the bodies to see Dr. Feist kneeling beside Tyler Yates' body, probing his arm for stiffness.

Josie walked up to Valerie Yates' side, across from Dr. Feist, and asked, "What do you think?"

"Time of death probably only a few hours ago. I think it was definitely something they ingested that made them sick and killed them. Perhaps some kind of poisoning. Hummel showed me what you found behind the tent. Whether it's accidental or not isn't really for me to say. That's your job."

Josie sighed. "Yeah, I'm working on that."

"I'll know more when I perform the autopsies. There is this, though."

She leaned over Tyler's body and lifted his large hand, uncovering Valerie's tiny palm that had been clasped inside it. She used her other hand to point to a mark on Valerie's wrist.

"Is that a cut or a brush burn?" Josie asked, leaning in.

"I don't know," Dr. Feist said. "But it's fresh."

"Ligature marks?" Josie asked.

"I can't tell for sure. Like I said, once I get her on the table, I'll have a better idea."

Josie sat back on her knees and examined Valerie's right wrist. "I don't see any marks over here."

Dr. Feist nodded. "Right. It's curious but could be nothing."

"We can revisit it once your autopsy is done," Josie told her.

Josie's phone rang. With mounting dread, she pulled it out and looked at the screen, actually relieved to see that it was Deputy Moore calling her back and not the prison again. She answered and he said, "There haven't been any reports of anyone acting suspiciously around the woods in Lenore County. I also checked with the nearest hospital to see if they've had anyone show up ill like they ingested something poisonous, and they haven't had anything like that in the last forty-eight hours."

"Okay, thanks," she said and hung up.

"Maybe the third camper did the poisoning and took off," Noah suggested, walking up beside her.

"I wouldn't rule out the third camper's involvement in whatever this is," Josie said, thinking of the menacing feeling she'd experienced earlier. "But if I'd poisoned a couple of people, I wouldn't leave evidence of my presence at the scene."

"Good point," Noah said. He looked at Dr. Feist. "Any idea what they might have ingested?"

Dr. Feist stood up and snapped her gloves off. She waved the paramedics over and they began to bag the bodies for transport out of the forest. Josie, Dr. Feist, and Noah stepped aside to let them work. "The only way to find out would be to run toxicology," Dr.

Feist said. "But as you know, that takes weeks, and it doesn't test for plants or berries found in the woods."

"You think it's something they found out here?" Noah asked.

Dr. Feist shrugged. "It seems the most likely explanation. Hummel says there were no prescriptions, illicit drugs, or alcohol found amongst any of their personal effects."

"There's also no food or water," Josie pointed out.

"Maybe the third camper took whatever was here when he or she left," Noah said. "Although it's weird that a couple would be camping with an extra person, don't you think?"

Josie nodded. "I've been thinking that all morning. Noah, you might be right. It would explain why so much is missing—or why the items you'd expect to find at a campsite are not here—and why we haven't found another dead person in the woods near here."

Dr. Feist fanned herself. "The lab will test for the usual stuff—alcohol, opiates, amphetamines, barbiturates, marijuana, that sort of thing, but your best bet is to bag up some of that puke and see if you can find any evidence of unusual leaves, roots, or berries that they might have found in the woods and eaten."

"I think that's Hummel's job," Noah said, wrinkling his nose.

From somewhere behind the tent came Hummel's voice. "Already did it."

"What kinds of plants would cause something like this?" Josie asked. "The sickness, cyanosis, and froth at the mouth? Jimsonweed? Bracken Fern? Foxglove?"

Dr. Feist nodded. "Sure, those. Or hemlock, oleander, water hemlock. There are also plenty of poisonous berries—yew and holly could cause death."

Josie recognized those as well. She'd grown up in the Denton woods and had spent most of her childhood exploring and playing in them. Before she was even six years old, her father had taught her the names of most wildflowers and made her memorize the plants and berries that were toxic to humans. He used to walk her through the forest and test her knowledge. Later, after he died, she used to test her then-childhood-friend, Ray, on which plants and berries were edible and which would make them sick or kill them.

"If I were you," Dr. Feist said, "and I wanted to really narrow it down, I'd search at least a mile in each direction and see if you can find anything toxic that this couple could have easily picked to use in their dinner or put in tea."

Josie nodded. The paramedics began carrying Tyler and Valerie Yates away. Dr. Feist followed. "I'll fast-track their autopsies and let you know if I find anything unusual."

Hummel emerged from behind the tent carrying a large cardboard box. "Boss," he said, walking over to Josie. "You'll want to see this."

CHAPTER SIX

Hummel fished inside the box until he came up with a clear plastic evidence bag containing what looked like a thin gold chain. Josie took the bag in her hands so she could get a closer look.

"Is that a necklace?" Noah asked.

"Yeah," she answered. "Looks like a gold chain with a heart-shaped charm on it." The golden heart was open in the middle and along its edges, small diamonds sparkled. "I would venture this belongs to a woman. Where did you find it? The chain is broken."

Hummel said, "The rolled-up sleeping bag."

Josie and Noah looked at one another. Noah said, "So we've got a husband and wife out in the middle of nowhere camping with another woman."

"Husband and wife are dead, and the woman is missing," Josie concluded.

Hummel said, "Maybe the female was their child?"

Josie thought of their faces and the dates of birth listed on their drivers' licenses. "I doubt that. Unless Valerie Yates gave birth as a teenager, any daughter they might have would have to be pretty young, and I'm not sure they would let a young child sleep out here. Wouldn't they keep her in the tent with them?"

"She could be a pre-teen," Hummel suggested.

"She'd have to be ten to twelve at most," Josie said. "I'm not sure this is exactly pre-teen jewelry, and I'm not sure that, as a parent, I'd let my pre-teen sleep in the woods alone while I was safely tucked away in a tent. There are wild animals out here."

Noah took the bag from her hands and held it up. "It could belong to a pre-teen. Hard to tell if it's expensive or not."

Hummel agreed. "Can't tell if those diamonds are real or not or if it's fourteen-karat gold."

"Okay," Josie conceded. "It's something we can't rule out." Her stomach turned at the thought of a young girl lost and sick in these woods—or worse. Again, for just a moment, the hairs on her body stood on end. Noah smacked his hand against the back of his neck. "Damn mosquitoes," he muttered.

Josie looked around them, studying the breaks in the trees around the campsite, searching for something out of place and finding nothing. She pushed the sensation away. The only thing that tempered her anxiety was knowing there were already searchers in the woods—at least until the thunderstorms came. She hoped they'd hold off another couple of hours. That could make all the difference. "We'll know more when we get back to the station and get some background on the Yates couple. For now, we'll let our team continue the search. Why don't the three of us take a look for poisonous plants nearby?"

Josie began walking out of the camp. Noah lingered, staring at his phone. "Everything okay?" Josie asked.

He looked up at her with a grimace. "I don't really know what I'm looking for."

Josie laughed. "Seriously?"

Noah shrugged. "I played sports."

Josie turned toward Hummel. He swiped sweat from his brow and gave a little smile. "I'm a hunter, so my dad made sure I knew what not to touch and what not to eat pretty early on. I'll stow this evidence and grab a couple of guys to help look."

Josie said, "Thanks, Hummel." To Noah, "Come with me then. I'll give you a crash course."

She and Noah went one way, and Hummel went the other.

They picked through the trees, checking their GPS units as they went to keep track of the area they were searching. Josie said,

"Since we got out here, have you felt like—?" She broke off. What could she say? Like someone was watching them? Like someone or something bad was waiting just out of their sight?

"Like what?" Noah asked.

Josie waved a hand. "Forget it. I'm just tired."

Noah stopped walking. "Tell me."

Josie stopped as well and put a hand on her hip. "If there was someone else out here with us, we would have found them, don't you think?"

Noah shrugged. "If not, we would have found evidence of them. Something they left behind or some trail. Why? You think there's someone else out here? Besides our officers and the third camper?"

"I don't know," Josie said. "No. I'm just—maybe I'm just having an off-day. Let's just keep going, okay?"

"Sure," Noah said. He set off again, Josie keeping pace with him. Beside her, Noah huffed. "I could take my shirt off and squeeze the sweat out."

"I know," she agreed.

Josie glanced over to see him beginning to limp. He had broken his leg several months earlier after jumping out of a burning building. He'd spent two months in a cast and another six weeks in physical therapy, but she knew it still bothered him on occasion. She stopped herself from pointing out his limp, knowing Noah would never agree to go back and wait at the car. She would have to rely on him to let her know when he hit his limit. Either that, or he would be hurting badly the next day.

"Tell me what we're looking for," he said.

She slowed down so he could keep up with her and ran through the toxic plants she knew could be found out in the Denton woods which could cause severe illness and even death: jimsonweed, oleander, foxglove, hemlock, water hemlock. She described each one in detail so Noah would know what to look for and then she moved on to the berries that could have sickened and killed the

Yates couple: American bittersweet, Cotoneaster, holly, juniper, and pokeweed.

Josie pointed ahead of them. "Is that a stream up there?"

"Looks like it," Noah said.

Josie stepped through a line of trees with Noah in tow to see a creek cutting through the forest. She took out her GPS unit. "Cold Heart Creek," she read from the screen. "We're about a half mile from the campsite. This is definitely Lenore County territory." She looked left to right. "This is kind of far, but it's possible the Yateses came out here to get water. Although, if they had, they would have needed a small portable water filter or at the very least, a pot to boil the water in. And something to drink it out of."

Noah used the hem of his shirt to wipe his face. "They could have been drinking the water without filtering it. Although I don't know that that would have killed them so quickly."

Together, they walked along the edge of the creek, small rocks crunching beneath their feet. Josie had a strong urge to jump into it and cool off even though from where they stood, it didn't appear that deep. As if reading her mind, Noah stopped and squatted down, cupping some of the water with his hands and splashing his face. "You think someone was at the campsite," he said. It was not a question.

"Yeah," Josie said. "I think someone took their stuff—whether it was part of the poisoning, or just someone stealing it after they died, I don't know." She didn't say that she thought that person was still out here. Noah was right—they would have seen or heard *something*.

"The bodies could have been staged," Noah agreed. "Someone slips something poisonous into their food or water supply, waits for them to die, lays them out next to one another, hand in hand, and then takes their stuff."

He stood and continued walking. Cold Heart Creek led further south of the campsite, deeper into Lenore County. Josie said, "That is the scenario that's entered my mind, except why would you bother to poison someone just to take their stuff? Someone could have just snuck into the campsite while they slept and taken whatever they wanted. Also, why leave them holding hands? That seems like something only a person who knew them would do."

"So, if this is foul play, we're back to the third camper as a suspect."

Josie sighed. "We just don't have enough information yet."

They walked in silence for a few more minutes until Josie could stand it no longer. She knelt on a large rock beside the creek and threw water on her face and neck. The cool moisture felt like heaven. As she reluctantly stood back up, she spotted a large hemlock plant on the other side of the creek. She pointed to it. "There."

Noah followed her finger. "That would be hemlock, wouldn't it?"

"Yes, it would."

They looked up and down the creek. There didn't look to be a way across it without getting wet. As if reading her thoughts, Noah said, "We might as well just walk across. We're already soaked in sweat. What difference will it make?"

Josie went first, walking slowly and carefully across the creek's rock bed. At its deepest point it only came to her waist. She had to admit, the water felt good, even though she knew she'd be risking blisters on her feet later from walking in wet sneakers and that her wet slacks would be heavier to maneuver in—although if they didn't beat the rain, they'd be soaked anyway.

When they reached the plant, Noah snapped on a pair of gloves, then looked at her. "Did you bring an evidence bag?"

Josie smiled as she produced one. "I got a couple from Hummel, yes. Just a minute though. Look at this."

She pointed to one of the smaller branches. "There's a broken stalk here."

Noah leaned in and examined it. "Take some photos," he told her. "And mark this on the GPS unit so we know how far it was from the campsite."

"Got it," she said, putting a marker into the GPS map and then taking out her phone. She clicked away, taking photos of the hemlock while Noah bagged some pieces of the plant. Josie was putting her phone away when something behind the plant caught her eye. "What is that?" she asked.

Noah pocketed the evidence bag and took his gloves off. "What's what?"

Josie took a few steps. "Behind those trees. There's something shiny. I think it might be a fence."

"Let's look," Noah said, walking in front of her and leading her through the dense copse of trees on this side of the creek bank. Josie estimated it was roughly twenty-five yards from the bank where they'd found the hemlock to the chain-link fence that stretched in both directions as far as they could see. On the other side was simply more forest. Josie walked along the fence until she came to a black sign with red lettering affixed to it that said: "Private Property. No Trespassing."

"Why is there a fence in the middle of the damn woods?" Noah muttered, coming up behind her.

"It's someone's private property," Josie answered, motioning toward the sign. "We should call and ask Moore about it. Might be worth looking into."

CHAPTER SEVEN

Hummel waited for them at the campsite, standing beneath a shady oak tree. The rest of the search had turned up nothing, so Noah gave him the hemlock they had bagged, and Josie released him so that he could go back to the station, log in the evidence, and deliver the specimens to the State Police lab's serology department and the casts from the footprints he'd found to the shoe and footwear department of the lab. The rest of the Denton PD officers were small push pins on the GPS map, meandering through the surrounding forest for miles in each direction. One uniformed Denton officer waited out by the road for the K-9 unit to arrive. So far, no one had found any evidence of the third camper.

Josie and Noah began the slow trudge back to the road where their vehicle waited. "We'll have to see what we can find out about the Yates couple," Josie said. "Do background checks, find some next of kin. See if we can figure out who was traveling with them."

Noah said, "Do you want to call Moore or should I?"

With a heavy sigh, Josie took her phone out. "I'll do it."

He answered after six rings.

Josie said, "We wanted to ask you about a chain-link fence we saw out in the woods. It's on the Lenore County side. Your jurisdiction. Marked private property. Any idea who owns it?"

Moore said, "That property belongs to a commune. They've got about a hundred acres, if I remember correctly. They keep it fenced off."

"A commune?" Josie said.

"Yeah," Moore answered. "A bunch of people live there, grow their own food, that sort of thing. It's been there for years. They call it The Sanctuary."

"Is it a religious thing?" Josie asked. "Or a cult?"

Moore answered, "I'm not sure. I don't know too much about it."

"How do you know it's a commune?" Josie asked.

"My—why do you need to know all this?"

"Because it's close enough to the campsite that the third camper might have made it onto that property. Is there a problem?"

A beat of silence, then a sigh. "No, no problem. Look, it's just a bunch of people living off the land, okay? We never have any trouble with anyone from the place. They pay their property taxes, keep to themselves."

"So they won't be upset if we go talk to them?"

More silence. For a moment, Josie thought Moore had hung up. "You shouldn't bother them unless you have to."

"I have to," Josie said pointedly. "Is there someone in charge there that I should ask for?"

"An older woman runs the place. Charlotte..." he trailed off, and Josie could tell he was mentally searching for the last name. "Fadden. That's it. Charlotte Fadden."

"How many people live there?" Josie asked.

Moore said, "Listen, I told you we don't know that much about it. Last I heard, there were about fifteen to twenty people living there but that was at least ten years ago."

"You were there ten years ago? Was there a crime?"

"No, no. I told you, they don't cause any trouble. I just happened to talk to someone who was living there at that time."

Josie couldn't figure out what he was hiding that was making him so cagey. Had he been a member of the commune at some point?

"Where is the entrance to the place?"

He told her.

"You think you could meet us over there? Make the introductions. We are in your jurisdiction, after all."

"You find any breaks in the fence?" Moore asked. "If there are no breaks, I don't see the point in bothering those people."

Noah, who had been standing at her side with his ear cocked toward the phone so he could listen to Moore's side of the conversation, looked at Josie and rolled his eyes.

Josie said, "I'm bothering those people, Moore. Now you can help smooth the way—this being *your jurisdiction* and all—or I can go over there with just my people. What's it going to be?"

Another heavy sigh. "Fine," Moore said. "I'll meet you there."

The Sanctuary was nothing more than an old farmhouse with white siding that had turned gray with age and harsh weather, and a porch roof that sagged. A short driveway led up to its wide steps, with fastidiously cut grass and small, colorful flowerbeds surrounding the outer edges of the large house. It was old but well cared for. Josie looked around. Toward the back of the house were several older-model cars parked in the grass next to a faded red barn. She caught a glimpse of the fencing behind the barn that snaked into the woods beyond. As Josie and Noah followed Moore onto the porch, she craned her neck to try to get a look around the other side of the house, but all she saw was a large field with rows of planted vegetables. A man and a woman worked among the rows with shovels. They were dressed in baggy khaki pants and faded tank tops, bandanas on both their heads, keeping the sweat from dripping into their faces. Every now and then, they looked up at the darkening sky.

Moore knocked on the heavy wooden door and waited. Josie noticed that the windows were open, the curtains inside fluttering as the wind picked up. No air conditioning. Josie wondered if they had electricity at all.

Noah said, "You sure someone's inside?"

"Well, if they're not, you can go talk to those people in the garden."

A few minutes later, the door creaked open and a woman's pale, thin face peeked out. She was young, perhaps in her thirties, and dressed in faded cut-off denim shorts and a plain white T-shirt. She took one look at the three police officers and said, "I'll go get Charlotte. Wait here."

The door closed. Josie glanced at Noah. Moore turned to them. "They're pretty isolated here. Don't get many visitors."

While they waited, Josie found a rocking chair on the porch, sat down and took out her phone to listen to her voicemail. Sergeant Dan Lamay's voice came across the line, letting her know that there hadn't been any reports of any females wandering out of the woods on the Denton side of the county line, nor had Denton Memorial Hospital had any related cases. With a sigh, Josie pocketed her phone. With the K-9 unit so far out and the storm coming in, they might have better luck figuring out the identity of the third camper by digging into the Yateses' social media accounts, phones, and speaking with their next of kin.

The door creaked open again and Josie jumped up as an older woman emerged, wearing a shapeless blue dress that fell to her ankles, brushing over a pair of sandals. Her white hair flowed down her back in waves. A hemp bracelet circled one of her thin wrists as she extended her hand in greeting to Deputy Moore. A warm smile lit her face. Her cheeks were full and shiny as her crepe-paper skin pulled taut across her cheekbones. Wrinkles creased the corners of her eyes and bracketed her thin mouth. "Hello officers," she said. "Charlotte Fadden."

She shook hands with Noah and then Josie. She took a moment to study Josie and then said, "I'm seventy-two."

"Excuse me?"

Charlotte kept Josie's palm in her own. "You were wondering how old I am. I'm seventy-two. What's your name, dear?"

Momentarily flustered, Josie took a beat to compose herself. "Detective Josie Quinn from the Denton Police Department. This is my colleague, Lieutenant Noah Fraley."

Charlotte let go of her hand, but the smile remained on her face. "Denton? What brings you to my door?"

Josie said, "We just recovered two bodies in the woods just within Denton's jurisdiction. They were camping. The site is about a mile from the fence that surrounds your property. We believe there was a third person with them, a female. We were wondering if you or anyone on your property had seen or heard anything? Have you had anyone come onto the property within the last twenty-four hours?"

Charlotte frowned. "Not that I'm aware of, but come in. I'll talk to some of my people. You'll want to have a look around, I'm sure."

"Yes," Josie answered. "That would be great."

"This is where I leave you," Moore said. He tipped his hat toward Charlotte. "Mrs. Fadden."

She peered at his nameplate. "Officer Moore."

So, they hadn't known one another. Or were they pretending, Josie wondered as Moore walked off to his cruiser and they watched him pull away. Noah grumbled, low enough for Josie to hear, "Guess we didn't need that introduction."

Josie and Noah followed Charlotte into the house, which was surprisingly cool without any air conditioning, through a foyer, and into a large kitchen where two women stood at a scarred wooden table chopping vegetables.

"Ladies," Charlotte said. "These police officers had some trouble in the woods nearby last night. They're looking for a missing woman. Can you gather everyone out by the barn so we can speak to them?"

With nods, the women shuffled out the back door. Josie looked around the room and spotted a refrigerator.

Charlotte said, "We have electricity here in the house. You two must be parched. How would you like some cold water?"

"We'd love it," Noah answered.

Charlotte pulled a large pitcher from the fridge and then found two glasses in one of the cabinets. They stood around the table as Charlotte poured them each a glass of water. Josie had to restrain herself from gulping it down. Smiling again, Charlotte placed the pitcher in the center of the table. "Have more if you'd like. Have you been working outside all morning?"

"Yes," Noah answered.

Josie placed her empty glass back on the table and pulled out her phone. On the way from the campsite to the Sanctuary, she had used a photo-editing app to crop Tyler and Valerie Yates' faces from their drivers licenses and put their photos side by side. She turned her phone so that Charlotte could see the smiling faces of the married couple. "Do either of these people look familiar to you?"

Charlotte studied the photos for a moment, her smile loosening and a small vertical line appearing between her eyebrows. "No," she said. "They're not familiar to me. I don't believe I've met them, but you should show that to the others. Someone else might remember one or both of them if they've ever been here. My memory isn't what it used to be."

Josie texted Noah a copy of the photo before pocketing her phone again. She said, "Deputy Moore told us that you have one hundred acres here."

"We do," Charlotte answered. "Although we don't use most of them. We have our garden, which is quite large, and there is a good deal of land devoted to living quarters."

"Living quarters?" Noah asked.

Charlotte laughed, the sound like the tinkle of windchimes. "Well, that's being generous, I suppose. Our focus here is on nature. We grow our own food and we use the land to sustain us. We don't really have any structures, per se. People live out of tents, mostly."

"What about the rain? Looks like a bad storm is coming in," Josie said.

"I ask that everyone gather in the barn or the house when we get thunderstorms. Simple as that."

"What about in the winter?" Josie asked.

Charlotte's smile didn't falter. "The house and barn are heated. People are welcome to sleep in there during the winter months, or they can live outdoors. There are provisions for camping outdoors in the cold weather, you know. We do have a few small cabins on the back end of the property, but I'm afraid they're not heated and in quite a state of disrepair. I don't believe anyone actually uses them."

"You don't know whether anyone is living in them?" Josie asked.

"No dear, I'm no one's mother. If the others want to use them, they're welcome to, but I don't dole out room assignments." She laughed. "We're all adults here. I was in that area about a month ago, and it didn't appear that anyone was staying in them."

"We'll need to have a look at those, if you wouldn't mind," Noah said.

"Of course," Charlotte said easily.

"What do you do for food in the winter?" Noah asked.

"We have a small greenhouse and we jar and freeze what we can."

"How many people do you have living here?" Josie asked.

Charlotte shrugged. "I'm not sure, to be honest."

"You're not sure?" Josie said, unable to keep the incredulity from her voice.

Charlotte laughed again. "Detective Quinn, people come and go from here as they please. We call it a sanctuary because we want people to feel free to come when they need to and leave when they want to. I've owned this property for decades. I've never felt any need to keep a log of people's comings and goings."

"Do you have some kind of vetting process?" Josie asked. "How do you know you're not letting someone dangerous onto your property?"

Charlotte reached over and poured more water into Josie's glass. "The people who come here are not the kind of people who would harm others. They come here because they're looking for peace."

"How can you possibly know that?" Noah asked, exasperation evident in his voice.

Charlotte was unfazed. "When we have a new arrival, I interview them. They stay here with me in the house for a few days. I have a series of sessions with them where we discuss their background and their needs. Then we tour the property, and I show them how they would be living. If it appeals to them, they stay for a bit. If it doesn't, they leave."

"Have you ever had to turn anyone away?" Josie asked. "Or throw someone out?"

"No, not in all these years. It's really quite extraordinary, isn't it? But I believe that the energy we put out into the world is returned to us on some level. I've only ever put positive energy out there and that seems to be what I attract to my home."

Josie and Noah exchanged a skeptical look. Josie asked, "What is it that you offer people who find their way here?"

"Whatever they need," Charlotte answered cryptically.

Noah said, "What do most people need?"

Charlotte answered easily. "Retreat. Refuge. The world is unkind. Here they find a place of peace where they can move at their own pace. They have food and shelter. I provide guided meditation and talk sessions for people dealing with psychological trauma. We don't allow drugs or alcohol so there's no concern about that. Most people just want to come here to be their most authentic selves without judgment."

"How do people find out about this place?" Josie asked.

"If you're wondering whether I recruit, I don't. I never have. It's simply word of mouth."

"Have you always lived here alone?" Noah asked.

The skin around Charlotte's eyes tightened. "This was my husband's land. He was older than me. We married when I was nineteen and I was thirty-two when he died of a heart attack. Then I went through a rather extensive grieving process that involved a lot of drink. Five years later, I met a woman at a bar looking to escape a violent home situation, and I offered her refuge here. She stayed with me for many years before she went back into the world again, and we invited a few more women as the years went by. Eventually, people just started turning up on my doorstep. It grew from there."

"Do you have any lifers?" Noah asked.

Charlotte gave him a quizzical look. "Lifers? You make it sound like a prison."

Noah cleared his throat. "I just meant any people who don't intend to leave?"

Charlotte nodded. "We have several people who seem very settled. But as I said, I don't keep track. I don't find it to be necessary."

Josie walked over to one of the windows and looked outside where several scruffily dressed people had gathered at the doors to the barn. "You're seventy-two," Josie said. "What happens to these people when you pass? Do you have children?"

Again, Josie saw the tension behind her smile. "No children. When I die? Well, I suppose it ends, doesn't it? Nothing can last forever."

"Do you have a will?" Noah asked.

"Well, that's a bit outside the purview of your inquiries today, isn't it, Lieutenant?" Charlotte said. The words were sharp, but her tone stayed the same—calm and kind. She pointed to the back door. "Shall we go speak to the residents? Show them your photo and find out if any of them have seen your missing camper?"

They followed Charlotte outside where roughly thirty people now sat and stood in the grass in front of the barn. Josie was going to ask if that was everyone but knew Charlotte would just say that she didn't know. As they walked, Josie spoke in a low voice to Noah. "I want the names of every person here, dates of birth, how long they've been here, and whatever else you can get out of them."

"Got it," Noah said, pulling a small notebook out of his jeans pocket.

CHAPTER EIGHT

As Josie and Noah spread out among the group, Josie noted that most of the people were between the ages of twenty-five and forty-five. Only a handful of people appeared to be over fifty. Most of the Sanctuary members kept their eyes on the ground or somewhere besides Josie and Noah. The ones who did look directly at them did so with wary eyes. Josie wasn't sure if it was the heat of the day or something else that made the majority of them seem almost zombie-like, their expressions blank. No one smiled. It seemed odd to her that a sanctuary that was supposed to be a place of peace and refuge was filled with people who looked so miserable. Momentarily, Josie wondered if they were all on drugs. Something homeopathic, maybe? Or perhaps it was just that the police presence made them uncomfortable.

She walked over to a tall man who looked to be in his mid-twenties with locks of blond hair shooting over a bandana he had wrapped around his forehead. Josie extended a hand. Nervously, he wiped his own hand on his cut-off jeans and shook, his grip limp. "I'm Detective Josie Quinn," she said. He was at least a head taller than her, but when he didn't look at her, Josie leaned in and looked up into his face to meet his eyes. "What's your name?"

He had blue eyes. "Tru," he said.

Josie took out her notebook and marked it down. "Tru?"

"Truman," he said. "You know, like Truman Capote or Harry Truman?"

"Got it," Josie said. "What's your last name, Tru?"

"Dreyer."

"And how old are you?"

"Twenty-six."

"How long have you been here at the Sanctuary?"

"About nine months, maybe."

His gaze wandered back to the patch of dirt between them. Josie wondered if his robotic answers were a result of his own uneasiness or if he'd been coached to say as little as possible to law enforcement.

"Where did you live before you came here, Tru?"

"Lewisburg."

That was almost three hours north. Josie looked around, noticing Charlotte's watchful eyes on them. "Why did you come to the Sanctuary?" Josie asked.

"I wanted to get back to nature, you know?"

Josie said, "What did you do before you came here? Did you go to college?"

He shrugged. "A little, you know. It wasn't really for me. I like—I like it here."

It certainly didn't seem that way to Josie. She glanced over at Noah who was talking to a young woman in a faded red shirt and khaki capri pants. Her hands were folded at her waist and, like Tru, her eyes downcast and her answers almost monosyllabic. It was strange, women usually responded to Noah, with his affable, sweet nature and easy good looks.

"What do you do here, Tru?" Josie asked, turning back to the man.

"I, uh, maintain the grounds sort of. Like keeping the grass down in the common areas."

"You must need a riding mower for that," Josie remarked.

"No, no. We have push mowers."

From where Josie stood, she could see that a great deal of the land was carefully tended. It would take days to mow it all with push mowers. Then again, with nothing to do but grow food and tend to the property, they probably had plenty of time to slog through a job like that. "Where do you sleep, Tru?" Josie asked.

He motioned behind him where a field stretched toward a tree line. Various colored tents peeked from beneath the trees.

"In a tent?" Josie clarified.

"Yes."

She put her notebook away. "Were you sleeping in your tent last night?"

He nodded.

"Did you hear anything during the night?"

Now he looked at her. "Like what?"

"Anything unusual? Someone in the woods. Someone getting sick. Someone calling out."

"Oh, uh, no. I slept all night."

"What time did you go to bed?"

"Oh, I don't know. We don't have clocks here. We go by the sun."

Of course.

Josie took her phone out and swiped until she found the photo of the Yates couple. She showed it to Tru. "Have you seen either of these people before?"

He studied the photos briefly and shook his head. "No. I haven't. I don't recognize them."

She put her phone back into her pocket and wiped more sweat away from her eyes. "How often do you leave the Sanctuary?" she asked him.

His eyes snapped back toward her. "What?"

"How often do you leave here?"

His eyes were wide and earnest. "Oh, I don't. I haven't left since I got here."

"Why not?"

"Well, I don't want to leave."

"You ever check out the woods beyond the fence?"

"No," said Tru. "There's no need to. Charlotte says it's state gameland. We try to stay out of the way of hunters and stuff."

She thanked him for his time and moved on to the next person, a woman named Jeanne Downey, in her forties, from Pittsburgh. She kept her answers just as brief as Tru. She'd been here for five years having struggled with opiate addiction after a back injury. She helped cook meals and mend clothing and tents. She stared at the photo of the Yates couple slightly longer than Tru had but then shook her head. "Never seen 'em," she said. "We done?"

"Not yet," Josie said, taking her time putting the phone back into her pocket. "Where do you sleep, Jeanne?"

"House."

"What time did you go to bed last night?"

"Don't know a time. It was after dark. After dinner."

She took her through the same questions she'd asked Tru, but the woman hadn't seen or heard anything unusual, and she said she'd never been beyond the fencing. The moment Josie thanked her for her time, Jeanne walked off at a brusque pace, headed for the house. Next was Megan Rodriguez, a twenty-nine-year-old nurse from Hazelton who had struggled with fibromyalgia as well as depression and anxiety until she found the Sanctuary.

"Since I came here, I haven't had any pain," she explained.

"What would you attribute that to?" Josie asked.

Megan's hands fluffed her long brown hair, lifting it off her neck and letting it fall. "I think the work Charlotte does with me."

"Which is what?"

Her eyes went everywhere but Josie. "Yoga. Meditation. Also, we eat what we grow. I think the diet agrees with me."

"How long have you been here?"

"A little over a year, I think. It's hard to tell, but I came last spring and now it's summer again."

Megan was the commune nurse, helping tend to people's scrapes and bruises; evaluating whether members needed more care than she could provide; driving members to the local hospital or clinic if necessary; dispensing medication but nothing stronger than Motrin or Tylenol. She slept in one of the tents, didn't leave the commune, and hadn't heard anything unusual in the last twenty-four hours. She did not recognize the Yates couple.

Josie looked over at Noah again who was busy questioning a sullen-looking African American man with his arms crossed defensively over his chest. Noah gave her a quick glance back and a barely perceptible shake of his head as if to say that he wasn't getting anything useful either. With his pen, he gestured toward the barn doors where Josie thought she caught a movement just beyond the darkness of the open doors. She thanked Megan for her time and casually made her way over.

It was only slightly cooler inside the barn than outside. In the stalls where livestock would usually have been kept were cots with pillows and light blankets folded neatly on each one. The hay stores up in the loft were filled with cardboard boxes, and dull light leaked from a hanging lightbulb in the middle of the space. Josie blinked as her eyes adjusted. Slowly, she walked along the row of stalls. Only the last one on the left was occupied.

The woman was young, maybe nineteen or twenty, Josie estimated. She sat on the edge of the cot, hugging herself. Behind her lay a rumpled sheet. Her brown hair was dull and fell in limp waves against her shoulders. Her skin was so pale, she looked nearly translucent.

She didn't look up when Josie walked into her private space. Instead, she began to rock gently back and forth, eyes on the wall across from her. A tan, long-sleeved man's shirt covered her upper body and oversized khaki pants stretched to her ankles, bunching over a thick pair of boots.

"I'm Detective Josie Quinn," she told the girl quietly.

The rocking stopped. She glanced up at Josie. She had blue eyes and a constellation of freckles along her right jawline. "Charlotte said to talk with you," she replied flatly.

Josie took another small step forward. "Did she tell you what to say?"

There was a sharpening of her gaze, microscopic, but Josie caught it. "Wh-what?" she stammered.

"What's your name?" Josie asked.

"Renee."

"Renee what?"

"Kelly."

"Well, Renee Kelly, it's nice to meet you."

The girl looked away and shifted her arms, uncrossing and recrossing them. Josie caught a flash of what looked like spots along the sleeve of her left arm. Dark. Red or brown. "Did you hurt yourself?" Josie asked.

Renee's eyes flashed. "What?"

Josie took yet another step so that she was standing directly in front of the girl and pointed to her sleeve. "That looks like blood."

Renee lifted her arm, saw the spots—Josie counted six of varying sizes—and then quickly pressed her arm against her body so that the stains were no longer visible. "I—I didn't."

"Did someone else hurt you?" Josie asked.

No response. Tentatively, Josie sat beside Renee. She waited for the girl to recoil but she didn't. Their knees touched for a moment, and Josie let out a breath and relaxed her posture, trying her best to give off a calm vibe. Two women just chatting.

Josie looked around the stall. "Is this where you always sleep?"

Renee nodded.

"I'd rather be in here than in a tent. Who are your roommates?"

She rattled off a few names that Josie didn't recognize, both male and female. Josie said, "Is it weird sleeping in here with men?"

Renee shook her head. "It's fine."

"I'm from Denton," Josie told her. "How about you?"

"Cherry Hill," she mumbled.

"Is that in New Jersey?"

A nod.

"How old are you, Renee?"

"Nineteen."

She was talking, at least.

"Do you like it here?"

A vigorous nod.

"I guess I can see the appeal," Josie said. "It's beautiful. Quiet. Getting back to basics, back to nature. Not sure I could stop my mind from racing though. I have a real problem with that."

Josie saw the smallest curve of a smile begin to form at the corner of Renee's mouth. "Charlotte says you guys do a lot of meditation. I've never tried it. Does it do any good?"

Renee met her eyes. "I think it does. I like the guided meditation the best. If I don't have a guide, my mind goes right back to circling."

Josie laughed softly. "That sounds like the kind for me too. It seems like everyone has a job here. Garden, kitchen, lawn care. How about you?"

"Oh, I help in the garden or in the greenhouse."

"What brought you here?"

"I felt like I wasn't really doing anything with my life. I couldn't afford to go to college. I was working a bunch of crappy jobs that I didn't like for almost no money. I got arrested for a DUI and someone in my counseling program told me about this place. It sounded perfect."

"Has that been your experience? Would you say it's perfect here?"

Her arms wrapped more tightly around her body. The rocking began once more. When Josie touched her shoulder, she flinched. "Renee," Josie said softly. "If there's something happening to you that you're not comfortable with, I can help you. You can walk out of here with me right now."

Nothing.

"I can protect you."

A whisper slipped from Renee's lips, barely audible. Josie couldn't be sure exactly what the girl said but she swore it sounded like, "No you can't."

"We don't have to talk here," Josie whispered, standing up to look over the other stall walls to check they were still alone. She extended a hand to Renee. "Come with me. We'll go for a walk or a ride if you'd like. I can tell there's something bothering you, Renee. I'd like to help."

A long awkward silence stretched out between them. Josie said, "Want to show me your arm? I could get some bandages from Megan."

"No, no," Renee said quickly. "Please."

Josie waited another minute, but Renee didn't speak again. Her rocking continued unabated. Finally, Josie took out her phone and pulled up the photo of Tyler and Valerie Yates, turning it toward Renee. "Do you recognize either of these people?"

She studied the photo for a few seconds and shook her head. "No. I'm sorry."

"Did you see or hear anything unusual last night or this morning?"

"No."

Josie pointed to the loft area above Renee's stall. "What's up there?"

"Supplies. Medications, old clothes, extra cots, blankets."

"Do you mind?" Josie said, pointing to the ladder.

Renee shrugged.

Josie put her phone back into her pocket and climbed the wooden ladder. The heat in the loft pressed in on her as she walked carefully around to ensure that no one was hiding there. She flipped open a few of the boxes and found that Renee was right. It was merely a storage space for supplies. Back on the barn floor, Josie studied Renee again. She thought about giving her a business card, but she wasn't sure that would do the girl any good.

"Renee," she said. "When people come here, what do they do with their cell phones?"

"We destroy them."

"What if you have an emergency?"

"We have a few drivers who can take people to the hospital. Don't get many emergencies though. Since I've been here, we only had one guy rupture his appendix. Megan took him to the ER. He was fine."

"What if you wanted to leave?"

"Charlotte or someone else would take us into the nearest town and drop us there."

"Do you want to leave?"

No answer.

Josie took out a card anyway and placed it in the girl's lap. "My cell phone number is on there. If you're in trouble and you're able to get to a phone, call me. Any time. Day or night."

Renee stared down at the card, her expression wavering from flat to distressed to hopeful and back to vacant. Josie turned to leave. As she reached the barn doors, she thought she heard Renee's voice again. "Th-thank you."

CHAPTER NINE

Outside, Noah was still interviewing Sanctuary members. A light touch on Josie's shoulder drew her attention, and she turned to find Charlotte standing close behind her. "Detective, one of my people tells me there is a breach in our fencing. He discovered it a week ago. Would you like to see it? I can walk you there while your colleague has a look around the property?"

Noah was only a few feet away, and Josie caught the warning glance he gave her. But she felt no threat from Charlotte. The woman was odd, for sure, but Josie couldn't see Charlotte attempting to harm her while Noah was on the premises, even though Josie was certain that something bad was happening to Renee Kelly. She couldn't prove it, but even if she was right, she doubted that whoever was hurting Renee would attempt to harm either Josie or Noah, especially since they'd shown up on official police business. A glance at the sky left her unsettled, but she hadn't heard any thunder or seen any flashes of lightning, so she still had time to search. "That would be great," Josie said, then loudly so Noah would overhear her, she added, "My colleague will have a look at the greenhouse and those cabins you mentioned."

"Of course," said Charlotte. She extended an arm, motioning toward the grassy field on the other side of the barn. Josie began to walk through the grass. Ahead of them, a line of trees came into view. As they walked closer, Josie could see several small tents erected beneath the shade of the trees. A few people had even put up clothes lines between the trees where their threadbare clothing hung. There were some camping chairs and a hammock. Josie did a quick count, noting about fifteen tents in all.

"Not all of them stay in the tents, as I said," Charlotte said. "We have the house and the barn."

For a fleeting moment Josie wondered if the woman was psychic—or was Josie just that easy for her to read?

"It's bothering you, isn't it?" Charlotte asked.

"What's that?" Josie replied without meeting the woman's eyes.

"I see your questions on your face."

Josie managed a tight smile. "I didn't think I was that transparent."

"I imagine you're not. I've had a lot of practice reading people. I hope you don't find it too intrusive."

"It's fine," Josie said.

As they picked their way past the tents and into the woods, Charlotte said, "Some of the residents share tents. I don't encourage relationships, but I don't discourage them either."

"There are no children here, are there?" Josie asked.

"I do discourage children. I have no experience with them, and I'm not sure this is the best place for them. I work with adults who are working through serious personal and emotional issues. If someone is ready to have a family, they don't belong here."

"If one of your people got pregnant, would you make them leave?" Josie asked.

"Not until they had somewhere to go. I'm not cruel. I would work with them in any way I could to make sure they had somewhere safe to go."

"Have any of your people ever gotten pregnant?"

"A few, over the years. It always worked out."

"As far as you know."

They were deep in the forest now, and Josie no longer had a clear view of the sky beyond the tree tops. She wondered how many miles she'd walked today so far. It felt like a hundred. She and Noah still had so much work to do when they got back to the station. Hoping to speed up the process, Josie walked faster. Charlotte kept up easily, and with some irritation, Josie noticed she wasn't even sweating. A few minutes later they came to the fence. Charlotte pointed to the left and Josie began following the fence in that direction, pulling out her GPS so she could see how far they were from the campsite—roughly four miles.

"How much longer till we get to the break?" Josie asked.

Charlotte smiled serenely. "Not much. You don't enjoy being out here? You spent a lot of time in the wilderness in your youth, didn't you?"

Josie raised a brow. "Figuratively or literally?"

"Both."

"Yes," Josie said. "I did. No, I don't enjoy it. I don't enjoy this heat, it's going to storm soon, and I have a lot of work still to do today."

"Is that all?" Charlotte asked.

"Is what all?"

"There's something else, isn't there? You're... struggling with something."

"I'm not..." But Josie didn't finish the sentence as her nightmare and the missed calls from Muncy prison came rushing back at her.

"I may be able to help you," Charlotte said. "If you'd like to talk about it." She stopped walking. Josie took two steps ahead of her before realizing she had paused. She turned back to find Charlotte staring at her with an unnerving steadiness, her dark eyes pensive pools. "It's to do with that wilderness, isn't it? The dark time in your youth. Figuratively."

Josie felt an involuntary shiver run the length of her spine and hoped Charlotte didn't sense it. She was beginning to feel completely disarmed and thrown off by this strange woman who smiled as though she knew something Josie did not, who didn't sweat in ninety-degree weather, and who seemed to know Josie's thoughts before Josie had time to articulate them. "Listen," Josie said. "I'm here as part of an investigation. We have two dead bodies and a missing female who may be ill. I don't have time for this."

Charlotte remained in place, still as a statue. "You've never made time for it, don't you see that?" She took a step toward Josie and touched her cheek, where the long, faded scar ran from Josie's ear to beneath her chin. She wanted to recoil, but her feet were frozen in place. "Now things are coming to an end of some sort, aren't they? Whatever it is, you'll only have one chance at it, and you're wondering whether you should take it or not."

Finding her composure again, Josie took a step back, away from the woman. "Mrs. Fadden," she said. "I need to focus on this investigation. Please just show me the break in the fence, would you?"

Charlotte gave her a knowing smile that only stoked the irritation growing inside her at the woman's overly familiar behavior. Trying very hard to keep her expression blank and professional, Josie watched as Charlotte turned and led the way in silence. Ten minutes later, they came to a portion of the fence that was bent into a V shape.

"Looks like a tree fell on it," Josie said. "Did anyone remove a branch?"

"It's certainly possible," Charlotte said. "We do use any branches found on the forest floor for firewood. We store it up for the winter."

"How long has it been like this?" Josie asked.

"Oh, we don't know. Could be weeks, could be months. As I said, one of my people just mentioned it to me, but he wasn't sure how long it's been like this. He only noticed it a week ago."

Josie sighed. She could find nothing suspicious about the damaged fence, but she snapped some photos of it with her phone anyway and marked it on the GPS map, noting it was nearly four miles from the campsite.

"Mrs. Fadden, we've got a K-9 unit en route to try to locate the missing female. The dog and handler may need to access your property. Would that be okay with you?"

"Of course, dear," Charlotte answered with a smile. "Anything we can do to help."

The faint rumble of thunder sounded in the distance. Before they started back to the farm house, she fired off a text to Noah. *Headed back now. Hope you're ready. Need to get the hell out of here ASAP.*

CHAPTER TEN

In the car, as they left to return to Denton Police headquarters, Josie put the air conditioning on full blast, turning the vent nearest to her so that it blew the icy air directly into her face. She groaned with pleasure as she weaved through the narrow rural roads, leaving Lenore County behind and entering south Denton. The sky had gone almost black with the impending storm. Thunder boomed in the distance.

Noah ran down the list of people he had interviewed. There were twenty-seven in addition to the people Josie had spoken to. Their ages ranged between eighteen and fifty-three. They'd been living at the Sanctuary anywhere from three weeks to seven years. They came from all over the state and others came from Maryland, Massachusetts, and Virginia. Each of them had sought out the Sanctuary after struggling with something in their lives: addiction, domestic violence, homelessness, depression, or just a general sense of aimlessness. All of them had given the shortest possible answers to Noah's questions. None of them recognized Tyler or Valerie Yates. None of them had heard or seen anything suspicious or unusual in the last twenty-four hours.

"I think they might have been coached," Josie suggested. "The girl in the barn—Renee Kelly—I think someone is hurting her." She recounted the encounter for Noah.

"You think whatever's going on with her had anything to do with the Yates couple or our missing camper?"

Josie sighed. "I don't know. Not without getting more out of her."

"You think you could get her to talk?"

"Given enough time, out of view of the others, yes, I think so."

"We might have to come back then," Noah said. "Depending on what else we find."

"There's a lot we don't know yet. We really need to dig into the Yateses' lives, see if we can figure out the identity of this missing camper, and I want to talk with Dr. Feist when she finishes the autopsies."

"What the hell was going on with that Fadden lady?"

"I don't know," Josie said. "She's very odd." She wanted to tell him her suspicions about Charlotte being some kind of psychic—even though Josie didn't believe in psychics—but then she'd have to tell him about the calls from Muncy prison. Instead she asked, "Do you think I'm easy to read? Like, can you tell exactly what I'm thinking by looking at my face?"

Noah laughed. "No. I mean, I probably can most of the time just because we spend so much time together, but you're not an open book. Why?"

"Oh, no reason. I was just curious. Did you find anything when you were looking around?"

"Nothing of interest at all. I mean, I don't know how those people live like that, but I didn't find anything that seemed connected to the investigation. We should have some units come down here and do a more thorough search of the entire hundred acres, though. I asked and Charlotte agreed to that."

Lightning flashed in the sky. Several seconds later, there was a sharp crack of thunder.

"Yeah, she agreed to letting our K-9 unit on the property as well," Josie said.

"They seemed pretty open. Cooperative."

"Charlotte did," Josie agreed. "The others seemed... so out of it. Either that, or they were coached."

"Well, yeah, there was that. Certainly none of them were volunteering anything. But they did make it pretty easy. Answered all questions, showed us around anywhere we wanted to look. I checked out the greenhouse. Nothing there. The cabins are practically falling down. No signs anyone is living in them. I don't think the third camper made it onto the commune."

"Me neither," Josie said. "But it's so close to the campsite, I don't think we can ignore it."

Raindrops began to fall on the windshield.

"Of course," Noah said. "I'll see if the units searching around the campsite can go over to the commune before the end of the day. Also, I called Mett while I was waiting for you to walk back. He ran the Yateses' names through the Penn DOT system and found a black 2017 Jeep Grand Cherokee registered in Tyler Yates' name. Moore said his team is going to see if they can locate it in Lenore County. Mett called dispatch and had them put out the word on the Denton side that we're looking for it."

"Great," Josie said. "What about their phones? Did Hummel get into them?"

"No," Noah said. "They're password protected, but Mett's writing up warrants to send to their phone carriers to see if we can access whatever's on them."

"Next of kin?" Josie asked.

"Dr. Feist is looking into it."

The rain began to fall harder and faster. Enough for Josie to turn her wipers on.

"Any chance you contacted the Fox Mill Police Department?"

"To see if Tyler and Valerie Yates had been reported missing?" Noah said. "I did. You were in the woods with that Charlotte woman a long time."

"I know," Josie said. "What did Fox Mill PD say?"

"Neither of them has been reported missing."

"Not surprising," Josie mused. "Their camping trip was probably planned. When we talk to their next of kin, we'll find out more. Social media accounts?"

"Didn't have time to look at those yet."

Rain poured down steadily now. Josie turned up her wiper blade speed, eyes straining to keep focused on the road ahead of them.

"We'll do it as soon as we get back," she said.

"After we eat. I'm starving."

"We'll order food," Josie agreed. "We can get something from that—"

Her words were cut off. Her knuckles suddenly went white on the steering wheel, and she swerved wildly to avoid a woman stumbling into the middle of the road.

"What the hell?" Noah said. He put both hands on the dash as Josie braked abruptly. She pulled the vehicle over onto the shoulder of the road and threw it into park.

"Did you see that?" she asked as she threw open her door. "That woman. She came out of the woods. Come on."

They raced out into the rain and back into the road to where the woman was now on her knees on the double yellow lines that ran down the middle of the tarmac. She was young. Her wet brown hair was long, tangled, and matted with twigs and leaves. Her skin was deeply tanned and streaked with dirt. The soles of her feet were black with bruising and a crust of dried blood. For a moment, Josie was confused. She was certain she hadn't hit the woman, so why had she fallen? Had she slipped in the rain? But as they drew closer, Josie saw that she was curled around her distended abdomen, both of her hands clutching the fabric of her saturated threadbare, plain shift dress where it gathered between her legs. She was pregnant. Very pregnant.

"Miss?" Josie said as she approached, shouting to be heard over the steady thrum of the rain. "Miss?"

The woman let loose a howl so loud and high-pitched that it startled both Noah and Josie.

"Let's get her out of the road," Noah said.

They each took one of the woman's arms. At first, she flailed against them, but then another howl tore from her body. As they dragged her toward Josie's vehicle, Josie noticed the bright red blood flowing down the insides of her legs.

"Good lord," Noah said. "What happened to her? Miss? Miss? Can you tell us your name?"

As they reached the rear of her vehicle, Josie popped the hatch. "She's having a baby, Noah."

He stopped, stunned. "Right now?"

"You didn't notice her belly? Help me get her into the back."

The woman grew heavier as another contraction took her, and she tried to curl into herself.

Noah said, "Well, yeah, but I didn't think— She's having a baby right now? We need to call an ambulance."

"And we will," Josie said, straining under the weight of the woman. "But help me get her into the back of the car so I can have a look at her. Noah, please."

They turned her back toward the opening of the rear of the vehicle, and each of them hooked their arms under armpit and thigh, lifting her quickly so that she was seated in the hatchback. The open hatch offered blessed cover from the sheets of rain falling down on them. In the distance more thunder cracked, and the black sky turned white with lightning.

"Miss!" Josie shouted over the woman's groans, trying to get her attention. But her eyes had glazed over.

Noah was on the phone with dispatch asking for an ambulance and trying to pinpoint their location.

"We're on Route 9227," Josie told him. "About three miles outside the Lenore County line. Mark us on the GPS unit and they'll be able to find us."

She didn't keep much in the back of her vehicle, just emergency items: a flashlight, portable car jumper, some bungee cords, a jack, a portable air pump, a blanket, and some paper towels. The only things of any use at the moment were the paper towels and blanket. The woman thrashed as Josie tried to put the rolled-up blanket behind her head.

"Miss," she said again, yelling over the sound of the rain pounding on the car's roof and open hatch.

The woman's eyes finally landed on Josie. They were wide with terror. "Help me," she said.

"We're going to help you," Josie told her.

Noah stepped forward and leaned in toward her. "Miss," he said. "What's your name?"

Josie held up the paper towels and pointed toward the woman's groin. "I need to have a look, okay? Try to clean you up a little? See what's going on?"

But as another contraction slammed into her, she reached out and grasped Noah's shoulder, pulling her into him. "Help," she screamed. "Help!"

Alarmed by the rate at which her contractions were coming, Josie snapped on a pair of gloves usually used at crime scenes and gently pushed the woman's knees apart. She lifted the hem of the woman's dress and pushed it toward her protruding abdomen. Josie used a wad of paper towels to clear some of the blood and fluid from her inner thighs. She wasn't wearing underwear. As Josie gently spread the woman's legs further, she gasped.

"What's the matter?" Noah said.

The woman now had his neck fully circled in her arms, pulling him off-balance. He was ash-white. Rain rolled down his nose and dripped into the woman's face.

"We don't have time to wait for the ambulance," Josie said.

"What? What the hell are you talking about?"

"The baby is crowning."

"What do you mean, crowning?"

Josie gave him a sharp look. "Noah," she snapped. "This baby is coming right now. I need your help. Push her leg up toward her head, would you?"

When he hesitated, Josie took one of his hands and fitted into the space behind the woman's knee. "Push," she told him. "Get it as far up toward her head as you can."

"Help," the woman screamed again.

Josie was counting in her head. The next contraction was seconds away. She reached up and pried one of the woman's arms from Noah's neck. Inches from the woman's face, Josie looked into her eyes. "The pain is going to come again," she told her. "When it does, I need you to push. As hard as you can. Do you understand? Push."

A long second ticked by and then the woman nodded vigorously. Josie lifted her other leg, pointing the knee toward the woman's head, and placed the woman's free hand on it. "Hold here," Josie told her.

The woman did as Josie said and with her other hand, she dug her fingers into the back of Noah's neck. He winced. Her eyes squeezed shut as another contraction began. "Push!" Josie shouted. "Push!"

The woman bore down, screaming with the effort. The baby's head pushed out, and Josie guided it along until the entire skull was in her palm. She glanced back up at the woman who was watching Josie with something that looked like horror. "Stop pushing! Stop!" Josie shouted. The tension drained out of the woman's body for a moment. Josie used a finger to clear mucous from the baby's mouth. She didn't have a bulb syringe, so this would have to do. She tried not to think about how unsanitary the entire scenario was; instead, she smiled at the woman. "Good," she said. "Very good. Get ready to push again, okay?"

The woman nodded. Then her gaze went toward Noah. Her hand slipped down to his shoulder and she fisted his shirt sleeve. He smiled reassuringly at her, and Josie saw her face go from a momentary calm to excruciating pain as another contraction set in. Josie tapped the woman's leg. "Time to push again," she said. "Push, push, push!"

She bore down again and this time, the baby's shoulders slipped out.

"One more," Josie said. "One more big push."

But the woman seemed not to hear her. Her eyes were focused on Noah. "Again," he told her. "You have to push again."

She seemed to understand, squeezing her eyes shut once more and half-grunting, half-screeching. A second later, the rest of the baby slid out and into Josie's waiting hands. She fitted one palm beneath him, and she used her other hand to clear his airway again. "It's a boy," she said.

"A boy," Noah said, looking from the baby to the woman's face. "A boy. It's a boy."

Josie kept trying to clear his airway, but there was no cry. He didn't move. In her hand, his little face began to take on a bluish hue. "Oh Jesus," she said. "Noah, something's wrong."

She laid the baby down on the floor of the hatchback next to his mother—as far as the umbilical cord would reach—and started to give him compressions with her index and middle finger. She fitted her mouth over his, gave him two rescue breaths and then resumed compressions. The mother's leg came down, bouncing off the side of Josie's body.

"Noah!" she shouted.

He reached across and gripped the woman's other leg, pulling her toward him and keeping her limbs from hitting either Josie or the baby. Josie repeated the compressions and rescue breaths again. Adrenaline coursed through her body. Sweat mixed with the rain and poured down her face. "Come on, little guy," she urged the baby. "Breathe for me. Breathe for me, baby."

Finally, the baby's limbs began to move and shift. Josie continued to rub his chest, trying to stimulate him further. Relief flooded through her as his mouth opened wide, and he sucked in a long, stuttering breath that he then let loose in a cry loud enough to rival his mother's. Josie scooped him up and held him against her.

"Should we cut the cord?" Noah asked.

"I don't know," Josie said, raising her voice to be heard over the baby's cries. "I think we should wait for the ambulance."

"What the hell is that?"

Josie looked down to where Noah pointed between the woman's legs. "That's the placenta," Josie said. "It's okay. It's supposed to come out."

She cradled the baby against her, looking into his tiny face. "Want to see your mom, little guy?" she whispered.

She looked up at the mother, ready to hand over her son only to see that all color had drained from her face. She tried to catch the woman's gaze, but her eyes rolled back into her head. Her death grip on Noah loosened and her arms fell slack to her sides. Blood began to pour from between her legs. Far more blood than could possibly be normal.

"Oh God," Josie said. She held the baby out to Noah. "Take him."

"What's wrong?" Noah asked, taking the baby in his hands, careful to maneuver the umbilical cord out of Josie's way.

"She's hemorrhaging," Josie said. She ripped off several paper towels and stuffed them between the woman's legs, but the blood kept pouring out. Josie reached behind the woman's head and extricated the blanket. "I can't stop this," she said. "She needs medication, a transfusion, something. Goddammit, where is that ambulance?"

Her words were swallowed by another jolt of thunder, followed quickly by a blinding flash. They had to get out of here, but all Josie could think of was keeping this woman alive. She kept the blanket pressed against the woman's pelvis with one hand while she reached up and felt her throat for a pulse. It was thready but still there. Lightly, she tapped the woman's cheek, trying to bring her back to consciousness. "Miss," she called. "Miss!"

Panic was starting to well in Josie's chest when she finally heard the wail of the ambulance siren. She left the woman unconscious in the back of the vehicle with Noah standing inches away, clutching the screaming infant, and went out to the road, waving her gloved, bloodied hands over her head to draw their attention.

They pulled over and two paramedics jumped out. Josie gave them a rundown of what had just transpired while they worked on mother and baby, loading them quickly into the ambulance and speeding away.

Noah stood on the side of the road, arms at his sides. The rain fell in torrents, soaking him completely. But he remained unmoving, staring at the back of the ambulance as it receded from sight.

Josie slammed the hatchback closed, leaving the mess inside. She couldn't worry about that now. "Let's go," she told Noah.

He didn't move, didn't even look at her.

"Noah, come on. We'll follow them to the hospital."

When he still didn't move, Josie hollered. "Noah, now!"

His eyes snapped toward her. He blinked and walked slowly toward the passenger's side of her vehicle.

Josie didn't wait for him to buckle his seat belt before tearing away, racing after the ambulance.

Noah said, "You just delivered a baby."

Josie said, "I know. We'll talk about it later."

CHAPTER ELEVEN

By the time they reached the hospital, some of Noah's composure had returned. Josie found a parking spot in the Emergency department lot, and they got out and walked toward the entrance where the ambulance was unloading mother and baby. Noah said, "How did you do that?"

"Do what? Deliver a baby? That's my second one. I did it once before when I was on patrol. Years ago."

"Really?"

Josie smiled. "Yeah. It's not ideal, but it happens."

"How did you know what to do?"

Josie shrugged. "The first time I did it, there was a more experienced officer with me. He's been retired for a while now, but he had done it a few times. He talked me through it. Afterward, he explained a bunch of stuff to me about childbirth. It helped that he had seven kids of his own and had attended all of their births."

They slipped inside the hospital doors, the cold air hitting them almost like a wall, freezing them now that they were soaked all the way through. "You think that was the third camper?" Noah asked.

"I don't know. She was nowhere near the campsite, and I'm not sure a woman that pregnant would go camping, miles from any help should she go into labor."

"Weird though, isn't it? We're looking for a female we think might be wandering around in the woods and then this lady stumbles out?"

"I don't normally believe in those kinds of coincidences," Josie said. "But I can't see her traveling that far from the campsite barefoot while in active labor. She came out of the woods almost ten miles from the Yateses' campsite."

Once past the security desk, they saw a doctor and nurse wheeling the baby down the hall in a bassinet. Noah raced over to them, flashing his badge. The nurse paused to look pointedly at the water dripping off him and pooling on the floor, but he didn't seem to notice. Over his shoulder, he said to Josie, "I'll go with him. Make sure he's okay."

"I'll see how the mom is doing," Josie replied.

As she walked down the hall, she found an unattended linen cart. She took a moment to use a clean towel to pat herself dry as well as she could. She found a laundry bin, deposited the towel into it and moved on. She found the baby's mother in one of the ER's private rooms, hooked up to an IV. A nurse hung a bag of medicine while another nurse hooked several leads onto her body to measure her heart rate as well as a blood pressure cuff and a pulse ox clamp on her finger. She had regained consciousness, though her eyes were hooded and sluggish. A doctor worked between her legs. He looked over as Josie walked in. "Heard you delivered her baby in the backseat of your car."

"The cargo area of my hatchback," Josie corrected.

"She doesn't have any tears. You did a good job."

"I didn't really do much," Josie said. "That baby was coming with or without my help."

The doctor laughed. "You probably saved her life—and her baby's—it's a good thing you were there. What do you know about this woman?"

"I know she just had a baby," Josie said. "That's it. We couldn't get anything out of her at the scene. How's she doing?"

"She had a small post-partum hemorrhage. We're administering some medication, running some tests. She may need a transfusion, but we need more information before we do that. We'll be admitting her." He pointed to her feet. "She's got some nasty lacerations on her feet."

"I saw that," Josie said. "She wasn't wearing any shoes when she came out of the woods."

"And she's got some scarring on her wrists," the doctor added.

Josie stepped up toward the head of the bed and looked at the woman's wrists. Thin, silvered scars encircled them. "I didn't notice these before," she told the doctor. "They look old."

A nurse on the other side of the bed squeezed the woman's shoulder. "Miss," she said gently. "Can you tell me your name? Miss?"

She didn't answer, didn't even look in the direction of the nurse. The doctor pulled a sheet up to the woman's waist and picked up her chart from the bottom of the bed without opening it. "I need a name," he said. "Miss? Can you tell us your name?"

Still, there was no response from her. Her eyelids fluttered. The nurse checking her vitals punched some buttons on the monitor over the bed. The woman looked over at the nurse, as if noticing her for the first time. "Help," she croaked.

The nurse was turned away from her, but she said, "We're helping you now, hon. Can you tell us your name?"

"Maybe we need some neurological tests," the doctor said with a frown.

Josie remembered that the woman had responded to her and Noah in the car during the birth. But only when Josie had been looking directly at her. "No," Josie said. "Wait a minute."

She squeezed the woman's hand and waited until her head turned in her direction. Josie made sure to look directly into her face when she said, "Can you hear me?"

The woman slowly shook her head.

Josie nodded. "Can you hear at all?"

A nod. "Not well," the woman said.

"But you can read my lips," Josie said.

Another nod. Then, "Is my baby okay?"

Josie smiled. "Yes. He's okay. They took him to the NICU. The Neonatal Intensive Care Unit. My colleague is with him now."

"A boy."

"Yes."

She closed her eyes momentarily, and Josie waited while she took several deep breaths. Josie noted that although she clearly didn't hear well, her voice had normal tone and inflection, and wondered when and how she had lost her hearing. When the woman opened her eyes again, they were brimming with tears.

Josie said, "My name is Josie. Detective Josie Quinn with the Denton Police Department."

"Denton?"

"Yes," Josie replied. "Can you tell us your name?"

"Maya Bestler," she said.

At the foot of the bed, the doctor jotted it down.

Josie asked, "Maya, what were you doing in the woods?"

The monitor emitted a small beep. Maya said, "I was taken."

"Taken?" Josie asked.

More beeps sounded from over the bed. "Her blood pressure is dropping," the nurse announced. "So is her heart rate."

Josie said, "Maya, what do you mean you were taken? Can you tell me what happened?"

But her eyes closed, her head lolling. The doctor had abandoned her chart and now pushed Josie out of the way. "I'm going to have to ask you to wait in the hallway, Detective."

Josie didn't argue. She backed out of the room while the doctor barked orders at the nurses. A security guard walked by, staring at her with wide eyes. She looked down at her clothes and realized that she must look like someone had dragged her behind a car for two hours. Her clothes were wet, rumpled, stained, and streaked with dirt, blood, and afterbirth. Had it really only been a matter of hours since she and Noah argued over the toaster oven? She proceeded down the hallway to the waiting room but thought better of actually sitting in one of the chairs. Instead, she found a cove next to one of the vending machines where she wouldn't scare anyone by sight and called the station, asking to be put through to Detective Finn Mettner's desk.

"Mett," she said when he answered.

"The K-9 unit has been called off because of the storm. Also, I've got nothing on the Yates vehicle," he said without preamble. "I think you'd have better luck in Lenore County. They probably went into the woods from there. Those state gameland areas have parking lots for hunters, hikers, campers, and such."

"I'll check with Deputy Moore," Josie said. "But listen, I've got something else I need you to look into for me."

"You find the third camper?"

"No, not exactly."

She told him what had happened on the way back to Denton. There was a long silence when she finished. Josie spoke into it. "Mett? You there?"

"Uh, yeah. I'm here. Sorry, I just—she had a baby in your car?"

"Not really the point, Mett."

"I know, I know. Sorry."

"Can you just look her up? She's probably mid-twenties. I'll interview her more extensively later when she's stabilized, but it would help if you could get me any background you can find."

"Sure thing, boss."

"It's just Josie," she corrected but he had already disconnected.

CHAPTER TWELVE

Noah stood outside the window of the NICU, staring at the small bassinets lined up on the other side of the glass. He looked only marginally better than Josie—not covered in quite as many fluids as she was—although the smell emanating from him was enough to make her gag. She could only imagine how badly she smelled. They would need showers before they returned to the station. She walked up beside him and followed his gaze, reading the small placards affixed to each bassinet until she found one that read: Baby Doe. Of course, they hadn't yet gotten word that the woman's name was Maya Bestler so they would have been referring to her as Jane Doe and her baby as Baby Doe. The staff had swaddled him in a white hospital blanket. Wires poked out from the bottom of his blanket, attached to a machine next to his bassinet. A small blue hat circled his head. Only his pink face peeked out, at peace now that he was warm and dry.

"You okay?" Josie asked Noah.

He cleared his throat. "You were amazing back there."

"Thanks," Josie said. "I'm just glad we were there to call 911."

He gave her a quick glance and for a second, she thought she saw tears in his eyes. "I didn't know it was like that."

"What?"

"Birth. I didn't know. When my sister had her baby, we weren't there. We just went to see her afterward."

"Well, I'm pretty sure you don't get to be in the delivery room unless you were an active participant in making the baby," Josie joked.

"You know what I mean. I've never seen anything like that. It was… amazing."

Josie felt a small bud of discomfort bloom in her chest. "Uh, yeah, it was," she said. "How is he?"

"They said he's stable. It could be apnea of infancy or bradycardia. Or it could just be a one-off thing. No underlying condition. It's too soon to tell. They've got him on a heart and lung monitor. They'll keep him here, watch over him, run some tests."

"That's great," Josie said.

"He's cute, isn't he?"

"He sure is," she said. "I got the mother's name but not much else." She kept talking, bringing him up to speed, until she realized that he wasn't listening. She put a hand on his shoulder. "Noah."

He looked at her again. "Yeah?"

She started to speak but her phone buzzed. It was Mettner. She swiped "answer" as Noah went back to staring at Baby Doe. "What've you got, Mett?"

"You're not gonna believe this, boss."

"Believe what?"

"You sure this lady said her name was Maya Bestler?" Mettner asked.

"I'm sure, Mett. Just tell me."

"Maya Bestler is a missing person."

Josie remembered Maya's words before her vitals had dropped: *I was taken.* "How long has she been missing? Where from?"

"She went missing from Lenore County two years ago. Get this. She was camping in state gameland with her boyfriend, whose name is Garrett Romney. Romney said that sometime in the evening during their second night in the woods, he blacked out. He woke up the next morning with a minor head injury, and his girlfriend was gone. That's all I've got so far. I'll dig up more, but I just thought you should know right away."

"Yes, thank you," Josie said. So Maya Bestler was not the third camper missing from the Yates scene, which meant another female was still out there somewhere—exposed in the middle of a raging thunderstorm.

"Where were Bestler and Romney from?" she asked.

"Doylestown," he said.

"That's a couple of hours away," Josie remarked. "Not the same place the Yates couple came from. Not far from them, though."

"Right," Mettner agreed. "I did some quick searches. Couldn't find any connections between Bestler and the Yates couple. But like I said, I will keep digging."

"Great," Josie replied. "See if you can get Bestler's driver's license photo and text it to me, would you?"

"Sending it over now," he said.

"Also, see if you can find anything on where Bestler went missing as compared to where the Yates couple were found, too, would you?"

"You got it, boss."

"One last thing, keep me up to date on the progress of the K-9 unit, okay? We've got to get cleaned up and then we'll be back at this."

"I'm on it," Mettner promised.

She ended the call to see Noah still in place, unmoving, his eyes locked on Baby Doe. Her phone chirped with Mettner's text message. She pulled up Maya Bestler's driver's license. Her hair had been darker when the photo was taken but there was no mistaking her. The woman who had given birth in the back of Josie's vehicle was the same woman who had gone missing from a campsite two years earlier.

Josie walked back over to Noah and took one of his hands, lacing her fingers through his and tugging him toward the doorway. "Noah," she said. "We have to go. We need to shower and eat. Then we have a lot of work to do. Come on. I'll catch you up on what Mettner told me in the car."

CHAPTER THIRTEEN

A hot shower never felt so good. Josie wanted to spend a half hour letting the water wash away the sweat and blood she'd been covered in so far that day, but she knew she couldn't linger. The thought of the mysterious third camper out there in parts unknown weighed heavily on her. Was the woman sick? Dead? Or was she some kind of twisted killer?

"Your turn," Josie told Noah as she returned to their bedroom.

Wordlessly, he stripped down and shuffled off to the bathroom. Josie watched him go, wondering if he was just as exhausted as she was or if he was still thinking about Baby Doe. Before she could go after him and ask, she heard the water turn on in the bathroom. She threw on some clean clothes and went to the kitchen, scarfing down some leftover pizza they'd ordered the night before. She checked her phone and found a missed call from Deputy Moore.

"Shit," she mumbled, pressing the call button beside his number.

"Detective Quinn," he answered. "I thought you might want to know that we found the Yates vehicle here in Lenore County."

Josie felt a flicker of hope. Perhaps there would be some clue in the vehicle as to the identity of the third camper. "How far from the campsite?"

"About three and a half miles south along Route 9227. There's a parking lot designated for people who want to use the state gameland along the road there. No way to tell how long it's been there."

"Locked?"

"Of course. It's still storming pretty bad so we haven't touched it."

Josie said, "That's fine. I'd like to send a team down there to process it if you don't mind. For prints and DNA. As you know, we're still trying to locate the female who was with them. If we can find anything, any clue, as to who she is, it might be crucial in finding her. Plus, we really don't know what happened at that campsite. There's always the outside chance that someone else was with them or encountered them at their vehicle."

"We'll hold off on looking inside until your evidence response team gets here."

"Thank you," Josie said. "I'll call Hummel right now. Oh wait—I wanted to ask you something."

"Go ahead."

"How long have you been working in Lenore County?"

"Oh, about ten years now. Why?"

"Do you remember a missing persons case about two years ago? A woman named Maya Bestler?"

"Oh yeah," he said. "Young brunette woman, mid-twenties. Camping with her boyfriend. Disappeared in the night. Bestler and her boyfriend were about five miles south of the Yates site—but the cases aren't connected."

"How can you be so sure?" Josie asked.

"Maya Bestler's boyfriend killed her."

"I don't think that's true," Josie said. "She—"

But he cut her off. "We could never prove it, but I'm telling you, that guy—Garrett Romney is his name—is guilty as sin. Every person we talked to who knew the two of them said that he used to beat her. We contacted Doylestown police. They had a few calls to the residence for domestic abuse, but Maya would never press charges. He had a history of violence with her, and besides that, his story never made sense. He claimed he was sitting at the campfire they'd built drinking beer with Maya after a long day of hiking and the next thing he knew, it was morning and he woke up in a mud puddle with a gash on his head. He said he didn't remember anything. Nothing at all. No struggle, no attacker. He didn't remember fighting with her. He said his mind was a blank slate. The head wound was superficial though, not enough to knock him out. He wasn't concussed."

"Did you run toxicology to see if he had been drugged?"

Moore laughed. "Drugged? Who would have drugged him?" When Josie didn't answer, he sighed. "Okay, okay, well as a matter of fact, we did run toxicology, but it came back negative."

"He could have been drugged with GHB," Josie said.

"What? The date rape drug?" Moore asked.

"Yes. It's usually not detectable in blood or urine after twelve hours, sometimes even less than that."

Moore gave another heavy sigh. "Look, I appreciate what you're trying to do here—like maybe if you can connect the cases, maybe there's some person out there in the woods taking women, you can stop him—but I'm telling you, Garrett Romney wasn't drugged. He was lying."

"But Moore," Josie insisted. "He didn't kill Maya Bestler. I know that because she's a patient at Denton Memorial Hospital right now."

"What?" he said, his tone sharpening.

She told him what had happened after they'd left the Sanctuary to return to Denton. When she finished, he said, "Are you sure it's the real Maya Bestler?"

"I had someone from my team pull her driver's license. It looks like her. I haven't had a chance to properly interview her or locate next of kin yet, but I'm pretty certain it's her. You think it's some kind of hoax?"

"I don't know what to think now. I'm just telling you that Garrett Romney is guilty of something. Mind if I drive up there? Talk to her? I can contact her family. She was taken from my jurisdiction."

There was the jurisdiction thing again. Josie let it pass. She would take whatever help she could get, even from someone as irritating as Moore.

"Of course," Josie said. "She's been admitted, so she's not going anywhere. Noah and I will head over there soon to check on her condition and see if we can get more information from her."

"Great," Moore replied.

"One last thing," Josie said before he hung up. "When you spoke with Maya's boyfriend and family, did they happen to mention that she was partially deaf?"

"What? No. It never came up."

CHAPTER FOURTEEN

By the time they got back to the hospital, Maya had been moved to a private room on the fourth floor. Her baby was still in the NICU. Josie and Noah met the doctor at the nurses' station on her floor. "She's stable," he told them. "We were able to get the hemorrhage under control. She's severely dehydrated. She's got a lot of cuts and bruises. Luckily none of the lacerations on her feet needed stitches. She's got some old scars around her wrists, as Detective Quinn saw earlier. We did some X-rays. She's got several old fractures—ribs, jaw, both forearms, and her left tibia."

Noah said, "She was abused?"

The doctor scratched his chin. "Well, I can't say that for sure but in someone her age, when we see that many old fractures, especially to the face and ribs, we do worry about domestic abuse."

"How old are the fractures?" Josie asked.

"Also hard to say but on average between three and five years old, I'd say."

"It fits with what Moore told me about her boyfriend," Josie said to Noah. "How about her hearing?"

"Well, you already know she's got hearing loss," the doctor said. "From what we can tell, it's from scar tissue."

Noah asked, "What would cause scar tissue in her ears?"

"Most likely untreated ear infections," the doctor said. "She has some hearing, but not much left. Other than that, she's in pretty good shape. Not malnourished. Appropriate weight. Since she can't tell us much, we took some blood for tox screens. We need to make sure she didn't have anything in her system that could affect the baby."

"How is he?" Noah asked. "Is he okay?"

"As far as I know, yeah. We're just covering all our bases."

"Has she said anything?" Josie asked.

The doctor shook his head. "No. We gave her something for pain so that made her a little sleepy. She just keeps asking us to help her. She asked if her baby was okay a couple of times. That's it. She's resting but lucid enough that you could ask her some questions if you'd like. Just not too long, okay?"

Quietly, they slipped into Maya's room. Someone had pulled the shades, closing off her view of the torrential downpour outside, although the occasional rumble of thunder could still be heard. A monitor above her head measured her heart rate, blood pressure, respirations, and oxygen saturation. An IV tube snaked from the crook of her right arm to a bag of fluids hanging next to the bed. Her eyes were open, staring straight ahead at a blank television across the room. Josie and Noah flanked the bed, and Maya startled when she saw them, her hands flying up toward her face.

"It's okay," Noah said.

"She needs to see your face, remember?" Josie reminded him. "She reads lips, like your ex-girlfriend did. Remember?"

"Right," Noah said. He leaned over the bed, keeping his movements slow and smooth. With a tentative hand, he touched her forearm. She tensed but then lowered it. Her eyes darted from him to Josie and back. Noah positioned his face so that she could see his lips move. "It's okay," he told her. "We're the police. We need to ask you some questions." He told her their names and each of them showed her their credentials.

Maya looked at Josie. "I talked to you earlier."

"Yes," Josie said. "You told me your name and that you were taken."

She looked back at Noah. "You delivered my baby."

He smiled and pointed to Josie. "Detective Quinn delivered your baby."

Her head swiveled again in Josie's direction. She reached out a hand and Josie took it, feeling a gentle squeeze. "Thank you," Maya said.

While she had her attention, Josie said, "Maya, I know you're exhausted, but I want you to know that you're safe now."

"Safe," she echoed, a tear rolling down her cheek.

"We'd like you to tell us what happened to you," Josie said. "Can you do that?"

"Where am I?"

"Denton, Pennsylvania," Josie answered. "About two hours west of where you live."

"What day is it? What's the date?"

Josie met Noah's eyes momentarily and then told her. More tears spilled from her eyes. She released Josie's hand and covered her face with both hands. Sobs rocked her body. They gave her a few minutes. When she peeked from between her hands, Josie offered her a tissue and she took it, dabbing at her eyes and nose.

Her gaze landed on Noah. "Is Garrett coming? My boyfriend?"

Josie had filled Noah in on everything she'd learned from Deputy Moore on the way to the hospital. Noah answered, "No, he's not coming. He hasn't even been notified that you've been… found."

"Someone should tell him," Maya said. "He'll be worried."

"Do you want to see him?" Noah asked.

She pressed the crumpled tissue to her mouth and nodded.

Josie touched her forearm to draw her attention. "Garrett told the police that the two of you were camping, and then he blacked out and when he woke up you were gone."

Another nod. Maya said, "We had a campfire. It was nice. A cool night. Clear skies. We were—we were having fun for once. Drinking beer. Then I—I woke up tied to a tree. Everything was gone. Garrett was gone."

"You don't remember what happened?" Josie asked.

"No. I was with Garrett. It was nighttime. Then it was morning and I was tied up. Somewhere else in the forest. I didn't recognize anything."

"Tied with what?" Josie asked. "Rope?"

"Yes, thick rope."

"Who took you?" Josie asked. "Who tied you up?"

"It was a man," Maya said. "I never saw him before. He looked like—like a monster. He was kind of old. He smelled and looked like he hadn't bathed or changed clothes in years. I didn't want him near me, but he was strong. I had no choice."

The monitor above the bed beeped softly. Josie glanced at it to see Maya's heart rate and respirations climbing. "It's okay," Josie said. "It's okay. We don't have to talk about that right now. Just breathe. Look at me." Josie pointed to her eyes. "Focus on me. Breathe. You're safe now."

Maya's gaze locked onto Josie's and the rise and fall of her chest slowed. When Josie saw her numbers go back to normal range, she asked another question. "Where did he keep you?"

Maya licked her lips. "In the woods for a long time. He kept my wrists tied." She lifted her hands and pushed her wrists together to demonstrate. "He dragged me around through the woods for days. At night he tied me to a tree. We moved every morning. Then we came to some caverns."

"Caverns?" Noah said but Maya didn't hear him.

Josie said, "What kind of caverns?"

"Underground," Maya said. "Not like a cave. Bigger. It was huge. There were tunnels and even a stream running through them. It was dark. So dark." She shuddered. "There was a place in there, almost like a room. He sometimes built a fire. It was so big in there and so cold. Other times he had flashlights. I don't know where he got them but when the batteries ran out, that was it. That room, it was pretty high up in the caverns. They would flood from time to time, and we'd have to stay up there until the water receded."

"What did you eat?" Josie asked.

"Plants. Fish. There was a creek nearby. He had this old wooden boat he would take out so he could catch fish. Sometimes he would trap a rabbit or a pheasant and cook those. I was sick a lot though." She touched her left ear. "My ears hurt. I got dizzy and nauseated. It seemed like it went on for weeks at a time, but I couldn't tell you how long any of it was—he kept me in the dark so much. Eventually, when I was too sick to even try to fight him anymore, he started taking me outside. I tried to get him to trust me so he'd let me out more without being tied up. So I could get away. I was trying to get better so I'd have the strength to run. He made stuff from plants and things and made me drink and eat them. He said it would make me feel less sick. Sometimes I felt better, sometimes not. I kind of got used to it, but then I realized…"

She drifted off, more tears rolling down her face. She touched her deflated abdomen. Clearing her throat, she started speaking again, "I realized I was pregnant. I didn't know how much time I had. I just knew I had to get away from him before the baby came. I would die giving birth in that place."

"How did you get away?" Josie asked.

"He was always making broth. It was so disgusting. He used to hit me when I wouldn't drink it. He said it had everything I needed to be healthy, and I should just be grateful I had something to eat. I snuck some foxglove into the cavern and when he was out trapping game, I crushed it up and put it into his broth. I had to wait a long time but eventually he got very sick. It went on for hours and then finally he fell asleep. That's when I left."

Josie glanced at Noah to see his curious expression. He touched Maya's arm and she turned her gaze toward him. "How did you know to use foxglove?"

Maya said, "One of the times he let me out of the caverns, he was foraging. He kept me tied to him and I saw the foxglove flowers. I thought they were so pretty. I hadn't seen anything pretty in the longest time. I picked some and he freaked out. He told me they'd make me very sick. Later, I saw some growing not too far from the caverns, and I knew that I'd have to get close to them and pick them without him seeing if I was going to have any chance of getting away from him."

She turned back to Josie. "I knew the baby was coming. I had to do it. I didn't think it would really work."

"When you escaped the caverns, was it daytime or nighttime?" Josie asked.

"Night," Maya answered. "I just started walking. I had no idea where I was—I just needed to get away. I started to have contractions—I guess that's what they were—and it got harder and harder to walk. Then I saw the road, and I thought maybe someone would find me if they drove past."

"We almost hit you," Noah said although Maya wasn't looking at him.

Josie said, "Did he ever tell you his name? Anything identifying?"

Maya shook her head. "No, nothing. I never even called him anything. He didn't talk much at all except to tell me to shut up or to—to give me commands whenever he—he f-forced himself on me."

Her shoulders quaked with a new round of sobs. Josie squeezed her hand again. "It's okay," she said. "I think that's enough for today. We just have one last question." She took out the photo of Tyler and Valerie Yates. As she had told Noah in the car, it seemed unlikely that the two cases were connected, but there was only one way to know for sure. She turned her phone so Maya could see the picture. Josie waited while she studied the two faces and then looked back at Josie's face. Josie asked, "Do you know either of these people?"

Maya shook her head. "I'm sorry, I don't."

"Didn't think so," Josie said. She smiled and was rewarded with a small return smile from Maya. "You need to rest now. Doctor's orders. We'll be back to check on you later, okay?"

CHAPTER FIFTEEN

Noah and Josie walked down the hallway to the bank of elevators. Josie checked her phone, but there were no calls yet from anyone on her team. "Let's go down to the morgue," she said. "See if Dr. Feist has gotten anywhere finding the Yates couple's next of kin."

She pressed the down button. Noah jammed his hands into his pockets. "You think she's telling the truth?"

Josie sighed. "I don't know. She's obviously traumatized. She's been missing for two years. She had someone's baby. But a man living in caverns in the woods?"

"There are a lot of underground caverns in Pennsylvania," Noah said. "Although I've never heard of anyone living in them."

The elevator dinged open and they stepped inside. Josie pressed the button for the basement. Noah reached across her and hit the button for the second floor. "I'm just going to check on the baby," he told her. "I'll meet you down there, okay?"

"The doctor said he was stable," Josie said.

"I know but I just want to see if there have been any changes."

Before Josie could say anything more, the doors opened on the second floor and Noah was gone. She watched him jog down the hall until the doors closed and the elevator proceeded to the basement. She emerged into a windowless, drab hallway lined with jaundiced tiles. The smell of chemicals and biological decay led her to the small suite of rooms that Medical Examiner, Dr. Anya Feist, presided over.

Inside the main exam room, the body of Tyler Yates lay on a table, a white sheet pulled up to his chin. Dr. Feist stood near the stainless-steel countertop that ran along the far wall, marking something down in a file in front of her. She smiled grimly when she saw Josie. "I'm glad you're here. I've autopsied the husband."

Josie said, "Where's Valerie?"

"Ramon has her. He's taking a full set of X-rays now." Ramon was Dr. Feist's assistant. "He'll be back in a few minutes."

"What's the verdict on Tyler? Respiratory failure?"

Dr. Feist raised a brow as she moved down the counter to where Josie could glimpse a specimen of some kind—pink and red with blood— laid out on a surface protector. "Well, he does have inflammation in his mouth and throat. There's excess blood in the vessels around his stomach. There wasn't much in terms of stomach content as it looks like most of that was vomited into the woods. He definitely ingested a toxin of some sort."

"We found hemlock in the woods, about a half mile from the campsite," Josie said.

"Yes," Dr. Feist said. "I was made aware. That could definitely have caused severe illness but that's not what killed this guy."

"It's not?" Josie asked.

Dr. Feist waved her over to have a closer look at the specimen. Up close Josie saw that it was horseshoe-shaped and probably only two or three centimeters in length. It almost looked like the tiny bones of a bird, but Josie knew it had come from Tyler Yates.

"That's his hyoid bone, isn't it?" Josie said, feeling a sudden chill shoot straight up her spine.

Dr. Feist smiled. "That's correct."

Josie saw the places where it had broken, and Dr. Feist had pieced it back together. "It's practically shattered."

"Yes," Dr. Feist agreed. "As you know, the hyoid is here." She pointed to her throat, just below her chin. "Trauma to the hyoid can cause asphyxiation."

"Someone strangled him."

"With great force, yes."

Josie turned back toward Tyler's body. "There was no bruising on his neck."

"Because he died quickly," Dr. Feist explained. "He was probably quite weakened from his illness. There are no defensive wounds. Whoever strangled him did it fast but with enough force to break the hyoid in four places. That's a lot of force."

"Could a woman have done it?"

"I can't rule it out, but I strongly doubt it. I think it's more likely that a man would have the hand strength for something like this."

"So the cause of death is asphyxia secondary to manual strangulation and the manner of death is—"

"Homicide," Dr. Feist filled in with a grim look.

"What about Valerie?"

"Like I said, I'll have to perform the actual autopsy but if her husband was murdered, it's not a stretch to think we might find further evidence of homicide. I did the external exam. She had bruising on her inner thighs but no signs of sexual assault internally. That doesn't mean she wasn't assaulted in some way. Certainly, the bruising is what I have seen in other cases where the victim was sexually assaulted, but I found no bruising or tearing internally and no DNA from another person."

Again, Josie felt cold dread envelop her. "Or maybe someone tried to assault her but didn't get very far?"

"Could be," Dr. Feist answered. "That seems the most likely explanation."

"What about the mark on her wrist?"

"It was fresh. It looks like a ligature mark except it's small. If someone tied her up, it either wasn't for very long or she didn't struggle."

"Can you say with certainty it's a ligature mark?" Josie asked. "Or could she have gotten it some other way?"

"I can't be certain. To me, it looks like a ligature mark, but if I had to testify in court as to the certainty of that conclusion, I'd have to say I'm only fifty percent sure that's what it is."

The double doors to the suite banged open and Ramon pushed through a transportable autopsy table, lining it up beside Tyler Yates. Valerie's body was completely covered with a sheet. Dr. Feist walked over and turned the sheet down, folding it beneath Valerie's chin.

She sighed as she stared down at the young woman's face. "I love my job, but I really, really hate my job."

Josie nodded, leaning a hip against the counter. Again, she thought of how close in age Tyler and Valerie Yates were to her and Noah. A wave of sadness washed over her. The Yates couple would never grow old together. They'd never again have the kinds of stupid arguments that long-time couples had—like whether a toaster oven was better than a toaster. "Me too," Josie said.

They let a moment of silence pass for the young couple. Then Ramon said, "Dr. Feist, you'll want to see this right away."

He walked over to an open laptop on the counter next to the Tyler Yates file and started clicking until he brought up a series of X-rays. He moved out of the way so that Dr. Feist could study them. Josie looked over her shoulder as she clicked through the digital images, settling on one that showed Valerie's upper ribs, shoulders, and the vertebrae of her neck as well as an object that was clearly not supposed to be there. It showed up bright white against the various degrees of gray, black, and hazy white on the X-ray. Something long and looped, almost like a string of some sort. Connected to it was another object, irregularly shaped but nearly round. It sat above the collar bones in the center of her throat.

Josie gasped. "What is that?"

Dr. Feist frowned. She snatched a pair of vinyl gloves from a box on the counter and walked over to Valerie's body. "Ramon," she said. "I need forceps. The ones that—" But he already had a small pair in hand which he gave her. He then went about flipping on the movable overhead lights that shone down on Valerie's body. Dr. Feist tipped Valerie's head back slightly and used both hands along her jawline to open her mouth. "I need my head lamp, Ramon," she said.

Seconds later, she was fitting it onto her head and peering inside Valerie's mouth. "I can't see anything from this angle."

She went around to the side of the table, climbed on top of it and straddled Valerie. Ramon moved the overhead lights to accommodate the doctor's new position. She pressed a finger into Valerie's chin, opening her mouth as wide as possible. Josie couldn't help but cringe as she watched Dr. Feist insert the forceps deeply into the dead woman's throat.

"It might be too deep," Ramon commented. "You might need to use the endoscope."

Dr. Feist's face was inches from Valerie's open mouth. Her eyes squinted in concentration beneath a pair of safety goggles. Her hand worked the forceps around inside Valerie's throat. "Nonsense," she mumbled to Ramon. "I can see the edge of it. If I can just grab onto a piece—got it!"

Squeezing the forceps, she gently tugged at the object inside. Josie knew she was trying not to damage any tissue inside Valerie's throat as she removed whatever it was that was lodged there. It was freezing in the morgue, but sweat beaded along Dr. Feist's upper lip.

Finally, the object slid out of Valerie's mouth, long and slick and covered in fluid. Ramon was ready beside the doctor with a small stainless-steel tray which she dropped the item into with a *thunk* sound.

Dr. Feist climbed down and followed Ramon over to an empty table where he set the tray. As Josie joined them, Ramon turned on the movable overhead light and shined it down on the tray. The three of them stared at it.

"It's a necklace," Josie said. She pointed to the long loop, which was only a couple of millimeters in width and perhaps twelve inches in length. It had no metal clasps, but its two ends were tied together in a knot. "Looks like leather."

"I'd say so," Dr. Feist said. She used the forceps to nudge the necklace so they could get a better look at the quarter-sized object attached to the leather. Again, there were no clasps but one end of the leather band had been fed through a hole in what looked like a small wooden item. The side facing them was brown and flat with two deep holes in its center, side by side, like two lobes or two sides of a heart. Around it were tiny, irregular, pin-shaped holes and deeper, longer indentations. Nothing about it was uniform. Dr. Feist turned it over to reveal that its underside was rounded, ridged, black, and rough. Almost like a miniature charred coconut.

Josie said, "That's a black walnut."

"What?" Ramon said.

Dr. Feist looked at her, waiting for her to continue.

"A black walnut," Josie said. "You can tell by the color on the back. It's been cut in half. Black walnut trees grow all over Pennsylvania. They grow in big green hulls. They're very difficult to harvest. I've seen people use hammers to break them open. That is the shell. The actual nut has been removed."

Dr. Feist said, "Someone made a necklace with half a black walnut shell and jammed it down this girl's throat?"

Josie felt a buzz of anxiety work its way through her body. She took out her phone and snapped a few photos. "Yes."

"But why?" Dr. Feist asked.

Josie took a step back from the table, finding a counter edge to lean against. She felt slightly dizzy. Exhaustion and sleep deprivation worked in tandem to slow her mind. "It's a signature."

This time, Ramon gave her a quizzical look and Dr. Feist said, "What do you mean?"

"A signature," Josie repeated. "Something a killer does for his own gratification, but which is not necessary for the commission of the crime. In other words, stuffing that necklace into her throat didn't kill her. He put it there for his own reasons. It means something to him."

"The necklace could have killed her," Dr. Feist pointed out. "Being that deep in her throat."

"That's true. It very well could have killed her, but I think when you do the autopsy, you'll find her hyoid was broken as well. Or she succumbed to the hemlock poisoning."

Ramon said softly, "Whoever did this was going to kill her one way or another."

Josie nodded. She closed her eyes for a moment. She felt Dr. Feist's fingers on the inside of her wrist and opened them again. Dr. Feist knew better than to ask Josie if she was okay. "Your heart is racing," Dr. Feist said. "Why don't you have a seat in my office? Ramon can stow Mr. Yates and get Mrs. Yates ready for autopsy."

Ramon nodded and immediately busied himself. He looked glad to have something to do besides talk about the black walnut necklace.

Dr. Feist's office was just off the examination room. Although the walls were blue-painted cinderblock, the lighting was softer, and the doctor had decorated said walls with several pastel abstract paintings which made the space seem almost soothing. Josie plopped into the guest chair in front of Dr. Feist's desk. "Take five," the doctor told her.

She left the room and Josie could hear her giving instructions to Ramon. When she returned, Josie had regained some of her composure. Dr. Feist perched on the edge of her desk and said, "So, is there some significance to the black walnut? The heart shape on the inside?"

Josie nodded. "It could be that. Some symbol of love—or what this sicko believes is love." Her mind ran through the scene again and the little that they knew. "I think the killer poisoned them with hemlock. Maybe he wanted her, but he couldn't get to her without eliminating Tyler. With both of them ill, he easily killed Tyler. Then he would have had Valerie to himself."

"Except that she was extremely ill," Dr. Feist said. "Like you said."

"And there was a third camper," Josie added, "but we don't know where they were during all of this. We're assuming the third camper was a woman because we found a gold necklace in the sleeping bag."

"Maybe he took her," Dr. Feist suggested.

"That's what I'm afraid of."

A moment passed between them while they each collected their thoughts. Finally, Dr. Feist said, "What else do you know about black walnuts?"

Josie rubbed her temples where a headache began to pound. "I know that the roots of black walnut trees exude something called juglone."

"That's a natural herbicide, isn't it?" Dr. Feist said.

"Right," Josie said. "It kills everything around it."

CHAPTER SIXTEEN

Ramon poked his head into the office. "Valerie Yates is ready for you, doc," he said.

Dr. Feist smiled at him. "Thank you, Ramon. I'll be there shortly." To Josie, she said, "I don't know about you, but I could use a cup of coffee before I dive into this next autopsy. How about if I run up to the cafeteria?"

"I need to get back to work," Josie said.

"One cup," Dr. Feist said. "Did Noah come with you?"

"Yes, he's in the NICU."

Dr. Feist raised a brow. Obviously, news of the morning's dramatic birth hadn't yet made its way into the bowels of the hospital. Josie recapped what had happened.

Dr. Feist said, "Then you need that coffee more than I thought. Stay here. I'll get the drinks and track down Noah."

Josie didn't have the energy to object. Remembering the main reason she had come to speak to the doctor, she asked, "Did you get anywhere with the next of kin?"

"I had a little help from your department. Detective Mettner is quite helpful."

"Yes, he's fantastic," Josie agreed. Discreetly, she checked her phone. "I'm actually waiting to hear from him on whether or not he could get into the Yateses' cell phones. I tried to check their social media profiles on my phone but there are about a dozen 'Tyler Yates' and almost as many 'Valerie Yates'. I didn't see any profile pictures that looked like either of them."

Dr. Feist smiled and motioned toward her desk chair where her laptop sat open. "Sit over there," she said. "We tracked down next of kin for Tyler. His dad is Wesley Yates and he, too, lives in Fox Mill. I called the coroner there, and they'll be making the death notification in the next twenty-four hours. You can have his number. I imagine you'll want to talk to him."

"Yes," Josie said as she moved over to Dr. Feist's desk chair. "That would be great."

Dr. Feist leaned over Josie's shoulder and clicked a few times, bringing up a document that included a photo of Wesley Yates' driver's license. Josie took out her phone and used a note-taking app to take down Yates' address and below the photo of his license, his phone number.

Dr. Feist said, "While you're there, you can log into Facebook if you'd like. Search for Wesley Yates."

"I can use my phone," Josie told her.

"I know. I like the company though." With that, she was gone.

The list of Wesley Yateses on Facebook was even longer than the list of Tylers and Valeries, but lucky for Josie, the Wesley Yates she was looking for used a clear photo of his face for his profile picture. She was able to easily match it with the driver's license photo. She checked his friends list and found Tyler's profile as well. He had used a photo of a forest at dusk for his profile picture, but several of his other photos were set to public. Josie clicked through them, finding several photos of him and Valerie. She was able to determine from the dates of some wedding photos that they'd got married four years earlier. It looked as though they went camping once or twice a year. Valerie was in almost all of the photos but not tagged in any of them. She was also absent from both Tyler and Wesley's friends lists which meant she likely didn't have a Facebook account.

Josie took one last look through Tyler Yates' photos, noticing that several photos of him and Valerie featured another couple who looked to be of similar age. The couple weren't tagged in any of Tyler Yates' photos. Josie searched the comments of many of the pictures, but no one mentioned any names besides Tyler's and Valerie's. She went back and studied the photos, noting the difference between the athletic-looking Yates couple and their friends. Tyler was average height and lean like a runner. In his photos he had a crooked smile and bright blue eyes. He kept his sandy hair cut short and sometimes spiked. The other male was taller with darker features, including shaggy brown hair that brushed his collar and shaded his deep brown eyes. His smile was restrained somehow, like he was gritting his teeth. The woman Josie assumed was his girlfriend or wife was short and curvy with ash-blonde hair that flowed down to her rear end, unlike Valerie who was a brunette, slightly taller and more angular. In the earliest photos, the mystery woman's wide smile revealed perfectly straight teeth and a dimple in her right cheek. As time wore on, the man with the shaggy brown hair disappeared and appeared to take her smile with him. In the most recent photos, she stood between Tyler and Valerie Yates, giving a thin, closed-lip smile that barely registered joy.

Josie checked the dates on the early photos, noting that they went back six years. The male partner in the second, unnamed couple stopped appearing in the photos two and a half years earlier. Josie wondered what happened to him. Had he passed away? Had they simply broken up, or divorced?

Dr. Feist sailed back into the room with a cup carrier containing three paper cups of coffee and an assortment of sugar, creamers, and stirrers. Noah trailed behind her. "Look who I found wandering around in the hall," Dr. Feist joked.

"Hey," Noah said. "Dr. Feist told me about the autopsy. I just had a look at the… necklace."

"Pretty disturbing," Josie said. "How's the baby?"

Noah smiled. "He's doing great. Also, I saw Moore upstairs."

"How lovely of him to travel out of his jurisdiction for us."

Noah laughed. "What've you got on the next of kin? Anything? Social media accounts?"

Josie told him about Wesley Yates and showed him what she had found on the social media profiles. "Look at this woman in these photos," she told him. "Her boyfriend or husband—or whoever that guy was— is gone, and she's still hanging out with these two."

"So? Maybe he died and they were consoling her," Noah said.

Josie clicked back through several of the pictures again. "But look: here's one of the three of them at a movie. Here are the three of them at a fireworks display. An art museum. A food festival."

"What are you thinking?" Noah asked.

"I'm wondering if this woman is the third camper."

"Because she hangs out with them a lot?"

"Not just hangs out with them. They take her everywhere with them."

"You're only seeing the photos that are set to public," Noah pointed out.

Josie made a noise of frustration deep in her throat. "There's a killer out there. He could have this woman, for all we know."

"Josie, you know we have to get this right. I agree that he could have the third camper. I understand she's in danger, but we need proof that the woman in these social media photos is the third camper before we get too excited."

Josie said, "There are enough photos of the three of them together to reasonably assume that she could have gone camping with them. We have to work with what we have. I'll take the risk of being wrong about her identity. But if we can find out who this woman is, we'll have a better idea of whether she is the person we're looking for or not."

"Wesley Yates probably knows."

"I don't know if the death notification has been made yet," Josie said. She pointed to the woman on the screen sandwiched between

Tyler and Valerie Yates at a Phillies game. "If she's the camper and she's missing, we need to know right away."

Dr. Feist said, "I'll call the Fox Mill coroner and see if they've made the notification yet, and if not, ask them to give me a time frame for doing so."

"Thank you," Josie said. "I'm going to send this profile link to Mett and ask him to start contacting anyone he can find on Tyler Yates' friends list to see if they know her name. I also want him to make sure our people are out in the woods looking for the third camper the minute the storm lets up."

She took out her phone but before she could dial Mettner, a call came in from Moore. She flashed her phone at Noah. "I'll call Mettner," he told her. "You take that."

"Quinn," Josie answered.

Moore said, "I called Mr. and Mrs. Bestler. They should be in Denton in the next hour. I'm at Denton Memorial Hospital now. You guys still around? You know what room this woman claiming to be Maya Bestler is in?"

"Fourth floor, room 428. We're in the morgue. We'll meet you there."

CHAPTER SEVENTEEN

Moore met them at the nurses' station. He must have gotten a shower as well, Josie thought, because his hair looked clean and freshly combed, and he had on a more casual uniform: a tan polo shirt with the Lenore County sheriff's insignia on it and navy-blue slacks. A manila file folder was tucked under one arm. Josie arranged for them to use the staff break room for ten minutes so they could exchange information. The file Moore had brought was a copy of the file on Bestler's disappearance. "You can keep that," he told Josie as she leafed through it. Noah recapped Dr. Feist's initial findings on the Yates couple and asked if he could arrange for units to search the Lenore County side of the campsite for the third camper.

Moore scratched his chin, his expression pinched. "I guess I could make a call."

But he made no move to take out his phone.

Noah said, "Yeah, you could make a call now."

Moore pointed to the ceiling. "You don't hear that? Rain's comin' down awful hard. Thunder and lightning, too. My boss isn't sending units out in this weather."

Josie said, "But he could have people on standby for when the weather clears."

Moore remained silent and unmoving. Josie saw a vein throbbing in Noah's neck. "Maybe we'll just call in the state police," she said, feigning a casual tone and returning to the file in front of her.

With a huff, Moore took out his phone and left the room.

"What an ass," Noah complained. "What's up with him? He doesn't even care that a woman is in danger right now."

"He's a jerk," Josie said. "We should go over his head. Have the Chief call his Chief."

"Cause that will go over well," Noah remarked.

Before Josie could answer, Moore stomped back into the room. "My boss is putting a search team on standby," he said. "You happy?"

"As a matter of fact, I am," Josie said.

Moore glared at her. She returned to the file while Noah gave Moore the rundown on what Bestler had told them.

Moore shook his head slowly. "I thought for sure Garrett Romney killed this woman and hid her body." He pointed to the file in front of Josie. "You'll see in that file our case was airtight."

Had the case really been airtight, Garrett Romney would be rotting in prison at that second, but Josie didn't mention this to Moore. His trip to Denton Memorial with the file was just his way of making sure they knew that his team had done everything they could to resolve the case. Someone in Lenore County didn't want to be blamed for zeroing in solely on Garrett and not looking any further. If Maya or her family could prove that the Lenore County sheriff's office had dropped the ball, they would have a pretty massive lawsuit on their hands.

"Well," Noah said. "I think it's safe to say that Romney is exonerated. We just have to figure out who did take her."

"I thought she told you who took her," Moore said.

Josie looked up from the file. "She says it was some guy living in underground caverns in the woods. Listen, I think someone definitely took her and kept her for the last two years. She's clearly traumatized. She's got scars on her wrists and hearing loss from untreated ear infections. I'm just not sure…" She searched for the right phrasing.

Before she could finish, Noah said, "We obviously have to investigate based on what she's told us, but we're concerned that it's a little far-fetched."

Josie said, "She went missing in Lenore County and came out only a few miles north of the county line, in our jurisdiction. We're talking state gameland, private property with hunting cabins and rural homes. While it's a large area to search by foot, it doesn't seem large enough for a man to be living out there for years on end without anyone reporting him—especially if he was as unkempt as she says he was. She described him as a monster."

Moore's face twisted in a grimace. He scratched his temple.

"What is it?" Josie asked.

Moore looked from Josie to Noah and back again. "Well, the thing is that we actually do have something like that in Lenore County."

"Something like a monster in the woods who kidnaps women and keeps them in underground caverns?" Noah asked.

Moore nodded and gave a little laugh. "Not the way you describe it, but there are some caverns in Lenore County."

"There are a lot of caverns in Pennsylvania," Josie pointed out. "Crystal Cave, Indian Echo Caverns, Lost River Caverns."

"Those are tourist attractions," Moore said. "I'm talking about caverns on state gameland property that aren't maintained or managed by anyone. The entrance is pretty difficult to find, if I'm remembering correctly, so wildlife management doesn't worry about them too much."

"Is there a man living in them?" Noah asked.

Moore said, "Well, five minutes ago, I would have said no, but now that I've heard this, I'm thinking maybe there is. We've got this guy down in Lenore County. Everyone calls him 'the hermit'. I've never seen him, but some people have."

"The hermit?" Josie asked.

"Yeah, it's a guy who lives in the woods. He doesn't bother anyone. Like I said, hardly anyone has even seen him."

"Then how do you know it's not some kind of urban legend?" Noah asked.

"Because enough people have seen him over the years that we know he's real. But like I said, he never bothers anyone. He's never caused any trouble with hunters or hikers or anyone else that we know of. He probably takes shelter in the caverns. That would make sense—especially in the winter time—and would explain how he's been able to keep largely out of sight most of the time."

"How old is he?" Josie asked.

Moore shrugged. "Not sure. Some people think maybe in his fifties."

Noah asked, "How long has he been living in the woods?"

"We think twenty years, maybe more. The lore around the county is that he's a widower. The story goes that after his wife died, he walked into the woods and never came back out."

"Who is he?" Josie asked. "What's his name?"

"Don't know. Nobody does."

"Then how do you know his wife died?" Noah asked incredulously.

"We don't. Like I said, it's county lore. Rumor."

"Can you find those caverns?" Josie asked. "Take us to them?"

"Probably, yeah. You sure this is a Lenore County case?"

"She came out of the woods on our side of the county line," Noah said. "So it might be our jurisdiction."

"But he took her, kept her, and assaulted her in Lenore County," Josie pointed out.

"I can get you a map, probably."

"Or you could do your damn job," Noah said, unable to keep his composure a moment longer. Quickly, Josie stood and stepped between the men, facing Moore who glared, red-faced, over her shoulder at Noah.

She snapped her fingers in his face, and he looked at her.

"If this is a Lenore County case, your team is going to need to prepare the case for trial. Your district attorney is going to have to prosecute."

He folded his arms across his chest. "So?"

Noah's chest bumped against Josie's back. "So stop trying to get out of doing work."

Josie held up her hand, silencing Noah. To Moore she said, "So we need to work together. In case you forgot, we now have a killer and a missing woman out in the woods somewhere. You tell me there's some guy living in the woods, and a woman reporting being kidnapped by someone who sounds a lot like him? It's not that big a stretch to worry that these cases could be connected. We need to find your hermit and make sure he's not the one who murdered the Yates couple and took their friend. I do not want another homicide on my hands and trust me, my friend, neither do you."

"I'm not your friend," Moore said.

"Fine with me," Josie said. "We don't need to have beers after work. I just need you to lead us to the caverns."

There was a brief knock at the door and then a nurse stuck her head in. "Officers," she said. "There are a couple of people here. They said they're looking for Maya Bestler."

"We'll be right there," Moore said.

CHAPTER EIGHTEEN

The Bestlers stood several feet apart from one another between the nurses' station and the elevators. Gus Bestler, as Moore introduced him, was tall and wiry, thin all over, with gray hair. He wore khaki shorts and a short-sleeved, button-down collared shirt and paced about in a pattern. Three steps toward the elevators, hands in his pockets, hands out of his pockets, three steps back to the desktop of the nurses' station. Josie didn't see a wedding ring. Mrs. Bestler didn't wear one either, Josie noted. She wondered if they'd been divorced a long time or if Maya's disappearance had destroyed their marriage.

Sandy Bestler stood still, but Josie could sense she was just as nervous as Gus. When Moore introduced her, she shook Josie's hand with a slick, sweaty palm. She kept looking inside the large purse slung over her shoulder, coming up empty, and then reaching up to straighten her bangs with her fingers. Her hair was cut in a short but chic style, all the ends of her hair brushed toward her thin face, softening her pointy chin. She couldn't decide which of them Maya looked most like but ultimately decided that she was a pretty even mix of them both.

After introductions, Moore spoke softly to them, relating the basics of what Maya had told Josie and Noah about her ordeal, including the birth of their grandson. Gus looked stricken but Sandy's face remained impassive. The only sign of her distress was the white of her knuckles around the black strap of her purse. "Is it really her?" Sandy asked.

Moore glanced at Josie who stood just behind him. "Detective Quinn was able to make a comparison with her driver's license photo. We believe it is Maya."

Gus's voice trembled when he asked, "Where is she? Can we see her?"

"Of course," Moore said.

Josie stepped forward and explained about her injuries, notably, her hearing loss. "You'll have to look directly at her when you speak to her. Make sure she can see you talking."

"Fine, fine," Gus said, bouncing from his heels to the balls of his feet.

Josie and Noah led them into the room. Maya looked as though she hadn't moved from when they had spoken with her earlier, although someone had taken the time to brush the tangles out of her hair. Her eyes widened as the five of them filed into the room. Before anyone could say anything, Gus pushed past all of them and ran to the bed. "Maya!" he cried, gathering her up into his arms. As the monitor above Maya's head protested, her heart rate and respirations increasing rapidly, Gus sobbed, squeezing his daughter tightly. Slowly, Maya's arms wrapped around her father's neck, and her eyes drifted closed.

Josie, Noah, and Moore waited near the door. Sandy hung back, standing near the foot of the bed, watching the scene unfold. She shifted her purse from one shoulder to the other and then back again. After a moment, she looked back toward the door, almost as though she wanted to leave. When she saw the three detectives lined up against the wall, she quickly turned back to her daughter.

Gus released Maya long enough to stare into her face. He cupped her cheeks with his palms and studied her for a long moment. "It's her," he said. He looked over and smiled at Moore. "It's really her." Then he kissed her forehead and tucked her head into the hollow of his shoulder.

With hesitant steps, Sandy walked around to the other side of the bed and took her daughter's hand.

"Let's wait outside," Josie said. "We can talk to Mr. and Mrs. Bestler after they've had a chance to speak to Maya."

Sandy emerged first, twenty minutes later, looking no less nervous, her fingers pushing her hair to and fro on her scalp. She didn't smile when she saw them, but she walked over anyway and said, "My... my grandson?"

"He's fine," Noah said.

"I'd like to see him."

Noah motioned toward the elevators. "I'll take you."

Moore waited until they were gone before he spoke, his ire from earlier replaced with confusion. "Why doesn't this feel like a happy ending? It should be a happy ending."

Josie sighed. "There's no such thing as a happy ending in this job."

"That's pretty cynical coming from you."

"What's that supposed to mean?"

"I've seen you on *Dateline*."

Josie groaned. In her tenure with the Denton Police Department she'd caught some of the state's most scandalous cases—some of them so shocking they'd snagged the attention of the entire nation. She'd had her reasons for participating in the press coverage, which were mostly to do with the fact that her twin sister was an anchor on one of the nation's most famous morning magazine shows. Trinity rarely took no for an answer and had managed to wear Josie down three times already with her requests that Josie do *Dateline* specials. It was still difficult to get used to her notoriety.

"Which one did you see?" Josie asked.

Moore blinked. "Which one?"

"There are three."

"Wow. I didn't realize. I only saw the one about you being reunited with your real family. That's why I said you sound cynical. You were separated from them at three weeks old. They think you're dead for thirty years. Then you find one another. That's a happy ending."

Josie gave him a pained smile. It was a happy ending, she supposed, and certainly not a day went by that she didn't feel grateful to have been reunited with her real family, but what Moore didn't understand was that they'd lost thirty years; three decades of holidays, birthdays, family vacations, memories, inside jokes. Thirty years of developing relationships. There was no getting that back. Josie and her biological parents and siblings tried hard, spending as much time as possible together, but nothing would give them that time back. Nothing would heal the wound that those thirty years had left. Even though Josie knew that her family's pain from having lost her ran deep, her own pain felt deeper and infinitely more complicated. The woman who had stolen Josie from her family and raised her had abused her horribly and nearly destroyed her. Josie still struggled with the emotional scars that Lila Jensen had inflicted on her. She would carry those her entire life. No happy ending would fix that. Nothing would fix it. Nothing would eliminate the nightmares. She thought of the calls from Muncy prison. They didn't matter, she decided. Nothing would fix her.

Josie pointed to the closed door of Maya's room. "This is a happy ending, but Maya will live with the trauma of what happened to her until the day she dies. Plus, she has a child to raise now whether she wants to or not, a constant reminder of what was done to her. That's why this doesn't feel like a happy ending."

She felt a small niggling at the back of her mind, something telling her that wasn't the only reason, that they were missing some important piece of Maya's story, but she couldn't think what that might be.

Maya's door opened again and Gus emerged, face streaked with tears, but his smile as wide as a proud father the first time he gets to hold his child. "Thank you," he told them, shaking both their hands and then pulling them both into hard, awkward hugs. "Thank you so much."

"We're just doing our jobs, Mr. Bestler," Moore told him.

Gus shook his head. "I just can't believe it. I really thought Garrett had killed her. In my heart, I believed that. We knew that he had hit her before. She wouldn't leave him. It wasn't a stretch to think he had done something to her. He was the only one there with her. His story was so lame. I can't believe this. I mean, I'm glad—thrilled—that he didn't kill her. It's just so unbelievable. It's a miracle, that's what it is, a miracle."

He paused to suck in several deep breaths. Then he looked around. "Where's Sandy?"

Josie said, "She went downstairs with Lieutenant Fraley to the NICU to see your grandson."

His smile widened. "A grandson! I can't believe it. I wish it wasn't under these circumstances, but we'll love that little baby just as much as we love Maya."

Josie thought of the tension that had been radiating from Sandy's frame from the moment she'd arrived and wasn't sure Sandy would love the baby the same way that Gus would, but she didn't say anything. Instead, she smiled and touched his arm. "I'm happy that Maya and her baby are safe and with you again, Mr. Bestler."

"I'm going to stay with her tonight. That's okay, right? I can stay?"

Moore said, "As long as it's okay with the medical staff, of course you can stay. We'll let you have some quiet time. If we need to ask Maya or you folks any other questions, we'll come by, how's that?"

"Yes," Gus said. "Thank you."

"Well, actually, I just have one question I need to ask her," Josie interrupted. "Then we'll leave you in peace."

"Of course," Gus said.

Josie left Moore in the hall with Maya's father and went inside to show Maya a photo of the black walnut necklace. She asked Maya if she'd ever seen anything like it; if the man who had taken her had ever had or made anything like it; but Maya said no.

CHAPTER NINETEEN

It was well past the end of their shift by the time Josie and Noah returned to the station house, but she knew they weren't going home any time soon. There were more leads she wanted to look into, and the paperwork they'd need to prepare after the day they'd had would take hours. Gretchen arrived a few minutes after they did for her shift, drops of water rolling off her raincoat and onto the floor as she deposited Styrofoam containers of takeout from Josie's favorite restaurant onto both Josie's and Noah's desks. "I was just downstairs talking to Sergeant Lamay. He brought me up to speed—including the news about the creepy necklace. Sounds like you two had a whopper of a day," she said.

Josie opened the container to see creamy, delicious pasta with chunks of lobster and shrimp mixed in and swallowed the pool of saliva her mouth immediately produced.

From his desk nearby, Mettner said, "Hey, what about me? I had a whopper of a day too!"

Noah laughed. "Did you leave this building at all today?"

Mettner feigned a wounded look. "I did *a lot* of work today."

"Did you deliver a baby?" Josie asked, around a mouthful of fettucine noodles.

Mettner looked down at his desk. "Well, no, but I've been coordinating the search for your missing camper."

"From your desk," Noah said. "In a thunderstorm, which means that you called the search off—that's the extent of your coordinating."

"I did more than that," Mettner protested.

Noah smiled at him to let him know he was joking and added, "You know it was ninety-two degrees today. Josie and I had to throw our clothes away when we got home. Those kinds of sweat stains don't come out in the wash."

Gretchen reached into the large paper tote bag she'd brought in and produced another container, which she placed in front of Mettner. "Come on, Mett," she said. "You think I'd forget about you?"

He smiled with childlike delight as he opened it and picked up a huge cheeseburger, slices of bacon hanging from beneath its bun, and bit into it. For a few moments, there was silence while the three of them ate.

Josie's pasta was gone in record time. "That was delicious. You always remember what I like. Thank you."

"Hey," Noah said. "*I* always remember what you like, too."

With a wide-eyed look of innocence, Josie said, "Yeah, but I bet Gretchen doesn't have a toaster oven."

Noah's plastic fork struck her shoulder and she laughed.

Gretchen hung her raincoat over a nearby empty chair and sat at her desk. She shook water out of her short, spiked, brown hair. In her hand she held only a cup of coffee. "I ate before I got here," she explained. "Fill me in. Where are we with the missing camper and this Maya Bestler thing?"

Noah said, "The death notification was made on Tyler's dad, Wesley Yates. I just left him a voicemail message."

Mettner said, "Boss found photos of a woman the Yateses hung out with all the time on Tyler's Facebook page. Thinks it might be the third camper."

Josie said, "We're hoping Wesley Yates can either tell us who went camping with them or the name of the woman in the photos."

"In the meantime," Mettner said, "I'm going to work through Tyler's friend list to see if anyone will talk to me and can tell me anything about the camping trip and whether they know the woman's name."

"We're also waiting for Hummel to get back. He was in Lenore County with the ERT processing the Yates vehicle," Josie added. "Right now, I'm going to call Garret Romney, Maya Bestler's former boyfriend; give him the news that she's been found; and ask if he knew the Yates couple."

Gretchen said, "While you're doing that, I'm going to search the National Crime Information Center database for any other homicides where a crude homemade black walnut necklace was found inside or around the body."

"Good call," Josie said. She picked up her phone and dialed. After four rings, a man's voice answered.

"Mr. Romney?" Josie asked. "Garrett Romney?"

Suspicion quickened his tone. "Who is this?"

"My name is Josie Quinn. I'm a detective with the Denton Police Department."

"Denton?" He said. "Where's that?"

"We're about two hours west of where you live," she explained. "North of Lenore County."

There was an icy silence.

"Mr. Romney?"

"When are you assholes going to drop this? I didn't kill my girlfriend. It's been two years. You need to let this go. I'm calling my lawyer."

"Maya's alive," Josie blurted.

Another beat of silence. Then she heard two small gasps. He said, "Maya's alive?"

"Yes. She was found today. She's hospitalized but stable. She thought you would want to know."

"I don't—I can't—" he stammered. "Why are you telling me this?"

Josie wasn't sure she wanted to put Maya Bestler back in touch with someone who had allegedly abused her, but she had asked for Garrett to be notified; and sooner or later he would find out. "I actually have some questions for you about an unrelated case—"

He cut her off. "You're trying to pin something else on me now? What did Maya say? She told you it wasn't me, right? She said that, right?"

"Yes," Josie said. "By her account, you had nothing to do with her abduction."

"Abduction?" he said and the question in his tone surprised Josie.

She said, "Yes, abduction. Someone took her and held her captive. What did you think happened to her?"

He laughed humorlessly. "Honestly? I thought she ran off, hid somewhere; let me take the blame for this whole thing. I know she wanted to leave me."

And yet, Garrett was the first and only person that Maya had asked about.

"Well, she was abducted," Josie told him. "Now she's safe. If you wouldn't mind answering a few questions for me—"

"I said no."

"Do you know anyone named Tyler or Valerie Yates?"

"Never heard of them," he said, hostility dripping from every syllable.

Before he could hang up, Josie slipped in another question. "When was the last time you were in Lenore County?"

"Eighteen months ago, and I'm not coming back there so don't even ask."

"There's no need for you to return to Lenore County," she said. "But you're welcome to come to Alcott County if you'd like to visit Maya."

"You think I want to visit that bitch? Tell you what—why don't you give her a message for me? Tell her to go to hell."

The line went dead. Josie pulled the phone away from her face and stared at it as if Garrett Romney's rage could be seen emanating from it.

"What was that about?" Noah asked.

Josie shrugged. "I'm not entirely sure."

She sincerely hoped that Garrett Romney decided not to visit Maya. "You would think that if your girlfriend went missing two years ago from a campsite in the middle of the night, and you knew you had nothing to do with her vanishing, you'd be happy to hear that she was found alive."

Gretchen said, "That would be the normal response."

"That guy obviously has some issues," Mettner interjected. "I could hear him all the way over here."

Noah said, "You think we need to talk to him in person?"

"No," Josie said. "I don't. Maya didn't implicate him."

"You think he could have been involved in the new case?" Mettner asked.

Josie said, "I strongly doubt it. I think a more likely suspect in the Yates case is the man who took and held Maya."

Noah said, "I checked that file Moore gave us. The Bestler/Romney campsite was only five miles from where the Yateses were camping."

"You think Romney was lying about not knowing the Yateses?" Gretchen asked.

Josie shook her head. "No. He didn't hesitate. I don't think he knew them. I didn't see his name on Tyler's list of Facebook friends either. We could look for other connections—workplaces, maybe—but I'm not sure they exist. I don't think he warrants any more of our focus at this point."

Gretchen said, "I agree. By the way, nothing in the NCIC about black walnuts or black walnut necklaces."

Hummel walked into the great room, carrying a small, brown paper evidence bag in his gloved hands. "Got something for you, boss."

Josie cleared some space on her desk, and Hummel shook out the contents of the paper bag. It was a dog-eared paperback book: *Strength: Mark of Nexus Book 1* by Carrie Butler. Noah walked over and stared at it. "Looks like a good book," he said. "But I'm not sure how this helps us."

With mock seriousness, Hummel said, "Watch it, Fraley, or next time you'll be bagging your own vomit." He used a gloved finger to open the front cover of the book. Inside, along the top left-hand side of the cover in thick magic marker someone had written: *E. Gresham.*

"Where was this?" Josie asked.

"In the back seat of the Yateses' car," Hummel answered.

Mettner came around and looked at it. "I'm not sure that means anything. It could be a used book."

"It's well-worn," Josie said. "Whoever E. Gresham is—she read this a lot."

"How do we know it's a she?" Gretchen said.

Noah examined the book and said, "This is a paranormal new adult romance, and it's got a shirtless musclebound man on the cover. The odds are the owner is a woman."

"Maybe it belongs to Valerie Yates," Mettner suggested.

"No," Josie said. "Valerie Yates had a paperback book in her backpack. Hummel, do you have a photo of it?"

"I uploaded them to the file already," he said as he slid the copy of *Strength* back into the evidence bag and took off his gloves.

Josie used her mouse to pull up the photos from the Yates scene on her computer monitor. She clicked through several before coming to the contents of Valerie Yates' backpack. "It's called *Too Blessed to be Stressed: Three Minute Devotions for Women* by Debora M. Coty," Josie said. She pulled up Amazon and looked the book up there. "This is a book aimed at inspiring Christian women and strengthening their faith. Not the same fare. I think we can assume that the book in the car belongs to E. Gresham."

Noah was already at his computer. "Was there anyone named Gresham on the list of Tyler Yates' Facebook friends?"

"Not that I remember," Josie said.

"There weren't," Mettner said.

Noah clicked a few times with his mouse. "Let me see if I can find any E. Greshams in Fox Mill, Pennsylvania."

Josie walked around the desks so she could peer over his shoulder. She watched as he entered the last name into the TLO XP database. No Greshams in Fox Mill. There were several Greshams in the state of Pennsylvania, however, seven of them with first names starting with E. Of those, four were female. Noah began pulling up their driver's license photos. On the third one, Josie said, "That's it! That's her!"

Over Josie's shoulder, Gretchen read the first name. "Emilia Gresham, twenty-eight. How do you know she's the one we're looking for?"

Josie said, "She's the one in the photos with Tyler and Valerie Yates."

"She lives in Furlong. Only a few miles from the Yateses," Gretchen said. "Call the police there and ask them to do a welfare check."

"On it," Noah said, picking up his phone.

Gretchen nudged him aside, clicked a few things on the computer, and across the room one of the printers started to spit out papers. "There are a few potential relatives here," she said. "I'll look them up."

"Perfect," Josie said. "I'd like to confirm that she was with Tyler and Valerie Yates if we can, but even if we can't, I think we should call WYEP and ask them to run her photo as a missing camper."

"Isn't that a little premature?" Mettner said. "We don't know one hundred percent that she was the other camper."

"True," Josie conceded. "But if I'm right, and it is her, and she's in trouble, we need to find her as quickly as possible. If her life is in danger, I don't want to take any chances. With this weather, we won't be able to use the K-9 unit until tomorrow—if it clears up. Maybe Gretchen can confirm with her known associates that she was on a camping trip. Regardless of what we turn up, I want her photo on the eleven o'clock news this evening. I'm not taking chances with her life. We can always retract the story later if we've got it wrong."

Gretchen said, "I'm on it. I'll get the Chief's approval for the press coverage."

"Thanks," Josie said. "Also, I want to go back over to the commune and show Emilia Gresham's photo to the people there."

Mettner jumped up. "I'll go with you."

Noah laughed. "Feeling guilty about being dry and in the air conditioning all day, Mett?"

Mettner bristled. "I'm feeling like maybe I should be in the field."

"Bring a poncho and prepare to sweat," Josie told him. "Let's go."

Gretchen waved them off. "I'll see what I can find out about Ms. Gresham."

Noah said, "I'll work on the Yateses' known associates."

"Someone should also go through the list of people actually living at the commune right now and do some background checks," Josie said.

"We'll handle it," Gretchen assured her.

CHAPTER TWENTY

Josie managed to avoid Charlotte during the trip to the Sanctuary with Mettner. The women who had worked in the kitchen earlier remembered her and let the two of them roam the property showing Emilia Gresham's photo to every person they could find. Wearing ponchos and using flashlights Mettner had pulled from his trunk, they slogged through the wet grass down to the tent area. Only a few people remained there, including Megan, the commune nurse, but none of them recognized Emilia Gresham. Luckily, the storm had sent almost all the residents into the barn to wait it out. Most were seated in the center, propped up against the fronts of the stalls, so Josie and Mettner worked their way to the back of the barn, getting blank looks and monosyllabic answers. Josie kept an eye on the last stall to the right—Renee's stall. Tru stood at the entrance to it, facing away from Josie and Mettner. His head was bent down, as though he was looking at the floor, or more likely, at Renee's cot. He spoke in a hushed tone and even as Josie drew closer, she couldn't make out what he said.

Finally, as she made it to the end, Josie stepped into the stall to find Renee curled up on the cot in the same long-sleeved shirt, pants, and boots as earlier. Her hands were tucked in fists beneath her chin. Tru looked at Josie, eyes wide. "You're back. Did something happen?"

Josie smiled reassuringly. "No, we just have one more photo we wanted people to have a look at." She showed him Emilia's picture, but his expression showed no flicker of recognition. "Sorry," he said. "Never saw her."

"Well, thank you for looking," Josie said, keeping the smile on her face. Pleasant. Non-threatening. "Do you mind if I have a moment with Renee?"

Tru looked from Josie to Renee and back. "She said she isn't feeling well."

"It will only take a minute."

He looked out over the tops of the stalls, as if searching for someone—Charlotte? Someone else? Josie wondered. When he didn't find who or what he was looking for, he said, "Um sure, I guess."

He stepped out of the stall but stayed clearly within earshot. Josie wondered if he had been assigned to guard Renee. She took out her phone and fired off a text to Mettner. *Blond guy in the back right. Distract him.*

She pocketed her phone and sat on the edge of Renee's cot. "Hi Renee," she said softly. "I'm back. Tru said you're not feeling well. I'm sorry to hear that."

No response.

Trying to buy time until Mettner got rid of Tru, Josie said, "I promise I won't take up too much of your time. It's just a photo of a young woman. Let me pull it up again. Now, where did it go?"

She saw the top of Mettner's head as he strode down the center aisle. When he was five or six feet away from Renee's stall, he went down. She heard his body thud on the floor, heard him mutter, "Shit," and then Tru rushed toward him. "You okay, man?" Tru asked before his head disappeared beneath the top of the stalls. While Mettner made a fuss over his "bad knee", fully capturing Tru's attention, Josie leaned closer to Renee's face.

Her heartbeat skipped when she saw a smear of blood on the outer edge of Renee's hand, disappearing into her sleeve. It was fresh. "Renee," Josie whispered. "I need you to be honest with me. Is someone here hurting you?"

The girl said nothing, but her eyes brimmed with tears. She closed them tightly, her entire body tensing. Josie continued, "You don't have to stay here. I know you think you do, but you really don't. I promise nothing bad will happen to you if you come with me."

"I—I can't," Renee said, her voice hoarse, eyes open again, glassy and wide.

Josie looked up but didn't see either Tru or Mettner. The heads of the people she could see appeared to be focused on Mettner's fake fall and knee injury.

"Okay," Josie said. "Tell me what's going on. I can help you."

"I can't tell." Her voice was so small, Josie could barely make out the words.

"You can tell me."

"That's not how it works here."

They were running out of time. "Then I'll leave, and I'll drive down the road and wait for you. At midnight—"

"No clocks," Renee muttered.

Mettner was now upright, leaning heavily on Tru, who kept glancing back at Renee's stall. "Right," Josie said. "Okay, let's do this. I'll take my colleague and leave. We'll drive down the road, to the right. There's a hill. We'll wait at the bottom for two hours. Say you're going to the bathroom or for a walk or whatever. Come find us and we'll take you away from here. You'll be safe, I promise."

She touched Renee's shoulder and the girl flinched. "Can you do that for me?"

No response.

"Can you try?"

She squeezed her eyes shut again and gave a small nod.

As Tru dragged Mettner back toward Renee's stall, Josie thought of something else. "Are you able to leave this stall? Or are they holding you here against your will?"

Before Renee could answer, Tru and Mettner stumbled into the stall. "Boss," Mettner said, his face twisted in imaginary pain. "I think I messed up my knee."

"Okay," Josie said. "We'll get going." She looked at her phone. "Here's the photo," she said. "Renee?"

The girl opened her eyes and stared at Emilia Gresham. "She's not here."

Josie and Tru spoke at the same time.

Josie said, "She's not here right now. But you saw her? You know her?"

Tru said, "Renee needs her rest."

He left Mettner leaning on the stall door and moved over, kneeling and inserting himself between Josie and Renee.

Josie calculated in her mind. If she pressed the issue now, they might clam up even more. She might cause more trouble for Renee. Then she'd get nothing. Emilia would still be missing, and Renee would be worse for wear. She thought about tracking Charlotte down and confronting her, but she didn't believe for a moment that Charlotte would be honest. Certainly, she wouldn't admit to Josie that anything criminal was happening on her property. If she was complicit in whatever was happening to Renee, then confronting her would only alert her to Josie's suspicions. What would happen to Renee then? No, Josie had to be very careful. Her only choice was to retreat and hope that Renee took her up on the offer to meet down the road later.

Josie stood and offered an arm to Mettner. "I'm sorry," she said to Tru and Renee. "We'll let her rest. Let's go, Mett."

CHAPTER TWENTY-ONE

Once they left the barn, they walked the rest of the property looking for stragglers, their flashlight beams sweeping back and forth in front of them. Mettner feigned a limp. They only found two more members in the greenhouse but neither of them recognized Emilia Gresham. Even in the rain, the heat and humidity hadn't let up. After covering a great deal of ground at the Sanctuary, they trudged back to Mettner's vehicle soaked with sweat. Mettner blasted his air conditioner as Josie pulled her seat belt on. "What was that all about? With that guy and the sick girl."

"I talked with her earlier today. I think she was injured. I think someone is hurting her. She wouldn't say it outright, but all the signs are there." Josie recapped both encounters with Renee Kelly.

"So the big blond dude was there to make sure she didn't say anything to the police," Mettner said.

"Great job distracting him, by the way," Josie laughed.

"Sorry, I couldn't think of anything else. Also, I figured if I caused a scene, that would also have everyone else's attention on me and not you."

"Good thinking."

At the bottom of the hill down the road from the Sanctuary, Mettner pulled over onto the shoulder of the road and cut his headlights. "So I guess we're waiting here for two hours, then."

"It will be worth it if she comes," Josie promised. "You heard what she said when I showed her Emilia's photograph."

"Yeah, 'She's not here,'" Mettner supplied. "Everyone else said, 'Never seen her' or 'Don't recognize her.'"

"Right. 'She's not here' implies that she was there at some point. Renee knows things that the others don't want her to tell."

"But I thought this Charlotte was some organic nature goddess or something—all about peace and love and that kind of stuff. That's how Fraley made it sound."

"He was right," Josie said. "That's exactly how Charlotte portrayed it, but those people are hiding something."

"Well, all cults have something to hide, don't they?"

"You could argue that," Josie said. "We need to know if whatever they're hiding has anything to do with the murders of Tyler and Valerie Yates or the disappearance of the third camper."

She leaned back into the seat and took her phone out, turning the brightness down to its lowest level where she could still see it, but it wouldn't attract attention, and shot off texts to Noah and Gretchen to let them know what was going on.

The rain pelted the car's roof, lulling Josie into a near-sleep. Her eyes burned with fatigue. The nightmare of the night before and the early morning lovemaking with Noah seemed like an eternity ago. They watched the road, eventually tossing out theories about the case in order to stay awake. One hour passed, then another.

Renee Kelly was not coming.

"Dammit," Josie said.

"What do you want to do?" Mettner asked.

Josie's head sank into her hands. "She knows something, Mett. She's in trouble."

"You can't make her come out, boss, and you can't storm the property and take her—or sneak her out. Shit, we're not even in our own jurisdiction."

Josie looked up at the rain-soaked windshield and swore.

Mettner asked, "You want to wait longer?"

"Gretchen's on all night, right? We'll ask her to come and wait. At least for a little while."

Mettner took out his phone and called the station. Twenty minutes later, Gretchen pulled up behind them. Josie got out of Mettner's car and ran to Gretchen's window. "Thanks for doing this," she said.

"Not a problem, boss," Gretchen replied.

"Is Noah still at the station?"

"He said he was going over to the hospital to check on the baby."

"Did someone call?" Josie asked. "Is the baby okay?"

"No one called. He finished up background checks on the list of people you guys talked to at the Sanctuary. No red flags. Nothing of interest. A couple of them had old DUIs and a few others had speeding tickets but that was it. Then he worked on the Tyler Yates angle and when he was finished, he got up and said he was going to the hospital to see how Baby Bestler was doing."

Josie felt a kernel of anxiety break open inside her, but she ignored it, focusing instead on the case. "Did he get anywhere with Tyler Yates?"

"He talked to a few friends who didn't know a hell of a lot. The Facebook friends he was able to get in touch with are people Tyler went to high school with or worked with at a fast food place when he was sixteen. They haven't actually talked to him or seen him in person in ten years. Noah did manage to find out where Tyler worked."

"That sounds promising," Josie said.

"He was a consultant for Bratina Property Management. Noah called and confirmed with them that he isn't expected back at work for another week. It was a pre-planned vacation."

Josie swiped at the rain falling into her eyes. Too late, she realized she should have gotten into the car for this conversation. "Well, that doesn't help much. What about Valerie Yates?"

"She was a schoolteacher at an elementary school in Fox Mill so she's off for the summer."

"Family members?" Josie asked.

"As it turns out, she's originally from Australia. Noah managed to get in touch with her parents, but they won't be able to get here for a couple of days. They weren't too sure about her friends. Noah emailed them a photo of Valerie and Tyler with Emilia Gresham to see if they recognize her or know anything about her. He's waiting on a response."

"He's waiting at the hospital, I guess."

By the low light of the dash, Josie saw Gretchen's quizzical look. "He's got the email app on his phone. I'm sure he'll let us know as soon as he hears anything."

Josie forced a smile. "Yes, he will. Did you find anything out about Emilia Gresham?"

"I asked the local PD to do a welfare check. There was no answer at her apartment. I found a work profile on LinkedIn. She's the director of the Stepping Stones Baptist Church Pre-K program. I was able to confirm that she just took two weeks of paid vacation. Although the Pre-K program is out of session, they're running summer camps that Emilia also oversees."

"She was probably camping with the Yates couple," Josie said.

"It's looking more and more likely. Here's where things get interesting. I asked who the emergency contact was, and they said her husband, Jack Gresham."

"He must be the man in Tyler Yates' photos," Josie said. "Did you check his driver's license photo?"

"He shows up in the database as a potential relative of Emilia's, and yes, I matched his driver's license photo to Tyler Yates' photos. It's the same guy. Same mailing address as Emilia. However, his cell phone has been disconnected, and his driver's license expired last year and was not renewed."

Josie frowned. "Did you check for a death certificate?"

"I did," Gretchen replied. "No death certificate. No obituary. Emilia's boss seemed to think he was alive and well. So did her family, by the way."

"What?"

"I was able to get in touch with a sister. Apparently, Emilia is from Rhode Island, one of seven children. Her mother passed away when she was a senior in high school, and her father is battling prostate cancer. Her sister said she calls once a week. They heard from her two days ago, but she didn't say anything about camping."

"Did you ask the sister if Emilia had mentioned her husband?" Josie asked. She had a creeping sense of dread thinking about Emilia and the way her husband, Jack, had disappeared from Tyler Yates' photos two years earlier.

"Her sister said that Emilia told her Jack was fine, just working a lot."

"Really? Where does Jack work?"

Gretchen put on her reading glasses, took out her notebook, flipped through some pages, and then held it up to the light coming from the dash, reading from her notes. "He worked in the service department of Cloudserv Technologies. They lease copiers and other office equipment."

"What did they say when you called them?"

"That he was laid off due to cutbacks three and a half years ago."

"Really?" Josie said.

"Yes," Gretchen answered. "Really. Like I said, I asked the local PD where the Greshams live to go to the residence for Emilia's welfare check, but no one was at their residence. They asked around about both Greshams. One of the neighbors said they haven't seen Jack in ages but couldn't say how long 'ages' was—could be months or even a couple of years. The same neighbor did say that Emilia left with some bags a few days ago."

Josie took this in. "I take it Jack Gresham was not reported missing."

"He was not."

"Did you tell Emilia's sister that we thought she might be missing?" Josie asked.

"I told her we had found the Yateses passed away during what appeared to be a camping trip. Didn't get into the homicide angle. She recognized their names. She said they've been friends with Emilia and Jack for many years. She was very upset. I told her we thought Emilia was with them, but she said Emilia hadn't mentioned anything about going camping when they last spoke to her. She asked me if Jack was with them because they always do everything together. I told her it didn't appear that he had been. She said she didn't think Emilia was with them. I texted her a photo of the gold chain and heart-shaped charm we found in the sleeping bag, but she didn't recognize it."

"But she lives in Rhode Island so she might not see Emilia frequently enough to be familiar with what jewelry she wears on a regular basis," Josie said. "Did you ask her about the book we found in the car?" Josie asked.

"Yeah, she knew the one I was talking about. She said that's Emilia's favorite series. She's read it dozens of times."

"Let me guess: she said because she spends so much time with Valerie and Tyler, she could have just left the book in the car."

Gretchen held up a finger, clarifying, "Because she and *Jack* spend so much time with them, yes."

"She's in denial. I would be too," Josie said. "No one wants to face something like this—that their sister's best friends were found dead and that she might be missing or worse—and if they're already dealing with their father's cancer diagnosis…"

"This would be horribly devastating," Gretchen finished.

"Where did you leave things?"

"She's going to drive down to Furlong tomorrow, she says, and talk with Jack. That is, if she can't get in touch with Emilia tonight. I got Emilia's cell phone number from her. I already got a warrant so we can try to locate her phone since it wasn't at the campsite. I sent it to her cell phone carrier and asked that it be expedited."

"Great," Josie said. "I'm getting soaked. Mett and I will go back to the station. I'll see you tomorrow unless Renee shows."

"You got it."

Mettner dropped Josie off at the station so she could finish up on some paperwork. She typed away at her reports as she thought about what they knew. Valerie and Tyler had been good friends with Emilia and Jack Gresham. They'd done everything together, which was evident from Tyler Yates' Facebook photos. They were four young professionals. Two married couples. Then something happened. Jack was laid off from work. He disappeared from the photos. His and Emilia's neighbor stopped seeing him.

She called Gretchen. "No sign of the girl," she told Josie.

"I don't think she's going to show. Listen, I've been thinking about the Greshams. It sounds like Jack has been MIA for a while now."

"If you put all the pieces we have so far together, yes."

"But it doesn't sound like Emilia has told anyone. If he was laid off three years ago, why would she tell her sister he was working a lot?"

"Maybe he had gotten another job?"

"Possibly."

"We don't know what his situation is," Gretchen said. "He could be having an affair; they could be separated; he could be hooked on drugs."

Josie nodded along with each suggestion even though Gretchen couldn't see her. "But in all of those cases, he'd probably still have a phone."

"Unless Emilia stopped paying for it, and he's got a new number now."

"True," Josie said, but her mind was working in a different direction. She thought back to the expressionless faces of the people they'd questioned at the Sanctuary that day. She didn't remember seeing anyone who resembled Jack Gresham, but the photos she had seen of him were a few years old. It was possible his hair might be different. He might have gained or lost weight. Grown a beard. "Where's the list of people living at the Sanctuary?"

"The middle of Noah's desk," Gretchen answered. "You think Jack Gresham is living at the Sanctuary?"

Josie reached across to Noah's desk and snatched up the list. She pored over it. "I don't know but it's pretty coincidental, don't you think? He's been somewhat unaccounted for, for a long period of time; his wife is covering up his absence; and then she and their two best friends go camping only miles away from the commune?"

Gretchen said, "I'm not sure we have enough information to draw that conclusion."

"It's a long shot," Josie conceded. She finished studying the list and let out a long sigh. "And you're right—he's not on this list."

She tossed the list back onto Noah's desk and plopped into her chair. The first thumps of a headache began to pulse behind her eyes. "How about the Yateses' phones? Did we get anything from the phone companies?"

"No. We probably won't until tomorrow or the next day."

From across the room, Josie heard the sound of Chief Bob Chitwood's door opening and then his voice boomed, "Quinn, where are the other three?"

Josie swiveled in her chair, feeling the usual mixture of dread and irritation that Chitwood inspired in her and just about every other officer on the force. Chitwood had been appointed chief by the mayor nearly a year ago, after Josie's short tenure as interim chief.

Josie said, "I'm on the phone with Gretchen, Noah's at the hospital, and Mettner had to go home to shower. He'll be back any second."

As Chitwood moved closer, white wisps of his thinning hair floated over his head. He folded his arms across his rail-thin chest and stared down at her. "Put Palmer on speaker, would you?"

Josie pressed the speaker button on her cell phone. Gretchen said, "Chief?"

Chitwood said, "We've got two dead bodies and a missing woman. You know how I feel about bodies and missing women, don't you?"

Josie stared at him blankly and said, "How's that, sir?"

He bent at the waist, looming over her, and shouted, "I don't want them in my city!"

Gretchen said, "Well, if it helps, Quinn *found* a missing woman today."

For just a second, the corner of Chitwood's mouth twitched as though he was fighting back a smile. Then he pointed a long, gnarled finger at the phone. Josie wanted to remind him that Gretchen couldn't see him, but she didn't dare speak. "Nobody likes a smart ass, Palmer." He turned his gaze to Josie, "Good work with that baby, Quinn."

The compliment was so unexpected and out of character for Chitwood that Josie barely got out the words, "Thank you, sir."

He went on as though he hadn't heard her. "I want to get ahead of both of these cases. I don't need another press circus so soon after the Ross case, you got that?"

Neither of them responded. Chitwood continued, "You need to split your resources. Quinn and Fraley are on the Bestler mess. Palmer, you and Mettner will take the Yates and Gresham fiasco."

"Quinn and Fraley caught the Yates and Gresham case," Gretchen said. "That's their case."

Chitwood rolled his eyes and leaned over to shout into the phone. "You have fifteen years of experience in homicide, and guess what? I'm your boss, so you're taking that case. Quinn hasn't done half bad at abduction cases in the past, so she's on Bestler. Speaking of you, Quinn." He looked at her once more. She fought the urge to squirm beneath his flinty gaze. "Go the hell home and sleep, would you? I just talked to the Lenore County Sheriff's department. You, Fraley, and a couple of their guys are going into the caverns tomorrow to try and find the guy who took Maya Bestler. Fraley told me Moore was dragging ass today so I called his Chief. He sent Moore to the hospital earlier to have Maya Bestler look at maps. He was instructed to have her draw a diagram of inside the caverns if she can. Meet them at the county line on Route 9227 at eight a.m., got it?"

Into the caverns.

She felt her throat closing, panic a vise around her neck.

"Quinn," Chitwood barked. "You got that?"

Unable to force words out, Josie nodded.

CHAPTER TWENTY-TWO

Josie hung up with Gretchen and left the station house, heading home. She thought about stopping at the hospital to speak with Noah, but the panic raging inside her was still at a fever pitch. She wasn't sure she could maintain her composure in a public place. Besides, she reasoned, Noah lived with her now. He'd have to come home eventually.

At home, she turned on all the lights on the first floor. Television couldn't hold her attention, so she paced from room to room, her nerves jangling like loose change in her brain.

Into the caverns.

She focused on her breathing. In, out. In, out.

Sitting at the kitchen table, she pulled out her phone to ask Noah to come home, but her eyes were drawn to the notifications over the voicemail icon. Without thinking, she opened the voicemail app and played the message. It was from the social worker at Muncy State Prison. "Detective Quinn," she said and introduced herself. "I'm just calling to let you know that inmate Lila Jensen is very ill. The last round of chemotherapy was not as successful as the doctors had hoped. We've placed her in hospice care. It's a matter of days, from what I understand. I thought you would want to know. She's been asking for you repeatedly. Please give me a call to discuss visitation."

Disgusted, Josie threw her phone across the room. It smacked into the cabinet door beneath the kitchen sink and fell to the floor. "*Discuss visitation*," she muttered. It implied that Josie didn't have a choice, that it was inevitable Josie would visit a dying woman.

Didn't it matter what Lila had done to Josie? Did Lila's dying wish trump all the horror Lila had inflicted on Josie when she was just an innocent child?

Without realizing it, Josie had crossed the room and opened one of her overhead cabinets. An unopened bottle of Wild Turkey stared back at her. Just one sip, she thought, then the demons swirling around her would be quiet. For a little while. But Wild Turkey had always been a short-term solution to her problems—and consuming it never ended well for her. Over a year ago, she'd sworn off drinking. Then five months earlier, after Noah's mother was murdered and he'd broken up with her, she'd taken it up again. The result of that night was not something she wanted to relive. She'd promised herself she wouldn't drink again.

Just one shot, urged a voice in the back of her head.

She slammed the cabinet door closed. It was never just one shot, though, was it? By the time Noah returned home, she'd be half a bottle deep and she'd say things she knew she'd regret. She'd ask questions she didn't want to know the answers to—like whether or not he'd stay with her if, ultimately, she decided not to have children. She realized now that that was a conversation they should have had before moving in together. When she was married to her late husband, Ray, they'd always been on the same page, having both survived horrific childhood experiences. Both of them had been abused, and they didn't want to pass down those genes. But since then, Josie had found out that the woman she had thought was her mother wasn't her mother at all, and that she actually came from a good and loving family. Her DNA wasn't tainted after all.

Still, she had so many reservations about her ability to be a good mother. She was happy serving and being of use to others through her job. A job that she worried would interfere with mothering a child of her own. It was fear, pure and simple. Now it was being compounded by the fact that Noah couldn't stay away from Baby Bestler. He had a niece and he often helped Josie babysit her friend

Misty's son, but he'd never been so enamored of either one of those children. Was it because he'd watched the baby come into the world, she wondered, that he couldn't tear himself away? Or had he reached a point where he wanted children of his own?

"It's only been a day," she muttered to herself. It felt like weeks since she had broken her coffee mug on the unwieldy toaster oven. She padded over to the kitchen table, pushing thoughts of the Wild Turkey out of her head.

She sat down and paged through the Maya Bestler file that Moore had given them earlier. Everything Moore had already told her was inside, including photos of the superficial cut on Garrett Romney's forehead. It was razor thin and only two inches long with little bruising; Josie could see why investigators had thought it was self-inflicted. The round, angry face beneath it did nothing to dispel the notion that Romney might be violent. His brown eyes were glittering marbles of hatred, and his thin upper lip lifted in a sneer. The initial reports described him as combative and uncooperative. Still, that wasn't enough to try him for murder. Exhaustive searches didn't turn up any sign of Maya, which was curious considering Maya's account of her abduction. Had the hermit moved her into the caverns before searchers gained on them? Had they not thought to check the caves? Josie made a note to ask Moore in the morning.

The file was thick, considering what little evidence police had been able to glean from the campsite and from Garrett Romney. It looked as though the prosecutors had tried hard to amass circumstantial evidence against him, perhaps with the hope of going forward one day without a body. There were statements from neighbors, friends, and coworkers of Maya stating that she often appeared bruised and in pain. Some neighbors reported often hearing her screaming behind closed doors. On four separate occasions, Doylestown police department had been called to Maya and Garrett's home for domestic disturbances but in all four instances, Maya had insisted that Garrett hadn't laid a hand on her. There were medical records as well documenting three of her fractures with ER visits. In each one of them, Maya said she had fallen. In spite of all of this, Garrett was the first and only person Maya asked for after she escaped. This didn't surprise Josie though; domestic violence survivors were often deeply entrenched in their abusive relationships, even when they didn't want to be. It was no easier to separate themselves emotionally from these men than it was physically. Going against their abusers could mean—and often did—death.

The sight of Renee Kelly cowering on her cot floated to the forefront of Josie's mind. Was she being abused by an individual on the commune or was there something more systemic going on? None of the other Sanctuary members appeared to be hurt or in distress. Coached, yes, but not despairing the way that Renee Kelly appeared.

But it wasn't her case anymore. Chitwood had taken her off the Yates/Gresham case and any connection it may or may not have to the Sanctuary. She would have been upset except that Chitwood was right—Gretchen was the best woman for the job. Her experience in Philadelphia's homicide department gave her an edge over Josie. That was fine. Josie cared more about the case being solved than her own ego.

She closed the file and rubbed her burning eyes. The bottle of Wild Turkey called to her again. She could practically feel its warmth sliding down her throat. But no. She needed sleep, she decided, not alcohol. She retrieved her phone from the kitchen floor. Upstairs, she stripped down to her T-shirt and crawled into bed. She didn't know if she'd still be awake when Noah got home, so she sent him a text letting him know they were due to meet Moore the next morning to explore the underground caverns in hopes of finding the hermit.

He responded almost immediately. *Be home soon.*

But she was asleep in minutes.

CHAPTER TWENTY-THREE

Josie cried until her thin, seven-year-old body had nothing left. Her tears soaked into the rough, smelly carpet on the closet floor. "You promised, Mommy," she said over and over again. "You promised." The words had started out loud and forceful and now they were weak and jagged, pushing out on the edge of the shudders that racked her tiny body. Lila had promised Josie that she wouldn't have to go into the closet as long as she didn't tell anyone that it was Lila who had sliced open her face. But Lila had tossed her in anyway.

"Shut up," Lila hollered from the other side of the closet door.

The darkness was absolute. Josie heard the scrape of a chair as Lila pushed it up against the closet door, cutting off the last sliver of light from beneath the door. Josie rolled back and forth, slamming herself against the door, then wall, door, wall. She pushed her feet against the wall and screamed. The closet wasn't big enough for her to stretch out. Staggering to her feet, she thrust her hands forward and suddenly the too-close walls of the closet were gone. She took a few steps, first walking, then running, but the darkness didn't end. No matter which direction she turned, there was no light to be found. She was trapped in the darkness forever. Panic squeezed her chest, crushing her so she could barely breathe.

"Mommy, please," she cried again. "I'm scared."

From somewhere came Lila's voice, spiteful and biting. "You're never coming out, JoJo. I told you, if you said one word, you were going into the closet forever."

"I didn't tell, Mommy," Josie insisted, lurching through the darkness, looking for something to grab onto. Anything besides the unrelenting, endless blackness.

Suddenly, a hand squeezed Josie's chin and the side of her face where her scar was burned. She flailed her arms but there was no one there. Then Lila's face appeared, bathed in light, inches from Josie's own. Her lips peeled back from her teeth, which were sharpened to points. "Not one word," she growled.

Josie slapped at her but hit nothing except air. Warmth poured down her legs and the smell of urine stung her nostrils. She tried to move her head, but Lila's ghost grip held it in place. Josie stared into Lila's mouth as it opened wide and a black walnut fell out.

Her screams echoed off the bedroom ceiling and walls. She followed Noah's voice out of the nightmare. "Josie, Josie wake up." She reached out into the darkness, relief flooding through her as she felt Noah's chest. "The lights," she gasped. "I need the lights."

He pulled her into his arms, rolling slightly to reach the bedside table. She heard a click and then soft light flooded the room. Her room. Their room. Her huge, beautiful king-sized bed. The bank of windows along one wall that would let the sunshine in the moment it peeked over the horizon. The closet with no door, her and Noah's clothes hanging from the rod, their shoes lined up on the floor. She clutched at him, the solid feel of his body in her hands bringing her back from the brink of hysteria. Gently, he stroked her hair away from her face and cupped her chin, his touch light and tender compared to the memory of Lila's fingers digging into her skin.

She looked into his hazel eyes.

His thumb traced her cheekbone, wiping away a tear. Jesus, she was crying. She wasn't a crier. Noah said, "We can sleep with the lights on if that helps."

The fact that he didn't ask questions or press her about the nightmares or why they were becoming so frequent made her tears come faster. She nodded and pressed her face into his chest. He held her, settling back against the headboard. She looked over and saw that his clock read four forty-seven in the morning. She knew she wouldn't be able to go back to sleep. When she closed her eyes, the image of Lila's face, her yawning mouth, the black walnut came rushing back, causing a tremble in Josie's body. Each time, Noah's arms tightened around her. He fell back to sleep but she stayed awake, inhaling his scent and studying him. Dark stubble dotted his jawline. She traced it with her fingers and stared into his face which was loose and expressionless in sleep. At once she felt grateful for his presence and fearful that what they had wouldn't be enough for him. Would he be able to withstand this? Her demons?

As the morning stretched on and daylight crept in through the windows, she set those thoughts aside and nudged him awake. "Hey," she said. "We have to get up."

He groaned something unintelligible but didn't open his eyes.

"Noah," she said. "Wake up."

She ran her fingers through his thick brown hair until he opened his eyes. She didn't bring up the nightmare. Instead, she asked, "How was the baby? Everything okay?"

For a moment, he looked confused. Then he blinked a few times and sat up straighter, disentangling from her. "Oh, yeah. He's fine. Everything's fine. Are you—are you okay?"

"I'm fine."

"Did you sleep at all?"

Josie smiled. "Yeah, of course. We have to get ready and get going if we're going to meet Moore and his team in Lenore County by eight."

"Yeah," he said. "I got your text last night. Caverns, huh?"

He reached out to pat her arm, but she hopped out of bed before he could touch her. She picked up her phone from her nightstand, searching for a text from Gretchen. It had been sent only moments ago. *Renee Kelly never showed. Sorry, boss.* She put the phone back on its charger and headed for the bathroom.

"Yeah," she answered Noah. "Caverns today."

"Josie," he said. "Look at me."

Reluctantly, she turned toward him. "What?"

"Maybe we should talk about these nightmares you've been having."

"Yeah, sure. Another time, though, okay?"

"Josie."

"We have to go to work, Noah."

He slid to the edge of the bed and put his feet on the floor. "You think you can do caverns? We could maybe station you outside, have the rest of the team go inside?"

"I'll be fine," she lied.

CHAPTER TWENTY-FOUR

Josie's anxiety was an undertow, tugging at her all morning. They drove to Lenore County and met up with Moore and another member of his team whose name was Nash. Parked in one of the state gameland parking lots, they reviewed the diagram of the caverns that Maya had drawn for them. Moore was brusque and businesslike, and Josie wondered whether his superior had dressed him down after Chitwood's call. It was raining lightly, the clouds overhead black and full. Josie addressed Moore and Nash. "They're calling for more possible thunderstorms today. You two okay with being out here in that?"

A muscle ticked in Moore's jaw but all he said was, "Your call."

So he had been reprimanded and likely blamed her and Noah. Josie glanced at Noah, who gave her a barely perceptible nod. He would defer to her. They could wait it out, and be safe should the forecast storms arrive, but Josie couldn't shake her suspicion that the man who had kidnapped and held Maya Bestler was responsible for the Yates murders and Emilia Gresham's disappearance. Maybe she was wrong, but if she was right, every moment they waited reduced their chances of saving Emilia in time. If there was even the slimmest possibility that the two cases were connected, and that finding Maya's abductor would solve the Yates and Gresham cases, then Josie had to take a risk.

"Let's go then," she said.

They set off into the woods in their rain gear, equipped with flashlights and headlamps. Five hours later, the rain, while still light, hadn't let up. Twice they were caught in a lightning storm, forced to stop, positioning themselves fifty feet away from one another and staying low to the ground until it passed. They discussed turning back each time, but they were so deep in the woods, the storms would be over by the time they returned to the cars.

Josie was regretting her decision to go forward with the search in the rain by the time they stopped to check the GPS units. She was sweaty and starving and the only thing her brain had room for were the blisters on her feet.

Noah addressed Moore. "I thought you said you knew where these caverns were."

Moore squatted next to a large tree trunk and drank what was left in his bottle of water. He wiped rain from his eyes with his thumb and forefinger. "I haven't actually been in them in twenty years. I thought they'd be easier to find."

Josie looked up from her GPS. "We've crossed the county line at least a half dozen times. We're actually in Denton right now. Are you sure we don't need to be further south?"

From his pack, Moore pulled out an old paper topographical map. He spread it out on the forest floor despite the rain soaking it through almost immediately. Noah walked over and knelt beside him to study it. Josie stood over them, her GPS unit out in front of her so she could compare it with the paper map. Noah and Moore argued for a few minutes over which direction to go while Nash stood several feet away looking annoyed. Once they came to a decision, Moore made to move his now soggy map, but Josie placed a boot on top of it. "Wait," she said. She squatted down and pointed to where Moore and Noah now believed the caverns were located, about four miles southwest. "How far from the caverns was the campsite that Maya disappeared from?"

Moore tapped a finger against his lips, studying the map. "I can't remember exactly, but I'm pretty sure somewhere over here." He pointed to another section of the map, far south of where he now believed the cavern entrance was located.

"How many miles is that?" Josie asked. "From camp to cavern?"

He shrugged. "Maybe twelve or thirteen."

"Did you conduct a large-scale search for Maya Bestler after she went missing?" Josie said. "On the Lenore County side?"

"Of course," he answered. "But obviously it didn't turn anything up."

"You used dogs?"

He stopped fidgeting with the map and really looked at her. Josie didn't miss Noah's look, either, which said: *you're going to do this now?*

Moore said, "Of course we used dogs."

"How soon after she went missing did you start the search?" Josie asked.

"Well, that's impossible to tell. We only had Garrett Romney's report, and we all thought he was lying. He said he woke up disoriented and injured and walked out of the woods until he could get cell service. But we don't know for sure how long it was between the time that she actually disappeared and Garrett reporting her missing. The hermit could have had a head start. Why?"

"It was just a question I had after I read the file, but now, we don't even know how far the caverns are from the original campsite—"

Moore stood up, crumpling his map in his hands. "I know where they are," he said.

Noah said, "Well let's go then. I don't want to be dragging this guy out of the woods in the dark—or get caught in more thunderstorms."

With that, he stomped off. Moore's colleague tromped off after him. Josie and Moore stared at one another for a long moment. She said, "I wasn't trying to imply your team didn't do a thorough job. It's just odd that Maya said the hermit moved her around for several days before they got to the caverns, but she couldn't be found, even with dogs."

Moore nodded. "You say an awful lot of shit for someone who isn't trying to imply that I don't know how to do my job."

"I never said anything of the sort," Josie said. "I'm just saying it's unusual that even the dogs couldn't find Maya Bestler. The K-9 unit dogs are very reliable."

"No shit," Moore said. "That's why everyone suspected Garrett Romney had done something with her. We brought in cadaver dogs, hoping we could find where he stashed her body. As you know, that didn't work out."

He left her standing there and started walking, following Noah and Nash. Josie trudged after him.

It took another hour and a half to reach the entrance to the caverns, which didn't look like an entrance at all. It was a rise in the terrain, a small hill where it looked as though several large stones had tumbled to the bottom followed by several tree trunks. Moore pointed to the mess. "I think this is it," he said.

"This is what?" Noah said. "It looks like a bunch of debris."

Moore turned away from the stones and tree trunks and pointed behind them. "Over there, about thirty feet, is a small tributary of Cold Heart Creek."

"I didn't see a creek when we walked up this way," Noah said.

"'Cause that's not the creek. It's just a little stream that fills up when the creek overflows. It's run-off, basically, but sometimes it's enough to flood this whole area."

Josie looked around, noting the mud puddles dotting the area which were wet and sticky from the recent rains. "Looks swampy to me," she said. She took several steps in the direction that Moore had indicated until something colorful caught her eye. "Over here," she said.

The others followed, picking through the trees until they came to an old wooden dory boat sitting on some rocks. The boat's hull was a faded teal color. All but one of the benches inside of it were broken, and a worn paddle rested at its bottom. Its back end was mired deep in mud, and Josie could see the long, wide rut in the forest floor where the Cold Heart Creek tributary carved its way through during the rainier parts of the year. It had already begun to fill with rushing water with the last day of rain they'd experienced. "This is the boat Maya told us about," Josie said. "We're in the right place."

They climbed back up the hill to where Moore had pointed out the collapsed stones and looked around.

"Maya said that you couldn't see the entrance because of rocks and fallen trees," Moore said.

He hopped over a tree trunk, and the rest of them followed. They climbed over a few large stones, getting closer to the base of the small hill. Another tree trunk barred their way and behind that, a thatch of weeds and vines hung down from a gathering of stones jutting out of the hill. It was a sort of natural curtain, Josie realized. But no one casually walking by would see it because it was blocked by so many fallen trees and stones, just as Maya had said. Moore pushed aside the mass of greenery and there it was—a crack in the earth. It was irregularly shaped, like a large, person-sized, scalene hexagon. At the base, it was about two feet across, then it widened and narrowed, widened and narrowed, and the top of the entrance was only a foot wide. Crouching, an average-sized person could fit easily through it.

Moore fit his headlamp onto his head and Nash and Noah did the same. Josie couldn't look at the opening for another moment. Her breath was coming faster and faster. She took out the GPS device and checked it. She blinked. "We're not in Lenore County," she said.

Noah looked at her. "What's that?"

She held out the device. "This is Alcott County. We're actually in Denton."

Moore walked over with Noah to look at the on-screen map. Moore pointed to Josie's right. "But another half mile that way and you're back in Lenore County."

"But if the caverns are in our jurisdiction, that makes things a little easier. Mark it so we know where the entrance is, would you?" Noah said to Josie.

She marked the entrance to the caverns on the GPS, hoping that no one saw her hand trembling.

Moore said, "If the caverns are in your jurisdiction that means you dragged our asses out here for no good reason." Without waiting for a response, he walked back to the entrance and put one foot through it, his entire lower leg disappearing into blackness. Josie sucked in a sharp breath. Her heart thundered in her chest. The nightmare-memory from last night came rushing back at her, the closet in which she had spent so many hours of her childhood transforming into never-ending darkness. "Just a minute," Noah told Moore.

"Give me your headlamp," he told Josie, his voice low.

Numbly, she handed it to him. He pretended to check the batteries, and she knew he was buying her time. He spoke so as not to be overheard. "You don't have to do this," he said. "We can leave you out here. You can be the lookout in case this hermit isn't in there and comes in after we've gone in."

"No," Josie choked out. "I have to do this. It's my job."

Noah met her eyes. She could tell he wanted to touch her. To comfort her, somehow, but he wouldn't do it in front of colleagues. She appreciated it even though she wanted nothing more at that moment than to let him wrap her up in his arms and tell her she should stay outside. Only Noah knew the true extent of the damage that Lila Jensen had done to Josie when she was a child. Only he knew about the endless hours locked in closets, the dark enclosed space pressing in on her until she couldn't breathe.

"No one questions your ability to do your job, Josie," Noah said. "One of us has to stay out here. So let it be you."

Josie looked over his shoulder to where Moore stood half in and half out of the entrance, chatting with Nash. It was tempting. Noah was right. Neither Moore nor Nash would think anything of it if she volunteered to wait outside. But if she did that, Lila Jensen would win. It would be just one more thing that the woman took from Josie even all these years later. Josie was a police officer. A good one. This was her life. She didn't have children. She had her job. She would be damned if she let evil Lila diminish that all these years later. Today they were looking for a kidnapper, but one day it might be a missing person, someone in need of help. Would she sit that out as well? She thought of her friend, Misty's son, Harris. At almost three years old, he had become an important part of her life. She loved that little boy so much, she'd take a bullet for him. What if he was stuck in a dark, enclosed place? Would she stand outside quivering at past trauma?

"This is my job," Josie repeated, thrusting her chin at Noah. "I'm damn well going to do it."

He smiled at her and she loved him for not looking doubtful. He fitted the headlamp over her hair, adjusting it and then testing it to make sure the light came on. For the benefit of Moore and Nash, he said loudly, "Now it's working."

Josie put the GPS into her pocket and took out her handheld flashlight. She walked over to Moore. "I'm right behind you," she said. With Noah at her back, she plunged into the darkness.

CHAPTER TWENTY-FIVE

Josie was startled by the cold, moist air that gripped her bare arms and the back of her neck as she plunged into the caves. Nash stayed outside. Josie, Noah, and Moore had handheld flashlights as well as headlamps, and the beams from all six light sources bounced chaotically around the area. The entrance was a short tunnel, maybe three or four feet in length, and then it gave way to something larger. Josie could feel the energy, the air around them change, as they moved into a large chamber. She swept her lights around, noting dirty white, yellow, and gray rock formations that looked like melted ice cream and other formations that looked like hundreds of hanging icicles. The ceiling above them was at least twelve feet high in some places, if not more. On the ground was a narrow path that looked like it had been made by someone repeatedly walking back and forth.

Noah put a hand on her shoulder, and she jumped. "It's just me," he said. "You okay?"

She barely heard him over the roar of her own heartbeat, but she nodded. Even with the high, misshapen ceilings and their lights bouncing around, she still felt the familiar clutches of panic enveloping her. She was a child again, locked in the closet, screaming and crying for Lila to let her out. She hadn't done anything wrong. Lila had promised not to make her go in there. But the darkness and the torture never stopped.

"What's that sound?" Moore said, stopping.

Josie nearly bumped into him.

"What sound?" Noah asked.

"Like a whistle," Moore said. "Is that one of you?"

It was her. She was starting to hyperventilate. She opened her mouth to say that she was fine, but nothing came out save for a high-pitched wheeze. Again, Noah placed a hand on Josie's shoulder, squeezing reassuringly.

Moore said, "Does she have asthma or something?"

Or something, Josie thought, but she couldn't force any words out of her throat.

Noah said, "Yeah. She'll be fine. Keep going."

As Moore turned and plunged deeper into the caverns, Josie squeezed her eyes closed for a split second. She opened them and concentrated on making her feet move. Noah kept his hand on her shoulder, guiding her forward. "Breathe," he told her in a whisper. "You're fine."

When she was a child, the boy who would become her late husband, Ray, had given her a backpack full of supplies to keep in the closet for when Lila locked her inside. So she wouldn't feel alone. Now, she reminded herself, reassured by the weight of Noah's hand on her shoulder, she wasn't alone.

They stepped into another tunnel, this one roomy enough for two people to walk side by side but longer, perhaps twenty or thirty feet, by Josie's estimation. Maya's diagram hadn't been exact, which Josie had expected. Her experience with the hermit had been disorienting and terrifying, Josie was certain, but so far, the descriptions she'd given Moore were accurate. They stepped out into another open area, their feet splashing into water. She looked down, directing her headlamp toward the ground. There was about two inches of water. Moore moved more slowly, sloshing along until he came to the other side, to another tunnel and then another cavern, this one so enormous that Josie's light didn't even reach the ceiling above them.

She shivered and Noah squeezed her shoulder. She thought of one of the last things Ray had said to her before he passed away: *the darkness can't hurt you.* His words played on a loop in her mind.

Between that and Noah's firm touch, her breathing started to slow, but only marginally.

Moore stopped and shone his flashlight overhead. Noah and Josie joined him but even with all their beams trained upward, the light didn't penetrate the darkness looming over their heads.

"You think this is it?" Noah asked.

Again, Josie tried to speak. Inside her mind, there was a logical part still working through their present circumstances. There was one more tunnel, to the left if Maya's map was correct, and then another large chamber.

Moore said, "I'm not sure."

Josie stepped in front of him, shrugging off Noah's hand, and veered toward the left. She felt along the uneven surface of the walls with one hand while using the other to direct her flashlight beam. Moore and Noah's lights bobbed behind her, casting a strange strobe effect all around her. A moment later, she found a small tunnel on the left. Just large enough for her to pass through if she crouched down. Moore and Noah were considerably taller than her so it was a tight squeeze, but she heard them moving behind her. Then the tunnel ended, and her foot stepped into air. She fell, hands out, flying toward the dark gray ground. Both knees struck stone and pain shot up her wrists into her arms.

Moore and Noah were beside her, lifting her to her feet. "You forgot," Moore whispered. "Maya said there was a big step into this chamber. But good work. We're here."

Josie nodded, still not able to form words. Her breathing had slowed but her heart rate had not. The three of them looked around at the massive space. Here, too, their flashlights didn't penetrate the darkness overhead. The smell of a doused fire filled Josie's nostrils.

As if reading her mind, Noah whispered, "We're in the right place."

Moore called out into the yawning darkness, "Hello? Sir? It's the police. We need to speak with you."

The silence swallowed his words, but he kept trying. There was no answer and no other sound but Moore's voice. Josie looked up, panning around her with the headlamp until she saw what looked like steps curving along one wall. They weren't manmade, just natural places in the stone where the surface had flattened somewhat—enough to hold a person's feet. She touched Noah's arm until she had his attention and then pointed.

"That must be the upper chamber," he said. "The one Maya called the bedroom chamber. I'll go up."

He caught Moore's attention and signaled to him that he was going up into the chamber. Moore nodded and followed along. Josie waited below, scanning all around her with her flashlight and headlamp but finding nothing but stone that looked like melted wax. Noah and Moore continued to call out for the hermit as they went up the steps.

"Police. Come out where we can see you. We need to talk."

Without Noah to anchor her, Josie's breathing began to speed up. Dizziness overtook her. The cavern seemed to spin around her, a vortex of blackness. One hand reached out, searching for wall. She stumbled forward. She was back in the nightmare. *The darkness can't hurt you*, said Ray's voice in her head.

Noah and Moore's lights shimmered above her head. Her gaze swept upward, hoping to glimpse them. A noise—something between a grunt and a shout— sounded from somewhere overhead and then she heard something rushing through the air. Every hair on her body felt as though it was on end. Then, something heavy slammed into her back, knocking her to the ground. Her handheld flashlight went flying. She heard her headlamp crack and shatter as her face crashed into the cold stone floor. The light extinguished. Her forehead was on fire, but she realized that the headlamp extending a couple of inches from her head had saved her from far worse facial injuries. There was a great weight on her back. She tried to push herself to her knees but something—no, someone—was on top of her. A smell like dead things and body odor made her gag.

Something bristly scraped the back of her neck, and it was then that her throat finally opened. A scream tore from her insides, animal-like and ear-splitting. The knot of panic building in her chest burst, the pain eclipsing every other sensation: the searing abrasion on her forehead, her bruised knees, her sore neck and ribs.

She was aware of people shouting—Noah and Moore—but her body was too focused on its own terror to process anything they were saying. There was a man on her back. She was in the dark, in an enclosed space, and there was a man on her back. He dragged himself upward like some kind of wet, slithering creature, his weight moving off her hips just slightly, relieving the pressure on her right side. Her legs kicked out, finding only air. Fingers crept up the back of her neck and into her hair. Foul-smelling breath tickled her cheek. Bile rose to the back of her throat.

"Get out," said a raspy voice in her ear.

Josie pushed her right leg up so that she was on her knee, each movement causing excruciating pain in her bones and joints. She put her right palm and forearm on the ground as well and with all her might, she pushed, rolling the man off her. As her body rolled on top of his, she jabbed with her right elbow, again and again, hitting him until she felt bone crack. He let out a grunt. She let the momentum take her, rolling all the way over until she straddled him. By feel, she found his chest and beard. His hands reached up, searching for her throat, but she batted them away, shifting her body upward until her knees rested in the hollows of his shoulders.

"Stop," she said, breathless. "Stop moving."

Finally, circles of light bobbed all around her. Noah dropped to his knees beside them, his headlamp illuminating the man's craggy face with its thin features; his long, tangled gray hair, and immense, unruly salt-and-pepper beard. His dark brown eyes bulged at her, flashing with hatred.

"Help me," Josie said. "Help me get him on his stomach and cuffed."

CHAPTER TWENTY-SIX

Josie held Noah and Moore's handheld flashlights while they took up position on either side of the hermit. His hands were cuffed in front of him. Flanking him, Noah and Moore dragged him along while Josie led the way back through the maze of tunnels and caverns. Her entire body was shaking, and she hoped none of them noticed. The hermit didn't speak. Moore repeatedly asked him his name but got only silence in return. When Josie finally saw the sliver of daylight at the entrance to the caverns, tears of relief gathered in her eyes. She blinked them away as they emerged into the gloomy daylight.

They all stopped to take a breath. Noah and Moore sat the hermit on a large stone near the entrance, and Nash stood guard beside him. Rain pelted them but the open air of the forest brought a relief so profound, Josie felt it in every cell of her body. In the daylight, Josie saw that Maya's description of the hermit had been correct; he looked exactly like someone who had spent decades living alternately in the woods and underground caverns. His wild, uncombed hair had the consistency of straw. A bushy beard that reached to his solar plexus was tangled with leaves and twigs and what looked like food particles snagged in it. His skin was pale but weathered. He wore an old, threadbare T-shirt that Josie thought might have been white at some point over cut-off denim jeans that hung low on his hips. Both were damp. His arms and legs were corded with muscles that rippled with the slightest movement.

The only thing that Maya hadn't prepared them for was his overwhelming stink. She had mentioned that he smelled but this was something altogether different. Even out in the open air, his odor radiated from him, stinging her nostrils. She didn't miss the looks of disgust on her colleagues' faces either. "This dude needs a shower," Moore muttered under his breath as he walked past her. He held up his phone, trying to get service.

Josie took out her GPS unit. "We're on the Denton side," she told him. "I'll call our guys."

Noah walked over. "There's a bunch of stuff in that upper chamber. We should have Hummel and his team come out and see if they can find Maya's prints or anything else connecting her to this guy and these caverns. That will strengthen the case against him. Plus, if there's anything in there to indicate he had something to do with Emilia Gresham's disappearance, the ERT will find it."

Josie pulled her phone out. No bars. She climbed over two tree trunks, moving away from the hidden entrance to the caverns toward the stream, checking her screen periodically until she reached a place where she had service. A thrill of excitement ran through her when she saw two bars on her phone. She punched in Hummel's cell phone number and, after a long discussion and comparison of GPS coordinates, they agreed to meet on the nearest road. Josie and her team would walk the hermit out to waiting patrol cars and then one of them would walk Hummel, his team, and their equipment back out to the caverns.

Hanging up, she turned back toward the caverns to see Noah standing there. For a moment, in his tactical gear, with his tousled brown hair blowing in the breeze, and his face steeped in concern for her, he took her breath away. He took a step toward her, reached up and brushed her hair out of her face. He touched two fingertips to her forehead.

"Ow," Josie said, backing away.

"You've got quite a bruise there," he told her. "In the shape of your headlamp."

"He got me pretty good," Josie replied.

"He jumped from the upper chamber. Saw us, took a few running steps and jumped right into the darkness."

"I know. He landed on my back."

He looked her up and down. "You okay?"

"What do you think?"

He gave her a wry smile. "I know what your answer will always be, but I'm asking you as your live-in boyfriend right now: are you okay?"

She looked up at the canopy of trees, heard the wind rushing through them, saw birds flitting about, looking for cover from the rain, and breathed in humid air. "Yeah," she said. "I think I am."

They walked back to where Moore and Nash were maneuvering the hermit over the rocks and fallen tree trunks. He struggled against them, demanding to know where they were taking him.

"You're under arrest," Josie said. "For the abduction and assault of Maya Bestler."

He froze completely for a moment. Something explosive passed over him like a shadow. Rage flashed in his eyes. A vein in his forehead pulsed. Then he was still again, his face impassive.

Josie recited his Miranda rights.

"I want a lawyer," said the hermit.

Silence. Josie and Noah exchanged a curious look. They hadn't even gotten him to the station yet, and he was already requesting an attorney. They weren't going to get anywhere with this guy.

"What's your name, sir?" Moore asked him.

"I want a lawyer," he repeated.

Noah sighed and said, "Let's just go."

Moore and his colleague began hauling him along through the forest with Josie guiding them using her GPS unit.

"I want a lawyer," the hermit said once more, in response to nothing.

CHAPTER TWENTY-SEVEN

Two hours later, Josie leaned back in her desk chair and pressed an ice pack to her forehead. She closed her eyes, listening to her colleagues move around the room. She could still feel the cool air of the caverns, the sense of dizziness and panic at looking up at the ceiling and seeing nothing but blackness. The man falling on her back, knocking her to the ground. Her eyes snapped open again, focusing on her present surroundings. The other desks were empty. Gretchen and Mettner were out working the Yates/Gresham case.

Noah appeared beside her and placed a cold bottle of water and a steaming mug of coffee on her desk. "You need to stay hydrated," he explained. "But I know you need coffee."

She smiled at him. "You're awesome."

He grinned at her as he plopped into his own desk chair across from her. "Awesome enough to be able to keep my toaster oven?"

Josie laughed, the movement hurting her forehead. She put the ice pack on her desk. "Don't push it. We'll talk about that later."

Noah said, "The hermit has been printed. We've asked the State Police to expedite running his prints through AFIS."

"Which will only tell us who he is if he's already in the system," Josie said.

Noah shrugged. "It's worth a try. I called the public defender's office. They've got a local lawyer taking cases pro bono. They'll get in touch with him and send him over as soon as they can."

"Which could be hours," Josie said. She sniffed the air. "I think I can still smell him."

"You can," Noah said. "The entire floor downstairs smells like him."

"The whole building is going to stink, at least until his lawyer gets here and we can get him booked and moved to Bellewood for processing. Fabulous."

"We've got time," Noah said. "You could go home and get a shower."

"And come back here only to get the smell stuck to me again? No thanks. I'll work on the reports."

Her cell phone danced on the desk. She pulled it toward her and saw the words *SCI Muncy* flash across the screen. Stomach turning, she sent it to voicemail.

"Everything okay?" Noah asked.

She nodded.

"Who was that?"

"Wrong number," she mumbled, pulling her chair closer to the desk and straightening her posture, ready to peck away at her keyboard.

Noah opened his mouth to speak again but Josie's desk phone rang. She snatched up the receiver. "Quinn."

Hummel's voice came over the line. "Boss, we got everything we could get from the caves. I've got some stuff you'll want to see. I'm down in the conference room."

"Meet you there," Josie said and hung up.

Noah followed her to the first floor, where the overpowering stench of the hermit was even stronger. "Glad we didn't eat yet," Josie muttered as they filed into the conference room and closed the door.

Hummel stood at the head of the long table, presiding over several paper evidence bags which he had spread out on the table's surface. He slid the largest bag toward him and, with gloved hands, took out a purple backpack. He set it on the table and turned it so that Josie and Noah could see the straps. Along one of them, in black magic marker, Josie read: *E. Gresham.*

Her heart did a double tap.

"Jesus," Noah said.

Hummel unzipped the bag and took out the items inside: a few T-shirts, bras, pairs of shorts, toothbrush, toothpaste, deodorant, tampons, hairbrush, a bottle of ibuprofen, and a phone.

"We have to go back," Josie said. "She could be in those caves."

"She's not," Hummel said. "We searched. She's not there. We also didn't find any blood. I used the luminol in there. Nothing. We also checked in and around the caverns for any possible recent graves. Nothing."

"He could have strangled her. She might still be there. We need dogs," Josie said.

Noah said, "The Alcott County sheriff's K-9 unit is supposed to meet Gretchen out near the campsite today if the rain stops. We've still got a couple of hours of daylight. They're not taking the dogs out in these storms. We shouldn't even have been out there."

Hummel packed the backpack up again and placed it into the evidence bag. One by one, he pulled the other items out of the various evidence bags. Water bottles, pots, pans, lighters, men's T-shirts, a small soft cooler, first aid kits, folding knives, a compass, several coils of nylon rope, lanterns, flashlights, even a camping chair. None of it was marked the way the backpack was. Based on the book and backpack, Emilia Gresham was someone who routinely marked her possessions with her first initial and last name.

"You'll need to print that stuff," Josie said. "See if you can get Maya Bestler's prints from anything so we can link her to the cave."

"We have her statement," Hummel said. "Her map of the caverns. Hell, we even have her baby."

Josie touched Hummel's arm. "This guy lawyered up before we even got him to the car. He's going to mount a defense. We need to have every base covered. It makes the district attorney's job easier, so please, just do it."

Hummel sighed and gave a half-hearted shrug as he gathered his evidence bags back up. "Fine," he said. "Whatever you say, boss."

"Hummel," Josie said before he left. "Check any rope you found for DNA. Maya had ligature scars on her wrists."

He nodded.

"Also, did you find any black walnuts in the caverns?"

"Nope," he said. "None."

Josie and Noah walked back up to their desks. "What do you think?" Noah asked. "The hermit crept through the woods, poisoned the campers, murdered them, ransacked the site, and made off with Emilia?"

"I just don't know," Josie said. "The caverns are almost ten miles from the campsite where Emilia Gresham went missing, although I suppose he could have traveled by boat up and down Cold Heart Creek."

"Maybe," Noah said. "But he'd have to drag that boat to the main creek. The tributary near his caverns wasn't full enough for that boat."

"True," Josie agreed. "I just thought we'd find Emilia Gresham, or some significant signs of her presence… more than a backpack."

"He took her somewhere else then." Noah suggested.

"We need to send units down there to search around the caverns," she said. "The moment the rain stops or even slows."

Noah made a few calls while Josie thought about the big picture. When he hung up, she said, "Why did he take Emilia's backpack but not Valerie's? They had virtually the same things in them."

"Maybe she brought it with her," Noah suggested. "He poisoned the Yates couple, killed them, threatened Emilia, forced her to come with him, and she brought her backpack with her. She had a phone. Maybe she thought she could make a call at some point."

"But he worked so hard to conceal Maya Bestler and keep her captive. Why would he risk letting Emilia bring a phone with her to the caverns?" Josie asked.

"Well, I would think that kidnapping a grown woman is a little stressful. Maybe he wasn't thinking that clearly and just took the backpack away from her once they reached the caverns," Noah argued.

"So then why didn't he keep her in the caverns?"

They both knew the answer to that but neither of them said it. Josie's desk phone rang again. This time it was their desk sergeant letting them know that the hermit's lawyer had arrived. Josie and Noah trudged back down the steps to the first floor. When they turned down the hallway toward the interrogation room, Josie froze in place. Noah bumped against her back. "What is it?" he asked. Then he looked toward the end of the hall where Denton's premier criminal attorney, Andrew Bowen, stood wearing a sharp suit and carrying a briefcase.

"Shit," Noah said.

Josie turned to him. "What are you worried about? You're not the one who sent his mother to prison for life."

"No," Noah said. "But I'm dating the person who did."

Lila Jensen was suddenly creeping into every facet of Josie's life. First the calls, then the nightmares, followed by the dark enclosure of the caverns reminding her of how Lila had kept her in a closet, and now the return of Andrew Bowen. A year and a half earlier, Lila Jensen had come back into Josie's life after a prolonged and blessed absence, digging up a decades-old murder case which Josie had solved, sending both Lila and her accomplice—Andrew Bowen's mother—to prison. The case had also unearthed some pretty ugly secrets relating to Andrew's family's past, none of which he had been happy to find out about. He was a criminal defense attorney, so he was at the police station often, but he always reserved his nastiest glares and most cutting remarks for Josie.

Today was no different.

As Josie and Noah reached him, he sneered. "I should have known. You. What kinds of outlandish crimes are you trying to pin on the innocent now?"

Josie crossed her arms over her chest and glared right back at him. She stated only the facts, nothing more, running through all they had learned in the last twenty-four hours about Maya Bestler and now Emilia Gresham.

Andrew Bowen's mouth was a thin straight line as he listened to her recount everything. Then he said, "Who has talked to him?"

"No one," Noah said. "He asked for an attorney right away."

Looking skeptical, Bowen said, "None of you have talked to him yet?"

"Other than to read him his Miranda rights, no," Josie said.

"You don't even know his name. How can you charge him?"

Josie said, "If you can point us to another man living in underground caverns in Denton who kept Maya Bestler prisoner and impregnated her, we'll be happy to direct our investigation to him instead."

Bowen's face flamed red. He pointed a finger at her face. "Don't think for one second I'm going to let you get away with your usual bullshit."

Josie felt Noah move behind her to step toward Bowen, but she put up a hand to hold him in place. To Bowen she said, "What bullshit is that? Doing my job?"

Bowen's finger jabbed the air in front of Josie. "You're not pinning every single thing going on in this town at this moment on my client. That's what I'm telling you."

Before Josie could respond, Noah growled, "Don't come into our station house thinking you're going to bully us. The evidence is what it is. You worry about your job and we'll worry about ours."

Bowen lowered his arm and then smoothed down the front of his suit jacket. "You're on notice," he muttered.

Noah started to speak again, but Josie elbowed him lightly to silence him. She could feel the anger radiating off his body. There was no point in antagonizing Bowen any further.

Bowen said, "I'd like to talk to my client."

"Of course," Josie said.

"Right this way," Noah said, walking past him to lead the way to the room holding the hermit.

As they reached the door, Bowen looked around the hall, wrinkled his nose and asked, "What is that smell?"

Noah smiled. "That's your client."

CHAPTER TWENTY-EIGHT

While Bowen went to meet with the hermit, Josie and Noah headed to the hospital, dropping in on Baby Bestler in his tiny bassinet, swaddled in a white hospital blanket with a blue knit cap on his little head. He slept peacefully. They watched him for several minutes before one of the nurses came out to speak with them. Noah flashed his credentials. "How's he doing?"

The nurse smiled. "He's doing great. No issues."

"Glad to hear it," Noah said, his gaze returning to the baby.

Josie asked, "Has his mother been to see him or asked for him?"

The nurse nodded. "She was here this morning to see him. Her parents too."

"Did she hold him?"

"Oh, yes. But she seemed very tentative. Like she was afraid she was going to hurt him. Her parents were trying to reassure her. It was very sweet, actually."

"Has she picked out a name?" Noah asked.

"No, not yet. Not that she's told us," the nurse responded. For a long moment, the nurse watched Noah gaze at the baby. Then she and Josie spoke simultaneously. The nurse asked, "Would you like to hold him?"

Josie said, "We should get upstairs and talk to Maya."

Noah answered the nurse as though Josie wasn't even there. "I'd love to," he said.

Josie wasn't sure that this was protocol, but she didn't say anything. Noah disappeared into the nursery with the nurse, leaving Josie standing there, open-mouthed. She gathered her composure and turned away from the window. She wasn't sure she could bear to watch Noah cuddle Baby Bestler. Her fingers punched the elevator's up button vigorously until it dinged, sending a wave of relief through her. She went up to the fourth floor to see Maya Bestler. The room was dim again. Maya rested in her bed, looking much better than she had the day before. She had obviously showered. Her brown hair was clean, dry, and combed. Her cheeks were rosy pink, and she now wore a pair of pajamas of which Josie could only see an oversized black T-shirt that said *Let Me Sleep* in white letters. Her father snoozed next to her in one of the visitor's chairs. No sign of her mother, Sandy.

Maya saw Josie peeking her head around the doorway and beckoned her inside. Josie walked up to the side of the bed opposite Gus Bestler and made sure to talk directly into Maya's line of sight. "How are you?"

Maya smiled. "Better." She looked down at her shirt. "My dad brought me some pajamas."

Josie smiled. "Those are way better than the hospital gowns."

Maya nodded. She pointed to Josie's forehead. "What happened?"

Josie touched the circular bruise which still ached. "I fell while wearing a flashlight on my head. I'm fine. I heard you saw your baby today."

Maya's smile widened. "He is beautiful. Thank you again for bringing him into the world safely."

"Just doing my job," Josie said. "Speaking of which, I have some news."

Maya stiffened. Her blue eyes grew wide. "What news?"

Josie motioned toward Gus. "I think your dad might want to hear this as well." She waited while Maya nudged her father awake. Josie reintroduced herself. When he was fully alert and standing beside his daughter, her hand in his, Josie looked into Maya's face and told her they had arrested the man they believed had abducted and held her.

A visible shudder worked its way through Maya's body. Gus reached up with his free hand and stroked her hair. "It's okay, Maya," he said, although Josie didn't think she could hear him. "You're safe now." He turned toward Josie. "Who is he? What's his name?"

Josie jammed her hands into her pants pockets. "We don't know yet. He won't talk. He immediately asked for an attorney. But we're certain he'll disclose his identity to his attorney. We did take fingerprints in the event that he is in the system."

"What system?" Maya asked.

"AFIS," Josie replied. "The Automated Fingerprint Identification System. It's a database we use in law enforcement to collect and store the fingerprints of anyone who has been arrested or convicted of a crime."

Maya swallowed. "You think… you think he's in the system?"

"Hard to say." She explained the county lore that Deputy Moore had told them about. "But you never know. Like I said, I think he'll have to disclose his identity to his own attorney."

Maya closed her eyes but after a few seconds, they blinked open and tears spilled down her cheeks. She looked at her father who smiled warmly. "It's over," he said. "It's all over."

Maya turned back toward Josie. "Did you call Garrett?"

Josie didn't miss the stiffening of Gus's shoulders. "I did," Josie said. "He indicated that he would not be coming to see you."

Maya's expression loosened, her eyes downcast. Josie couldn't tell if it was disappointment, confusion, or both. Gus caught his daughter's eye. "Honey, you have to understand that the police believed that Garrett had killed you. We all did. I think it's best if we just let him move on with his life now."

Maya didn't look convinced, but she nodded.

Josie stepped forward, looking into Maya's face again. "Maya, we need your permission to take a DNA sample from your son."

"Wh-what?"

"A DNA sample," Josie said. "So we can prove the paternity of the man who took you. That will prove the district attorney's case, and we have a much better chance of keeping him locked up if we can match his DNA to the baby's."

She nodded along with Josie's words, but her eyes were wide with fear. "Will it—will it hurt him? My baby?"

Josie smiled. "Oh no, not at all. They can do it by just swabbing the inside of his cheek."

Maya didn't look convinced. She glanced at her father and back to Josie. "I don't want him to be traumatized."

"Of course not," Josie said. "If I have your permission, later I'll bring by some forms for you to sign."

Maya nodded. Her father squeezed her shoulder and assured her she was doing the right thing.

"I just have a couple more questions," Josie said.

"Yes," Maya said. "Anything."

"When you were in the caverns, did the…" She almost said hermit but instead went with, "… man ever bring anyone else with him?"

Surprise slackened Maya's face. "What? No. I mean, I don't think so."

"You were the only one?"

She nodded. "As far as I know. But I only ever stayed in the upper chamber unless he took me outside. There could have been others. He could have kept them in other parts of the caverns. I wouldn't have heard anything. I didn't search the caverns though. When I had the chance to escape, I didn't explore. I just got the hell out of there."

"Were there any items in the upper chamber when you were there?" Josie asked.

Maya nodded. "Sure. He was always bringing things into the caverns. Things he said he found. He said people who hiked and hunted in the woods left things behind, but honestly, I always wondered if he stole them. I even wondered if he had, you know, hurt anyone. Certainly, he was capable of it."

"Do you remember any of the things he brought?" Josie asked.

Maya's eyes flitted to the ceiling as she considered this. "Pots, pans, sometimes clothing. Coolers. Bottled water. Pretty much anything he could find."

"Before you left," Josie said when Maya's eyes were on her again. "Do you remember him bringing anything specific into the chamber?"

"Oh," Maya said, lifting a finger into the air. "A backpack. I think it was a woman's backpack because it had tampons and stuff in it."

"Did you go through it?"

Circles of pink colored her cheeks.

"It's okay," Josie said. "You wouldn't be in any trouble. In fact, in those circumstances, I would have ransacked anything he brought into the place looking for something I could use for comfort or to help me get away."

Maya gave a weak smile. "I did look through it for those reasons. There was a phone inside, but it was password protected. I tried using the 911 feature because you can make emergency calls without signing in, but it wouldn't work inside the cavern. I wanted to keep it on me and try it outside, but all I had to wear in there was that horrible dress—God knows where he got that old thing—and I had nowhere to hide it."

Josie said, "Why didn't you take it with you when you left?"

"The battery was dead. I didn't think it would be of any use to me in the woods. Besides that, I was so scared he would catch up to me, I wasn't thinking clearly. I just ran and ran."

Josie touched her arm. "You did great, Maya. I'm so glad you're here with us. We'll speak again soon, okay? I'll leave my card here if you or your parents have any questions."

CHAPTER TWENTY-NINE

Noah was no longer in the nursery. Josie took one last look at Baby Bestler—noting how hopelessly adorable he really was—before heading downstairs and out toward the parking lot. She fired off a text to Noah asking him to meet her at the car and lingered at the main entrance to the hospital under the alcove roof, watching the rain fall down in sheets. When she didn't hear thunder or see any lightning after ten minutes, she sent a text to Mettner to see if the K-9 unit was still on hold because of the weather. His reply came back almost immediately, confirming that it was. Josie was about to step into the downpour when she noticed Sandy Bestler several feet away from the door, at the end of the overhang, smoking a cigarette. Josie walked over to her and she put the cigarette down at her side, blowing smoke away from Josie and out into the rain.

Josie laughed. "It's okay. I'm not going to tell anyone you were smoking. I don't think anyone would begrudge you a cigarette after the last twenty-four hours."

Sandy's shoulders sagged with relief. She brought the cigarette back to her mouth and took in a long draw. As she blew out the smoke, she used her other hand to push her gray-blonde bangs out of her eyes. "It's certainly been…" She searched for the right word, but it was clear that she wasn't finding it.

Josie filled in, "Shocking?"

Sandy laughed, but her smile was tight. "Yes, very shocking."

Josie would have expected any other mother to gush over how wonderful it was to have her child back, especially after thinking she'd been murdered, after living with that grief for two years, but

Sandy didn't go there. Then again, Josie thought, what did she know about mothers?

"I just spoke with Maya and your husband," Josie said.

"Ex-husband," Sandy corrected. "Our divorce was finalized last year."

"Oh?"

Sandy looked away. "We had different approaches to dealing with the grief of losing our daughter. Of course, now…" she trailed off.

"Well," Josie said. "I just brought them up to date on the investigation."

Josie explained that they had the hermit in custody; that he hadn't told them his name; and had asked for an attorney. She also mentioned that Maya had consented to having a DNA test performed on Baby Bestler.

Sandy nodded. "That's good news," she said, her tone flat. "Maybe Maya can move on from this."

"I'm sure she will," Josie said. "It looks like she has a good support system."

Sandy scoffed. "If only that were enough. She might move on from this but right back into Garrett's arms."

"I don't think that's likely," Josie said. "Garrett wasn't exactly receptive to me when I called. He has no interest in seeing Maya. He made that quite clear."

Sandy took another drag of her cigarette and shook her head. "But all it will take for her to go back is him changing his mind. He could show up here tomorrow, and my daughter would be lost again—this time with my grandson."

Josie said, "I looked at Lenore County's file on Maya's disappearance. It looked as though Garrett may have been abusing her, but she wouldn't press charges."

Sandy rolled her eyes. She threw her cigarette butt onto the ground and stepped on it. Then she took out another and lit it. "She would never leave him. No matter how bad things got."

"Did she tell you things were bad?" Josie asked.

"Not at first," Sandy said, beginning to pace. "We knew he was hitting her, though. There were too many unexplained bruises and a couple of fractures. Finally, we got her to admit it. She wouldn't leave. We told her she could come home to us. We'd protect her. We'd take her to the police. We would support her. But Maya was never very good at getting herself out of things."

It seemed a strange thing to say about a domestic abuse survivor and her own daughter, but Josie didn't press the issue. She had no idea what the true dynamic between Sandy and Maya had been, but it didn't seem as though their relationship had been pleasant. Instead, Josie said, "She got herself away from the man who abducted her."

Sandy nodded but her eyes had taken on a faraway look, as if her mind were somewhere else. After a moment, she seemed to snap back, blinking and shaking her head. "I must sound cold. My daughter was missing for two years. Presumed dead. Here I am complaining about how she wouldn't leave her abusive ex-boyfriend. I'm happy she's home. I'm grateful to have a grandchild—even under these circumstances—but I'm worried for my daughter and her future."

"I can understand that," Josie said.

"If she goes back to Garrett, though, I'm suing for custody of that little boy."

Josie waited for her to say more, but just then Noah came jogging up from the parking lot, his raincoat pulled low over his face. "Mrs. Bestler," he greeted Sandy. To Josie, he said, "I thought you said you'd meet me at the car."

"Sorry," Josie said. "Let's go. We've still got a lot of work to do."

Before she left with Noah, she pressed one of her business cards into Sandy Bestler's hand. "If you need anything," she told the woman.

CHAPTER THIRTY

The rain had stopped by the time they returned to the station house. Josie prepared the consent forms for Maya to allow them to get a DNA sample from her son while Noah went downstairs to check on the hermit. He sent her a text a few minutes later saying Andrew Bowen wanted to speak to them. She found her way to the conference room where Noah and Andrew Bowen waited. Bowen stood beside the table. His suit jacket was folded and draped over a nearby chair. He had rolled up the sleeves of his blue dress shirt. He folded his arms when Josie walked in.

"Do you have a name for us?" she asked without preamble.

Bowen said, "My client's name is Michael Donovan." He rattled off Donovan's date of birth, putting him at fifty-eight years of age. "He doesn't know Maya Bestler. He's never met her."

"Maya Bestler would disagree," Josie said. "Did you show him a photo of Ms. Bestler to confirm he never met her?"

Bowen's lips parted slightly, and Josie knew that he hadn't. He hadn't asked anyone there for a photo of her although he could have easily found one on Google to show Donovan. He said, "My client has lived alone in the woods for several years. He doesn't entertain female guests."

Behind Josie, Noah laughed. "That's one way of putting it," he said.

Bowen's eyes flashed. "You think this is funny, Lieutenant? These are serious charges you've leveled against my client."

Josie said, "A DNA test should confirm whether or not Donovan knew Maya Bestler. Will you consent to him submitting his DNA?"

"Yes," Bowen answered. "If it will get him out of the county jail system quickly and back to his home."

"You mean the wilderness," Noah said.

"That's where he lives," Bowen replied. "Yes."

"There's still the matter of Emilia Gresham," Josie said. "Her backpack was in his... home."

"My client knows nothing about Ms. Gresham."

"Then how did he come to be in possession of her backpack?" Noah asked.

Bowen sighed. "My client frequently scouts the surrounding woods for items that hikers and campers may have left behind. He says that he came upon a campsite several miles from his cavern two days ago. It was unoccupied. He returned to the site in the early morning hours yesterday—at dawn, he says. All he saw were two people, a man and a woman, sleeping on the ground near the fire."

Josie narrowed her eyes. "Sleeping? That couple was murdered, Mr. Bowen."

"Well, my client didn't kill them. As I said, he came upon them, they were asleep, he didn't want to wake them, so he took what he could carry and left."

She thought about the scene and also about what had been found in Donovan's cave. She could have Hummel print any items that would yield fingerprints and prove that Donovan had taken the Yateses' and Emilia Gresham's things. She could also have Hummel process those same items for any DNA that Donovan might have left behind, but he'd already admitted to being at the scene. His defense would be that of course his prints and DNA were all over their things—he ransacked their camp after the murder. She had nothing at all to prove that he had murdered Tyler and Valerie and abducted Emilia. From what Maya had said, Donovan knew which plants in the forest were edible and which were toxic. He could have somehow poisoned the Yates couple, but again, there was no way that Josie could prove it. Everything she had linking him to the Yates/Gresham case was circumstantial at best. She didn't even know if the district attorney would go forward to trial with so little hard evidence.

They already had him for the Maya Bestler case. He would go away for a long time. But Emilia Gresham was still missing. Finding her alive was looking less and less likely. Josie wanted badly to go at Michael Donovan but she couldn't. Bowen now stood in the way, and she knew with certainty that he was going to be no help whatsoever. It was a stalemate. All of them knew it.

"Let's go," Josie told Noah. "The rain stopped. We'll go assist Detective Palmer with the search for Emilia Gresham."

She turned to leave and Noah followed.

"Detective," Bowen said. "If you have any way of expediting the DNA testing, I'd like my client to be able to resume his normal life as soon as practically possible."

Josie stared at him for a long moment, watching a slow smile spread across his face. Wordlessly, she left.

CHAPTER THIRTY-ONE

"That guy's a real dick," Noah said when they were out of earshot.

"I agree," Josie said.

"Why would he agree to let his client do the DNA test?" Noah said as if he hadn't heard her.

"That's what I'm wondering."

"It's a huge risk."

They walked toward the stairwell so they could go back to their desks. Josie shrugged. "But what's the alternative? We could probably get a warrant to get his DNA based on the evidence. By refusing, all he does is drag things out and clearly, his client doesn't want to spend one more second than he has to behind bars."

"How long has he been in the woods?" Noah asked. "Didn't Moore say like twenty or thirty years? Does this guy even know what DNA is?"

Josie laughed. "Even if he doesn't, Bowen does. It's fine. When the results come back, Bowen will want to negotiate a plea deal. The district attorney can deal with that. Right now, we've got to help Gretchen find Emilia Gresham."

Noah opened the door and motioned Josie to go ahead of him. Before she could step through the doorway, she saw Sergeant Dan Lamay lurching down the hallway toward them, face flushed. "Boss!" he called.

Dan had been with the department for over forty-five years. In spite of his age and a bad knee, Josie had kept him on as a desk sergeant during her tenure as chief because his wife was battling breast cancer, and his daughter had just started college. Since that time, he'd proven an invaluable asset to her when she needed him most. "What's going on, Dan?"

He caught up to them, huffing out several breaths before he said, "We just got a call. Body in the woods in South Denton."

It felt like every drop of blood had drained from her body. She put a hand on Noah's shoulder to steady herself. Only one word made it out of her mouth. "No."

Noah said, "Where in South Denton?"

"Cold Heart Creek," Lamay answered. "A couple miles down from the South Denton bridge close to where it empties into the Susquehanna river. Pretty remote area. Some fishermen found her."

"A woman," Josie choked out. Of course it was a woman. They were too late. Emilia Gresham was dead.

Lamay continued, "We've got patrol units there. Hummel's on his way. You want it or should I get Detective Mettner?"

Shaking her head briskly, Josie said, "We'll take it. Call Dr. Feist, would you?"

They followed the riverbank past the South Denton bridge, driving until they saw the flashing lights of two Denton police cruisers. Noah parked on the shoulder of the road, behind one of the marked vehicles. They stepped out into a light mist and picked their way down the muddy riverbank. One of their uniformed officers waited outside a copse of trees. He pointed between two trees. "Go through there about fifty or sixty feet, and you'll see Cold Heart Creek. Follow it about a half mile. You'll know when you get to the scene."

They thanked him and hiked off into the forest, their shoes squishing in the mud. They heard the rush of Cold Heart Creek before they saw it. It was brown, swollen, and churning from all the recent rain. They walked carefully along its rocky banks until they saw police activity. Hummel's team had already cordoned off a large area with yellow crime scene tape and erected a pop-up tent over the body.

Just outside the tent stood Officer Jenny Chan, a member of the ERT, with a clipboard in her hand. A Tyvek suit, complete with a skull cap and booties, covered her uniform. Behind her, the other members of the team, including Hummel, worked slowly and methodically through the mud- and stone-covered bank, collecting whatever evidence they came across. The only sound was the rush of the creek just beyond the scene.

"Can't let you go in yet, boss," Chan told Josie.

"Of course," Josie said. "You guys have suits that we can use?"

"Sure thing," Chan answered, pointing to a large pile of supplies they had dragged along with them and left several feet from the perimeter of the scene. "There's a box over there."

Noah started toward the box to suit up. Josie remained, craning her neck to peer over Chan's shoulder. All she could see was the white of naked flesh. "Jesus," she muttered.

Chan said, "Female in her twenties. Still in rigor. I'm not a doctor, but I'd say she's been dead maybe four to six hours."

Josie knew that Chan had a few years of crime scene experience under her belt. She had come to Denton from a larger city that saw more crimes. "Thanks," Josie said.

"Shouldn't be much longer."

Josie turned away and walked toward the box of crime scene supplies. With every step, her heart felt heavier and heavier in her chest. She took her time pulling on her own Tyvek suit. Once she was finished, she and Noah waited side by side, leaning against a nearby tree trunk. They didn't speak. Dr. Feist arrived fifteen minutes later. She took one look at them, and her thin lips turned downward. She shook her head and suited up.

None of them spoke, even when Hummel gave them the signal that they could enter the cordoned-off area. They went over to the tent single file and immediately surrounded the body. The woman was completely naked, arms at her sides, legs pressed together and laid out straight. She looked as though she had simply lain down and gone to sleep. Except that her eyes were still open, as was her mouth; her last expression of fright embedded in her skin forever.

Noah stood near her head, peering down at her face. "Holy shit," he said.

It took a second or two for Josie's brain to process exactly what she was seeing. Once she got past the horrific look on the girl's face, and saw her brown hair, she realized that her assumption had been completely wrong.

"Josie," Noah said.

"I know," she answered.

"That's not Emilia Gresham."

Josie knelt beside the woman's head. "No," she murmured. "This is Renee Kelly."

"From the Sanctuary?" Noah said.

She nodded. Tears burned the backs of her eyes. Behind her, Noah placed a hand on her shoulder. "There was nothing you could have done," he said.

"Wasn't there?" she said, her voice scratchy. "I could have gone back. Made something up, maybe, to get her out of there. Told Charlotte I needed to take her with me."

"You know damn well that if she wasn't ready to leave on her own, anything you did would have just made things worse for her. Josie, this isn't your fault."

She didn't believe him. Pursing her lips, she willed herself to focus. She would not cry. She would not shake. Whether Renee Kelly's death was on her or not, the only thing Josie could do for her now was to find her killer.

Hummel walked around and stood beside Josie. "Boss," he said softly, drawing her from her thoughts. "I think she was killed somewhere else and moved here." He pointed down toward her feet and beyond. "See the drag marks in the mud?"

Two long marks in the shapes of Renee's heels led up to where her feet rested.

Josie said, "Did you find any footprints?"

Hummel shook his head. "It's weird, but no, we didn't. I guess he could have walked on the stones but that would be a lot carrying a body in full rigor, and I'd expect to find muddy shoe impressions on the stones themselves. There's nothing. It's like this guy is a ghost."

Josie stood up. "The boot impressions you found at the Yates campsite—did you get anything on those yet?"

"We found three different types of boot prints," he said. "Two of them we matched to the Yates couple. The other one we were able to match by brand and size in the SICAR database."

SICAR stood for Shoeprint Image Capture and Retrieval, which was a footwear database used by law enforcement to identify shoeprints left at crime scenes. It contained the sole patterns for thousands of different types of footwear.

"What was the brand and size of the third boot?" Josie asked.

"It was a Keen Terradora, women's size six."

Josie sighed. "So that was probably Emilia's footprint."

Noah said, "The hermit didn't have shoes on when we arrested him. He could have done this. That's why there are no shoe prints. We know he was at the Yates campsite but there were no additional shoe prints there. We picked him up this afternoon. He could have taken this girl after you and Mettner left the Sanctuary last night, killed her, dumped her body, and made it back to the caverns before we got there. He had a boat. He could have used it to get her here and then gone back. We're closer to his caverns than the Sanctuary."

Hummel said, "We processed that boat when we were out there working in and around the caverns. Didn't find anything."

Noah said, "That doesn't necessarily rule out the hermit. He still would have had time to do this without using his boat. All he had to do was follow the creek. It goes past the Sanctuary and the tributary runs past his caverns." He moved around to stand near

Renee's feet, studying the scene thoughtfully. "Look at her. She's naked, sure, but the way she is staged here is almost..."

Dr. Feist said, "Modest. He didn't leave her spread-eagled or in some humiliating position. He left her here because he needed to get her away from wherever he killed her. Not because he was making a statement of some kind."

"Right," Noah said. "Like the Yates couple. They were laid out straight, side by side, just like this except holding hands."

"But Renee was living at the Sanctuary. Something was happening to her there," Josie said. "I don't think it was the hermit sneaking onto the place and abusing her. I can't see Charlotte allowing that."

"But you said yourself that those people were coached. Why coach them if you're not hiding something?" Noah countered.

Frustrated, Josie threw her hands in the air. "I don't know. They're definitely hiding something. I'm just not sure what it is. Maybe these cases aren't connected at all. But I think that Renee recognized Emilia Gresham. When I showed her the photo, she didn't say she had never seen her, she just said that Emilia wasn't there."

Noah said, "We know the last place she was seen was the Sanctuary. So either she tried to escape—maybe even made it off the property—and someone took her and killed her, or whoever was hurting her on the Sanctuary premises killed her and brought her here."

"We can go there but we're not going to find the crime scene. They'll have cleaned it up by now," Josie said.

Dr. Feist said, "Whoever was hurting her had been doing it for some time." She knelt and pointed to one of Renee's wrists. Josie had been so shocked to see Renee Kelly instead of Emilia Gresham, she hadn't yet taken the time to search for injuries. There were several ligature marks around both of her wrists. Some were old and silvered and others were new, raw, and caked with dried blood. Josie studied the rest of her body. There was bruising around her throat.

"Manual strangulation," Dr. Feist said. "That's what I'd guess. Of course, I've got to get her on the table and do the autopsy."

Noah said, "Didn't Maya have scars on her wrists from being bound?"

"She did," Josie said.

"So, we're back to the hermit."

"But the hermit doesn't have a connection to the Sanctuary. His cave isn't anywhere near it," Josie insisted.

"Unless that's the thing they're hiding over there on the Sanctuary," Noah pointed out.

Hummel, who had been silent while they tossed ideas around, said, "Want me to call Mett?"

"Yes," Josie said. "Please. Ask him to do some digging to see if Charlotte Fadden and Michael Donovan have any past associations."

"You got it, boss."

"Well," Dr. Feist said. "I've got my third strangulation case in two days. It seems like there must be a connection somewhere, although I know we can't force it. We can only work with what the evidence shows."

"Valerie and Tyler didn't have bruising on their throats," Josie said. "Not like this."

"Because they died quickly. Too fast for bruising to take place. This girl was likely repeatedly strangled over a matter of hours before she was finally killed."

Josie stared at Renee's open mouth. "Do you think—"

"That she's got a black walnut in her throat?" Dr. Feist asked. "Only one way to find out. Get her to the morgue. I'll do the autopsy right away. Maybe we'll get lucky and find some of this bastard's DNA on her body."

CHAPTER THIRTY-TWO

They waited until an ambulance had taken Renee's body away before heading back to Noah's vehicle. The rain had begun again as a light mist, but the air was still thick with humidity. Noah started the car, put the air conditioner on, but made no move to pull away.

"I want to go to the Sanctuary," Josie told him.

"It's late."

"I don't care. I want to go there."

"I know."

She motioned toward the steering wheel. "Let's go."

"I need to know you're okay."

"What does that even mean? Okay for what? To work? Yes, I'm fine." She looked out the window, concentrating on the flashing red lights of Hummel's cruiser. The ERT packed their things and left, headed back to police headquarters.

"You're not sleeping. You're barely eating. The nightmares—"

"They don't matter," Josie said. "They're not related to work."

She felt his eyes on her. "You can't tell me these things aren't affecting you in some way."

Finally, she turned and met his gaze. "That girl died because I didn't save her."

Noah's expression went from frustration to something between shock and sympathy. "Josie, no. That girl died because some psychopath killed her. You know that. Her murder is not on you."

She looked away. "Please take me to the Sanctuary."

"What could you have done?" he said. "Forcibly removed her from the premises? The law doesn't work that way. We're not allowed to do that. You know this. You gave her an opportunity to leave. You waited down the road for her for hours. Then Gretchen waited for hours."

Through gritted teeth, Josie said, "We need to go to the Sanctuary."

"How many domestics have you worked in your career? Dozens? Hundreds? How many times do we have to let those women walk back into the house after they refuse to press charges, knowing full well they're going to be beaten again or killed? How many?"

"Too many," Josie mumbled.

"You can't control everything. You gave Renee Kelly an opportunity to get away, and she chose not to take it."

"Or she tried, and they killed her for it."

"You think Charlotte is in on whatever was going on with Renee?"

"You think she's not?"

Noah put the car in gear. "Let's find out."

At the Sanctuary, Josie and Noah waited ten minutes on the porch while the same women from before—the ones who had been working in the kitchen—went to get Charlotte. She smiled when she saw them and invited them in, making a small comment about the time. It was after eight p.m. Josie didn't bother with an explanation for the late hour or with pleasantries. Once they entered the house, she said, "We'll need to talk with Megan and Tru as well. Have your people bring them up here."

Charlotte stared at her for a brief moment, uncertainty in her eyes. For once, Josie was glad to have the woman off-balance instead of the other way around. "Of course," Charlotte said, beckoning them into the kitchen where two women were working on a pile of dirty dishes. One washed while the other dried and put them away. "Ladies," Charlotte said. "Can you please fetch Megan and Tru for me? Bring them back here right now?"

Without a word, they left. Once the back door closed, Charlotte folded her arms across her chest and raised a brow in Josie's direction. "What's going on, my dear? You seem more troubled than usual."

Noah said, "Do you know who Renee Kelly is?"

Charlotte looked at Josie and slowly her composure cracked. She pressed a hand to her mouth. The lines around her eyes and face slackened. Tears glistened. "Something's happened."

Josie took a step closer to her. "Do you know what happened to Renee?"

Charlotte shook her head.

Josie said, "Charlotte, now is the time to be honest with us. It's extremely important that you tell the truth right now."

Charlotte pulled her hand away from her mouth. Tears rolled down her cheeks. "What happened to her? Where is she?"

"She's dead," Noah said flatly. "Someone murdered her and dumped her body near the creek last night."

"No!" Charlotte's legs gave way, and she grabbed onto the edge of the counter behind her before she fell. "No. She's here. She's in the barn. I saw her last night. She wasn't feeling well—she—"

"Someone was hurting her, Charlotte," Josie said. "Here. On your property. Your 'sanctuary.'"

"No," Charlotte said. "That's not how it works here."

"But that's what happened," Noah said. "She had wounds, Mrs. Fadden. Someone had been torturing her for some time."

"No," Charlotte said. "That's not what happened."

Josie asked, "Do you know a man named Michael Donovan?"

Charlotte looked startled by the change in subject. "What? I don't know. I don't think so. Who is he?"

The back door banged open. Megan and Tru walked into the kitchen, a look of surprise taking over when they saw Charlotte crying.

Tru said, "What's going on here?"

"It's Renee," Charlotte told him as he went over to her and put an arm around her shoulders protectively. "She's been killed."

"When?" Megan said. "How?" She looked back and forth between Josie and Noah. "You're mistaken. Have you checked the barn? She's been in her stall for days. Her stomach has been bothering her. I gave her an antacid, but it didn't do much good."

"She's not in the barn," Josie said. "When's the last time you saw her?"

"Last night," Megan said. "After you and your colleague left."

"What time?" Noah asked.

"Oh, I couldn't say. We don't have clocks here."

Josie looked at Tru. "You were with her. How long did you stay with her?"

Tru said, "I don't know. A few hours after you left? I was worried about her. She didn't seem right."

"Were you sleeping with her?" Noah asked him.

Tru's head reared back. Charlotte looked at his face. "Tru?"

"What? No. We were just friends. I mean, I liked her, but it wasn't like that. I was just, I was worried, and she asked me if I could sleep next to her cot."

So, he had been guarding her but not because Charlotte or someone else had ordered him to do so.

"Did you?" Josie asked. "Sleep next to her cot?"

Tru nodded.

"Did she leave the barn at any time during the night?"

"Well, yeah. I woke up at some point and she wasn't there. I just thought she went to the bathroom or to find Megan."

Noah turned toward Megan. "Did Renee come find you last night?"

"No," Megan answered. "I checked on her before I went back to my tent for the night."

"Where's the nearest bathroom to Renee's stall?" Josie asked.

"There's an outhouse behind the barn," Tru said.

"Did you check there?"

"Well, no. I—I figured, you know, if she didn't feel well, she wouldn't want people knocking on the bathroom door. I just figured she would come back when she was finished. Then I—I fell back to sleep."

"She wasn't in her cot when you woke up, was she?" Josie asked.

"No. I don't know where she went. I asked around but no one had seen her. Then I had to get to work in the greenhouse. With all the rain, part of it flooded and so a bunch of us went over there to try to get that in order. We need the food for the winter, you know?"

Josie said, "We need to talk to every person here. Again."

Charlotte's head fell onto Tru's shoulder. "Of course," she said.

CHAPTER THIRTY-THREE

This time, they set up shop in the parlor area of the house, questioning each and every Sanctuary member one at a time without anyone else present. Two other people had seen Renee leave her stall the night before, although they couldn't say what time, of course. No one thought it unusual that she would leave her sleeping quarters in the middle of the night. There were no rules in place about comings and goings, and plenty of the rest of them used the facilities during any given night.

Four other members confirmed that Tru and Renee had become friends since Renee's arrival two months after Tru. No one seemed to think they were intimate. None of them could think of anyone else Renee spent a lot of time with—or they could but they weren't willing to tell Josie. She had the sense that several of them were lying, but she couldn't say what they lied about. They brought Tru in last to interview him without Charlotte's—or anyone else's—presence, and his earnest assertion that his relationship with Renee had been platonic seemed truthful.

"Did she ever confide in you?" Josie asked. "About anything going on here at the Sanctuary?"

"Like what?" Tru asked. He sat in an old, brown wing-backed chair. Josie pulled the matching ottoman close to him so that she was positioned almost between his legs while Noah stood at the door to make sure no one lurked in the hallway to eavesdrop.

"Someone making her uncomfortable? Maybe making her do things she didn't want to do?"

"No. She didn't say anything like that," he insisted.

"Who else was she friends with?"

He shrugged. "I don't know. Probably whoever she worked with."

"What did the two of you talk about?"

"Actually, we mostly talked about life outside of here. We were missing it, I guess. I mean, a little."

From his position by the doorway, Noah said, "She had scars on her wrists, Tru. Old and new. Someone was doing something to her."

True looked nonplussed. "Doing something to her? Like what?"

"Tying her up," Noah answered.

"For what? Why?"

Josie leaned in until her face was only inches from his and touched his arm. Her voice was soft, intimate. "What do you think men do to women when they tie them up against their will, Tru?"

"What?" he said, his voice quavering. "No. Who would do that to her? Renee was a good person."

"You never saw her scars?" Noah said. "I thought you were friends."

Tru gave a vigorous shake of his head. "No, no. She always wore long sleeves and long pants. I never saw her, like, undressed or anything."

"It's over ninety degrees," Noah said. "Has been for weeks. You didn't think it strange that she dressed like that?"

"Well, sure, but I figured she had her reasons and I didn't want to pry and, like, make her uncomfortable."

A loud crack of thunder sounded from outside, causing all three of them to jump. Josie sighed. "Guess the K-9 unit will be on hold till tomorrow."

Lightning flashed outside, followed by more thunder. Noah met her eyes, silently communicating that they weren't getting anywhere here. "It's late," he said. Noah pointed at Tru. "We'll be back," he promised.

*

Noah drove back to the police station so Josie could get her vehicle. Rain thundered against the windshield. "What do you think?" he asked as the green wooded hills of Lenore County gave way to Denton's southernmost edge.

"I think Charlotte is lying."

"You think she knew Renee was murdered?"

"No. I don't think any of them knew, but I still think they're hiding something."

"Any idea what?"

Josie reached up and squeezed the bridge of her nose between her thumb and forefinger. Sleep deprivation, fatigue, and stress were conspiring to give her the headache of a lifetime. She reached into Noah's glove compartment, looking for the ibuprofen she knew he kept inside. "I don't know," she told him. "I still think we're missing something. Something big."

The pills rattled as her hand closed around the bottle. Her phone rang. Dread was a lump in her throat as she took it out of her pocket, expecting to see the words *SCI Muncy*. She was relieved when she saw it was Dr. Feist. Until she remembered why the doctor would be calling her. She swiped to answer.

"Josie," Dr. Feist said. "Your girl, Renee? I was right. She died from manual strangulation. Crushed hyoid bone. On internal exam we did find evidence that she had had intercourse with someone anywhere between just before her death to two days ago. I can give you that range with certainty based on what I found during the internal exam, but I can't narrow it any more than that."

"Intercourse?" Josie said. She squeezed the phone between her ear and shoulder as she twisted the pill bottle open and tapped three ibuprofen into her palm. "She wasn't assaulted?"

"Well, I can't say for sure, but there's no evidence that she was assaulted. No bruising, no abrasions, tears, or lacerations. Basically, nothing to suggest that the sex was not consensual."

"She let someone tie her up and have sex with her?"

Josie didn't miss the look Noah shot her as he listened in on her half of the conversation.

"I don't know," Dr. Feist said. "I'm not sure the two are related. Given her scars and the fresh ligature marks, it appears as though she did try to escape from her bindings. If she hadn't, her wrists wouldn't have been so damaged. But I can't say she was sexually assaulted, and I can't make any connection based on the evidence between intercourse and her being bound at the wrists on several occasions in the past few months. The good news is that we've got DNA. I've sent it off to the lab and asked that it be expedited."

"DNA from the person she had sex with," Josie said. "We don't know if that's the same person who killed her."

"No," Dr. Feist admitted. "We don't. But if you get a hit on the DNA it's one more avenue of investigation."

Unless it was a Sanctuary member. They could just say that they'd had an intimate relationship with Renee but hadn't killed her. Josie would have no way to prove them wrong.

Josie didn't want to ask, didn't want to know, in her heart, but knew she had to ask. "How about her throat? Did you find anything?"

Dr. Feist's silence spoke volumes. Josie felt sick even before she answered. She tossed the pills into her mouth and swallowed them dry while Dr. Feist told her exactly what she didn't want to hear. "Yes. There was a thin leather strap looped through half of a black walnut pushed deep into her throat. Just like Valerie Yates."

CHAPTER THIRTY-FOUR

By the time they arrived at the station, Dr. Feist had texted Josie a picture of the necklace found in Renee's throat. It was nearly identical to the one found inside Valerie. No clasps, the leather was tied together at the ends. The inside of the black walnut was an imperfect heart shape. The outer hull was dark, ridged, and rough. Josie stared at it for several seconds until Chief Chitwood called them both into his office for a briefing.

He didn't like anything they had to say.

He sent them home to rest, against Josie's protests. She was exhausted but the thought of another night filled with bad dreams was enough to set her teeth on edge. Noah left the light on for her in the bedroom. He was asleep within minutes. Josie spent the night sitting up in bed, shaking herself awake each time she started to doze. Her eyes burned with fatigue by the time they drove into work for the day. Besides the two cups of coffee she'd already had, the only thing that perked Josie up was a text from Gretchen saying the forecast called for no rain in the morning and that the K-9 unit was ready to go.

I'll meet you there, Josie texted back.

Back at their desks, Noah printed out the consent forms for Maya Bestler to allow them to take a DNA sample from her son. "I'll grab Hummel and run this over to the hospital while you meet Gretchen."

Josie watched him go, trying to ignore the knot forming in her stomach. All she wanted to do was go home, crack open the bottle of Wild Turkey in her cabinet, and drink for days. Until oblivion took over. No more dead bodies. No more calls from Muncy prison. No more serial killers lurking in the woods. No more nightmares.

But she had work to do. She checked her phone and saw a text from Gretchen:

Meet us at the Yates car.

Josie weaved through the rural roads that stretched like thin black ribbons through the forest back to Route 9227 passing a large orange flag along the side of the road, which Hummel had positioned, marking the place where officers had entered the forest to walk to the campsite. She found the parking lot a few minutes later and pulled in. Gretchen's unmarked vehicle was parked next to a large truck with a spacious cover over its bed. A large Aluminet tarp was draped over the truck. Its hatch was open and inside it, Josie saw the large, brown face of a German Shepherd, its tongue lolling and its bright eyes flitting all around.

Between the two vehicles stood Gretchen with the Alcott County sheriff's deputy K-9 handler. They both wore raincoats even though the rain had now receded to a light but persistent mist. As Josie stepped out of her own vehicle, the heat hit her like a wall. The heavy rain had done nothing to relieve the humidity. If anything, it had made it worse. As she got closer to the other two women, she saw drops of sweat slide from the deputy's hairline down the sides of her face and to the tip of her nose. Her gray-brown hair was slick, the wisps that had escaped from her ponytail clinging to her face and neck. Josie estimated her to be in her fifties. On their last case working with the Alcott County sheriff's K-9 unit, they'd been assigned a male handler.

The deputy smiled, wiped her hand on her slacks, and extended it for Josie to shake. "Deputy Maureen Sandoval," she said. She pointed to the back of her truck. "You probably saw Rini in there."

Josie said, "We appreciate both of you working out here in this heat. Do you mind if I speak with Detective Palmer privately for a moment before we start?"

"No problem," Sandoval said.

Gretchen, looking every bit as hot and bothered as Deputy Sandoval, followed Josie a few feet away so that Josie could bring her up to speed on the many developments of the day before. Gretchen scribbled furiously in her notebook while Josie talked, muttering things like, "good lord" and "sweet Jesus" on occasion. When Josie was finished, she used her pen to point at the circular purple bruise in the center of Josie's forehead. "How's your head?"

"I'm not concussed if that's what you're worried about," Josie answered.

Gretchen tucked her notebook back into her pocket. "Fair enough."

They returned to Deputy Sandoval, and Gretchen pointed to a Jeep Grand Cherokee on the opposite side of the parking lot. "That's Tyler and Valerie Yates' car. Lenore County didn't have a chance to move it."

"That's better for us," Sandoval said. "I prefer to start at the vehicle, especially in cases like this."

"Why's that?" Josie asked.

"Most of the time, we know for sure that the missing person was in their car at some point before they went into the woods. That's a good place to start. I had a case once—a hunter who got lost, and we started at his tree stand. Couldn't find him. Came back to the car, scented Rini on the vehicle, and she found him within an hour."

"He never made it to the tree stand," Josie said.

Sandoval smiled. "Right. He got lost before he even got out there. If we hadn't started at the car, we might not have found him. So even though I know you have a scene that looks as though the woman was there, I'd still prefer to start down here at the car.

Detective Palmer has the sleeping bag in her vehicle. We'll use that to put her onto Ms. Gresham's scent."

"Of course," Josie agreed.

Gretchen asked. "Mind if we follow along?"

"Be my guest."

Sandoval reached into her truck cab and pulled out a long black leash and a harness. From the truck, Rini began to whine. Her body wriggled with excitement. "She likes to work," Sandoval explained. While she took Rini out of the truck and hooked the leash onto her collar, Gretchen went to her vehicle and took out a large plastic bag containing what they believed to be Emilia Gresham's sleeping bag.

"Down," Sandoval commanded Rini. Dutifully, she lay on the hard-packed dirt, but continued to make high-pitched noises, as though complaining to Sandoval that the preparation for the search was taking too long.

Once Sandoval gave the command, Rini stood and went to the bag that Gretchen held up, sniffing aggressively. "Good, that's good," Sandoval murmured. She slipped the harness onto the dog. "Now it's time to work, Rini."

Rini loped in the direction of the Yates vehicle. Gretchen tossed the sleeping bag into the back of her car, and she and Josie jogged after the handler and her dog. Rini sniffed around a bit more and then took off into the woods. Josie and Gretchen had to run to keep up.

"She's in-scent," Sandoval called over her shoulder. "Try and stay with us."

Sandoval kept Rini on an extremely long lead which trailed behind the two of them. Josie and Gretchen stumbled several times in their attempts not to step on it or trip over it. Eventually, they let handler and dog work several yards ahead of them so that they weren't in the way.

Rini worked without cease, laser-focused on her task, her nose sometimes in the air and sometimes near the ground as she weaved and zig-zagged through the forest. Both Josie and Gretchen were soaked in sweat and gasping for air by the time they reached the Yates campsite, which was just over three miles from the car. They didn't even have time to discuss the fact that Emilia had obviously been at the campsite, because Rini was already plunging deep into the forest beyond, with Sandoval at a brisk walk behind her, offering encouragement as they worked together.

Rini turned south from the campsite, moving through the thick undergrowth of the forest with speed and assurance until she came to Cold Heart Creek where she lingered, pacing back and forth, tongue lolling as she panted. "Hang on, girl," Sandoval said as Josie and Gretchen caught up. Gretchen bent at the waist, bracing her palms on her legs, just above the knees, breathing heavily.

"What's wrong?" Josie asked Sandoval, wiping sweat from her eyes.

"We have to cross this," Sandoval told them.

Gretchen straightened up. She ran a hand through her short, brown spiked hair. "You think this woman crossed the creek? Wouldn't water destroy the scent?" Gretchen asked.

"That's a myth, Detective," Sandoval answered. "Humans carry their scent all around them all the time. Imagine an invisible cloud around you, almost like an aura. That's your scent. We all have it. That scent is falling from you wherever you go. Even in water, Rini will still be able to scent her. In fact, scent needs moisture to survive. Now the wind—that's another matter."

There was barely even a breeze, Josie thought. Or maybe it just seemed that way because every square inch of her body was soaked with perspiration, and the air around them was thick with humidity.

From the pocket of her vest, Sandoval pulled out a small bottle of baby powder. She twisted it open and squeezed it so that a bit of powder puffed out. Josie and Gretchen watched as the white powder floated along on the air, all the tiny particles drifting in the same direction—across the creek. Sandoval met Josie's eyes. "The water's not very deep, is it?"

Josie said, "No. I crossed it yesterday. It only came up to my waist. Might be deeper today with all the rain, but we could definitely cross it."

Sandoval urged Rini forward. "Let's go girl."

Rini splashed through the water and Sandoval followed her, keeping the lead long. When it got too deep for Rini to stand, she paddled until she came to the other side. Josie and Gretchen splashed behind them. Once Rini was on the opposite shore, she took off in her frantic trot, nose searching the air, the scent of Emilia Gresham leading her ever forward. Although Josie had her GPS unit with her, there was no time to take it out and study it. She wasn't sure how much ground they had covered by the time Rini led them to the break in the fence that separated the state gameland from Charlotte Fadden's Sanctuary.

Sandoval pulled the dog up short before she leaped over the bend in the fence. "Private property," she said.

Breathless, Josie shook her head. "We have their permission to search on their land."

Several feet behind her, Gretchen huffed. "I'll go back to the car and drive around, let them know we're bringing the dog onto the property."

"You gonna make it?" Sandoval asked Gretchen, giving her a raised brow.

Gretchen waved a hand in the air. "I'll be fine. You go ahead."

Sandoval gave a command, and Rini hopped gracefully through the bend in the fence. Sandoval followed with Josie trailing behind her. Josie knew they were far from the main house and barn. In her mind, she tried to orient herself, but the dog moved too quickly. Josie's breath came in gasps as she jogged after dog and handler through one of the many wooded areas of the Sanctuary. Everything looked the same. Josie was grateful to have her GPS tucked away in her pocket. No matter how deeply they went, she was sure they'd find their way out. After what felt like an eternity, they emerged into a clearing. Ahead, Josie saw the cabins that Noah had told her about. Noah had been right about their state of disrepair. Josie counted five of them, faded brown, leaning against one another as though they might fall down if one was knocked out of place. One had a collapsed roof. The others had rotted and sagging steps. They were oddly shaped, and Josie had a feeling that they'd been built by former members of the Sanctuary with whatever materials they could find at hand. Rini ran up the steps to one of them, nudged the door open with her long nose, and went inside. Josie's heartbeat sped up. They had checked the cabins. They hadn't found anyone. She knew Noah would not have missed something so major.

But then Rini emerged and was back on the ground, running the length of the front of the cabins and plunging back into the woods. Josie had only a moment to look inside the cabin. There was no furniture, only wooden plank floors and crude wooden bunk beds without mattresses. Something beneath the lower bunk caught her eye—she took another step inside, squatted and peered at it. It was a thick piece of rope, about two inches long. Taking out her phone, she quickly swiped the flashlight app and shone it on the object. What looked like some kind of dried brown substance crusted along the fibers. Josie's heart did a double tap. She snapped a few photos and then searched her pockets. She had gloves and, luckily, deep in one of the pockets of her rain jacket, a single crumpled evidence bag. With a sigh of relief, she dropped the rope into the bag and raced back outside. Could this be part of the rope used to bind Renee Kelly? Had someone been taking her to this cabin, tying her up and doing God-knows-what to her? Rini had specifically entered that cabin. That had to mean that Emilia had been inside at some point.

Was it where Renee had seen Emilia? Had someone brought Emilia here? Or had she taken shelter here only to find herself in whatever hell Renee had caught herself up in?

Josie didn't have time to think about it. Outside the cabin, Sandoval and Rini were gone. Anxiety pricked at her. She sprinted in the direction they had set off, crashing through brush and thick vegetation until she could hear Sandoval's voice, gently praising and encouraging her dog. Josie caught up with them just as they emerged into an open field. Ahead, they saw the Sanctuary house sitting on the crest of a small incline and beside it, the barn. Rini jogged across the field, occasionally zig-zagging. Sandoval was sure-footed behind the dog, but Josie slipped in the wet grass, falling forward onto her hands. She scrambled back up and ran after Sandoval and Rini. When they reached the house, several people stood around, staring at the dog. Some of them shrank back, away from Rini, but as Sandoval had said, the dog was in-scent. She was tracking Emilia Gresham's scent and that was her one and only focus. Josie was one hundred percent sure that any one of the Sanctuary members could have dangled a steak in Rini's face, and the dog would bypass it completely in search of her quarry.

She sniffed around the house as Sandoval adjusted the lead. Then she veered off, crossing over to the barn. But then, after sniffing the door, Rini abandoned the barn and started off along the driveway, out toward the road. She weaved in and out of the parked cars along the way but didn't stop. As they came around the front of the house, Josie saw Gretchen standing on the porch, speaking with Charlotte. The two paused in their conversation to watch Rini and Sandoval move along. Josie tried to keep pace with them while still avoiding the long leash that trailed behind dog and handler.

Had Emilia passed right through the Sanctuary? Where the hell had she been heading? If she'd been in trouble, why wouldn't she have stopped at the house or the barn to ask for help? Or had she known that she'd get no help here?

Rini reached the road, where she stopped, pacing frantically and scenting the air. Finally, she stopped pacing and looked up at Sandoval. Josie knew that search and rescue dogs gave active indications when they found the person they were looking for. From her observations on previous cases, it was usually a bark. But Rini didn't bark. Sandoval took out her puff bottle again and squeezed some baby powder into the breeze. She urged Rini in its direction, goading her down the road a bit, but Rini had none of the urgency she had had only moments ago.

With a sinking heart, Josie already had a pretty good idea what Sandoval was going to tell her before she even opened her mouth.

Josie said, "She got into a vehicle, didn't she?"

Sandoval frowned. "You know I can't say that for certain. I can only tell you the scent stops here. Rini doesn't lose a scent. At least, if she does, she usually regroups and finds it again. So what I can tell you is that it's just not here."

Gretchen ambled over, picking up the end of their conversation. "Could all the rain we just had have washed it away?"

Sandoval said, "I doubt it. I don't think there's enough run-off right here for it to have done that. Even so, Rini would still be able to pick up the scent, I'm sure."

Gretchen sighed and looked up and down the road. Josie turned back toward the house to see Charlotte watching, her face carefully blank. Softly, for only Gretchen to hear, Josie said, "We're missing something."

"A connection to the hermit," Gretchen said.

"Right."

Emilia Gresham's backpack had been found in Donovan's cave and yet, Rini hadn't even sniffed in the direction of the caverns. The dog would follow a person's scent, not the scent of a backpack. As Deputy Maureen Sandoval had said, people carried their scent all around them like an aura, and the scent falls away from them everywhere they go. Emilia Gresham's backpack would have her scent on it, but it would not constantly be shedding her scent as Michael Donovan carried it through the woods.

Josie said, "Emilia Gresham went from the campsite, through the Sanctuary, out here to the road, and we are now theorizing that she got into a vehicle there. Either she was running from someone, came to the road, and flagged down a vehicle, or someone took her and brought her here and then put her in a vehicle."

"Maybe it was someone from the Sanctuary," Gretchen suggested. "Someone who is no longer here. Everyone here's been questioned more than once, but we haven't accounted for anyone who might have left between the night the Yateses were murdered and now."

Josie sighed. "Right." She looked back at the barn and driveway where several people stood staring at the three officers and Rini standing in the road. "They'll all say that no one left or that they don't keep careful enough track of who comes and goes to say who might have left recently. They'll all lie."

Gretchen lowered her voice to match Josie's. "You want to talk to Charlotte again?"

Josie met Charlotte's gaze and held it.

"No," Josie said. "Not yet. We need more information."

CHAPTER THIRTY-FIVE

Josie found Hummel in the first-floor break room. He sat at one of the tables, a takeout container open before him and a big hamburger in his hands. "Boss," he greeted her around a mouthful of food.

With a sigh, Josie sat down across from him. "Hummel, how many times do I have to tell you? It's just Josie. I'm not the boss anymore, remember?"

Hummel swallowed and grinned at her. "You're my boss."

Josie raised an eyebrow. "No, Hummel, I'm not."

He pushed the takeout container over toward her and pointed to the French fries, indicating for her to have some. She hadn't even realized how hungry she was until she looked at them. As if sensing how ravenous she was, Hummel said, "Have the rest."

He finished his burger while she polished off the fries. When they were done, he closed up the takeout container and pushed it to the edge of the table. Then he leaned in toward her. "I don't care who's in charge around here," he said. "You'll always be the boss to me."

Josie shook her head, but a smile spread across her face. "Thanks for the fries," she told him.

She reached into her pocket and pulled out the bag with the piece of rope in it. She explained where she had found it. Hummel looked inside the bag.

Josie asked, "Do you think there's enough there to do a presumptive blood test and have enough left over to get DNA?"

Josie knew that a Kastle-Meyer test was a simple, quick way to figure out if the crusty substance on the rope was blood or not.

All Hummel had to do was swab the stain with a cotton swab, moisten it with one or two drops of ethyl alcohol and then apply one to two drops of phenolphthalein followed by one or two drops of a hydrogen peroxide solution. If the substance on the swab turned bright pink within six seconds, they were dealing with blood. The problem was that the phenolphthalein used to do the test would destroy DNA so whenever they worked with a limited amount of a substance, they had to make sure there was enough to test for both blood and DNA. If there wasn't enough for a presumptive blood test, she'd send the entire thing off to the state lab for a DNA test, which could take weeks or months, unless she could get it expedited, and even that was a challenge. But if there was enough to do both, and the substance was blood, she'd have something she could use to rattle Charlotte Fadden and perhaps get her to talk about whatever she was withholding from the police.

Hummel looked up from the bag. "Let me see what I can do."

She opened her mouth to thank him, but Noah appeared in the doorway. "Got something for you," he said.

"Gresham?" she asked hopefully.

"No," he said. "Bestler."

She hefted herself up from the chair and followed him back upstairs to their desks. "What've you got for me?"

Noah leaned across her and used her computer mouse to bring up a PDF document. Josie leaned forward and began to read. "Are you kidding me?" she asked.

Noah went around to his own chair and sat, leaning back, fingers laced behind his head. "Nope. Our hermit, Michael Donovan, killed his wife thirty-three years ago. He beat her to death in their home and then served ten years in prison."

Josie scanned the details of the case. "He pleaded down to voluntary manslaughter. Only ten years? That's terrible."

"It is," Noah agreed.

"This is an Allegheny County case. Pittsburgh area. So how did he get from there to Lenore County?"

"He did his time just west of Lenore County. When they released him, he had nothing. No money, no home. Nothing to go back to. I guess he hung around for a while, told enough people a story about how his wife died, then walked off into the woods and didn't come back. That's where the lore comes from. He's got a history of violence, so it's not a stretch that he'd take Maya Bestler, or that he may have killed some or all of our recent victims."

"No, not a stretch." She still wasn't completely sold on Donovan as Renee Kelly's killer. It seemed too coincidental that Renee was being abused, living in a state of terror on the Sanctuary, and then just happened to be killed by Donovan when she left. Still, she couldn't deny the presence of the black walnut necklaces. Tyler and Valerie Yates and Renee Kelly had definitely been killed by the same person.

"But this doesn't help us find Emilia Gresham," Josie said.

"I know," Noah conceded. "Speaking of that, where are Gretchen and Mett?"

"Gretchen went home to take a quick shower. Mett's not on shift yet, but he should be here soon."

Josie's desk phone rang. She answered, had a brief conversation and hung up feeling a little better about the Gresham and Yates cases than she had minutes earlier.

"What's that look for?" Noah asked.

"That was Dr. Feist," Josie said. "She just met with Wesley Yates. He came to claim his son's body. She told him we needed to speak with him. He'll be here in fifteen minutes."

CHAPTER THIRTY-SIX

Wesley Yates was a bear of a man, tall and broad with white hair tied back in a ponytail and a well-trimmed moustache and beard. He wore a plain black T-shirt and denim shorts. His arms were decorated with tattoos from wrist to shoulder. Many of them were old and faded but from what Josie could see, the theme was carnivorous animals. In spite of his size, he shuffled into the conference room where Josie, Noah and a freshly showered Gretchen waited, and when he looked up to greet them, Josie could see his brown eyes were red-rimmed from crying.

She stood and took his large hand. "Mr. Yates, we're deeply sorry for your loss."

He nodded, seeming numb while Josie, Noah, and Gretchen made introductions, offered him coffee, and waited until he was seated comfortably in one of the chairs across the table. "I can't believe this is happening," he muttered. "It doesn't seem real."

Josie knew from personal experience just how surreal it was to lose someone you loved suddenly and unexpectedly. Her heart ached for this large man.

"The doctor at the morgue said they were poisoned and then… strangled?"

Gretchen said, "Yes, that's correct. We believe whoever killed them poisoned them with hemlock found in the forest and then when they became ill, he strangled them both. I'm so sorry, Mr. Yates."

He swiped at a couple of rogue tears that slipped from his eyes. "I just can't believe it. My son, he was no slouch. He could have protected Val. I don't—I don't understand. I guess if he was that sick… it's just so hard to take in."

Noah said, "We understand. If you need a few minutes, we can come back."

Wes shook his head. "No, let's get this over with."

Josie asked, "Did he and Valerie go camping a lot?"

"No," Wesley answered. "Maybe a couple of times a year. They were hoping to travel more, do more of it. Maybe go back to her country. She's from Australia—was from Australia. Jesus."

He looked away from them, more tears spilling from his eyes. Josie got up and retrieved a box of tissues from the other end of the table, sliding them over to him.

"Mr. Yates," Gretchen said.

"Wes," he interrupted. "Call me Wes."

"Wes, we believe that someone else was camping with Tyler and Valerie. A woman. Do you have any idea who that might have been?"

"Yeah, probably Emilia."

"Emilia Gresham?" Josie asked.

"That's right. She's their best friend. Well, she was Valerie's best friend since college. Emilia was married to a guy named Jack. The four of them used to do everything together. They were inseparable. Till Jack went off the deep end."

Josie and Noah exchanged a curious look. Gretchen stayed focused on Wes. "Off the deep end?" she coaxed.

Wes folded his beefy hands in front of him on the table. "Yeah, he went a little coo-coo, if you know what I mean?"

"In what way?" Noah said.

"He wouldn't leave the house for weeks on end. Emilia thought he was depressed. He wouldn't do any of the usual things those four did together. Tyler said once he went over there and Jack was holed up in their spare bedroom. He hadn't bathed for a long time. Tyler said the smell almost knocked him out."

"Sounds pretty depressed to me," Gretchen said.

Josie felt a cold shiver down her spine. She thought of how Jack Gresham had disappeared from Tyler's photos. She hoped he hadn't committed suicide.

Gretchen said, "We were trying to locate Jack. So far we haven't had any luck. We talked with one of Emilia's sisters who had no idea that anything was wrong. She seemed to think he was working regularly and would be at their home."

"He's not there," Wes said. "He hasn't lived there for a long time. He joined a cult, last I heard."

Josie sat up straighter in her chair while Gretchen leaned in closer to Wes. "Where was this cult located?"

"I don't know. Tyler never said."

"Did he mention what kind of cult?" Josie tried.

"Nah. Are there different kinds of cults?" Wes said with a weak laugh. "They're all bad news, aren't they?"

Gretchen smiled. "One could probably make that argument."

Josie tried a different tactic. "When did he join? Do you have any idea?"

Wes scratched his forehead. "Oh, a while back. Couple of years ago? Could be longer. It was after he got fired from his new job."

"Fired for what?" Noah asked.

"Don't know exactly, but I know he was fired. Tyler told me."

Gretchen flipped open her notebook and turned back a few pages. Josie watched her run a finger down the lines of writing until she came to Jack's employer. "This wasn't at Cloudserv Technologies, was it?"

Wes waved a hand in the air. "No, no. That's the place he got laid off from. That's what he told everyone. Never heard different. It was after the layoff he got real depressed. Then he worked at this other place a few months. After he got fired, he and Emilia had a big blowout. That's when he left. About six months after that, he came home and told her he was leaving for good. Joining some cult—

I mean, I'm sure he didn't call it that. He probably said something else. That's just how Tyler put it. Tyler told me that Emilia didn't believe Jack at first but then after he was gone a few months, she went there to try to talk him into coming home. He wouldn't hear of it. She went a few times, I guess, and couldn't convince him. Tyler said he even went himself and joined up for a couple of weeks but as soon as it became clear he was only there to talk to Jack and try to get him to come home, they asked him to leave."

"Tyler went to this place and didn't tell you where it was?" Gretchen asked.

Wes shrugged. "Tyler's a grown man. He—" He broke off and horror shaded his face anew as the realization hit him once more in its finality. "He *was* a grown man," he added. "Oh Jesus." He took several deep breaths, trying to compose himself. Then he went on. "He didn't tell me until after the fact. It was over and done with. I just figured that was it—they were going to let Jack be."

Noah said, "Did Tyler ever mention why Emilia didn't tell anyone else what was going on?"

"I guess she was embarrassed. Tyler told me what was going on, but he didn't want me repeating it. Didn't even want Emilia to know he'd told me. He said she was sure she could get Jack to come home and things would go back to normal, so she didn't want anyone to know."

That would explain why she hadn't told her parents or neighbors or anyone else they'd been in touch with during their search for Emilia.

"What about Jack's family?" Gretchen asked. "Have they been involved at all? Are they aware of the situation?"

"Jack's only got his mom. She was a single mother. After he was out of high school, she remarried and moved away with her new husband. They live in Georgia from what I remember. She never had much to do with him though. Came to his wedding and that was the last he heard from her."

Josie went back to the workplace issue. "What was the name of the place that Jack was fired from?"

"Oh, it was Lantz Snack Factory. They make chips and stuff. He just worked in the loading docks, putting boxes onto their trucks."

Gretchen marked the name of the company down on her notepad.

Noah asked, "Did Tyler and Valerie mention to you that they were going camping?"

Wes shrugged. "Well I knew they had a vacation coming up. I hadn't talked with them in a few weeks. I wasn't sure what they'd decided to do. I know they were saving money to buy a house. They only live—lived—in an apartment. So they wanted to do stuff that was cheap. Camping would make sense. I never expected…"

Again, words failed him. More tears streamed down his face. He snatched a tissue from the box and wiped his cheeks.

Josie stood up and moved to the other side of the table. When she touched his shoulder, she could feel him shaking. Sadness gnawed at her. "Wes," she told him. "You've been very helpful. We won't take any more of your time." She placed her business card on the table before him. "We're going to do everything we can to find the person who killed your son and your daughter-in-law and bring them to justice. In the meantime, if you need anything, please don't hesitate to call."

CHAPTER THIRTY-SEVEN

Exhaustion weighed down Josie's limbs. It was hard to believe that only two days ago she and Noah had been called out to the Yateses' campsite. So much had happened, so many leads had been chased and so much conflicting information had been collected, she felt overwhelmed by it all. As if reading her mind, Noah said, "Let's talk this out."

They sat at their desks—Noah, Josie, Gretchen, and Mettner, who had just arrived for his shift.

Gretchen said, "Someone should get Chitwood. He'll want to be briefed."

A collective groan went up from the rest of them. Mettner stood, trudged over to Chitwood's office and knocked on the door. A brusque "What?" came from the other side. Mettner poked his head inside the door and said a few words. Then he closed the door behind him and walked back to his desk. "He'll be out in a few minutes."

Nearly a half hour later, Chitwood emerged from his office. He stood near their desks, arms crossed over his thin chest as he listened to their updates. When they finished, he was silent for a long moment. Josie was beginning to think he had fallen asleep with his eyes open when finally, he said, "Tyler and Valerie Yates went camping with Emilia Gresham a couple of miles from the Sanctuary because Emilia's husband, Jack, joined the cult and she wanted to get him back. Tyler and Valerie were poisoned and strangled—and our killer left a nice little gift for us in Valerie's throat in case we weren't convinced of just how sadistic he really is. Emilia either left or was taken from the campsite, went through the Sanctuary property, and out to the road where she was likely picked up by a vehicle. But her backpack, as well as several other items you believe are from the Yateses' campsite, were found in Michael Donovan's cave."

"That's correct, sir," Gretchen said.

"In the meantime, while you guys were questioning these clowns at the Sanctuary, Quinn talks to this Renee Kelly who seemed afraid, hinting that someone there might be hurting her."

"Well," Josie clarified. "She didn't actually hint at it—that was my assessment."

"Fine," Chitwood said. "Quinn told her to leave the premises and meet her down the road. Kelly left the Sanctuary during the night but never made it to where Quinn or Palmer were waiting."

"Correct," Noah supplied.

"The next day, you guys apprehend Michael Donovan and take him into custody. Renee Kelly's body is found on the bank of Cold Heart Creek, miles from both the caverns and the Sanctuary but closer to the caverns. Evidence suggests she was killed elsewhere and dumped there. She had old and new ligature marks on her wrists indicating that she had been bound by the wrists several times in the weeks or months before her death. Like Valerie Yates, she may or may not have been sexually assaulted, she was manually strangled, and this sicko left a black walnut necklace in her throat."

"Yes," Josie said.

"All right," Chitwood said. "What else have we got?"

"I found a piece of rope in one of the cabins on the Sanctuary property. Hummel is testing that for blood now," Josie said.

"Michael Donovan has been charged with the abduction of Maya Bestler as well as multiple counts of rape. You guys do DNA testing?"

"We did," Josie said. "Maya consented to us taking a sample from her son which Noah and Hummel took care of this morning.

Andrew Bowen, Donovan's attorney, also agreed to his client giving a sample. Hummel took that as well."

"Those are gonna take weeks to come back. But that's not our problem. That's the DA's problem. The Bestler case is wrapped up, then?"

Noah said, "Well, yeah, but we can't rule out Donovan for the Yates and Kelly murders or Emilia Gresham's disappearance. Like you just said, Donovan had Gresham's backpack as well as several items from the Yates campsite in his cave."

Chitwood waved a hand in the air. "But searches turned up no other evidence of Gresham in or near the caverns, right? The dog from the K-9 unit didn't track her to the cave. Donovan says he ransacked the campsite after the fact. We can't prove him wrong. You guys have no DNA on either of the Yates bodies, do you?"

"No sir," Gretchen answered.

"But we have DNA from Renee Kelly's body," Josie said.

Noah added, "He would have had time to kill her and move her body before we apprehended him."

"But until those DNA results come in, we can't charge him," Chitwood pointed out. "Wrap up the paperwork on the Bestler case and send the file to the DA. I'll be happy to have that off my desk. The press is gonna be all over me on this one. They don't seem to have a clue yet, but it's only a matter of time before they figure out a missing woman was found alive. Held captive by some feral mountain man? That's press gold. Let's go back to Gresham."

Mettner said, "WYEP is still running her photo. I called her sister as soon as I got in. She said there was no sign of her or of Jack at their apartment. Of course, now we know why."

"How about warrants to get into the phones?" Chitwood asked. "We've got three phones belonging to Tyler Yates, Valerie Yates and Emilia Gresham."

Gretchen said, "We're still waiting on those. It could be another day or more, but I'm not sure they'll be of any use. We already know where our focus needs to be now."

Josie said, "Jack Gresham—he's missing, too, as far as we know—and the Sanctuary."

Chitwood said, "You guys were there a few times in the last forty-eight hours. You showed them photos of Emilia. What about Jack?"

Josie said, "We didn't know he was a player until just now, so no, we didn't show them a photo of him. I also didn't see him there. But no one admitted to having seen Emilia or Tyler, both of whom had been there before to try to get Jack to come home, so they're a bunch of liars. They've obviously been coached not to tell us anything of use. Noah and I even conducted private interviews and got nothing."

"We need more information," Noah said.

"Like what?" Chitwood asked.

"Like someone who used to live there. Someone who can tell us more about them and their inner workings."

"Where are we gonna find that, Fraley?"

Noah ran a hand through his hair. "I don't know," he said. With the circles under his eyes, his five o'clock shadow, rumpled clothes, and slumped shoulders, he reflected the exhaustion they were all feeling.

Mettner said, "Everyone there said they heard of the place through word of mouth, right? So obviously there are people who leave there and go back into the world. We have to find one of those people. I read the reports from yesterday—a good percentage of the people there are recovering addicts. Maybe we start visiting rehab facilities. See if any of the patients there know the place."

Gretchen groaned. "That's going to be a lot of work, but it's a solid idea. I can start making a list of rehab facilities. We can hit them tomorrow morning."

Josie said, "Moore knows something."

Everyone looked at her. Chitwood said, "How do you know?"

"Because when we first asked him about the Sanctuary, he got defensive."

"That guy's a douche all the way around," Noah remarked. "Doesn't mean he knows anything."

Josie thought of the way Moore had answered almost all of her questions with a question when she'd asked about the place. "No," she said. "He knows more than he's letting on. I think he either knows someone who lives there now or someone who used to live there."

Gretchen said, "Or *he* lived there at some point."

Noah said, "So what do we do? Ask him? He's been a pain in the ass since this started, and he's even more pissed at us since the Chief called his boss to give him an attitude adjustment. What makes you think he's just going to tell us? Especially if he was the one who used to live there? He's not going to want to admit to that. Not to us."

Chitwood walked over to Josie and looked down at her, arms still crossed over his chest. "Quinn," he barked. "You sure about this?"

"Moore definitely knows something."

Chitwood nodded slowly. Then he turned to Mettner. "Mettner, you call Deputy Moore. Tell him I need to talk to him."

"Sir," Mettner said. "I don't—"

"Don't argue with me, Mettner. The man's got a cell phone. Call it."

Mettner began shuffling papers around on his desk, looking for Moore's cell phone number. "I'll text it to you, Mett," Josie told him.

Chitwood pointed a finger at Josie. "Finish up your paperwork and then Quinn, Palmer, and Fraley, go home and get some rest. I expect all hands on deck tomorrow. I want this Gresham woman found yesterday!"

CHAPTER THIRTY-EIGHT

The paperwork took a few hours. Then Josie, Noah and Gretchen went out to dinner, discussing the case as they ate but coming no closer to any firm conclusions. At home, Josie and Noah stripped down to nothing and fell into bed. Noah fit his body against Josie's, wrapping her in his arms and nuzzling her ear. Josie laughed softly. "You're going to be asleep in thirty seconds."

His breath was warm on her neck. "Truth."

"What do you think Chitwood's up to?" Josie asked.

"I don't know. Guess he's going to try to find out what Moore knows about the Sanctuary. Man, I'd love to be there when he talks to Moore. I can just hear him now: 'son, I've been doing this since you were in diapers!'"

Josie giggled. "If I had a dollar for every time he's said that to me, I wouldn't have to work."

"Me either."

Noah kissed the nape of her neck, his arms pulling her in closer. "Do we have to talk about work right now?"

Josie turned into him, kissing him deeply. In spite of how tired they were, their lovemaking was slow and purposeful. Josie tried to commit every touch, every kiss, every movement to memory. She wanted these moments to replace all the horrors of the last few days inside her brain, if only for a little while. Afterward, she fell asleep feeling comforted and content.

But it wasn't enough to ward off the nightmares.

She was running through the woods this time. The night was inky black. Branches of barren, gnarled trees reached out for her from every direction. No matter how far or fast she ran, there was no way out of the forest. When she saw a sliver of moonlight ahead, her feet pounded harder against the leaf-strewn ground. Almost there, her hand shot out to grab the shaft of silver light, but something snagged her ankle. She fell as it dragged her backward into the darkness. She was small again. Six years old. "You're a feather!" her daddy used to tell her before he threw her up in the air and caught her again. She used to laugh so hard. "Again, Daddy!" she would shriek. "Again!"

In the dream, she cried for him as the thing in the night pulled her back, away from the light. "Daddy, help!"

Lila's voice cut through the blackness. "You want your daddy?" she growled. "I'll show you your daddy."

Josie's limbs scrabbled against the roots of trees, trying to get away. She knew what was coming, and every cell in her body screamed in protest. She didn't want to see him. Not after what Lila had done to him. Even as she screamed the word "no" longer and louder than she ever had, a spotlight shone down on her. She wasn't being hauled through the forest anymore by some unseen creature. Now she stood in the center of the spotlight with Lila behind her. Lila's hand reached around and gripped Josie's chin, squeezing hard enough to bruise, and forcing her to look.

In front of them, Eli Matson sat slumped against a tree, the back of his head splattered across its trunk. "You think your daddy is so great?" Lila growled. "Look what he did. He left you."

"No," Josie cried. "You killed him. You did this."

Lila's grip tightened on Josie's jaw, cutting off her words. "That's right, girl. I'll destroy everything you love. You don't say one word, you got that? Not one word."

The spotlight extinguished and Josie wriggled from Lila's grasp, racing away into the night. But everywhere she went, Lila was there. Every time she got away, Lila captured her again. There was no end, no rest, no peace. Sweat seeped from every pore. Her lungs screamed for air. Every muscle in her body burned. Her mind felt foggy. Exhaustion tugged at her, and hopelessness knocked her to the ground. She no longer had the energy to even stand up. She told her body to get up, to keep running away, but it wouldn't.

Lila was there, holding her down, looming over her. "I've got something for you, JoJo," she said in a singsong voice.

With one hand, she pried open Josie's mouth. The dream was pitch black and yet with perfect clarity, Josie saw the black walnut necklace dangling from Lila's other hand just seconds before she jammed it deep into Josie's throat.

CHAPTER THIRTY-NINE

Josie woke on the bedroom floor, legs kicking, hands clutching at her throat until an ear-splitting scream came out. They had left Josie's bedside lamp on and in the glow of it, Josie's eyes fixed on Noah. He squatted next to her, calling her name, touching her arms and her hair, trying to bring her back from the depths of the nightmare. Her fingers found his face and she cupped his cheeks, staring desperately into his eyes, trying to anchor herself in reality.

"It's okay," he said. "You're safe. Everything's okay."

He waited for her breathing to even out before helping her back up into bed. Her bedside clock read three forty-three a.m. Josie knew she wouldn't go back to sleep. Noah settled in beside her, holding her and pulling her head gently down onto his chest. Josie focused on the steady thump of his heartbeat.

"What's going on, Josie?" he asked.

"Nightmares," she said.

He chuckled. "You don't say."

"Bad memories," she said. "From when I was a kid. Also, these cases we're working on. It's all jumbled in my head. I can't—I can't stop them."

"Is there something about these cases that's reminding you of that stuff?"

"No, I don't know," Josie answered. She didn't want to tell him about the calls. She already knew what he would say: she should go see Lila. They had unfinished business. But did they? Lila had destroyed not just a good portion of Josie's childhood but a part of Josie's sense of self and security. Lila had tortured her, and Josie hated her for it. That was Josie's truth, plain and simple. She didn't need to visit Lila to know that. She didn't need to give Lila that last bit of satisfaction in life by coming when she called.

"I guess just being out in the woods," Josie lied. "My mom took my dad out for a walk in the woods before she killed him and staged it as a suicide. She used to take me out to the tree where she did it when she was feeling especially cruel."

His arms tightened around her. "I'm sorry."

"Me too," Josie whispered. "Me too."

She didn't sleep after that. Her mind was a taut string about to snap. Her bones and muscles felt weak and heavy. At six she left Noah snoring in bed and went downstairs for coffee. She waited another hour before waking him and tried to put on a smile for him as they got ready for the day and drove to police headquarters.

Mettner had gone off shift, but Gretchen was already there. She stood outside the conference room door, her brown eyes gleaming with excitement. When she saw Josie and Noah, she rolled up onto the balls of her feet and back.

"Wow," Noah said. "I haven't seen you this excited since Komorrah's came out with a toasted pecan frappuccino."

Gretchen slapped his shoulder as he and Josie stopped next to her. "This is better than that," she said. "Josie was right."

"About Moore?" Josie asked.

Gretchen nodded. "He has a younger sister, Haylie. Ten years ago, when she was eighteen and just out of high school, she went to live on the Sanctuary."

"Really?" Noah said, eyes widening. He nudged Josie with an elbow. "Good work. Did Moore say why he didn't mention it when we asked him about the Sanctuary?"

"I guess he didn't want her getting caught up in this case by association. She only lived there for six months but when her brother asked her to come in and meet with us—at Chief Chitwood's urging—she said no problem."

"She's in there?" Josie said, a stab of excitement piercing the cloud of fatigue she couldn't shake off.

Gretchen nodded. "You guys ready to talk to her?"

Haylie Moore looked like she was ready to take a jog——in a Penn State T-shirt and blue running shorts, her shoulder-length blonde hair pulled back from her face with a black cloth headband. When they walked in, she was standing at the window, looking outside. The sky was still a bruised gray. Haylie turned when the three of them entered. She smiled easily at them, walking over to shake each one of their hands. Josie was happy to see that law enforcement didn't intimidate her.

Gretchen had brought in several cups of coffee, and Haylie accepted one with a soft "thank you." Once they were seated, she said, "My brother said you wanted to know about the Sanctuary."

"Yes," Gretchen said, pushing a basket of sugar and creamer across the table toward her. "Anything you can tell us about how it works and the people there would be extremely helpful."

Haylie stirred cream and sugar into her coffee. "Where should I start?"

Josie asked, "How did you hear about it?"

"I was working at this restaurant, The Dogwood Diner, as a waitress, and one of the other girls told me about it. Well, I shouldn't say girl. She was way older than me. She was in and out of rehab like crazy. Lost her whole family 'cause she couldn't stay off drugs. Anyway, she was getting her life back together, and she told me she owed it all to the Sanctuary. I asked her what that was—I thought it was some rehab facility, but she said it helped her way more than any rehab place ever did."

"What was that woman's name?" Noah asked.

Haylie frowned. "Oh geez, I don't remember. Theresa, maybe? It was years ago. She left the restaurant, moved away to be near her kids. I didn't hear from her after that."

"She told you how to get there?" Gretchen asked. "Before she left town?"

"Oh yeah, one night after our shift, she drove me past it. At first, I thought she was a little nuts, you know? But the more she talked about it, the more I thought maybe I should check it out. It didn't help that I was having a lot of problems at the time. I was really struggling, like, with depression and anxiety. I didn't know what I wanted to do with my life. My parents wanted me to get into farming cause that's what they did, but I didn't want to do that. I had dreams of going to college, which they said we could never afford. We were fighting all the time. It didn't help that I was a lesbian and in total denial. There was no way I was coming out to them. I told Josh, and he was cool about it, but I knew they would freak out."

"You were under a lot of pressure," Gretchen said.

"Yeah, exactly."

Josie said, "The woman who runs the Sanctuary says that people come there to find peace. Is that what your friend Theresa told you? That you would find peace there?"

Haylie sipped her coffee. She picked at the discarded sugar packet wrappers. "Not so much that I'd find peace, but that I could be myself there—whatever that meant to me. Like she could go there and be like 'I'm an addict and I screwed up my life so bad, my kids got taken away from me' and everyone there was fine with that. I think it was the idea of acceptance more than anything else that made me curious."

"So you decided to check it out," Gretchen prompted.

"Yeah, eventually I drove up there. At first, I just met with Charlotte. We talked. She walked me around the place. She told me to go home for a few days and see how I felt. If I still wanted to stay at the Sanctuary after that, I could come back. So I did that. Have you met Charlotte?"

"Yes," Josie answered. "We have."

Haylie smiled but tense little lines pulled at the corners of her eyes. "She's very… well, she's got this way about her. Like she knows what you're thinking. It's really weird at first but then it becomes kind of comforting. I was really mesmerized by her, I guess."

Gretchen asked, "What happened when you first joined the Sanctuary?"

"Well, back then, I spent a week or two in the main house with Charlotte. It was like this intense therapy. I talked with her for hours on end. I did some stuff like cooking and helping in the garden or doing laundry, but mostly I talked with her and I meditated. They used to have a lady who taught a yoga class at the house for new people. It was all about relaxing and 'shedding the trappings of the outside world.' Like a retreat."

"Were there other people in the house with you?" Josie asked.

"A few, yeah. People in various 'stages of arrival.'" She used her fingers to make air quotes. "That's what Charlotte called it."

"So she had a system of some kind?" Noah asked.

"Oh yeah," Haylie said with an eye-roll. "They have a very strict system there."

"Really?" Josie said. "She made it sound like there was no organization at all. She said she didn't even keep track of who came and went or how long they stayed."

Haylie picked up her coffee but put it back down without taking a sip. "Well, that is true. She didn't keep a list or anything. I mean, not that I know of, and you could come and go as you pleased. I could have left at any time."

Josie asked, "What were the stages?"

"It had mostly to do with the work that needed to be done there and where you got to sleep. When you first arrived and stayed at the house it was great. I mean, it was like a vacation. You didn't mind helping out with cooking or cleaning or whatever. I felt like someone saw me—really saw me—and accepted me for the first time in my life. I think I had been in the house about three weeks. Maybe a month. Then she said if I was going to stay, I'd have to really 'immerse myself in the work' which basically meant toiling all day. It wasn't boring at first 'cause I was all into it, and I thought I was having some kind of awakening. But it got old quick."

"What was the work?" Gretchen asked.

"Like, literal work. They live off the land, you know? So the work is never done. There's gardening, laundry, cooking—they're mostly vegetarians though so we didn't have to worry about killing animals, although some would go fishing and cook that."

"Sounds like they kept you pretty busy," Josie said. "What else did you do there?"

"Not much. There's no internet or television. No radio. No connection to the outside world at all. Oh, and the bathroom situation is gross. You can't have that many people going in the house, so they put outhouses in certain places. The smell was horrific. Anyway, when you have to do everything from scratch, there's really no downtime. Sometimes we'd get books when someone went on thrift runs." At their puzzled faces, Haylie added, "That's where you would take a drive with another member and visit a bunch of thrift stores to buy second-hand clothes for everyone who lived there."

Gretchen asked, "Where do they get their money?"

"You give them whatever you can when you get there and they kind of live off that. They sell produce too. I don't know much about that part of it. It never seemed like something that was discussed. That was one of the cool things about living there. Money was never a stressor. If it was for Charlotte, she never showed it."

That hardly seemed enough to house, clothe, and feed up to thirty people but just because Haylie didn't know the Sanctuary's full financial picture didn't mean that there wasn't more to it. It was possible that Charlotte's husband had left her a good chunk of money. One hundred acres of land was quite a lot. Perhaps he had also left her other assets that she'd been able to live off all these decades. Or maybe he had had a sizeable life insurance policy.

"What were the other people there like?" Gretchen asked.

Haylie shrugged. "They were all nice. Most of them were either struggling with drug or alcohol addiction or running from bad relationships. Then there were one or two like me who had bad anxiety or just didn't know what they wanted out of life."

Noah said, "Were they… did they…" He hesitated, and Josie knew he wanted to ask her about how tight-lipped everyone had been.

Josie jumped in. "We met some people there the other day. They all seemed very reserved. Almost as if they had been coached not to speak to law enforcement. Was it like that when you were there? Was anything ever said about dealing with outsiders?"

"I was never coached. I never heard anything like that, but a lot of them had had bad experiences with the law so they would have gotten real spooked if police came around asking questions. This was ten years ago though."

Josie asked, "Was there some kind of guiding principal at the Sanctuary?"

"You want to know if they're religious? Well, it wasn't religion, I can tell you that. Charlotte isn't like that. I mean, she wanted people to meditate all the time. She's a big believer that meditation helps people overcome their problems and anxieties, but she doesn't believe in organized religion or in God. She believes that we only get one life and this is it. There's no afterlife, no heaven or hell. No purgatory. No paradise. There's just this. This life. So while you're there, you should be focused on becoming your 'whole, authentic self' is what she always said."

"What does that mean?" Josie asked.

Haylie shrugged. "To be honest, I don't know. I never really understood what she was going on about most of the time. I was so tired all the time, and I started not to care what she was talking about. Plus, I never got to the commitment stage."

"What's that?" Gretchen asked.

"Okay, so you can go to the Sanctuary and stay there for a while, like you said: like a retreat from the world. But after you're there for a while you have to make a commitment, or leave and go back into the world. You can return to the Sanctuary, but you can't stay forever unless you make the commitment."

"Which is what, exactly?" Noah asked.

Haylie's brow furrowed. "Well, I'm not sure. I didn't do it, so I don't know what really happens to you. Except you get to live in some cabins or something."

"Those cabins are all unoccupied now," Josie said. "People lived in them when you were there?"

"Well, that's what I heard, but I never actually saw them."

"Did making the commitment mean you had to stay forever?" Noah asked.

"No, I don't think so. She just said it meant I would always be loyal. I didn't really understand the whole thing, to be honest. But it was the branding that really turned me off. Like, I'm not gonna let some strange person put a permanent mark on me for something I don't really understand."

"Branding," Josie said. "What kind of branding?"

"I guess like with a piece of metal and some fire or something. I don't know. I never saw it done. I just heard about it. I saw some people's brands, but I never asked about it."

Josie felt an uptick in her heartbeat. She thought back to all the people she'd seen and spoken with at the Sanctuary. Besides their demure demeanors, she hadn't noticed any strange markings. Then again, she hadn't been looking for them. She hadn't seen any markings on Renee Kelly's body nor had Dr. Feist noted any, although perhaps Renee hadn't made the commitment. "What does the brand look like?"

"Like two Cs facing one another, except that the top of one C goes into the opening of the other C. Do you have a piece of paper?"

Gretchen tore a blank page from her notebook and handed it to Haylie along with her pen. The three of them watched as she drew the letter C. Then she drew a backward C, the top of which started inside the opening of the first C. "Almost like a broken infinity sign," Haylie murmured as she finished.

"What's it supposed to mean?" Noah asked.

"Charlotte said it's supposed to represent dark and light being connected or some weird shit like that. She was always talking about how we all have dark and light inside of us, but that we shouldn't have to choose just one or the other."

"Did she ever give you any examples?" Gretchen asked.

Haylie shook her head. "No, and I didn't ask. Honestly, the longer I was there, the weirder the whole thing was. It really started to feel like a cult."

"Where did they brand people?" Josie asked. "Which part of their body?"

"Charlotte said I could have it done wherever I wanted, although they didn't like for it to be visible. So it couldn't be on your wrist or ankle or whatever. I saw some on the backs of people's necks, like under their hair, or on their hips or lower backs."

"Why didn't she want it to be visible?" Gretchen asked.

"Because the Sanctuary is a kind of private place. If people go back out into the world and are asked about the brand, it might gain notoriety. Charlotte didn't want that."

"Aside from the branding," Josie said. "Did you witness or hear of any other kinds of violence at the Sanctuary?"

Haylie shook her head. "No. Everyone there was really nice. It was just super boring. When I turned down the commitment and left, Charlotte was great about it. She said I'd always be welcome."

There was a knock at the door, and their desk sergeant, Dan Lamay, poked his head into the room. "Boss," he said to Josie. "Can I talk to you for a minute? Lieutenant Fraley, too?"

Josie and Noah excused themselves and walked out into the hallway. When Josie pulled the door closed behind them, Lamay said, "We just got a call from the hospital. Maya Bestler is missing."

CHAPTER FORTY

Twenty minutes later, Josie and Noah followed a guard into Denton Memorial's CCTV viewing room. It was dark with a bank of screens, each one split into four different views, showing various locations in and around the hospital. A laptop sat open on a nearby table. The guard sat down and manipulated the software program to bring up the nurses' station on the fourth floor.

"Her baby's fine," the guard said. "He was down in the nursery with the grandmother. Ms. Bestler's father was in the room with her. She got up and said she was going to take a walk around the unit. This was about an hour ago. She didn't come back, so the dad reported it."

On the laptop in front of him, the guard rewound the footage from the fourth floor until they saw Maya Bestler, in her pajamas and a pair of slippers, walk past the nurses' station. She stopped for a moment and chatted with one of the nurses before slowly moving on.

"No IV," Noah noted.

Josie squinted at the screen. "She still has the port in her hand."

The guard said, "We talked with the nurses. They said she came around and asked them about the lunch menu, so that's probably what they were talking about here. She didn't get into any of the elevators. We checked all the fourth-floor rooms and didn't find her."

"What about the stairwell?" Josie said.

"Well, that's what's strange," he said. "Watch this." He switched to another view of a door. "This leads to the stairwell."

They watched for several minutes before Maya ambled onscreen. She walked right through the door without hesitation. She didn't look around to see if anyone noticed or if there was even a camera. She didn't open the door tentatively as if she didn't know what was behind it. She knew exactly where she was going. But where was that, Josie wondered?

"We need to see the cameras over the entrances to the stairwells on every floor," Josie told him.

"Already did that," the guard said. "No sign of her."

"What about cameras inside that stairwell?" Josie asked.

The guard shook his head. "Don't have any."

Noah said, "How can you not have security cameras inside the stairwells?"

The guard sighed. "The Joint Commission's Life Safety Code—"

Noah cut him off. "Wait, what?"

Josie said, "The Joint Commission. It's an organization that accredits healthcare facilities."

"Right," the guard said. "In their rules, it says that stairwells are only there to provide egress. We can't put anything into stairwells unless it 'serves the stairwell.' That includes cameras. Apparently you can put cameras in the stairwells if you make a special application for them, but we're not a big hospital. We haven't had any incidents of escaped patients or violence in the stairwells for at least fifteen years, maybe longer. So upper management decided not to apply for cameras in the stairwells. Like I said, egress only."

Josie said, "Okay, if you wanted to exit the building from this stairwell, where would you do that?"

"Basement," the guard said. "And yeah, we have an exterior camera over that door. I checked it. Maya Bestler didn't exit there."

Josie thanked the guard, then asked him, "You mind if we have a look around? Maybe check out the stairwell ourselves?"

"Be my guest," he said. "You know where to find me if you need anything else."

They made their way down to the basement stairwell exit, where they checked the staff parking lot, and then back up, headed for the fourth floor.

Noah said, "Where do you think she went?"

"My first best guess would be that she went to see the abusive ex-boyfriend," Josie offered. "Maybe she feels like they have unfinished business and wanted to go see him. She probably doesn't feel like she can really talk to him with her parents hovering the way they are—especially her dad."

"But why take off without a word?" Noah asked. "She must know that would devastate her folks."

Josie said, "She's a grown woman. She can do whatever she wants, really."

"But she left her baby behind."

Josie stopped walking, her right foot on one step and her left foot below it on another. Her hand held tightly to the metal railing that lined the stairwell. "Noah, has it ever occurred to you that she might not want that baby?"

"How could she not want her own baby?" he blurted.

"Noah," Josie said. "She didn't exactly have a choice in making that baby. Sure, he's innocent and beautiful, but even if she loves him with all her heart, she'll always associate him with trauma. Two years of trauma. Maybe she got scared. She's a single mother now with no resources. She just lost two years of her life and everything she knew. Maybe she feels like she can't handle raising a child."

"But her parents clearly love that baby," Noah pointed out. "They haven't left her side—or the baby's. She has help."

"Help, yes, but ultimately she is the mother of that child. He's her responsibility. At the end of the day, no amount of help will change that."

"But why just… leave? Without a word?"

Josie thought about what Sandy had said about her daughter: *Maya was never very good at getting herself out of things.* "Maybe

Maya didn't think there was any other way to get out of raising the baby."

They began climbing the stairs once more. When they opened the fourth-floor door, they could hear Sandy Bestler yelling at her husband all the way down the hall. "I told you, Gus. She was up to something! She held that little baby how many times, Gus? How many? Once? She left."

"She didn't leave," Gus Bestler shouted back, his voice thick with tears.

"Get a grip, Gus, would you? Your daughter isn't the perfect angel you think she is—she just abandoned her own son. She's not missing. She left."

Josie pulled the door shut, muffling the shouting.

"Wow," Noah said.

Josie pointed upward. "Let's check the upper stairs."

On the sixth-floor landing, Josie stopped when she saw a little square of black fabric peeking out from behind the long, thick pipe that went from the ceiling to the floor. She knelt and took a pen out of her back pocket, using its blunt end to probe the item. Behind her, Noah snapped on gloves and knelt beside her. He used his hands to pull and out slid a large black T-shirt emblazoned with the words: *Let Me Sleep.*

"Shit," Noah said.

Also stuffed behind the pole were a pair of pajama pants and slippers. "These are hers," Josie said.

Noah carried them in his hands as Josie moved through the door and onto the sixth floor. They went to the nurses' station. Josie showed them a photo of Maya Bestler, but no one recognized her. Josie said, "Is there a way to check with all the staff on the clock right now to find out if any of theirs or their patients' personal possessions are missing?"

One of the nurses started making calls. Ten minutes later, they hit pay dirt. A nurse on the second floor was missing her backup scrubs which she'd left in a tote bag behind the nurses' station on that floor the day before. Roughly ninety dollars and her sneakers were missing as well.

Josie and Noah put Maya's discarded pajamas into a Patient Belongings bag that one of the nurses provided. Then they took the elevator back down to the first-floor security suite. The same guard who had helped them earlier was there. Josie explained what she was looking for and within a few minutes, he was able to find Maya Bestler, dressed in nursing scrubs and sneakers, her hair pulled back in a ponytail, walking casually from the sixth-floor stairwell to the elevator. Then he found her again, exiting the same elevator on the first floor. She didn't leave through the main lobby as Josie suspected, however. Instead, she turned and exited through the Emergency Room, where everyone was far too busy to notice a nurse who was probably taking a smoke break.

They checked the exterior cameras, watching her stroll out of the parking lot onto the sidewalk, where she crossed the street and disappeared from view.

"Shit," Noah said.

CHAPTER FORTY-ONE

Two hours later, Josie and Noah were back at their desks, Chitwood looming over them once more. "This is not good, kids," he said. His pockmarked cheeks were pink and wisps of his white hair stood up from his scalp, as though the angry energy emanating from him had set them afloat. "Bowen is already demanding we release his client. Without Maya Bestler's testimony, the case against Michael Donovan falls apart. The District Attorney said even with the baby's DNA, he's not putting this guy on trial when the victim and main witness ran off. It doesn't look good to a jury."

Noah said, "We canvassed around the hospital, checked exterior cameras of other businesses. No one remembered seeing her, and we couldn't find her on camera anywhere, but how far could she possibly get on foot?"

Chitwood said, "Maybe she wasn't on foot. Maybe she hitched a ride."

"From who?" Noah asked.

"We only canvassed a small area," Josie said. "She could have gone out of that area and easily hitched a ride with some unsuspecting stranger or solicited help from someone on the street. She had ninety dollars. She could have gotten on a bus or train for all we know. No one knows who she is, so she wouldn't be recognized."

"We could call the press," Noah said. "Put word out that we want to find her. Release a photo."

"We can't," Josie said.

"Why not?"

"For the same reason we couldn't call in patrol units to canvas for her. It's not like we can detain her even if we do find her. She's a grown woman. She left the hospital of her own accord. We have no evidence that her life is in danger, and she has no obligation to anyone in this situation."

"She stole the nurse's things," Noah said.

"We can't prove that," Josie replied. "She wasn't caught on camera doing it."

"But the baby," Noah argued. "That's child abandonment."

"Not according to the Safe Haven law in Pennsylvania," Josie said. "She left him at a hospital in the care of medical staff. The charge would never stick."

"And it makes her look like shit to a jury," Chitwood added. "Even though she was kidnapped and raped by this guy, a jury is still going to hate her for walking out on her kid. I don't know how long we can hold this hermit guy."

"The DA is going to release Donovan." Josie said, feeling defeated. "Just like that." Without definitive proof that he had also killed the Yates couple and Renee Kelly or that he had taken Emilia Gresham, they couldn't charge him for any of those crimes. Chitwood was right. They wouldn't be able to hold Donovan much longer. If he was behind the recent deaths, they'd be letting a sadistic killer loose.

Noah said, "He stole items from the Yates campsite. Can't the DA charge him with theft?"

Josie shook her head. "There's no one to press charges and no witnesses. Tyler and Valerie Yates are dead. Emilia Gresham is missing. That would never hold up in court. Even if the DA charged him with theft to buy time, he'd be released on his own recognizance. The county isn't going to spend money housing a prisoner on a misdemeanor offense like that."

"Shit," Noah muttered. He looked at Chitwood. "Can you get us some more time? Maybe we can find her and talk her into coming back."

"You think you can find her?" Chitwood asked.

Josie said, "We can try. I don't think she'll want to come back, but we can give it a shot."

"Where do you think she went?"

Josie said, "The ex-boyfriend. That's the first person I'd check with."

Chitwood rolled his eyes and then looked at the clock on the wall. "Jesus," he said. "That guy lives a couple of hours away, doesn't he? Who's working the cult?"

"Gretchen," Josie said. "And Mett will be in this afternoon. She's going to check property records. Try to get more information about Charlotte Fadden before we go back in to rattle her."

"Fine," Chitwood said. "Go see if you can find Bestler. But you only get one day. If she doesn't want this guy prosecuted, I'm not wasting any more manpower on this. Especially when the Gresham woman is still missing."

Josie and Noah nodded.

Chitwood's voice rose to a shout as he waved his hands upward, motioning for them to stand up. "What are you still doing here? Go, go!"

CHAPTER FORTY-TWO

Josie took the interstate. Luckily for them, it was early afternoon, so the traffic was light. They made it to Doylestown in just under an hour and a half. It was a sprawling, mid-sized town just north of Philadelphia. Josie and Noah stopped first at the local police station to let their department know that they were in town and what they intended to do, which wasn't much more than asking Garrett Romney some questions. With the local chief's blessing, they drove to the address they had for Romney. He lived in a large, blocky, four-story apartment building. The foyer was unlocked. They passed a row of metal mailboxes and found a staircase to take them to the third floor. Loud music could be heard behind the door to apartment 310. Noah rapped his knuckles against the door.

"Just a minute," a male voice called.

They waited five. The door didn't open. Noah knocked again. After a few seconds, the music cut off and the door swung open. Garrett stood before them. Josie had only seen photos of him in the press stories from two years earlier when Maya went missing. Time and the cloud of suspicion hadn't been kind to him. In the photos she had seen, he was lean and well-groomed. The man before them now had a round, bearded face and a sizeable paunch. He wore a gray Lehigh University T-shirt with various food stains on it and a pair of cut-off sweatpants. His dark brown hair was greasy and uncombed. His small, dark eyes narrowed when he saw them. "Who are you?"

Josie and Noah flashed their credentials and introduced themselves. Garrett started to close the door, but Josie put her foot near the doorframe, preventing him from shutting it in their faces. "Mr. Romney, you're not in any trouble. We just have a couple of questions."

He scowled. "A couple of questions. That's how it starts. The next thing I know, you're trying to charge me with murder. Well, I didn't do anything wrong."

He tried to close the door once more, but Josie's foot stayed firmly planted in the doorway. "Mr. Romney, we know you didn't do anything wrong. We're not even here for you. We're looking for Maya Bestler."

He stopped pushing against the door and looked from Josie to Noah and back. "What?"

Noah said, "We were wondering if you'd seen Maya Bestler today."

He gave a nervous laugh. "Are you crazy? The cops called me and said she was found. It was some guy who took her. I'm innocent."

"We believe you," Josie said. "The facts bear that out. We're not disputing that you're innocent. But the fact is that you had a prior relationship with Ms. Bestler. She asked for you when she was brought to the hospital. I made it clear to her that you didn't want to see her again."

Noah said, "But today she left the hospital of her own accord. Since she asked about you several times, we thought she might come see you. We still have some things we need to discuss with her about her case."

Now Garrett's laughter was deep and raucous. He opened the door slightly and put a hand over his stomach. "You guys lost her! You lost her!"

Josie said, "She wasn't in our custody, Mr. Romney. She was in the hospital recovering. When she left, she didn't notify us of where she was going."

Garrett's hand moved from his stomach to his chest. "You think she came to see me? You think that bitch would have the nerve to show up here and ask me for help?"

"Would you help her?" Josie asked.

For a beat, Garrett looked stunned. Then he quickly collected himself. "Uh, no. I wouldn't. She ruined my life. I'm done with her."

"You wouldn't want to give her hell for what she did?" Noah asked conversationally.

Garrett leveled a finger at Noah. A smile curved his lips. "I see what you're doing. You're trying to get me to admit to shit so you can pin me with her disappearance for a second time. No way, pal. Not gonna happen. You think if you act like my friend and say some shit like, 'Oh, don't you want to hit her for what she did?' that I'll say something incriminating. Well, I got nothing to hide. I didn't do anything."

"Mr. Romney," Josie interrupted, but he kept going.

"You all thought 'cause I got a little rough with her when we were going out that I killed her and buried her body. You were wrong. You know, if you knew her, you'd understand why it happened."

"Why what happened?" Josie asked.

"Why I had to hit her. She can really twist a person up. You have no idea what she's like. She pushed me. She pushed and pushed until I snapped. But I never meant to hurt her—and I didn't. She wasn't really injured. I sure as shit wouldn't have killed her and buried her body. But none of you believed me. Now I've been proven innocent. I want her and everything to do with her out of my life. In fact..." He swung the door open wide. "You search my apartment right now."

Noah held up a hand. "Mr. Romney, we're only here to talk."

Romney motioned them into his small apartment. "We can talk in here while you look around. Then you'll see I have nothing to hide."

Josie and Noah walked in. There wasn't much to the place. In the small kitchen there was a dining table with four chairs tucked underneath it and a pile of mail, some unwashed dinner plates, and a tie were scattered across its surface. The small living room had only one gray couch with a pile of clothes—clean or dirty, Josie couldn't tell—covering one cushion. More random items covered the coffee table: a couple of remote controls, a cell phone, keys, magazines, and a cardboard box. Noah poked his head into the bedrooms, bathroom, and closets while Josie asked, "So you haven't heard from Maya since she was found? No phone calls? She didn't show up here?"

Garrett shook his head emphatically. "Nothing." He walked over to his coffee table and picked up the cardboard box. "Actually, after you called me, I dug this out of my closet. I was going to mail it to Maya's parents' house but since you're here, you can have it."

Noah came back into the room and took the box from Garrett. "What is this?" he asked.

"A bunch of shit from when Maya and I lived together. We used to rent a house across town. After she went missing, the police came and ransacked the place. They took a bunch of her stuff. Then her parents came and took the rest. Well these are things they both missed. I don't want them at my place anymore. I told you, I'm done with her."

Noah looked at Josie, one brow kinked slightly. It wasn't really their job to courier belongings from one person to another, but in this case, it couldn't hurt. She gave him a barely perceptible nod and to Garrett, she said, "We'll make sure Sandy and Gus get this. They can give it to Maya when she comes home." She almost said "if she comes home" but corrected herself before the words came out.

"Thank you for speaking with us," she added. She pressed a business card into his hand, which he would probably toss into the garbage as soon as they left, and asked him to call them if Maya showed up on his doorstep.

As they walked back to their vehicle, Noah asked, "You think this guy is telling the truth?"

"Actually, I do," Josie said.

"He was awfully insistent. I don't know if I trust someone who tries to convince me with that much force."

Josie laughed. "I think he's just angry. I don't think he's over-compensating."

They got into the car and she pulled out of the parking lot and started driving through the streets of Doylestown. "Maybe we're just too early. She only had a couple of hours' head start on us and she was on foot."

Noah said, "You think he'd call us if she showed up?"

Josie shrugged. "Probably not. I think he'd slam the door in her face and that would be that. But we can stop at the police station again and ask the Doylestown PD to check in on him in the next couple of days and ask if she's been by. That might buy us some time with Bowen, keep Michael Donovan behind bars a little longer."

"Let's do that," Noah said. "Then we'll head home."

CHAPTER FORTY-THREE

After a quick stop back at the local police station, they got back on the road to Denton, but an accident near the interstate forced them to take a detour. Josie was two towns over when she spotted a building with the name "Lantz Snack Factory" above its front doors in large, glowing yellow letters. Without warning, she put on her turn signal and made a right into the parking lot.

"What are you doing?" Noah asked.

"This is where Jack Gresham worked right before he left to join the cult. That's what Wes Yates told us."

"We don't have a warrant," Noah said. "If you're thinking of getting his personnel records."

"We don't need a warrant to ask questions," Josie said.

She parked and they got out of the car. Josie pointed toward the side of the building. "There," she said. "I see the loading docks. That's where Wes said Jack worked. The front office isn't going to tell us anything without a warrant. You're right about that. But it's not his personnel file I'm interested in. I want to know what people thought of him, how he acted when he was here."

Together, they walked past several tractor trailers that were backed up to the massive loading dock, their doors yawning open, their cargo areas in various stages of loading. Men and one or two women moved briskly from the warehouse onto the dock. Some had clipboards, some drove forklifts with pallets of boxes on them, and others unloaded the boxes from the pallets and fit them into the backs of the trucks. Josie and Noah stopped for a moment to watch. Finally, Noah pointed to a man wearing a black Philadelphia Eagles T-shirt with the sleeves torn off, a hard hat, and goggles. He was leaning on the back of a truck while a much younger man loaded boxes into it, trying to strike up a conversation with every person who walked by. Noah said, "We should start with him."

Josie smiled and followed Noah over to the loading dock steps. Sure enough, the moment they alighted onto the dock, the man in the hard hat called out. "Hey, you can't be up here. Hey!"

Josie and Noah had their credentials ready, flashing them at him as he jogged over. The man squinted at their badges and IDs. "Denton?" he said. "Where's that?"

Noah answered, "About an hour and a half west of here. We're sorry to bother you, uh...?"

"Tim," the man filled in.

"Tim," Noah repeated. "We have a case right now involving a guy we think used to work here."

Tim looked over his shoulder, but all of his colleagues had gone back to work. Probably getting more done now that he was distracted, Josie thought. "Well, the front office could tell you..."

He drifted off and Josie filled his silence. "We were told that this gentleman worked back here with you guys. Maybe you remember him. Jack Gresham?"

She took out her phone and swiped until she found one of the photos of Jack she'd saved from Tyler Yates' Facebook pictures.

Tim's lips twisted in thought, one hand reaching up to scratch the top of his helmet. "Sure, I remember him. Didn't remember his name, but I remember him. Couldn't get a smile outta that guy if you offered him a million dollars."

Noah said, "Guess he didn't make a lot of friends here, then?"

Tim shook his head slowly, his eyes still drawn to the photo. "No, no friends here. You know, we're a pretty close group, but there was no getting to that guy. He was a weirdo."

"We were told he got fired," Josie said.

The man's eyes flicked from Josie's phone to her face. "Oh yeah, there was that business with the girl in receiving." He gave a nervous laugh. "Shana. Been in the office up there about five years. Nice kid."

"Is Shana still here?" Noah asked.

"Oh yeah. She's still here. Just got married. Nice gal, like I said. You can talk to her. If you go in that door…" He pointed to a nearby door and reeled off an elaborate set of directions that would take them deep inside the building, but Josie didn't want to risk them getting thrown out of the place for not having a warrant.

"We don't want to make Shana relive the whole thing," Josie said. "Especially if she's in a good place now, having gotten married and all."

Josie could feel Noah's eyes on her. She shot him a look that said *trust me*. Tim had mentioned "trouble". The most likely trouble between male and female coworkers was harassment. She was taking a gamble, but her instincts turned out to be right.

Tim nodded vigorously. "Oh yeah, you're right. That's true. It was hard on her. Brave of her to speak up, I said."

"You're absolutely right," Josie said. "If you don't mind then, maybe you could just clarify a few things for us? That way we don't have to bother her with it."

"Oh, well sure. Like I said, I don't want to upset her."

Josie's mind worked at warp speed, trying to think of questions that would bring out the information she needed without tipping him off that she didn't actually know a damn thing. "When did it start?" she tried.

He scratched under his helmet, just above his ear. "Oh, maybe about a month after they hired him. Someone said they saw him follow her after work, like out to her car, and that he hid behind someone else's car. At first she just, like, blew it off. Everyone thought he had a crush on her. She's a cute girl, Shana."

"Did anyone say anything to him? I mean, that's pretty creepy."

"After maybe the third or fourth time. When Shana started asking people to walk her to her car, then someone talked her into reporting it to the bosses. They brought him in and gave him a warning."

"It was all very innocent, according to him, wasn't it?" Josie said, hoping she was reading things correctly.

"Of course. He said he was just making sure she got to her car safely. But then he gave her flowers."

"How did Shana react to that? Seems like it could go either way: creepy, or a nice gesture," Josie said.

"Well, like I said, Shana's a sweet girl so she thought it was nice. They started talking a little. Saying hi and stuff. Nothing serious. But then he kept asking her to go places with him after work and she didn't want to. He wouldn't take no for an answer. Started waiting by her car at night again—you know, more obvious this time."

"She must have had to be really firm with him," Josie said. "It doesn't sound like he took no for an answer."

Tim shook his head and gave a short laugh. "He didn't take it well, that's for sure."

Here, Josie had to be careful and open-ended. She said, "We heard a couple of different versions of what happened to actually get him fired."

"Yeah, that happens in a place this big. Lots of different stories floating around. But two guys from my department were out there that night when she finally told him nothing was going to happen between the two of them. They said he lost it, man. Started shouting at her, cursing up a storm. Then he kicked her car real good. Put a big old dent in her door. Then the guys went over and told him he had to leave. They made sure she got home okay, and the next day they all went to the bosses. They called him at home before he came on for his shift and told him not to come back."

"We were told that was the end of it," Josie said.

Tim nodded. "Thank goodness. Yeah. No one saw him again after that."

She extended a hand. "You've been very helpful. We really appreciate it."

"Oh sure," he said. "Happy to talk."

Josie could practically hear Noah's thought: *No kidding.*

CHAPTER FORTY-FOUR

Back at the station house, they got coffee from the break area and gathered with Mettner and Gretchen in the conference room so they could update each other on everything they'd found out that day. They took seats around the table, which had already been covered in paperwork on the Bestler, Yates, Gresham, and Kelly cases.

Mettner took notes using the note-taking app on his phone while Josie and Noah spoke. When they finished, he looked up and said, "Jack was married and he's at a new job hitting on someone else?"

"Not hitting on her," Josie said. "Stalking her."

"He gets fired for harassing this poor woman and leaves to go to the Sanctuary," Gretchen said, jotting something down in her notebook.

"He'd been out of sorts for a long time before he even started at the factory," Josie pointed out. "Remember Haylie said that Charlotte told her to leave and then come back? I bet he had been there already. When the job at the snack factory didn't work out and Shana spurned his advances, he gave up. I think that's when he went to the Sanctuary and stayed."

"But he didn't stay," Mettner said. "He wasn't there when we questioned everyone. Either he left or they're hiding him."

"How did he get there in the first place?" Noah asked. "Mett, did you get anywhere checking for the owners of the vehicles we saw at the Sanctuary?"

Mettner tapped the screen on his phone and then scrolled until he found what he was looking for. "There are thirty-two people presently living at the Sanctuary if you include Charlotte. Five of them have vehicles registered in their name, and all five of those are on the premises. That includes a car registered to Charlotte. Jack Gresham has no vehicles registered in his name. Emilia Gresham has one car, and it's outside of her apartment."

"We can't say how Jack Gresham got to the Sanctuary then," Noah said. "That's a dead end."

Josie sipped her coffee. "Can we run a background check on Charlotte Fadden? See if we can turn up anything unusual? Something we can use when we go talk to her?"

"Already did," Gretchen said. "Let me pull it up." She reached toward the end of the table where Noah had placed the box of Maya Bestler's belongings from Garrett Romney. Next to the box was a laptop which Gretchen pulled over and booted up. After a few clicks, she turned the screen so that all of them could see it and she began talking them through what she had found. "She's lived in the farmhouse that then became the Sanctuary since she was nineteen, so there wasn't much in terms of old addresses. No known jobs. We'd need authorizations from her to ask the IRS for her records, but I can't find any evidence she's worked on any of the databases I used. She's got the one vehicle, as you know, registered and on the premises. One old phone number—a landline. No email addresses. No social media. No criminal record. Husband died in 1978. Charlotte was thirty-two."

"He must have left her a chunk of change for her to be able to live off the Sanctuary land for forty years," Josie said.

"He was fifty-one. Much older. Like nineteen years older than her," Mettner said.

"Double her age when they got married," Noah said. "What else did you get? Anything?"

"Not on her," Gretchen said. "But a report was filed with the Lenore County sheriff's office against Mick Fadden in 1974 for inflicting injury on his wife. I called the Lenore County sheriff's office, talked to someone besides Moore, and asked them to look up the file. Everything from before 2005 was scanned into their computer system so, the file was easily accessible. I had them email it to me." She clicked a few more times and brought up a police report.

Josie leaned in closer to read it. "Mick Fadden beat Charlotte pretty severely according to this," Josie said. Her eyes skimmed the report. "Why does this officer keep mentioning that the beating took place after ten p.m.? It shouldn't matter what time it happened. A beating is a beating."

Gretchen said, "Apparently, in the seventies in Lenore County there was still a law on the books that said that husbands couldn't beat their wives after ten p.m. or on Sundays."

"Are you kidding me?" Noah blurted. "So it was okay for husbands to beat their wives the rest of the time?"

Gretchen nodded solemnly. "In Lenore County in the seventies, yes."

Mettner gave a low whistle. "That's disturbing."

Gretchen continued, "I don't know what the laws were in the rest of the state. Every county is different. Anyway, that law was removed from the Lenore County books in the eighties. I guess the only way Charlotte could have him charged was if he beat her after ten p.m. or on a Sunday."

Josie reached over and clicked through, past the report, until she found photographs of a barely recognizable, twenty-something Charlotte. She took in a sharp breath. "Wow. I can't believe she survived that."

The photos were in black and white but there was no mistaking the effects of the beating that Mick had inflicted on his young wife. A chunk of her hair had been torn from her scalp, blood dripped down her forehead, and her eyes were slits swallowed up by puffy, blackened skin. Her bottom lip was almost split in half. There were other photos of her arms and legs, also swollen and dark with bruising. In some of the photos, they could clearly see boot prints on her thighs, buttocks, and where her kidneys were.

"1974," Josie said, reading off the date on the photos. "Four years before he died. Did he go to prison?"

Gretchen shook her head. "No. The charges were dropped."

"She went back after this. Jesus," Josie said. "How did the husband die?"

"Car accident."

Josie closed the lid of the laptop as a shiver ran through her. She'd seen a lot on the job, but few domestic violence cases as severe as this.

Mettner pointed to the box at the end of the table. "What's with the box?"

Josie said, "That needs to go to the hospital, to the Bestlers."

"Come on," Noah said. "You're not even a little curious about what's in here?"

Josie shook her head but pulled the box over to her and opened it. She asked Gretchen, "Has anyone heard from Hummel about the piece of rope?"

"Oh yeah," Mettner said, bouncing in his chair with excitement. "He tested it. It was definitely blood. He already sent it to the lab for DNA testing. Chitwood asked that it be expedited, but it could still take weeks."

Josie opened her mouth to speak but Gretchen held up a hand to silence her.

"Before you ask," Gretchen said. "We already got a warrant for our ERT to process the cabins at the Sanctuary since that's where you found it. Hummel and the team are over there now."

"That's great," Josie said. She started taking items out of the box of Maya Bestler's things: a neck pillow, a Chris Stapleton CD, a pair of sunglasses, a blanket, a candle, a half dozen bottles of nail polish, a lanyard, and a mug from the Cancer Survivors' Alliance for Hope, the non-profit organization Maya had worked for. Then there were some random work items: a policies and procedures handbook, a keycard, and a company newsletter.

Gretchen said, "By the way, I got the phone records for Tyler and Valerie Yates and Emilia Gresham, including text messages.

They definitely believed that Jack was at the Sanctuary three days ago when they went camping. They were there to get him out. The plan was to sneak onto the property in the middle of the night, try to find him, and convince him to come home. Apparently, Emilia thought if the three of them showed up together as a united front, it would be more like an intervention, and they'd have a better chance of convincing him."

As Gretchen spoke, Josie's eyes roamed over the various photos in the Cancer Survivors' Alliance for Hope newsletter from almost three years ago. It outlined all of the non-profit's efforts to raise money and where the money went, which appeared to be mostly to local families struggling financially with their cancer diagnoses.

A headline caught her eye: *Lantz Snack Factory Teams Up with CSAH to raise over $50,000 for Community Survivors.* She skimmed over the article which discussed a joint fundraiser between Lantz and the non-profit which had raised a large amount of money for the cause. She turned the page and came to a color photograph taken in front of the Lantz building. Roughly thirty people gathered beneath the large sign, squishing together to get in the frame. All of them were smiling broadly and wearing matching teal T-shirts displaying the words *"Nurture Hope"* and the name of the non-profit. Josie's gaze took in the faces until she found Maya. How different she looked back then. Not just younger but more innocent. Her smile was still relatively untouched in spite of the abuse she had suffered at the hands of Garrett.

"Tyler and Emilia had already tried to get Jack to leave the Sanctuary on prior occasions with no success," Noah said.

Josie studied the other faces in the photo.

Gretchen said, "Right. I don't think Jack would have left with the three of them. I think he was there to stay."

Josie's gaze landed on a familiar face, and she gasped.

"What is it?" Noah said.

She held up the newsletter with the photo. "I think that Jack Gresham and Maya Bestler knew one another."

CHAPTER FORTY-FIVE

Noah, Gretchen, and Mettner stood up and crowded around Josie, staring down at the photo as she pointed out Jack in the far left, back row of the photo and then Maya front row, center. She checked the date. "This picture was taken just over two years ago. Two years and four months."

Gretchen said, "I thought that Maya Bestler and the Greshams lived in different towns."

"They did," Josie said. "But still relatively close to one another. Maya's organization did charity events with businesses all over the southeastern Pennsylvania area."

Noah said, "This doesn't mean they knew one another. It just means that they were in a photo together."

Gretchen said, "I have to agree there, boss. This was a one-time event. They're not even near one another in the photo and there are at least thirty people there. We really don't know that they ever actually met."

"But Jack Gresham had stalking tendencies. He wouldn't have had to officially meet her to see her and fixate on her. This is only a few months before Maya was kidnapped."

Mettner said, "But we already know that the hermit took Maya from her campsite. That's what she said."

"Plus we've got her prints from inside the caverns," Gretchen agreed.

"What are you suggesting?" Noah asked.

Josie stared at the photo. Maya and Jack had been in a photograph together. Maya's non-profit had done a charity event at Jack's place of employment sometime during the three months he worked there. Jack had joined a cult in Lenore County, roughly eight miles from where Maya went missing while camping with her boyfriend. Maya had then disappeared from that campsite months after Jack joined the cult. Two years later, Jack's wife went camping near the Sanctuary and disappeared after her—and Jack's—best friends were murdered. Renee Kelly, a girl living on the Sanctuary, had then been murdered in exactly the same way that Valerie Yates had been. All these things had proximity but that didn't mean they were all connected. Ultimately, it was her job to follow the evidence. Gut feelings, hunches, suspicions were all fine and good, but she had no evidence that Jack Gresham and the Sanctuary were somehow connected to Maya's abduction, or that anyone besides the hermit was responsible for the recent murders.

What were the odds, she wondered, of one woman going missing and another being found within hours of one another, both connected to the same man: Jack Gresham? Although, admittedly, Maya's connection to him was tenuous at best.

Josie sighed. "Nothing," she said. "It's just strange."

Gretchen and Noah looked at her, as if waiting for her to say more. She tossed the employee newsletter back into the box and said, "I think we've got enough to go back and speak with Charlotte again. We'll go to the Sanctuary tomorrow and see what we can shake loose. This time we need to show everyone a photo of Jack Gresham. Someone should recognize him, even if he's left. Although, I expect they'll all lie. In the meantime, someone can take this box over to the hospital and give it to one of the Bestlers. Show them a photo of Jack Gresham as well, just for the hell of it."

"I'll do it," Noah said. He packed the box again and carried it out of the room.

Josie watched him go. In her pocket, her phone buzzed. She took it out to see that the display read *SCI Muncy*. She sent it to voicemail.

Gretchen said, "You okay?"

Josie managed a smile. "Yeah, fine. I'm going home. I need some rest. We'll head over to talk to Charlotte and her people first thing tomorrow. See what we can turn up."

"You got it," Gretchen answered.

Josie took the long way home, not wanting to be alone with the bottle of Wild Turkey in her kitchen for longer than she had to. Luckily, Noah arrived home a few minutes after she did.

"Did you show the Bestlers a photo of Jack Gresham?" Josie asked him as they trudged upstairs to their bedroom.

"I did."

"Did they recognize him?"

"Nope. Not at all."

CHAPTER FORTY-SIX

Josie left the light on in their bedroom. Noah was too tired to even notice, sleeping deeply within minutes of climbing into bed. She watched his eyelids twitch as her head sank into her pillow beside him. Sleep drifted in, wrapping her consciousness in a fog and carrying her away. But some part of her brain remained alert, so that when she found herself in childhood again, begging Lila not to hold her fingers over the blue flame of their stove, she fought her way back to wakefulness with a jolt. Her chest heaved as she sat up in bed. Sweat poured from her scalp. She dared not go back to sleep. She couldn't face another night of reliving the unspeakable horrors Lila had inflicted on her. She got out of bed and went downstairs to review her case notes until it was time to get ready for work.

Fat gray clouds rolled overhead as Josie, Noah, Gretchen, Mettner, and two marked units from Denton, together with Moore and his colleague, Nash, pulled into the driveway of the Sanctuary. As they got out of their vehicles, Charlotte appeared on the front porch in a flowing dress the color of gold. She seemed to float down the steps and across the grass toward them, her signature smile now a thin line. She held up a hand as she reached them. "I'm sorry, officers," she said. "Now is not a good time."

Moore stepped up next to Josie and handed Charlotte the warrant. "Mrs. Fadden, this is a time-sensitive issue. We've got a missing female, and we believe that her husband is either in residence here, or he used to be. If any of your people have seen him or know where he is, we need to talk with them immediately."

Charlotte folded her arms across her chest. "Your people were here almost all afternoon and evening yesterday messing about in our cabins. You've been traipsing all over our property for days now. One of our own was murdered. People are upset. All of this activity is extremely disruptive. We're trying to grieve as a family and the police presence is… I'm afraid it's too much right now. I can't let this continue."

Josie said, "We have a warrant, Mrs. Fadden. I understand that with Renee's murder, people are very upset, but we're just doing our jobs. Now, if you don't mind—"

Charlotte cut her off. "You brought a photo of a missing female the other day. No one had seen her. What does her husband have to do with anything?"

Josie said, "We believe he might be with her. We need to locate him. His last known whereabouts are right here on your property."

Charlotte panned the group of them and said, "Does it need to be all of you?"

Josie said, "It will go a lot faster if we all work together."

Charlotte looked reluctant. Josie could see her mind working, calculating how hard she could push back. Finally, she gave a tight smile and waved a hand in the direction of the house. "Then please," she said. "Be quick about it."

The team dispersed, armed with notebooks and their photos of Jack Gresham. Josie remained in place, hands on her hips. Charlotte's smile loosened a little into something more genuine. "You want to talk to me."

Josie reached into her back pocket and pulled out a photo of Jack Gresham. She showed it to Charlotte. "I know he was here."

Charlotte took it in her hands and studied it. Without looking at Josie, she said, "Yes, he was here for a long time. Jack."

"You remember him?"

"Yes, he was quite troubled."

"Do you remember his wife showing up here, demanding to talk to him on several occasions?" Josie asked.

Charlotte handed the photo back. "No, I don't. But it's possible I was working elsewhere on the property when she came."

"His best friend came here and tried to join your people. Tyler Yates. Yet, when I showed you and the rest of your people his photo the other day, no one recognized him."

"Then there must be some mistake," Charlotte said. "Or perhaps he wasn't here long enough for people to remember him."

"Tyler's dad said that he was kicked out of the Sanctuary when it became obvious he was just trying to get Jack to come home," Josie challenged.

Charlotte laughed. "Now I know there's been a mistake. I don't remember any such thing. Whoever you're getting your information from is simply wrong."

Josie knew Charlotte was lying but pressing her seemed to do no good. She moved on. "Where is Jack now?"

"I don't know."

"Is he here?"

"I don't think so," Charlotte said. "You would know better than I would. You've been speaking to people the last couple of days."

Josie took out her phone and pulled up a photo of Maya Bestler. She showed it to Charlotte. "How about this young lady?"

Charlotte sighed. "Detective Quinn, I have told you before that we have many, many people pass through here. I simply can't remember every single face."

"So she may have been here?"

"What's her name?"

"Maya."

Charlotte shook her head. "I don't think we've had a Maya here, no."

"You said that Jack Gresham was troubled. What do you mean by that?"

Charlotte motioned toward the house. "Would you care to come inside while we talk?"

"I'd like to know what you know about Jack Gresham."

Charlotte smiled. "Let's walk," she said, strolling off toward the area behind the house.

Josie followed her for several yards, growing more annoyed by the minute. But she knew the woman was playing some kind of game, and Josie wasn't about to let her get the upper hand. She waited until Charlotte spoke again. "Jack had a difficult childhood. Single mother. Not attentive. There were some other issues. He came to me very depressed and confused. I daresay he was suicidal."

They passed the garden where Josie saw several Sanctuary members gathered around Mettner. Their faces looked drawn. One woman pressed a tissue to her cheeks, dabbing at tears. Clearly, the death of Renee had affected the other Sanctuary members. Josie said, "You nursed Jack back to sound mental health?"

Charlotte laughed. "That's not what we do here, Detective."

"Then what did you do for him?"

"I tried to help him align the darkness inside him with the light."

"What does that mean?"

"Jack had demons. Like all of us. Like you."

Josie said, "Why are you bringing me into this?"

Charlotte stopped walking. Josie took a few steps before realizing the woman had stopped moving. Charlotte stepped toward Josie, getting so close her face was only inches away. It was a space Josie usually reserved only for Noah. She fought the urge to back away. Charlotte said, "There is a darkness in you, Detective Quinn."

"There is a darkness in all of us, Mrs. Fadden."

Her eyes lit up, as if Josie had answered a test question correctly. "You're right! There is darkness in all of us. Some people come into the world wielding their darkness. Doing terrible things that come easily to them. Their light is buried so deeply, most of them never find it. Others, like me, like Jack, and like you—we are victimized so much, so often, or so badly that our own darkness is buried too deep for us to access. People like us, if we want to fully *become*, we've got to access that piece of ourselves. That's what Jack needed."

"What does that mean? To *fully become?*"

Charlotte stepped back and Josie tried not to show her relief. "It means to align your darkness with your light and vice versa, to become the fullest, truest version of yourself that you can in this one life you get. Embracing yourself completely. All of yourself, not just the pieces of you that society deems acceptable."

They began walking again, now taking a path that Josie knew led to the cabins. Again, she wondered if Charlotte was somehow psychic; part of Josie's plan had been to confront Charlotte about the bloody piece of rope found inside one of the cabins.

Josie said, "Did Jack have to make the commitment in order to fully become?"

Josie caught the slight tensing of Charlotte's shoulders, but when she looked at Josie, her smile was firmly in place. "You've done your research, I see. Yes, Jack made the commitment. He was here for some time, if I recall. At a certain point, if I see that a person is here a long time but not making any progress, I'll ask them to make the commitment."

"What is the commitment to?" Josie asked.

"To continue personal growth, to not let anything impede it, to commit to protecting the Sanctuary and its members, to commit to living an authentic life. That's what the commitment is about."

"Why would you insist on branding?"

Charlotte ducked beneath a low hanging branch. "The branding is symbolic of how painful personal growth can be, but it's also a physical reminder of a person's evolution to a new level of being. Here we don't believe in an afterlife, so we strive to ascend to new levels of existence and enlightenment in this life." Her palm circled Josie's wrist. "You know, I can help you."

Josie tried to pull her wrist away, but Charlotte's grip was firm. She said, "Help me what?"

"Evolve. Embrace your darkness."

Josie snatched her hand back. "Embracing my darkness won't help me find Jack and Emilia Gresham."

"Burying yourself in work won't help you avoid the thing you're running from."

"I have work to do," Josie said and stomped ahead.

The cabins came into view. Josie stopped in front of the one she had been inside the other day. "I found a bloody piece of rope in this cabin," she told Charlotte.

Charlotte bunched the front of her dress in her hands, revealing a pair of old flip flops, and went up the steps. She took a long moment looking inside, and Josie wondered if she was thinking of something that would explain away the presence of the rope. When she turned back, she said, "Yes, we had a member keeping a dog here. I allowed it until the dog bit him. That was probably the blood you found."

"Renee Kelly had ligature marks on her wrists. Old ones and new ones. Someone was tying her up. Someone here in your Sanctuary."

Charlotte descended the steps. "Renee would not have done anything she didn't consent to, Detective."

"What does that mean? She agreed to be tied up? She was terrified the last time I saw her. How do you account for that?"

Charlotte stepped toward her again, this time reaching out and touching Josie's cheek. Fatigue and sleep deprivation slowed Josie's reflexes. She wasn't able to stop herself from flinching. Charlotte said, "You're not the only one scared of the dark."

CHAPTER FORTY-SEVEN

Josie and her team gathered in the conference room again to compare notes. Outside, rain fell in sheets, pelting the windows in a steady roar. She looked around at Noah, Gretchen, and Mettner, all of them looking exhausted. Boxes of pizza sat in the center of the table, but no one touched them. Mettner took a long sip from his bottle of water and said, "I talked with three people who recognized Jack. They said he had lived there for a very long time; had very little contact with other members; and had left the property a few months ago."

Gretchen flipped a page in her notebook. "I had two people confirm the same. Same time period. 'A couple of months.' When I asked them how he left—by car, on foot—they said they didn't know."

"Same from the people I interviewed," Noah said. "They said they just stopped seeing him around one day. One person said he didn't speak and didn't engage with any other members. She said he left three weeks ago."

"What did Charlotte say?"

Josie filled them in on what Charlotte had told her both about Jack Gresham and about the bloody piece of rope. She left out the parts about Charlotte wanting to help her get in touch with her dark side. "She's lying," Josie concluded. "I pressed her on the ridiculous dog story and the fact that someone was tying Renee up and doing something to her, but she wouldn't budge. All I got out of her were cryptic non-answers. She definitely knows something, though. They all know more than they're saying." She thought about what Charlotte had said about the commitment. Renee Kelly hadn't made the commitment to protect the Sanctuary. In fact, she had left the night that Josie gave her an out. She just never made it to Josie or Gretchen's car.

But Jack Gresham had made the commitment. He had pledged loyalty to the Sanctuary. So why had he left? Where had he gone?

"Has someone tracked down Jack Gresham's mother?" Josie asked.

Mettner raised his hand. "I talked with her on the phone last night after you went home. She lives in California. She said she hasn't seen him since his wedding and that they talk once a year at Christmas."

"Caring mom," Noah remarked.

Josie thought about what Charlotte had said. Jack had been troubled. He'd been raised by an inattentive mother. She had referenced other issues. Having spoken with his coworkers at Lantz Snack Factory, and learned about his stalking activity, she could guess what those issues might be. Josie wondered what exactly Charlotte had done to help Jack access his "dark side".

"I think Jack Gresham is still there, or he is still in the area."

"On the Sanctuary?" Noah asked. "We've searched that place a half dozen times now. Where would they be hiding him?"

"I don't know," Josie answered. "But he wouldn't leave the place for long. He wouldn't want to."

"Why would he hide?" Gretchen asked.

Josie suggested, "Maybe he was the one abusing Renee Kelly."

"You think he killed her?" Mettner asked. "If he killed her, that means he killed his best friends, too, and did something to his wife."

"Or maybe," Gretchen said, "his friends get killed and his wife goes missing while on a mission to get him away from the Sanctuary, and he's afraid he'll be looked at as a suspect."

"Could be," Josie agreed. "Maybe he and Charlotte were thinking that whatever he was doing to Renee Kelly would come up in the police investigation and make things worse for all of them—for the whole Sanctuary. He could have been there the day we found Tyler and Valerie. Charlotte could have sent him away until things died down and told the rest of her people to lie about his presence."

Gretchen said, "She could have told Renee not to breathe a word about what was happening to her."

For just a moment, inside her head, Josie heard Lila's voice from her nightmares. *Not one word.*

Noah said, "He stalked a coworker. Got depressed, joined a cult. That doesn't necessarily mean he's someone who tortures young women or that he's a murderer. The hermit still looks good for these murders."

"I think we need surveillance," Josie said. "We don't have to go onto the Sanctuary premises. We'll set a perimeter and see if Jack Gresham comes on or off the property. If we see him leave, we'll follow him and see where he goes. Then we'll talk to him and see what he has to say about his missing wife. What if he knows where she is?"

Mettner said, "It's pretty far out in the middle of nowhere. You can't exactly sit in your car for a stake-out."

Josie said, "So we'll sit out in the woods. We've pretty much been out there for the last three days as it is, and now Noah knows which plants not to eat."

Mettner laughed. "You guys have Ghillie suits?"

Gretchen said, "What's a Ghillie suit?"

Mettner looked at Josie as if to say, "Is she serious?"

Josie said, "Gretchen's a city girl, remember? They don't have much use for Ghillie suits in Philadelphia."

Gretchen repeated, "What's a Ghillie suit?"

Noah laughed. "It's clothing. It's a kind of camouflage you wear when you go hunting to blend in with your surroundings. Makes you look like walking brush—or like a walking tree covered in vines. Google it. You'll see."

Gretchen took out her phone and punched it into her browser. A smile lit her face. "Oh, I need one of these," she said.

They got Chitwood's approval for surveillance after he spoke with law enforcement in Lenore County to let them know what was going on. Most of the land surrounding the Sanctuary belonged to the state, so there was no issue of getting warrants or permissions from property owners to set up out in the woods. Mettner and a few of the other officers on Denton's police force gathered as many of their hunting clothes as they could find to camouflage themselves, as well as some night goggles. The sun set just after eight in the evening. Once darkness descended, they set out in teams.

Unmarked police vehicles were left in strategic places outside their perimeter, and Josie had the uniformed officers don plain-clothes and wait in those vehicles in case they needed to pursue any vehicle leaving the Sanctuary. The other teams split up, moving on foot. Mettner and two other officers took up the area in the woods between the Yates campsite and the Sanctuary fence, spreading out to cover as much ground as possible and forming a loose circle around the place. Noah, Josie, and Gretchen took up position on the other side of the Sanctuary, in the woods across the road from the farmhouse. Gretchen concealed herself in the trees at the bottom of the hill south of the Sanctuary. Josie positioned herself directly across the road from the Sanctuary driveway. She found a downed tree trunk about roughly ten yards away from the shoulder of the road, well-hidden by brush and trees. Noah traveled farther up the hill, north of the Sanctuary. Josie estimated that there was a quarter mile between them. It wasn't far, but in the dark, quiet forest, she felt like Gretchen and Noah were worlds away from her. She kept checking the back pocket of her jeans to make sure her radio was still there. The teams had agreed to only contact one another if there was a sighting so that the radios didn't draw unwanted attention.

Luckily, it had stopped raining. Even though the sun had gone down, the heat and humidity hadn't let up. Josie had declined a Ghillie suit, instead wearing black jeans and an olive-green raincoat to help her blend into the forest. Still, sweat poured from her skin and pooled at the base of her spine. She ached for a breeze or even for more rain, but none came. Beside her on the tree trunk she set out her thermos of coffee and a pair of binoculars which she used to zoom in on the farmhouse and barn. Dim light glowed from inside both structures. People moved back and forth between the two, some of them abandoning both and walking off into the field behind the house where the tents were set up. An hour passed, then another and another. No vehicles came in or out of the property. Eventually, the lights in both buildings were extinguished. A single exterior light behind the barn illuminated an outhouse.

By midnight, from what Josie could see from her perch across the road, all the members of the Sanctuary had retired to their sleeping quarters. Josie sipped her coffee, waiting. Twice, she saw shadows moving along the outer barn wall, but then the figures emerged in the circle of light around the outhouse. Two female members using the facilities. Josie checked her cell phone and noted the times. The first woman came out at one fifteen a.m. and spent ten minutes using the facilities. The second woman used the outhouse at two forty-three a.m. and emerged only a minute later, hurrying back toward the front of the barn.

Josie sighed and hopped down from her seat on the tree trunk. Looking from side to side, all she could see were varying degrees of darkness. It was a moonless night and the light from the outhouse lamp didn't reach across the road and into the trees. By feel, she picked her way to a spot several feet away where she relieved herself. Returning to her spot, she shook her thermos, relieved to hear coffee slosh around inside. She sipped the rest of it slowly.

By three, the temperature had finally dropped slightly, and the breeze she'd longed for so badly earlier ruffled the tops of the trees.

Initially, Josie was afraid that the quiet dark of the woods might lull her into sleep, especially since she hadn't had more than a couple of hours over the last few nights combined, but as the Sanctuary descended into complete stillness, her surroundings reminded her too much of her recent nightmares for her body to rest. Every small noise startled her: the rustle of the wind through the trees, the chirp of crickets, the buzz of cicadas, and the low hoot of an owl. Her sweat cooled on her skin, leaving it clammy. A shiver ran through her.

Something cold caressed her neck. Her body leaped from the tree trunk and whirled around, staring into the blackness. She pulled her gun from its holster, holding it out in front of her. She swore she saw a shadow pass between two nearby trees. Her legs went weak and she stumbled, her head slamming into a branch behind her. An involuntary gasp escaped her. A noise to her left froze her in place. Footsteps? She remained silent, ears straining to pick up any noise. The gun felt heavier than usual. Her arm trembled holding it up.

Was her mind playing tricks on her? Blinking, she took a few steps back toward her seat. Suddenly, she had that feeling again. The same one she'd had the first day at the Yates campsite. Every hair on her arms and the nape of her neck stood on end. Her head whipped around. Was that someone breathing? She lowered the gun to her side and sprinted toward the road—or where she thought the road was—but she was disoriented, her heart pounding, and the further she ran, the more lost she became. Stopping to regroup, she pressed herself against a tree and pointed the gun out in front of her once more. Her eyes panned back and forth but nothing moved. She waited, listening for more sounds, but there was nothing. Eventually, the sensation went away. She took one hand from the pistol grip and reached into her jacket pocket for her cell phone, but it wasn't there. She touched her other pocket. Her GPS unit was gone as well.

"Shit," she muttered under her breath. They must have fallen out when she was running. Or had she left them on the tree trunk? Why were her thoughts so muddled?

She pointed her gun toward the ground and closed her eyes, trying to gather her composure. Eventually, she opened them and blinked, trying to bring the shadows into focus, but it didn't work. One of her hands fumbled for the handheld radio in her back pocket, but her fingers wouldn't work. The simple movement sent a wave of dizziness through her.

From her periphery she swore she saw movement. The shadow again. The thundering in her chest overwhelmed her. Was there someone really there? Or was her exhaustion-addled brain making her crazy? Should she stay or run? She tried to bring her gun up in front of her again, but it was too heavy. Instead, her fingers reached back and tried once more to find the radio. There was another noise.

Breathing, she thought. The forest was breathing.

Had she fallen asleep? Was this another one of her nightmares? Would Lila step out from behind a tree, grip her chin, and scare the piss out of her?

The sound was all around her now. The trees and the leaves were alive. Something wet slid down her cheek.

A voice beside her said, "You're here."

She opened her mouth to scream, but nothing came out. *Move! Run!* A rush of fatigue overcame her so quickly and so completely that she could barely lift her limbs. She was vaguely aware of her gun falling from her limp hands. If this wasn't a dream, then something was horribly wrong. She felt breath on her cheek. Hands touched her. She wanted to recoil but no part of her body would work. One word appeared in the front of her mind in neon letters: RADIO.

She thought hard about making her hand move, visualizing it in her head, seeing her fingers find and grip the radio, pull it out of her pocket, and push the buttons. Opening her mouth to tell her team she was in trouble.

The hands lifted her and her head lolled. The Sanctuary driveway came into view briefly from across the road and then receded. Her radio dropped into the mud.

The voice came again.

"You won't be needing that where you're going."

CHAPTER FORTY-EIGHT

Josie woke with a start, her body thrashing, pushing up, away from the shadows in her mind. As her eyes searched her surroundings, she saw that she was in a bedroom. It was small with wood paneling, an old rust-colored carpet on the floor, and a thin twin mattress beneath her. Daylight streamed through the gauzy curtains hanging from the single window over the bed. The door, which was on the other side of the room, was closed. Josie stumbled up, out of the bed, her legs like jelly, and staggered to the door. She turned the knob, pushed, and pulled but it didn't budge. She went back to the mattress, falling to her knees at the head of it and wrenching the curtains open. Trees surrounded her. She was on the second story of some structure, but beyond a small strip of grass below, there was only forest.

Am I still dreaming? She wondered as scraps of the last few days mingled with slices of her nightmares. Her brain tried to put things in order, to reorient itself, but everything around her was unfamiliar. What the hell had happened?

Her mouth felt like someone had stuffed it with cotton and a pounding headache finally began to register now that she had been awake for a few minutes. She looked down at her clothes, patted her pockets. Everything was gone. Her gun, her holster, her wallet, her flashlight, radio, phone, keys, GPS unit.

"Shit," she muttered.

A wave of nausea rocked her, and she lay back down, staring at the white, water-stained ceiling until it passed. She thought back to the last thing she remembered. It had been night. She'd been stationed in the woods across the road from the Sanctuary. She'd been finishing her coffee. Then she had felt something touch her neck, freaked out, and ran, becoming increasingly disoriented.

"Oh no," she said.

She'd left her equipment unattended, including her thermos, when she relieved herself. Had someone slipped her something, or had her own extreme fatigue done her in? More likely it was the combination of the two, she thought. How had no one on her team noticed? They had vehicles stationed at both ends of the road, so anyone who drove out would have had to pass one of her unmarked police vehicles, not to mention either Gretchen or Noah. There was only one way, Josie realized. The woods behind her, opposite the Sanctuary. Whoever had taken her would have had to carry her out that way. Had someone carried her miles through the forest? It didn't matter now. She'd been taken. Here she was—in a strange room in a strange house.

A shudder worked through her as she thought of the man's mouth against her cheek, his breath in her ear, his hands on her body. She thought about screaming for help but what were the odds that she was in a place where someone who might help her would hear her?

Noah, she thought. He and her team would have figured out that something was wrong by now. They would have looked for her, realized she was gone. But they wouldn't be able to track her using her phone because she had lost it in the forest before she was taken. She couldn't sit around waiting for a rescue that might or might not arrive.

Her feet were a little steadier this time as she made her way to the door. She pulled with all her might, even putting her foot up against the wall beside the door to give her more leverage. But after a few minutes she was soaked in sweat, shaking, and no closer to getting out. Panic rose in her chest as she looked around the room once more. All she could think of was that this was just one big closet, just like the one that Lila Jensen had trapped her inside so many times when she was a child. Except it wasn't pitch black.

The window.

Josie wiped her clammy palms on her jeans and walked over to the window again, tearing the curtain down and tossing it aside. The window frame was old and wooden, its locking mechanisms petrified and unmovable, and the place where the window fit into the frame had been painted shut long ago. She swore again and leaned her head against the window, trying to figure out whether she could jump. There was a sizeable tree branch not too far from the window. If she knocked out enough of the glass and perched just right, she could push off the sill and reach it on her way down. It would slow her fall and maybe keep her from breaking a leg. But she'd only have one chance at it.

There was nothing in the room to break the window with. Nothing to use as a weapon. There was a mattress. That was it. She went back to the door and pressed her ear against it, waiting. No sounds came from the other side. Back at the window, she gathered up the curtains and wrapped them around her right boot. Then she tossed the mattress out of her way, against the door, so she could brace her left foot firmly on the floor and kick with her right.

She was weak with exhaustion and hunger and whatever drug she'd been given. It took a good half dozen kicks to break the glass. Once she'd kicked a hole in the middle, she unwrapped her boot and then wrapped the curtain around her right hand, using that to punch out the remaining shards. The creak of a floorboard sounded behind her. Then someone grunted. Josie glanced over her shoulder just long enough to see a man struggling to get the mattress clear of the door. She turned back to the window, gripped the frame with one hand on each side, and prepared to jump.

Rough hands yanked her by the waist, pulling her back into the room. She let her weight fall back on him, sending him off balance. Her left hand grabbed a shard of glass as the two of them fell, landing half-on, half-off the mattress. The moment they hit the floor, Josie turned her body, slicing with the glass, hoping to hit something. When the man sucked in a sharp breath, she was sure she'd gotten him. But strong arms looped around her, over the top of her arms, holding her in place. Her stabs became weaker and weaker until there was no more area to slice.

"Stop," the man said. "Drop that."

But Josie held tight, even as she felt her own blood seep through her fingers. She wriggled in his grip, pushing her body upward. She whipped her head back, smashing the back of her skull into his face. His grip loosened. Josie used her elbows as daggers in his soft abdomen until he let go of her and she scrambled to her feet, racing toward the door. His hand wrapped around her ankle, pulling her back.

"Dammit," he said. "Stop."

She shook his hand loose and sprinted through the doorway, down a short hall toward a staircase. Just as she reached the crude wooden bannister, the man tackled her from behind, knocking her to the ground. Her breath left her as his weight crushed her. Blackness encroached on her vision. Then his large hands seized her throat, pressing on her carotid artery, sending her spinning into unconsciousness.

CHAPTER FORTY-NINE

Josie felt the hardness of the chair beneath her before she even opened her eyes. She tested her limbs, but they were tied down. Her left palm burned, and warm air caressed her face. She thought she heard birds. Was she outside? Her eyes fluttered open, blinking against the light. She was in a different room. This one was obviously a sitting room with its saggy, threadbare couch and well-worn floral-design area rug. On one side of her was a fireplace. On the other was a set of large wooden sliding doors, closed almost completely with only an inch left open. Gauzy curtains billowed over the windows, and her heart sank. She was being held somewhere so remote they felt comfortable keeping the windows open. Where no one would hear her scream for help.

She wriggled in the chair. Her wrists were bound tightly to the arms of the chair, her ankles to the chair legs. Blood dripped from beneath her left hand where she'd gripped the shard of glass to defend herself. She stilled as she heard the sound of a door creaking open elsewhere in the house. She leaned her head toward the crack in the door. Voices came, muffled and indistinct. It took several moments for her to determine that one was a man and one was a woman.

The woman's voice was angry, her words a hiss. "What were you thinking, bringing her here?"

The man's voice was so low that Josie couldn't make out the words.

"This was a mistake. This is how we got here in the first place. You can't keep doing this. This is not what we're about. You know that."

The man spoke again.

The woman replied, "No, absolutely not. I'm going to talk to her."

Josie tensed as the door suddenly swung inward, and Charlotte Fadden stepped through it. "Hello, Detective," she said with her calm smile.

In her hands she held a small black bag with blocky red writing on it: *First Aid Kit*. Trailing her through the door was a tall, shaggy-haired man in bare feet, threadbare khaki shorts, and a stained white T-shirt. On his side there was a slice in the shirt and through the opening, Josie could see a bandage. His face was bearded, his eyes vacant, but she recognized him from the photos she had seen. Jack Gresham.

He stood silent and unmoving by the wall while Charlotte knelt in front of Josie and slowly, gently, began to untie Josie's left arm. "I'm so sorry that it's come to this."

"What's that?" Josie asked. "Kidnapping? Assault?"

Charlotte's smile didn't falter. "Jack," she said. "Go get me some warm water, would you?"

He left the room. Charlotte continued, "As I told you before, Jack is troubled. I do not and would not ever condone this type of behavior."

Charlotte turned Josie's palm up, revealing a mess of wet and congealed blood in various stages of drying. Josie tried not to make a sound as Charlotte probed it. Jack returned with the water, placing it beside Charlotte and then resuming his position against the wall. Charlotte fished out a piece of gauze from the first aid kit, wet it, and began to clean the blood away from the slice in Josie's hand.

Josie said, "You knew where Jack was all along. Why didn't you just tell me? Why did you hide him?"

"I was trying to protect him, dear. He needs a safe haven. That's what the Sanctuary was for him."

"A safe haven to act out his deranged fantasies? He was the one hurting Renee Kelly, wasn't he?"

"He and Renee had an agreement."

"An agreement? What kind of agreement?"

"That's not important now, dear."

Trying another tactic, Josie said, "I thought you didn't condone violence."

"I don't. Not generally."

"Not generally? What does that mean?"

Charlotte cleaned away the last of the blood and studied the wound. "I think you'll be fine without stitches, but you'll have to be careful. We'll wrap it up, but it will be up to you to keep it immobile so that it heals."

Josie saw that Charlotte wasn't going to give her any real answers. Not easily. So she changed course again. "Where am I?"

Charlotte squeezed a glob of bacitracin from a tube and onto Josie's hand. "You're in a safe place."

Josie looked over her shoulder at Jack. She doubted that. "Where's Emilia?" she asked, her question directed at him. Something passed over his face, but it was so brief, Josie couldn't tell what it was. Shock? Dismay? Fear? Regret? Had the hermit been telling the truth about ransacking the campsite after Emilia was gone and the Yateses were already dead? Had they been completely wrong about him? Did that mean that Maya had lied? Josie's thoughts swirled in a fog. She was too tired, too traumatized to make sense of everything. She couldn't think clearly. Her mind tried to grab onto one line of thought and stay with it: getting the hell out of here.

Charlotte pressed a clean gauze pad into Josie's hand, cut open a fresh roll of sterile gauze and began wrapping the wound. "You ask a lot of questions," she mused.

"That's my job," Josie said. "To ask questions. But if you're tired of questions then how about this: both of you are actively breaking the law right now by keeping me here against my will. The longer you keep me, the more trouble you're making for yourselves. Let me go now or bring me a phone and I'll call my team, and I promise to work with the district attorney to get you a reasonable plea deal."

Jack's voice was low and gravelly. "I told you we can't trust her."

"Hush," Charlotte told him. She taped the rolled gauze in place and put Josie's hand in her lap. Looking up into Josie's eyes, her smile widened. "I need you to see past your job for a moment. I need you to see what's really important. It's true that I am not happy with what Jack's done, but don't you see that by bringing you here he's given you a gift?"

"Did you give me something to make me high, or are you just that crazy?" Josie retorted.

Jack mumbled, "This is a waste of time."

Charlotte laughed. "Your walls are so high. Your resistance so fierce! But I promise you, you are exactly where you need to be right at this very moment."

"A prisoner?" Josie said.

"No, my dear. Not a prisoner. Well, no more than you've always been. But right now, here with us, you're on the precipice of true freedom. Freedom like you've never known. You've been brought here at exactly a time when you need to embrace yourself the most. When you need most to fully *become*—light and dark, married, together as one."

Josie leaned forward as much as her bindings would allow and stared into Charlotte's eyes. "Let me go right now."

Charlotte backed away, packing up her first aid kit. Josie felt a small satisfaction that she'd won the staring contest, but she had a feeling she was no closer to being free. She slammed her injured hand down hard against her thigh and hollered, "Let me go!" Ignoring her, Charlotte got to her feet and stood beside Jack. They watched as Josie's left fingers worked at the bindings, trying to free herself, struggling with the ropes until blood seeped through her new bandage. Finally, she stopped, panting and exhausted, sweat pouring down her face, stinging her eyes.

Charlotte said, "Jack, wait here. I'm going to get Detective Quinn something to eat."

Josie worked more slowly at her bindings while Jack stood over her. She freed her right hand and began to work on her left leg. He did nothing to stop her. A voice in the back of her head shouted panicked warnings at her. Why would they let her free herself? This made no sense. Why wasn't he trying to stop her? What would he do when she got completely free? Just let her walk out? Strangle her into unconsciousness again? Tie her back up? What the hell kind of game were they playing?

Her legs were still bound when Charlotte returned with two tray tables. She opened them up and set one in front of Josie. "Jack," she said. "Be a dear and get the rest from the kitchen, would you?"

He left and returned with another chair for Charlotte, and then returned again with two trays of food. Charlotte sat down across from Josie. "Please," she said. "You must be starving."

"Let me go," Josie said, leaning down and trying to squeeze her upper body between the tray table and the chair so she could continue trying to free her legs. With no success, she pulled her head back up to see that Charlotte was already eating. There was a bowl of noodle soup with vegetables in it, some bread, an apple, and a large glass of water.

Calmly swallowing a mouthful, Charlotte said, "Either you're going to cooperate with me and give me a chance to show you the benefits of what we do at the Sanctuary, or you're going to escape. No matter which option you choose, you'll need your strength. At the very least, you'll need to stay hydrated. Wouldn't you agree?"

Josie said nothing.

Charlotte reached over and pushed the glass of water closer to Josie's face. "This means nothing, Detective. You're not yielding. Just surviving. Everyone has to eat and drink."

It was a trap, Josie thought. It had to be. There was something in the food, in the water. Hemlock, or something else. Something that would render her unconscious while they decided what to do with her.

Charlotte sighed. "We're not poisoning you."

She stood and beckoned Jack. He picked up Josie's tray and Charlotte picked up her own. They switched them so that now Josie had Charlotte's and vice versa. Charlotte sat back down. She took a drink of Josie's water and then began to eat Josie's soup. Josie waited several minutes before reluctantly picking up Charlotte's water and gulping it down. Next she ate the apple. Then the bread. She didn't want to eat the soup in case there was something in it, but then she realized that Charlotte had been eating it before they switched the trays. Charlotte was fine. Josie, too, felt fine. Slowly she began to eat the soup, astounded at her own hunger. Jack left the room and returned with a pitcher of water which he used to fill both their cups. They each took a drink.

Josie said, "You're just going to let me go? You're not going to try to stop me?"

Charlotte frowned. She looked pointedly at Jack. "No, we're not going to try to stop you. But you'll have a long journey ahead. You're quite far from civilization. It would be better if you stayed with us for a spell. If you gave me a few days to help you."

"The only help I need is to get out of here."

"I know that's what you think, but you're wrong. You're fighting an important inner battle right now. One that could possibly set the tone for the rest of your life. I'd like to help you."

Josie replied, "Maybe under other circumstances, but I need to find Emilia Gresham." She looked at Jack. "As you know, she is missing. I believe she could be in danger. I don't have time for this. I need to leave now." She pushed her tray table away and reached down, fingers back working at the bindings on her legs.

Charlotte said, "What if I told you Emilia is safe?"

Josie's head shot up. "How can I believe you?"

Charlotte said, "Jack."

Jack stepped forward. "My wife is safe," he said.

Josie looked at Charlotte. "After what he did to me, you expect me to believe you? I need to see her."

"You can't see her, Detective," Charlotte said. "You'll have to live with my assurances. Not Jack's. I understand that he has betrayed your trust. I hope you'll believe me. I wouldn't lie about something like this."

"You've lied about a lot of things," Josie pointed out.

"But I'm telling you the truth about Emilia."

"Is she here?" Josie asked.

Charlotte smiled. "You only need to know that she is safe and unharmed."

"Did she come here willingly?"

The answer was a little slower in coming. "She came to be with Jack. Now please, would you give me some time to help you?"

Josie looked at Jack. "What about Maya Bestler? Do you know her?"

There was a brief flicker in his eyes. Not anger or distrust. Hurt, perhaps? Regret?

"You knew her, didn't you?" Josie went on. "You met her at a charity benefit at Lantz's and you fixated on her."

His mouth hung open. Charlotte looked back at him, but Josie couldn't see the look that passed between them.

"Was it you?" Josie asked. "Were you the one who took her? Did she lie about the hermit? Why did she lie? She's afraid of you, isn't she?"

Charlotte told Jack, "That's enough for now, Jack. You can go."

Josie opened her mouth to ask more questions, but she was struck by a sudden wave of dizziness and fatigue. No, she thought. Not again. She tried to hold on, to hold fast to her consciousness, to the light, but she couldn't. It fell away and blackness enveloped her.

CHAPTER FIFTY

She woke in yet another room, now on a mattress that sat in a black metal bedframe. Her wrists were bound with rope and tied to the bedframe. Her feet were tied together. An ache spread through her shoulders as she began to move, to test her bindings. She couldn't help but think of Renee Kelly; this rope looked the same as the kind Josie had found in the cabin at the Sanctuary. What had Jack been doing to her? Would Josie be next? Charlotte seemed to have some control over him, but he had brought Josie here against Charlotte's commands. That's what they'd been arguing about when Josie heard them outside the door of the other room.

She pushed the jumble of thoughts aside and concentrated on her present situation. This room was almost identical to the last one, with its ugly wood paneling and rust-colored rug. Rattling the bedframe did nothing to loosen her ties. She tried to cry out, but her voice was squeaky and weak. Her mouth felt dry as paper, but at least she hadn't had nightmares. Whatever they were doping her with was strong. So strong that it was dragging her back under as the exertion rushed the blood round her body. Still fighting against the ropes that held her, Josie fell back into a deep sleep.

When she woke again, Charlotte was there, sitting on the edge of the bed, wiping Josie's face with a wet washcloth. Josie didn't want to admit it, but it felt wonderful. She helped Josie sit up and offered her a glass of water. Nothing had ever looked so inviting, but Josie couldn't drink it. She couldn't risk being drugged again.

"You said I was safe here," Josie said in her scratchy voice. "Is this your idea of safe? Keeping me tied up?"

"I'm sorry, Detective, but we needed a little more time with you. Please, you must drink."

"No," Josie said.

Jack came in and untied her feet. Josie tried to leap up, but her legs were so wobbly she fell to the ground, hanging awkwardly from the bed. "Not so fast," Charlotte told her as they untied her from the bed but left her wrists bound together. Charlotte took her into a bathroom next door and waited while she relieved herself. Josie's mind was muddled, but still racing to find a way out of this. They clearly didn't want to hurt her. Although she didn't appreciate being drugged, it was preferable to being beaten into submission. She had the feeling that given some time alone with her, Jack would have different ideas about how to treat her. Somehow, she needed to convince Charlotte to let her go. She knew her team would be working hard to find her, but she was losing hope that they'd be able to.

Back in the room, Josie refused food and drink. Charlotte promised to return later to try again. The hours passed with Charlotte and Jack hovering over her, offering her food and drink, and Josie refusing. She lay tied to the bed, her feet bound together, trying not to drift back to sleep, trying to keep her wits about her. Her whole body ached with the inactivity.

The daylight coming into the bedroom window receded and night crawled in. Josie had been listening intently for any noise outside all day, but there was only the wind in the trees, birds chirping, and Charlotte moving in and out of the room. Josie rarely heard Jack. As big as he was, he moved noiselessly through the house. It was not a reassuring thought.

She had no way to keep track of the hours. No way to know what time it was when she finally fell back to sleep. The drugs Charlotte and Jack were giving her must have finally left her system enough for her nightmares to return. She was a child again, trapped in the closet. From outside the door she heard Lila talking with one of her "special friends"—men who came to deal her drugs or to do them with her. Sometimes Lila didn't have enough money, so she did other things with them. Sometimes she didn't feel like doing those other things and would offer Josie up as payment for whatever she owed them.

"Mommy!" Josie's dream-self cried out as the dark space closed in on her. She banged on the closet door until her hands hurt. "Please, Mommy, let me out!"

"Shut up, girl," came Lila's reply.

"Come on," a man's voice said. "She's just a kid."

"Help!" she shrieked. Backing up, she lifted a leg and kicked at the door. After three tries, it burst open, and Josie tumbled out. But she wasn't in her mother's trailer. She was back in the forest, and it was just as dark as it had been in the closet. Something heavy and foul-smelling crawled on top of her. Its hot breath and wet mouth hung just over her head. Her small body was paralyzed, the sound of her heartbeat like a bass drum, rattling her chest.

"Jo!" The voice came from the direction of where she'd toppled out of the closet. Familiar and grounding but also surprising. The creature on top of her vanished. She scrambled to a sitting position. A single bulb hung from an invisible ceiling above. Below it was her late husband, Ray. He was grown up, dressed in his police uniform. He was clean-shaven, his blond hair neatly combed. Josie opened her mouth to speak, but he raised a finger and pressed it to his lips.

Shhhhh.

The sound hadn't come from him, but Josie kept her gaze glued to him. He held up two fingers—index and middle finger—and then slowly pointed them toward his own eyes. *Look*, he was trying to tell her. Or *watch*. She wasn't sure.

Shhhhh.

The noise was coming from next to her. A breeze caressed the nape of her neck. That feeling of being watched came again. Except she was no longer in the dream.

Josie opened her eyes to see a tall shadow looming over her, just a dark shape against the muted gray moonlight that flooded through the gauzy curtains on the window.

Jack.

She didn't move. Didn't even breathe. She was bound and help-less. Just one of his large hands could cut off her screams before Charlotte heard them. Still, she would be damned if she showed him her fear. Her voice came out far steadier than she felt.

"If you touch me again, I will break every one of your fingers."

He didn't respond. She couldn't make out his expression well, but for a second she saw the white of his teeth. Was he smiling?

She lurched away when he leaned over, but he simply placed something next to her on the bed, turned and left, all without making a sound.

Josie blinked until she was able to make out the small, quarter-sized object he had left on the mattress beside her. When she finally did, her body let out an involuntary cry which the conscious part of her brain immediately strangled in her throat.

He had left her half of a black walnut.

CHAPTER FIFTY-ONE

Resisting sleep became a fight for survival. She could not risk falling into slumber again and leaving herself vulnerable. In her fright, she had knocked the walnut to the floor. Hopefully, she'd be able to point it out to Charlotte in the morning, tell her what Jack had done, and then—

What?

Charlotte would make him leave? Free Josie and turn him in to the police? The idea was absurd. Charlotte had to have known all the terrible things he had done and still, she protected him. She had been protecting him all along, even after Renee's murder. They were keeping Emilia against her will. Charlotte was in charge, not just complicit with the things Jack did. She gave the orders. She believed she could control Jack to some extent, but that didn't mean she could stop him from torturing and killing Josie.

Josie's limbs strained against her restraints, the rope digging into her wrists and ankles. He had killed his friends—Tyler and Valerie. He had taken Emilia. Then he had killed Renee. He'd lived at the Sanctuary. What had Charlotte said? He and Renee had had "an agreement"? She didn't know what that meant, but she knew that whatever he'd done to the girl had caused the scarring on her wrists and the terror in her eyes before her death. Josie was certain from Charlotte's initial reaction to the news of Renee's death that she had never intended for Jack to kill the girl. But he had and she continued to protect him.

After having been drugged twice, eating and drinking hardly anything, and resisting sleep, she felt dizzy and disoriented. When

Charlotte appeared at dawn, untied her and offered her an apple, she accepted. What could they do to an apple? Then she accepted bread. Charlotte urged her to drink water, but the only way she would do it was directly from the faucet in the bathroom, cupping the water with her hands and splashing it up into her mouth.

Charlotte returned her to the bedroom, binding her again. At some point after that she fell asleep, jerking awake in a panic, unsure how long she'd been out. It was still daytime. The room was empty. She pulled at her restraints. The skin on her wrists had blistered and burned every time she moved. She focused on the pain to help keep her awake, but hunger and sleep deprivation dulled her. When she tried to think—about how to get away, about Noah and the team, about her family—her mind went blank. Her world had narrowed to a single focus: not ending up strangled to death with a black walnut necklace pushed down her throat.

When Charlotte returned and untied her, she couldn't even muster relief to be free of her bindings. Her body was weak, her mind still dim. Charlotte led her downstairs and outside. Sunlight stabbed her eyes. She used a hand to shield them as her vision adjusted. They were on a small porch. Beyond it was a stretch of grass and then trees in every direction. She looked back from where they had come and saw Jack's shadow through the doorway. He was always there. Lurking. Josie felt a twinge of panic, but she pushed it down.

"Come, sit," Charlotte told her.

Josie hadn't even noticed the small outdoor table and chairs or the food and drink waiting there. She didn't protest when Charlotte offered one of the chairs in front of a meal of vegetable soup and more bread. Josie ate slowly, on alert for signs that she'd been drugged again. She had to eat something to maintain some sort of strength or she'd never be able to escape. Charlotte waited several minutes before she said, "When I met you, there was something you were struggling with—that you're still struggling with—and

I believe it is time-sensitive. This is where I believe I can help you. Are you ready to talk about it?"

Josie didn't want to talk about Lila Jensen. Didn't want to think of her ever again, but she didn't have the mental energy to keep up a lie. "There's a woman," Josie said. "In my childhood she did terrible, terrible things to me. She's dying and she wants to see me."

"You don't want to see her?" Charlotte asked.

Josie shook her head. "No."

"Why is that, dear? Do you think if you go and see her, she'll still have the upper hand? Even in death?"

Josie looked around at the swaying trees. She listened to the birds chirp. In spite of herself, she thought how peaceful it was here. It felt cooler. Either the August heat wave had finally broken, or they were high up in the mountains.

"No," she told Charlotte. "I don't want to see her because she doesn't deserve to see me. She doesn't deserve to have anything she wants after the things she's done, after all the lives she's destroyed."

"You want to keep this one thing from her," Charlotte said.

Josie held up a hand. "Don't talk to me about forgiveness. It's not going to happen."

Charlotte laughed, this time a full-throated, genuine bray. "You don't have to worry about that. I don't believe in forgiveness."

Josie said, "Don't you need to show forgiveness to 'fully become'?"

"That's nonsense," Charlotte said. Josie had an inkling then as to how people could get sucked into this woman's world. She rarely said what Josie expected. She tried to remind herself that Charlotte was a consummate liar, but she was too intent on staying focused on the conversation to think of much else.

Charlotte leaned forward, pushing her fingers through her gray hair, feeling along her scalp until she found what she was looking for. She kept her right hand in place and used her left hand to part the hair and reveal an old lump of scar tissue. Josie felt nausea swirl in her stomach, remembering the photos she had seen of Charlotte in the decades-old domestic violence case. "Do you think I could forgive this?" Charlotte asked. She stood and lifted her dress, pointing out the scars on her crepe-paper skin from her ankles to her ribs. "Do you think I could forgive these? My husband—my loving husband—did this to me. And these are just the ones on the outside. I didn't forgive him when he was alive, and I felt no such impulse after he died."

"If not forgiveness, what then?" Josie said.

Charlotte rearranged her dress and sat back down. She took a long sip of water as her eyes traveled the yard. "When a person victimizes you, they make you less. They diminish you."

"You're saying I should rise above?" Josie asked.

Charlotte looked back at her, eyes flashing. "No, I'm saying you should become whole again. There's only one way to do that."

"How is that?"

"You've got to embrace your own darkness. Your impulses. Just the way this woman you're telling me about did. I bet she embraced her darkest desires every single day."

Josie nodded. Her fingers gripped her water glass, knuckles turning white. She wanted so badly to drink, but couldn't risk it.

Charlotte went on. "She knew her dark side and she lived it fearlessly, recklessly even. That gave her power. Power over you, and I imagine power over many people."

"You want me to become an evil bitch?"

Charlotte laughed again. "I do like you, Detective. I like you very much. No. You shouldn't just become an evil bitch. That's not fully *becoming*. That's only living in the shadow of one side of yourself. A half of the whole. You have to be able to access both. I believe you've long had access to the light inside you. You fight for people, to protect people, to help them. I see that in you. What I don't see is your ability to tap into your own darkness and wield it. The abuse you received at this woman's hands, it went on for a very long time, didn't it?"

Josie nodded.

"Chronic victims can only become whole again, powerful in their own right, if they are able to tap into their dark side. Tell me, if there were no rules in the world, what would you do to this woman?"

Josie had had her entire life to fantasize about what she would do to Lila if only given a chance. If she had a free pass. No consequences. The answer seemed so obvious: torture her in the same way she had been tortured as a child, or kill her. What else was there? But those were hollow choices, weren't they? Josie had seen enough death and despair in her career. If she could hurt Lila Jensen, would that give her back what Lila had stolen? Logically, Josie knew it wouldn't. Life just didn't work that way. The one and only thing that had given her any peace over the last year and a half while Lila rotted in prison was knowing that she couldn't hurt anyone else.

So why were these calls from Muncy prison bothering her so much? Why were the nightmares so frequent and intense?

Charlotte said, "Close your eyes. I want you to imagine something. Go ahead."

Josie didn't want to close her eyes. The soup and bread had already made her full and drowsy. She didn't want to risk falling asleep at the table. But Charlotte was right across from her, she reasoned. Surely, Jack wouldn't try anything under Charlotte's watchful eyes. Reluctantly, Josie put her hands in her lap and closed her eyes, feeling the gentle summer breeze on her arms and face.

Charlotte's tone was soft. "You're with this woman. She's lying in bed, dying. You're alone with her. Maybe she is still lucid. Maybe she's so close to death that she's out of it. Regardless, you sit down next to her. You look at her face and you feel all the horrors she inflicted on you. You feel weak and victimized all over again. But you don't have to feel that way. Not ever again. You've got the power inside you if you'll just take it. All you have to do is reach for her, wrap your hands around her throat, and squeeze. Feel her panic set in as she realizes what you're doing. Her eyes bulge open and you see the fear, the terror in her eyes. The same feelings she's always inflicted on you, except now you're on the other side."

Josie's fingertips dug into her thighs, making the vision of Lila that Charlotte had created disappear, replaced with an image of Renee Kelly on the mortuary table. Through gritted teeth, she said, "Is that what you do at the Sanctuary? You hurt each other? You abuse one another—even kill one another—so you can feel powerful?" Josie opened her eyes to see that the fire in Charlotte's eyes still burned bright.

"Of course not. We *help* one another."

"By hurting one another?"

"If that's what's necessary."

"I don't understand."

Charlotte shifted in her seat. "Our members—once they've made the commitment—make pacts with one another. These pacts allow them to fully bring out other members' power, and get in touch with their dark sides."

"I don't understand how that makes someone whole," Josie struggled. She thought she'd feel better after eating, but her mind was clouding over. Her body wanted desperately to sleep.

Charlotte said, "You can't have light without dark."

Josie fumbled to follow her logic. "You find the darkness in each other."

"We help people to bring out their darkness so it can sit next to the light and take up an equal amount of being. I know it's difficult to grasp, but at the Sanctuary we rid ourselves of the norms and expectations of society. That's the first step. You can't think through the filter you've used your entire life. Take Jack for example. All of his life he was horribly abused by multiple people—usually his mother's boyfriends. Yet he was a good man, he held fast to the light inside himself and tried to do what he believed was right in his life. But he was horribly depressed and incomplete. Almost to the point of being suicidal. He came to me like this. I helped him access that other side of himself and in doing so, he became a more complete person."

Some part of her brain wanted to point out to Charlotte that all she had really done was create a killer, but she was still struggling to understand the framework Charlotte was trying to lay before her—the guiding principles of the Sanctuary. Instead, she asked, "What does that entail exactly? Helping a person access the other side of themselves?"

"Well, for every member it's different."

"What was it for Jack?"

"For each member, including Jack, it's a personal decision. Though some of our other members were willing to help him with it."

"Like Renee? Had she even made the commitment? She wasn't branded."

"She passed out each time we tried to do the branding ceremony. You have to be awake for it—fully aware of what you're receiving. But she was committed. She would have gotten there eventually."

"Jack hurt her, didn't he? Her and the 'other members' you're talking about, didn't he?"

"It's not hurting them if they consent."

"Hurt is hurt, Charlotte. Murder is murder. What you're alluding to sounds like a crime."

Charlotte looked away for a moment, her face flushing. "He wasn't supposed to kill anyone."

"But he did."

"You're thinking too much like a police officer, Detective."

"That's who I am, Charlotte. Who were the others? What happened to them?"

Charlotte met her eyes again. "They're all alive, if that's what you're asking."

"Where are they? Are they still at the Sanctuary? Did you tell them to lie to us? Did you coach them?"

Charlotte sighed. Her fingers smoothed the cloth napkin beside her bowl of soup. "There was one member who tried to help him, but he was—he couldn't—he hadn't yet tapped into his impulses. She left over a year ago."

"Who else?" Josie pressed. She looked again at the water, wanting so badly to pour the entire glass down her throat. Or even better, an entire cup of coffee. She missed coffee.

"She's gone," Charlotte said. "No one knows where she went."

"How do I know these women are still alive?"

"You've met one of them."

Josie's addled brain worked for several seconds to put the pieces together. Finally, she said, "Maya Bestler? She joined the Sanctuary?"

"She didn't join," Charlotte said quietly. "It was a mistake."

Josie heard Jack take two steps toward the door, but he didn't emerge right away. The fatigue that had threatened to overtake her minutes earlier was gone.

"What happened?"

Charlotte wouldn't look at her now. "I didn't know about her. Not at first. I only found out after. You see, Jack had long been nursing fantasies of kidnapping a woman, tying her up and... doing things to her. These were his dark impulses. Evidently, he wasn't satisfied letting other members fulfill his fantasy. He brought Maya onto the property without my knowledge. Once I found out, I made him release her. She promised she wouldn't tell what had happened."

"You believed her?"

Charlotte shifted again in her seat. "She was so afraid of Jack, that yes, I believed she wouldn't tell. I had Jack take her off the property and release her."

"Where? Where did he release her?" Josie asked.

"Honestly, I don't know. He set off one day into the woods with her and then came back without her. I didn't ask questions. The police never came."

Had Jack delivered her to the hermit or had the hermit found her wandering through the woods and taken her? Why hadn't Maya just told them what really had happened? Was she really that terrified of Jack?

Of course she was. Hadn't Josie herself just spent hours—possibly days—staying awake to protect herself from him? How long had she been in this place? One day? Two?

"What did you say, dear?" Charlotte asked. She leaned forward and peered into Josie's face, her brow furrowed in confusion. "Are you… counting?"

Had she talked aloud? Josie shook her head, trying to concentrate.

Was Jack the reason Maya had run away? Not because she didn't want to be a mother but because she was afraid he would come for her? He had obviously perfected his stalking skills. His efforts with Shana at Lantz Snack Factory had taught him a valuable lesson. Josie could attest to that.

Josie looked at her lap. Her mind worked to focus once more on the conversation. Becoming. Wholeness. Light and dark. Getting in touch with your darkest impulses. Chronic victims becoming whole again, grasping power. "You said 'becoming' is different for everyone. You believe I need to kill the woman who hurt me to get there?"

"I told you, dear, I don't condone violence. But I can help you with your struggle. I can help you *become*."

CHAPTER FIFTY-TWO

"How?" Josie asked. "How do I become?"

Charlotte beamed at Josie. "It doesn't happen overnight," she said. "It's a process. It takes time."

Josie thought about all the calls from the prison. "I don't have time," she said. "This woman I've told you about—she could be dead already. I have to go back."

"Nonsense, dear. I'll help you. I'll make the pact with you. You can act out your impulses on me."

Josie stared at her, disbelieving. "You want me to… you want me to kill you?"

Charlotte laughed, the light, musical laugh this time. "Of course not. Jack will help us. I believe he owes you some redress for bringing you here before you were ready."

Josie's body lunged forward. She clasped a hand over one of Charlotte's forearms. "I don't want to work with Jack. Only you."

Charlotte looked at Josie's fingers digging into her skin. "I won't let him hurt you. You have my word."

Josie almost pointed out that Charlotte's word was meaningless, but she didn't have it in her to get on the conversational merry-go-round with the woman again. Instead, she pulled her hand away and asked, "How? How will Jack help us?"

Charlotte leaned back in her seat and picked up a piece of bread, nibbling on it. "He'll make sure you don't kill me. You may choke me into unconsciousness, but you may not kill me."

Josie thought of the visualization Charlotte had just done with her. "You think that this will help me with my conflicted feelings over her death?"

"You'd be surprised how much tapping into the darkness helps. Trust me, you'll feel liberated."

"But you're not her," Josie said.

Charlotte stood up and extended a hand toward Josie. "Walk with me, dear."

Slowly, Josie stood. She refused to take Charlotte's hand but followed her off the porch and around the house. From the outside, Josie saw that it was a small two-story home. It had probably been used as a hunting cabin at some point. Its siding was faded blue wood, paint peeling in many places. Even the window frames sagged like tired eyes. At the rear of the house were two windows set against the ground, which meant there was a basement. The glass was dirty and the view into the house was blocked by what looked like cardboard on the other side. Josie wondered if that was where they were keeping Emilia. Obviously, they weren't keeping her at the Sanctuary. That explained why the K-9 Unit's Rini had lost her scent at the road just outside the Sanctuary property. If Jack had taken her, and Charlotte had allowed him, they would have moved her right away, brought her here. Josie kicked herself for not checking the property records in both Lenore and the surrounding counties. Then again, Gretchen's background check on Charlotte would have turned up any other properties that she owned anywhere in the entire country. So why hadn't it turned this up?

Charlotte had stopped walking, looking back at Josie with a puzzled expression. "Are you alright, dear?"

"Oh yes," Josie said quickly. "I'm just enjoying the outdoors. It feels like forever since I was outside."

Charlotte's smile returned. "Being outdoors is restorative, isn't it?"

Josie nodded and Charlotte walked on. She waited until the woman was a few steps ahead of her and then her eyes studied the surroundings for any clue as to Emilia's presence, and any avenue of escape. But there seemed to be none. There wasn't even a driveway or any vehicle nearby. Josie theorized that the driveway or vehicle entrance to the place must be somewhere on the other side of the trees, but in which direction, she couldn't tell.

Charlotte led her to a flat rock beneath a large weeping willow tree. "Sit down," Charlotte instructed. The tree's branches fell almost to the ground, shielding them from the sun or a view of the house. The rock next to its trunk looked as though it had been dragged there. It was a natural bench. As Josie walked up to it, she saw a break in the branches on the other side of the tree, and beyond that, a faint trail leading away, into the woods.

She could barely contain her excitement as she dutifully sat on the rock. When Charlotte told her to close her eyes, she felt relief. She didn't want the woman to see the elation in her face at having found a potential way out. She tried to relax her posture as Charlotte talked about reaching into the darkness. Charlotte wanted to take her back to many of the incidents of abuse at Lila's hands, but Josie didn't want to go there. She had spent her entire life fighting to get out from beneath the specter of those awful hours.

"Please don't," Josie said.

She felt Charlotte's hands in hers. "Fine then, dear. We don't have to go backward. We'll go forward instead. She pulled Josie's hands from her lap and wrapped them around her own throat. Josie's eyes snapped open. She tried to pull her hands away, but Charlotte held them fast around her paper-thin skin. Josie wasn't applying pressure, so she was able to speak easily.

"You're in control now. You have the power. Tell me what you would say to her. Imagine her face. Imagine making her pay for all the things she's done to you, all the ways she's made you suffer. The ways she still makes you suffer even though the damage was done long ago."

Josie tried to pull her fingers loose again, but Charlotte tightened her grip. "Don't fight it. What did she do to you, Josie? What did she do? She gave you that scar on your face, didn't she? She cut your skin. She tried to kill you."

Josie squeezed her eyes closed as the memories came rushing back at her. The gleam of the knife. The pool of blood in the kitchen where she dropped her stuffed dog, Wolfie. The feel of Lila's fingers bruising her chin. The stitches. The fear. The rage. The sense of betrayal that had lasted her entire life right up to this moment.

Charlotte said, "What is it she said to you? 'Not one word.'"

Josie's mind went completely blank. Charlotte disappeared. There was nothing in front of her. Nothing existed. Not light or dark or anything at all. Then the world crashed back in around her. Charlotte was pulling Josie's fingers away from her throat, gasping and coughing. Josie pushed her away and stood up from the bench, backing away.

Charlotte bent at the waist, hacking. She held up a hand in Josie's direction. When she could speak, she sputtered, "It's okay, dear. It's okay. I'm fine."

Josie's entire body shook. "I want to go back inside," she said.

Once Charlotte regained control of her breathing, she stood up straight. "Of course, dear. You've done so well. This is truly a breakthrough. Come, you can rest."

On trembling legs, Josie followed Charlotte back to the house. As they walked, a flicker of movement near the base of the house caught Josie's eye. It came from one of the basement windows. Josie looked at Charlotte's back. She didn't turn around.

One corner of the cardboard peeled back just a fraction.

Josie swore she saw a finger digging at the corner, trying to pull it away from the glass.

Her heart pounded like a jackhammer. Still, Charlotte didn't turn around. Josie slowed her pace.

Two fingers, then three, appeared in the corner of the window. Long, delicate fingers. A small diamond sparkled on one of them. Emilia. Josie almost gasped.

"We'll try again tomorrow," Charlotte said over her shoulder.

Suddenly, the fingers were snatched back into the darkness. Was Jack in there with her? Preventing her from escaping? Josie looked at Charlotte just as they rounded the house to alight onto the porch.

"Yes," Josie said. "Tomorrow." But she already knew that the only thing she'd be doing tomorrow was leaving this place. She now knew where the trail was to get out and where Emilia was. She only had to find a moment when Charlotte and Jack weren't breathing down her neck and she could escape.

CHAPTER FIFTY-THREE

Every muscle in Josie's body seemed permanently tensed. That night she had no trouble staying awake. Charlotte had left her untied and her legs bobbed against the thin mattress as Jack occasionally passed through the hallway. She could tell not by the creak of the hallway floor—he made no noise, he never did—but by the shadow that passed through the slit at the bottom of the door. She wondered if he ever slept. Getting past him was going to be the real problem, she realized. Even if it came to fighting, she knew she could take Charlotte, but Jack was large, strong and, it seemed, without humanity. Josie knew from the black walnut he had delivered to her that very little stood between her and Jack carrying out whatever sick fantasies he harbored about her. She knew he was itching to break every one of Charlotte's rules.

She thought of her team and wondered how close they were to finding her. She was certain Noah wouldn't sleep until she was safe. Imagining them out there searching for her buoyed her but she knew, deep down, that it was up to her to rescue Emilia and escape. If she could make it out of the house, she could easily kick in the glass of the basement window—she still wore her boots—but that might make too much noise. Although, she might not have a choice. She hadn't seen an entrance to the basement inside the house the entire time she'd been there.

After Jack's shadow passed her doorway for the second time, she waited as long as she could stand it. She had no idea what time it was, but she knew it was deep into the night. Surely he was asleep by now. When her heart started thudding so loudly in her chest she felt as though it might burst through bone and skin, she decided to just go for it.

Her heart hammered all the way through the upstairs hallway, down the steps, and into the foyer. As her fingers trembled on the front door lock, her heart skipped two beats, then roared back to life in double time as her hands worked slowly and methodically to unstick the screen door. She stepped through it, took three steps, and jumped from the porch. Her feet landed softly in the grass. It was a clear night. The moon shone overhead, lighting everything around her in a silver glow. The house sat silent and dark. No movement caught her eye.

Adrenaline had driven away all her weakness, dizziness, and exhaustion for the moment. With swift feet, she rounded the back of the house and found the two basement windows. Josie went to the one where she'd seen the fingers trying to pry away the cardboard. Someone had pushed it back into place. Feeling around the window frame, she tried to determine if she could somehow push it in or pull it out toward her. It wasn't meant to open at all, it seemed. It was just a long, flat pane of glass in a wooden frame, painted in thick blue. But the frame, like the other window frames on the outside of the house, looked semi-rotted, moist, and saggy.

Her knees sank into the damp grass. She had no idea what kind of sleeper Jack was, but she guessed he would wake at the slightest sound. Still, she had no choice. Josie sat down and then leaned backward, bracing her hands against the ground. She raised both feet, aimed at the small pane of glass, and with a heaving chest, kicked as hard as she could.

The entire window caved in with more of a *thunk* sound than a crack. Turning onto her knees, she used her bandaged hand to clear as much of the glass and wood as she could. Some of it fell into the darkness of the cellar, and the rest she tossed to the side. Poking her head in, she saw nothing but blackness. "Emilia," she whispered as loudly as she dared.

Nothing.

She pushed her shoulders into the opening. "Emilia," she called, raising her voice a little more.

The sound of a whimper came from the darkness.

Josie said, "Emilia, can you hear me?"

Another low whine.

Jack wouldn't have left her unbound after discovering she'd tried to peel away the cardboard covering the window, Josie realized, feeling sick. She'd have to go inside. There was no way to tell how steep the drop was, or how big the space inside. It mattered little: if Josie wanted to take Emilia with her, she was going to have to squeeze through the tiny hole into complete darkness and get her.

Terror clawed at her, making it hard to breathe, as she rolled onto her stomach and slid into her own worst nightmare. Into her past. Into her personal hell. Her late husband Ray's voice came back to her: *the darkness can't hurt you.*

He had been right; the darkness had never hurt her. It was always the monsters in the light, and she wasn't about to get caught by the one sleeping two floors up. Pushing her upper body through the opening, she fell, hands first, onto a hard-packed dirt floor. A stinging vibration shot from her wrists to her shoulders. Turning quickly onto her back, she was relieved to see a slice of moonlight illuminating the small rectangle that led back outside to freedom.

On her hands and knees, she felt her way around the room, calling out Emilia's name in a hiss. Each time she was rewarded with a small cry, and she changed her direction to match it until her hands bumped up against something that trembled beneath her touch. It was her. She squirmed madly beneath Josie's hands.

Josie said, "Emilia, my name is Josie Quinn. I'm a detective with the Denton police department. I've come to help you. I'm going to get you out of here, but we have to be very quiet."

Emilia stilled. Josie felt the limb beneath her with both hands until she realized she was touching Emilia's thigh. Moving her hands upward, she reached Emilia's face. Cloth was tied around her head, covering her mouth. Josie tore at it until she heard the woman take a deep, shuddering breath.

"My hands," Emilia said urgently. "Untie my hands and I can help you with my feet."

Relief washed over Josie. Emilia was ready and willing to get the hell out of there. Hands poked at Josie's neck. She reached up and grasped Emilia's bound wrists, feeling her way around the thick rope until she found the knot. Sweat poured from Josie's scalp and into her face as she tried to loosen it. The slice on her own hand burned. Her wrists ached. Finally, after what seemed like hours, she freed Emilia's hands. Their heads clashed together as Emilia sat upward like a shot. The impact caused a flash of light behind Josie's eyes. She fell backward, holding her head.

Emilia whispered. "I am so sorry. Are you okay? Tell me you're okay."

"I'm fine," Josie croaked, feeling momentarily disoriented. "Can you get your legs free? We have to get out of here."

There was a rustling as Emilia tried to untie her ankles. "Where's Jack?" she asked.

Josie said, "Sleeping, I hope.

"He sleeps pretty deeply," Emilia said. "But only a few hours at a time."

Josie heard rope drop to the floor. Then Emilia said, "Let's go."

They found each other's hands and stood up. "There," Josie said, pointing to the smashed-in window. "When you get out, run in a straight line, do you understand? Into the trees. Wait for me there. If anything happens—if you see Jack or Charlotte or you hear any-thing—just run. Don't stop. Not for anything. Do you understand?"

Emilia squeezed her hand and Josie took that as a yes. While Emilia pulled herself up and through the opening, gasping as she scraped over shards of glass, Josie pushed her thighs and rear-end from the cellar floor. Once she was through, Josie listened for her footfalls through the grass, flinching when she heard the crunch and snap of twigs which signified that Emilia had made it to the treeline.

Josie scrambled up, feeling her pants tear on the glass, hearing it crunch beneath her body as she fit herself through the opening. The night air was thick and humid but after the close confines of the cellar, it felt heavenly. Josie got to her feet, swaying with fatigue, her nerves jangling. Emilia hissed, "Over here," and Josie followed the sound until her own feet crunched over the debris on the forest floor. They clung to each other. Out here, as her eyes adjusted once more, Josie could see the other woman's dirt-streaked face. Emilia smiled at her, then reached down and took her hand.

"Thank you for coming," she said.

Josie nodded. "We have to get out of here right now. As fast as we can. There's a trail." She pulled Emilia along. "This way."

All Josie could hear was a roar inside her head and somewhere beneath it, the sounds of their labored breath mingling. They found the willow, then the trail behind it, and raced along it as quickly as they could. It felt like miles. Josie had no way of knowing where it came out, and she knew she didn't have time to stop and question Emilia as to what she might know about where they were.

Josie's lungs burned with the effort of running so fast and so far after being kept prisoner for so long. Emilia slowed down incrementally, and Josie urged her on, driven by desperation.

Then something hard hit Josie directly in the chest, sending her flying backward. Her hand tore from Emilia's and then a scream ripped through the night. Her head hit the trunk of a tree. Josie blinked and realized she was flat on her back. The moonlight filtered through the treetops in eerie slants of dull light. She searched for Emilia, her ears pricked for the sound of her crying or breathing—something.

Then a long, dark shadow blotted out what little moonlight was left.

"Where do you think you're going?" said Jack.

CHAPTER FIFTY-FOUR

A primal shriek rose from the depths of Josie's diaphragm, bouncing and echoing off the trees around them. Every ache and pain in her body forgotten, she clambered to her feet and charged at Jack, driving her shoulder into his hip. As her body made contact with his, he buckled but didn't fall. When she realized he wasn't going down, Josie stayed close and rammed her elbows into his mid-section. He was an impenetrable wall. Jack swiped at her head, catching her temple and sending her back to the ground. As one of his hands clamped down on her upper arm, another howl reverberated through the surrounding trees. Emilia was a black shadow flying through the air as she jumped onto Jack's back. He whirled around, hands reaching behind him to try to grab her.

On the ground, Josie felt around her until her hand closed around a large tree branch, a little longer than a baseball bat but thick enough to do some damage. She hoped it would be enough to help them get away. Jack thrashed with Emilia tight on his back, her thin arms wrapped around his throat. He reached up with both hands, trying to pull her loose, but she held tightly. Josie ran at him, drawing the branch back and swinging with all her might. It hit his midsection, but he barely seemed to notice. He whirled around and slammed Emilia against a nearby tree. With a broken cry, she slid off his back and slumped to the ground, unmoving. Fear drove a spike through Josie's heart. Had he killed her? Had the two of them escaped and come all this way just for Emilia to die?

Josie swung at him again as he turned to look for her, this time hitting him in the kidneys. He grunted but kept coming. Next she aimed for his knee, making solid contact, causing him to stumble. But he was too strong, too energized. He was enjoying this, she realized. This was his darkness. Not just the stalking or the imprisonment. It was the violence of the chase that brought him to life. Regaining his footing, he reached for her. She backed up and swung the branch again, missing him and losing her balance. As she fell forward, he caught her. Lifting her as though she weighed nothing, he pressed her back against the nearest tree and then held her there, one hand pinning her sternum and the other closing around her throat. She clawed at his eyes, but he merely straightened his arms so she couldn't reach his face. She scratched her nails along his arms, up his wrists, feeling for the pinky fingers on each of his hands. If she could just peel one finger away and snap it like a twig, she might stun him long enough to get away.

His fingers didn't budge. Josie felt her consciousness unmoor, felt herself floating off into the deep blackness of oblivion. *No*, a voice in her head cried. *Not like this. Not now.* Even as she willed her body to keep fighting, her arms fell away, slack and useless.

Then the pressure was gone. Josie's upper body folded in on itself. She braced her hands against her knees, trying to stay upright. From somewhere to her left came the sounds of grunts and the crunch of bone, as well as the rustle of the forest floor being disturbed. Josie blinked several times, trying to bring the shapes into focus. Two bodies on the ground. Jack and someone else. Far too large to be Emilia. Josie looked in the other direction and saw Emilia, still motionless on the ground.

She looked back to see that one of the men had straddled the other. She took a step closer and saw that it was Jack pinned down on his back. The other man rained down blows on his face. She heard a crack. Definitely bone. Something wet slapped against her face. She reached up and touched it. The coppery smell told her it was blood. She stepped forward again and grabbed at the attacker's shoulder. "Stop," she said. "Stop."

The man ceased punching. Breathing hard, he hefted himself from Jack's immobile body and stood. Turning, she saw his face in the moonlight and stumbled backward. "Donovan?" she said.

The hermit stood before her, his dark, flinty eyes gleaming. For a moment, Josie wondered if she was hallucinating. "What are you—what are you doing here?" she asked, realizing that she must have been at Charlotte and Jack's hideaway long enough that Andrew Bowen had managed to get Michael Donovan released from jail.

"Come on," he said roughly.

"No," Josie said. "I'm not going anywhere with you. I'm going home."

He shook his head, as if annoyed with her. Then he walked over and knelt beside Emilia.

"Leave her alone," Josie said but as she drew closer, she saw he was checking Emilia's throat for a pulse.

"She's alive," he said flatly.

Relief flooded through Josie. She moved closer and knelt beside him. "I'll take care of her, but we're not going with you."

He chuckled. "I'm not going to hurt you. I don't care about you—or her."

"Then why are you here?" Josie asked. "Where are we?"

"North of Denton." He leaned forward and slid his hands under Emilia's body. Lifting her easily, he slung her over one of his shoulders. He stood and started walking, stepping over Jack's body. Josie didn't stop to see if he was alive or not. She had no idea what the hell was happening, and she didn't have time to help the man who had just tried to kill both her and Emilia.

"You didn't answer my question," she said as she jogged to keep up with the hermit's long and easy strides. "What were you doing here?"

"Looking for supplies," he said gruffly.

"You must be miles from your caverns," she said.

"You want to go home or not?" he snapped.

"You're taking us home?"

"Shut up and walk."

She followed him until the first fingers of light crept up the horizon. Occasionally, Emilia groaned, the sound a sweet relief because it meant she was alive. There was no way for Josie to know how far they had walked but by the time they reached a road, she felt so weak that she was afraid if she stopped moving, she'd never start again. Dawn was pink and yellow, and fog rose from the asphalt as the hermit stopped at the shoulder of the road. Josie saw nothing in either direction but more trees.

"Where are we?" she asked.

"A road."

He walked along the shoulder until he found a spot where a large oak tree shaded the side of the road. "Sit," he told her.

"What?" Josie said. "Why?"

"Shut up and sit."

Too tired to argue, she sank to the ground. Carefully, he laid Emilia down with her head cradled in Josie's lap. Then he turned and began walking away.

"Wait," Josie called. "Where are you going?"

He didn't turn to look at her, just called over his shoulder. "Someone will find you here."

"You can't just leave us here," Josie shouted after him. "Emilia is hurt. She needs medical care."

"Shut up and wait," he said and disappeared into the trees.

CHAPTER FIFTY-FIVE

The sun was high in the sky by the time Emilia's eyes fluttered open. The day grew hotter with each minute, it seemed. Even in the blessed shade, both of them were drenched with sweat. Josie's lower body was numb. She'd fallen in and out of sleep, perking up when she thought she heard a vehicle, only to realize it had been in her head. She wasn't even sure at this point what was real and what was not. She stroked the hair away from Emilia's face and looked into her eyes.

Emilia said, "Where are we?"

Laughter bubbled up from Josie's stomach, uncontrollable. Emilia's head bobbed in her lap as it escaped from her mouth. "I d-don't k-know," she stammered.

Emilia turned her head toward the road. "How did we get here?"

"You wouldn't believe me if I told you," Josie answered.

"Tell me."

Josie recounted the night's events and then explained who the hermit was and how Josie had come to know of him. As she spoke, Emilia tested out each of her limbs. She tried to sit up, but fell back immediately, squeezing her eyes shut. After a few moments, she tried again, moving slowly with Josie's help. "There's two of everything," she said.

"Yeah," Josie said. "You took a pretty good hit. You need to go to the hospital."

Emilia leaned against Josie, fitting her head on Josie's shoulder. "We're just waiting then?"

"Yes," Josie said. "Someone has to drive down this road at some point today. I hope."

They sat in silence and Josie wondered about Jack. What if he looked for them? What if he found them? They were far too weak and injured to fight him off. Had the hermit killed him or just injured him? Had Charlotte gone looking for him? She certainly couldn't mobilize anyone else from the Sanctuary. Josie knew that her team would have questioned everyone there and when they found Charlotte absent, zeroed in on her and her people. They would be watching the Sanctuary members to see if they'd lead them to Josie's location.

Emilia said, "I'm so thirsty."

"Me too," Josie replied.

"What do we do if no one comes?"

"Someone will come."

"What if they don't?"

To distract her, Josie asked, "My team responded to the scene at your campsite. That's when we realized you were missing. Do you remember what happened when you were camping with Tyler and Valerie?"

Emilia's head sagged against Josie's shoulder. She sniffled. "We were camped there for two days. We'd looked around a bit and found a break in the fence around that place—the Sanctuary or whatever. We'd been out all day figuring out the best way to get on and off the Sanctuary property and then we came back to camp to eat. Soon after that, Tyler and Valerie got sick. I was packing up my backpack to go and get them help when I saw Jack in the woods. At first, I was so happy to see him. So relieved. I just dropped everything and ran to him. I thought he would help me. But he was so… weird. So still. Just watching. He said to come with him, and we'd get help together. I followed him into the Sanctuary. He took me to this old, broken-down cabin and told me to wait there. I did at first, but it was so creepy there. Then, he took a really long time, and I was worried that Val and Tyler wouldn't get help in time. So I left and walked and walked. Then I saw the house. All these people were working in the garden. I started toward them but then Jack came out of the house."

"Did he tell you about Valerie and Tyler?" Josie asked gently.

She felt Emilia's nod against her shoulder. "He told me they didn't make it. That he thought they had eaten something toxic, probably from the woods. But I was with them the whole time. They didn't eat anything they weren't supposed to."

"He told you he'd take you into town, didn't he?" Josie asked. "To get you into a car."

"Yes. It wasn't until we were already on the road that I realized he was lying. You have to understand. He's my husband. I thought—I thought that deep down the man I married would shine through. Val and Tyler were our best friends. It was unimaginable to me that he'd harm them and then turn on me as well."

"But he did."

"I panicked in the car and then he told me he hadn't meant to kill them, only to make them a little sick so he could get me alone. He just wanted to talk, he said. He wanted me to join him. He kept talking about all this weird stuff like becoming—and embracing—the darkness inside. He said all his life he had fought against the darkness within him, but at the Sanctuary he didn't have to fight. He could be whoever he wanted to be. He didn't have to be ashamed anymore. It was just weird. It made no sense. I told him to stop: stop talking and stop the car and let me out."

"But he didn't."

Josie felt the shake of Emilia's head against her body.

"I tried to open the door. I was going to jump from the moving car. He hit me. That's the last thing I remember. Then I woke up in the cellar. I don't even know how long I was there. Do you know how long it's been? Since Val and Tyler died?"

"I'm sorry," Josie said. "I don't. I lost track of how long I was at that house."

Emilia reached down and squeezed her hand. "We're free now, and soon we'll be found."

It was nearing dusk when a vehicle finally appeared on the horizon. Josie staggered to her feet, pulling Emilia behind her. The car rolled to a stop as Josie and Emilia made it to the double yellow lines in the middle of the road. A woman Josie didn't recognize got out of the vehicle, squinting at them as if she wasn't sure of what she was seeing. "Hey," she said. "You're those women on the news. The ones they're looking for."

"Yes," Josie said. "We are."

CHAPTER FIFTY-SIX

True to his word, the hermit had left them along a rural route in a town north of Denton. Their rescuer used her cell phone to call 911 as she drove them to Denton Memorial Hospital. Noah, Gretchen, Mettner, Lamay—and even Chief Chitwood—were standing in a line outside the Emergency Room entrance as the woman pulled up. Each of them looked haggard and hopeful at the same time. A patchy beard covered Noah's face. Circles smudged the skin beneath his eyes. Before the car even pulled to a stop, he flung the back door open and reached inside for Josie. He lifted her out and enveloped her in his arms, burying his face in her matted hair. She felt his body shake around her. Into her ear he said, "I thought we lost you."

Josie inhaled his scent and closed her eyes, collapsing into him. "You can't get rid of me that easily."

A hand touched her shoulder. She opened her eyes to see Gretchen staring at her, tears streaming down her face. "I know you're not crying, Palmer," Josie said.

Gretchen wiped the tears away and grinned. "I've got allergies," she choked.

Mettner and Lamay approached, each one of them reaching forward and gently squeezing her arm. They flanked Noah as he walked her toward the hospital doors. Josie looked back to see Chitwood and two nurses lifting Emilia from the back of the car into a wheelchair.

"You okay?" Noah asked.

"Yes," Josie answered. "I am now. Just tired and bruised."

*

Emilia was admitted for severe dehydration and a small subdural hematoma. Josie was discharged after a few hours, having received IV fluids, a new dressing on her left hand, and some pain medication. Noah wanted to take her directly home, but she wanted to go to the station and give her statement right away so they could figure out where Charlotte and Jack had been hiding her and track them down. She recounted her ordeal in as much detail as she could muster, leaving out the parts about Lila Jensen, only saying that Charlotte had tried to recruit her to avoid kidnapping charges.

It was almost morning by the time Gretchen came into the conference room with a sheaf of papers. "I found it," she said.

"Found what?" Noah asked.

"The property. I mean, I think. Charlotte's husband inherited several properties from his mother. While she was living, she transferred the largest property into his name. That was the Sanctuary. But these other properties—" She spread several pages across the table. "They stayed in her name. He never transferred them. They passed to him after her death, but he never had the titles changed. Then he married Charlotte. Everything he owned became hers when he died."

"But she didn't bother to change any of the properties over into her own name," Josie said. "Except the Sanctuary."

"Right. It would have been a project. She would have had to get a death certificate for Mick Fadden's mother to prove that she had passed. Then there would have been the issue of her will—did she have one or didn't she? She would have had to provide proof one way or another that the properties passed to him and then to her."

"It wasn't worth it," Mettner said.

"Right," Noah agreed. "As long as she paid the property taxes on these premises—"

"All of which were paid off, so there was no mortgage," Gretchen put in.

"Then she could just keep them," Noah finished.

"We should have thought of this before," Mettner said, a look of defeat on his face.

Josie said, "Don't beat yourself up, Mett. I didn't think of it either. We really didn't even know Charlotte was a threat until it was too late."

"She ran a cult," Mettner replied. "Seems like that's a pretty big red flag."

"Okay," Noah said, gazing at the pages Gretchen had spread before them. "Let's see what we've got."

They pored over the deeds and then several maps. Only one of the properties was near Denton, toward the north where Josie and Emilia had been found. The other two were in Lenore County, far south. Gretchen pointed to the property on a satellite map she'd printed out. "It has to be this one."

Josie leaned forward and studied the map. She found the faint trail through the woods that she and Emilia had taken. What she hadn't been able to see, especially in the dark, was that about a half mile down that trail was another path that veered to the right. That led to a gravel driveway which led down to a road. Still, it was extremely remote.

Gretchen said, "Chitwood wants a team to go in at first light. If they're still there, we'll get them."

"I'm going," Noah said.

Josie reached over and clutched his forearm. "Please," she said. "Don't. Stay with me."

He stared at her. She could see the conflict in his eyes, but ultimately, she won. He put a warm hand over hers. "Fine," he said. "Let's go home."

"No," she replied. "I want to stay until I know they've caught Charlotte and Jack."

Gretchen said, "Komorrah's will be open in a half hour. I'll run down there and get reinforcements."

Mettner and Gretchen led a team of uniformed officers onto Charlotte's property north of Denton. Josie and Noah waited with Dan Lamay behind the front counter at the station house, listening to the radio calls coming in. Jack was still alive—in need of medical attention, but alive—and once Denton PD had both him and Charlotte in custody, Josie turned to Noah and said, "Take me home. I'm going to sleep for days."

CHAPTER FIFTY-SEVEN

Josie did sleep for almost twenty-four hours straight. Noah tried to wake her a couple of times to eat, but her exhaustion was so bone deep, she could only eat a few bites of whatever he made her before falling back into a deep, dreamless sleep. When she finally woke, he brought her eggs, pancakes, and bacon in bed and updated her. Jack and Charlotte had been booked on so many charges Noah couldn't even remember them all. Charlotte wasn't talking at all and had already hired an attorney, but Jack talked almost immediately, corroborating what Emilia had told Josie. He had used the wild hemlock on the Yates couple but for Josie he used GHB, a date rape drug that was usually undetectable in a person's system soon after it was used. He'd gotten it from a dealer under Denton's Eastern Bridge when accompanying one of the other Sanctuary members on a thrift run. He'd been watching Josie and her team as they came and went from the Sanctuary and become fixated on her. It had been his idea and his choice to take her, not Charlotte's.

Josie had told her team that Jack had brought Maya Bestler onto the Sanctuary for some period of time but when they asked him about her, he would only say he had seen her at the charity benefit when he worked for Lantz. He had found her attractive and wanted to approach her, but things hadn't gone well with Shana so he didn't. Josie knew he was lying but couldn't prove it. No one had seen or heard from Maya. Sandy and Gus Bestler had taken their grandson and returned to their hometown.

The best news was that Emilia was doing well. Her sister was already in Denton when she was found and had not left her side in the hospital. Noah said Emilia was filing for divorce from Jack at her first opportunity.

After breakfast in bed, Josie showered and dressed, feeling like her old self finally. As she descended the stairs, she heard female voices coming from her living room. On her couch sat her grandmother, Lisette Matson, and her mother, Shannon Payne. Noah stood in the foyer. Josie hugged the two women but gave Noah a questioning look. Something wasn't quite right. She could feel the tension in the room.

"What's going on?" she said.

Noah jammed his hands in his jeans pockets. "We know about Muncy, Josie."

She was going to ask how, but then she remembered Noah telling her that they'd found her phone in the woods not far from where Jack had taken her. They would have checked it to see if there was anything on it to help them find her.

She sank down to the couch between Lisette and Shannon. "Is she dead?" Josie asked.

"No," Shannon said. "Not yet. But she's very sick, they said. It won't be long now."

Lisette took Josie's hand and squeezed it. "You know," she said. "She hurt you most of all, but she also hurt us."

Lisette and Shannon exchanged a look over Josie's head and for the first time in their presence, Josie felt like a small child whose mother and grandmother had been conferring about. Shannon said, "We have a right to speak to her before she passes. I hope you understand that."

Josie said, "You don't need my permission to see her. You know that."

Lisette said, "We're not asking your permission, Josie. We want you to come with us."

"I don't want to see her," Josie said.

Shannon said, "Josie, you do understand that this will be your last chance to say anything you might need to say to her. We're worried that if you don't take it, it will harm you."

"I'm not going to forgive her just because she's dying," Josie said. "The things she did were unforgiveable."

"We're not suggesting you forgive her," Lisette said.

"Then what?" Josie said, irritation sharpening her tone.

Shannon shrugged. "We don't know. But it might come to you when you see her. Whatever it is that you might want or need to say."

"Or you might not need to say anything at all," Lisette said.

Josie looked at her grandmother, then at Shannon. "You two have things to say to her?"

"Yes," they said in unison.

Josie sighed. "Then let's go."

CHAPTER FIFTY-EIGHT

Lila Jensen didn't look at all like the woman Josie had put behind bars nearly two years ago. In her hospice bed she was a shrunken bag of bones, her cheeks sallow and sunken. Her hair was gray and thin. She looked as though she had aged a thousand years since Josie had last seen her. When she breathed, a sound like a child's rattle shook from her chest and bubbled up in her throat. The smell in the room was at once musty and moist, foul and sweet. It was the smell of impending death, Josie realized. This was it. This woman would finally be gone from Josie's life, from the world, forever.

Josie watched as Lisette went into the room. She stood over Lila and spoke in a firm but low voice. Josie couldn't make out any of the words, but Lisette stood tall and resolute while she delivered her speech over Lila's withered form. She held her head high as she pushed her walker back out into the hallway where Josie and Shannon waited.

Shannon went in next. She touched Lila's arm, letting her fingertips linger. Then she leaned down and whispered into Lila's ear, making her jump and squirm. She let go and walked toward the doorway, holding herself carefully as if it hurt to move. "What did you say to her?" Josie asked.

Shannon gave a sad smile. "That's between me and her, honey."

Josie stood in the doorway for a long time, debating whether to go in or not. She didn't have to do this. She didn't care what everyone else thought was good for her. She didn't care what Charlotte had tried to tell her about killing Lila—about tuning into her basest impulses the way that Lila had done since birth. None of that mattered. If Josie didn't want to give this one last thing to Lila, she didn't have to. She could turn and walk away and let Lila die without ever having seen her or heard her voice again. But before she even realized it, her feet were carrying her across the room. She stood looking down into Lila's wretched face. "It's me," she said. "I'm here, like you asked."

The name scraped over Lila's chapped lips. "JoJo."

Josie winced. Lila's hand reached up, searching. Her eyes blinked, trying to bring Josie into focus. "JoJo."

Josie recoiled but the hand found her wrist anyway, clutching it with a strength Josie hadn't expected from this dying shell of a woman. What was Josie supposed to say? Lisette and Shannon had come prepared. They had obviously been thirsting for this opportunity, but Josie was at a loss. What should she say? *You stole my life? Destroyed my childhood? Killed the man I believed was my father? I hate you?*

But Josie didn't hate her. That was the problem. That had always been the problem. Her entire life, she had grown up believing that Lila was her mother, trying and failing to figure out what was so wrong with her, so terrible about her, that her own mother couldn't love her. Her entire life, Josie had struggled to figure out why her own mother was so cruel toward her. She must have come into the world broken, flawed, unlovable. Why else would a mother treat her own child with such brutality? All Josie had ever wanted from the woman was love.

Even though she now knew that Lila wasn't her mother and wasn't capable of love, the wounds in Josie's psyche remained. Knowing that Lila hadn't really been her mother, that she had taken her from a loving stable home—in some ways it felt worse. On top of the abuse she had suffered and the deep scars that Lila had left, now there was bitterness for all that had been lost.

No, not lost. *Stolen.* By a woman who cared for nothing and for no one but herself. A woman who was so selfish that on her deathbed she made demands of the girl she had tortured for so many years.

Josie tried to twist her wrist from Lila's grip, but she couldn't. She looked to the doorway where Lisette and Shannon stood huddled together for comfort, their backs to Josie and Lila. No one else was near. She could so easily reach out with her free hand and squeeze Lila's frail neck, strangle the life out of her, rid the world of the terrifying darkness she'd wielded for so long. Shatter her hyoid just like Jack had done to his victims.

But then she'd be just like Jack.

Maybe there had been light in him like Charlotte said. He must have had some good in him to draw a woman as gentle and kind as Emilia. But the Sanctuary had vanquished any goodness left in him. It had snuffed out the light inside of him.

Josie looked from Lila's ravaged face back to Shannon and Lisette again. Lisette's gnarled hands drew Shannon's face to hers. They pressed their foreheads together. Tears glistened on both their cheeks. They spoke softly to one another and then they both laughed quietly. Not the kind of laughter that came from finding something funny but the kind that had to come out just to break unbearable tension. The kind that came from trying hard just to breathe beneath the weight of something heavy and horrible, if only for a few precious seconds. The kind that came when nothing was funny—not even a little bit—and because nothing was funny. It was humanity clawing its way out of hell, demanding optimism that didn't yet exist.

Josie felt a yearning break open inside her, tugging at her like the earth's gravity. Away from Lila, back toward the people who loved her. Back toward the light. Josie had seen what happened when a person embraced their darkness. She'd been on the receiving end of it for years. She didn't need more darkness. She wanted to stay in the light, where she could help people. Charlotte was wrong, Josie realized. Her power came not from killing Lila but from helping put people like Lila behind bars where they couldn't hurt others ever again. She could hold onto her light and her power, and Lila couldn't take that away from her—in life or in death.

With her free hand, she reached down and smoothed the hair away from Lila's forehead. "M-mom," she choked out.

A smile spread across Lila's face. She pulled Josie down closer and said, "You're a good kid, JoJo." Then she released Josie's arm and drew her last breath.

CHAPTER FIFTY-NINE

A week later, Josie returned to her desk at the station house only to find it piled high with paperwork. She fished through it as Chief Chitwood passed by her desk. "That's the Bestler crap," he said. "Put it in some order so we can get rid of it. It's a closed case."

She wanted to tell him that he could have done that himself, but he was already in his office with the door slamming shut behind him. Gretchen appeared beside her with a coffee and a cheese Danish.

"You're the best," Josie said with a smile.

"I'll help you," Gretchen told her.

They began thumbing through reports and photos, maps and statements, organizing everything. "Did the DNA come back on Bestler's baby?" Josie asked.

"Oh yeah," Gretchen said. "But it wasn't a match to Michael Donovan."

Josie looked up. "The hermit wasn't the father?"

"Nope."

"Did they figure out who?"

Gretchen said, "Nope. They ran it through the database. Didn't get a hit."

Josie shook her head. It didn't matter now. They no longer needed to solve the mystery of the baby's paternity. There was no case. The baby was safe and being raised by Maya's parents. Of course, Josie had her suspicions but thus far, she hadn't been able to prove a damn thing.

"Do you have the section of the file with the photos?" Gretchen asked. "I need to put these photos in there with the rest of them."

Josie riffled through the folders in her hands. "Yes, right here."

She took the stack of photographs Gretchen held out to her. They were of Maya Bestler when she was examined at the hospital and had been taken to document her injuries. Josie went through them, grimacing at the lacerations on her feet. She stopped at the photos of the scars on Maya's wrists. Josie had had similar marks on her own wrists after a few days in Jack and Charlotte's custody, although she'd been told by the doctor they wouldn't leave permanent scars. She kept going until she came to a photo of a bruise on Maya's right hip. The skin next to it, where her abdomen began, was stretched and loose from her pregnancy. Josie was about to put it back into the pile when a small line of scar tissue caught her eye.

"Gretchen," she said.

"Yeah?" She walked over and put her reading glasses on, looking at the photo over Josie's shoulder.

Josie pointed to the lines of thick, lumpy skin that stood out from the depressions of the stretch marks surrounding it. "What does that look like to you?"

Gretchen studied it for a long moment. "Well, the skin is really stretched out but I think it looks like a C and a backwards C."

Josie shot out of her chair, heart pounding. "I need that list of properties still in Charlotte Fadden's mother-in-law's name."

"You got it, boss," Gretchen said, moving around to her own desk and shuffling papers around.

"And call the lab, would you? See if they got any results on that piece of rope I found in the Sanctuary cabin. Also, have them run Baby Bestler's DNA through CODIS again. This time, they should get a hit."

CHAPTER SIXTY

"I want to go in alone," Josie said.

"Absolutely not," Noah protested.

The team, which consisted of Josie, Noah, Mettner, Gretchen, and Lenore deputies Moore and Nash, stood at the foot of a long, paved driveway in lower Lenore County. It was a half-mile long, by Josie's estimate, and the house at the end of it, a squat rancher with tan siding, was almost entirely obscured by tall evergreen bushes. The property was well-kept, and Josie knew from the records it consisted of six acres. Most of those acres were in the woods behind the house.

"She's almost completely deaf, remember?" Josie said.

"You don't know who else might be in there," Noah pointed out.

"I'll have my radio on."

"No," Noah said.

"We'll move the perimeter closer to the house," Moore suggested.

"Right outside the house," Noah said. "That's the only way you're going in alone, Josie."

Josie rolled her eyes. "Fine, but stay out of sight. She's not going to tell me anything if she sees what looks like a damn SWAT team waiting outside for her."

Gretchen held out a bullet-proof vest to Josie. "Let's do this."

They crept up toward the house, moving in columns on either side of the driveway. Once past the bushes, they fanned out, staying low and running until they reached the sides of the house. No vehicles were visible although there was a detached garage with its doors closed. Josie, gun holstered, walked casually up to the door and knocked. She waited several minutes and knocked again. Then she jiggled the doorknob.

"Josie," Noah hissed. "You can't just go in there."

"I can if I think someone is in danger," she said.

The knob twisted in her hand and the door swung open. "Hello?" Josie called.

There was no answer but Josie heard the sound of a woman crying.

Josie signaled to the team to move in behind her but quietly. She walked into a sparsely furnished living room with plain white walls. A brown couch with a standing lamp beside it sat along one wall. A purple fleece blanket was crumpled on one end of the couch. The place looked unlived-in and impersonal. Josie kept walking. Next was a dining room with an old wooden oval-shaped table and six matching chairs pushed beneath it. Again, there was no evidence that the room had been used recently.

Beyond that was the kitchen, decorated in cheery yellow colors with gray tile. Maya Bestler stood in front of an island countertop. She wore a form-fitting black cotton top and khaki shorts. Her hair was in disarray; her face pale; eyes wide. Both her hands were fisted and pressed up under her chin. She looked up as Josie came closer. Her face filled with shock or relief, Josie couldn't tell which.

"Maya," Josie said, taking care to look right into Maya's face. "Are you here alone?"

Maya turned her body and jerked her head toward the area behind the island countertop. Josie's heartbeat picked up. She noted the bowls and utensils on the counter as she moved slowly past it. One bowl was overturned, its soupy liquid congealing on the countertop. A spoon lay a few inches away. The next thing she saw were a pair of feet on the floor. Her eyes moved from the bare feet to the man's face. His eyes bulged over a pale face and blue lips. Froth and vomit leaked from his mouth, down his neck and onto the floor beneath him.

Josie knelt and pressed two fingers to the hermit's throat.

"He's dead," Maya said.

She was right. Josie could tell from his glassy, vacant stare, but the first responder in her had to check for a pulse. As she stood, she saw Noah, Gretchen, and the rest of the team crowding in the doorway, silent. She gave a little shake of her head, willing them to stay there for a moment. She stood back up and looked at Maya. "What did you give him?"

Maya's voice was a barely audible squeak. "Foxglove."

Josie nodded. "This was the first time you gave him foxglove, wasn't it? He didn't take you, did he?"

Maya shook her head.

"Want to tell me who did?"

"You already know, don't you? Or you wouldn't be here."

"I do," Josie said. "Tell me, did Jack take you by force or did you go willingly?"

Maya didn't answer.

Josie moved closer and pointed to the scars on Maya's wrists. "You made a pact with Jack, didn't you? You helped him."

A little bit of air seemed to go out of her. "Yes," she breathed.

"You met at the charity benefit," Josie said. "Jack became fixated on you."

"He talked to me. Began stopping by where I worked for lunch every day. We had a connection."

"Then he started talking to you about the Sanctuary."

"Yes. He wanted me to come with him, and I wanted to go but I knew Garrett would kill me. I told him that. I told him I'd tried to leave Garrett many times, but I couldn't. He really would kill me. Jack came up with this idea."

"You staged your kidnapping," Josie said.

"No, Jack staged it. It was all his idea. I didn't actually think he would go through with it. But he did. Then I was at the Sanctuary. It was wonderful. I kept waiting for the police to show up or for

Garrett to come after me, but they didn't. I felt so at peace there for the first time ever. When Charlotte asked me to make the commitment, it was a no-brainer."

"You didn't worry about your family? They thought you'd been murdered," Josie said.

A tear rolled down Maya's cheek. "I felt bad about my dad. For sure. I thought about him every day. But I didn't feel bad at all for my judgmental bitch of a mom. She was probably glad to be rid of me."

Josie thought Maya had misread Sandy Bestler, but she didn't bother to correct her. "If it was so wonderful, why leave?"

"Because of Jack. Sort of. The Sanctuary is all about balancing your inner self. Light against dark. Dark against light. Well, really it's about finding your dark side, I guess."

"Because you're all victims?" Josie said, unable to keep the note of sarcasm out of her voice.

"But we *were* all victims," Maya said earnestly. She pointed at her own chest. "Especially me, and when I got there and started helping Jack, I realized I was just being victimized all over again. He just wanted to act out his sick fantasies on me." She held up her wrists. "And it was okay because I consented to it."

"But it wasn't okay," Josie said.

"I didn't like it," Maya admitted. "It wasn't—it wasn't what I signed up for. I went along with it because I was kind of in love with him, but he changed. He became harder, colder, and me? I never got to find my own darkness. It was all about him and his impulses and him finding his power."

"I found a piece of rope in one of the cabins," Josie said. "DNA showed that it was your blood on it."

"Yes, that's where he would take me to act out his… scenarios. He tried to give me this necklace he made—a leather band with a walnut on it. A black walnut. He liked it because it was kind of heart-shaped when you split it open and looked inside. Also, he said there was something about the roots of the tree it came from. Something they gave off. It was toxic, like him, he said. But his love for me balanced it out. Some weird stuff like that." She gave a nervous laugh. "He wanted me to wear it while we… did things. It was a gift, he said. Like tying me up and having sex while he strangled me half to death was so romantic. I don't think it was ever love for him. I think it was some twisted desire. 'Cause I know that eventually he started acting his fantasies out with some other girl there too. He always said he didn't really like her, but it didn't stop him from being with her. Anyway, things with him could get rough sometimes."

"I know," Josie said. "That girl's name was Renee Kelly. After you left, he murdered her. The medical examiner pulled a black walnut necklace out of her throat."

Maya's eyes widened. A hand flew to her chest. "Oh Jesus."

"When things got bad with Jack, why didn't you just leave?" Josie asked.

"Because I had made a mess of things, hadn't I? I couldn't just waltz back into the world and tell everyone I faked them out. But I did try to leave a few times. I mean I got so far and then I chickened out."

"The break in the fence," Josie said. "Did you do that?"

"No. A tree fell there, but I used it to get on and off the property without anyone realizing it. Well, until I met Michael."

She glanced past Josie to where the hermit's body lay on the tile.

Josie caught her eye again. "He didn't force you back to his cave, did he?"

"No," Maya said softly. "I didn't even go there at first. We just started to meet up sometimes in the woods. He was so… fascinating."

Josie thought about how little Michael Donovan had said even after saving her and Emilia. How he wouldn't answer any questions. Under other circumstances, perhaps his mysteriousness would have held some allure. Maybe not to Josie but to someone like Maya, trapped and looking for a way out that didn't involve her returning to civilization.

Josie couldn't believe the words were coming out of her mouth, but she said, "You had an affair."

Maya nodded.

"But you were already pregnant with Jack's child."

"How did you know that?"

Josie pursed her lips and then said, "DNA. Michael Donovan was already in the system because he killed his wife many years ago. Jack wasn't in the system until he was arrested for murder and for kidnapping me and Emilia. I had the lab run your baby's DNA through the database again, and he came up as a familial hit."

"Michael wasn't happy. He figured out very quickly that I was pregnant and when he did the math it was pretty obvious it wasn't his."

"But you had told him he was the only one you were sleeping with?"

"Well, yeah."

"He became violent with you, didn't he?"

Another nod. More tears. "I stopped seeing him after that. Went back to the Sanctuary. I told Jack he couldn't do those things to me anymore because I was pregnant. Charlotte wanted me to make arrangements to leave. She said no children on the property."

"But then you were about to give birth, and Jack killed two people and took Emilia."

"Yes."

"And when you take the commitment, you promise to be loyal to the Sanctuary and do whatever it takes to protect it."

"Right," Maya said.

"Whose idea was it to frame Michael for your abduction and Emilia's disappearance?"

"Jack's," she said, and Josie suspected this was a lie. If it had been Jack's idea, he would have made sure that the Yateses' and

Emilia's things were in Michael's cave before Maya stumbled out of the woods. Instead, it was Maya, at nine months pregnant, who had gone.

Josie said, "You went to the campsite first, but Michael had already taken enough from there to make himself look guilty."

"Yes," Maya said.

"And when you got to his cavern, you knew the things were there."

"Yeah. I went in to check. He was off trapping or foraging or whatever."

"So you framed him and once he was released, he went looking for you. He checked all of Charlotte's properties."

Maya said nothing. Josie went back to Michael's body and looked from it back to Maya. "Where is the mark?" she asked.

"What?"

"Michael made the commitment. Where is his mark? The back of his neck? His hip?"

Maya's body began to tremble. "How do you know that?"

"Charlotte was holding me and Emilia at one of her other properties. The one north of Denton. When Emilia and I escaped, we ran into him. He helped us get away from Jack. I kept asking him what he was doing there, and he wouldn't give me a straight answer. He was miles and miles from his caverns. He was looking for you, and the only way he would have known about Charlotte's other properties is if he'd been a member of the Sanctuary. A long-time member. After he had served his sentence for killing his wife, he didn't walk off into the woods. He joined the Sanctuary. But he was too violent, too volatile. Charlotte made him leave, didn't she?"

Maya nodded. She walked over, edging around Michael's body. She reached down and lifted his shirt until Josie saw the symbol of the Sanctuary just below his left rib cage. "He found me here. He wanted to teach me a lesson after I framed him. It was bad at first. He was very angry."

She pulled at the hems of her shorts, revealing deep black bruises on her inner thighs. "Eventually he calmed down. But I knew I couldn't get rid of him or outrun him. We're still in the middle of damn nowhere out here."

"The game was up," Josie said.

Maya stared down at her ex-lover, her ex-abuser. "Yes," she said softly.

Josie motioned for the rest of her team to come closer. "Maya," she said. "Deputy Moore is here. This is his jurisdiction."

Maya watched, expressionless, as everyone filed in and Deputy Moore stepped forward. He read her Miranda rights and when he pulled out his cuffs, she offered up her wrists. In that motion, Josie thought she saw a degree of relief. So much running, so much deceit. Now it was over.

Before Moore led her away, Josie went over to her, leaned in and said, "Did you ever get in touch with that dark side that Jack and Charlotte always went on about?"

Maya looked past Josie to Michael once more. "What do you think?"

CHAPTER SIXTY-ONE

Josie pushed a small table against one of the walls in her kitchen. Once it was in place, she unplugged the toaster oven and carried it over to the table. Relieved that it fit just right, she stood back and surveyed it, trying to decide if it would look better elsewhere in the kitchen. No, she decided. It was perfect right there. She heard the front door open and close. Hearing Noah moving around, she waited for him to come into the kitchen. After a few minutes, she called for him.

"Just a minute," he said.

A minute went by, then another. "Noah," Josie said.

He came in then, his face flushed. He almost had a look about him like a child who'd been caught doing something wrong. Josie raised a brow. "What's going on?"

"There's something I need you to see."

"There's something I need *you* to see," she replied. She pointed at the table with the toaster oven on top of it. "Ta da! Not only do you get to keep the toaster oven, but it has its own space now."

Noah laughed. He walked over, gathered her in his arms and kissed her. "I love you."

"I know that," she said.

He gazed down into her eyes. "But?"

She pushed away from him, but he didn't let her go.

"I saw the way you looked at Baby Bestler."

His brow furrowed. "What? Josie, what are you talking about?"

She pushed again and this time, he let her go. The words were a struggle to get out. She wasn't good at talking about her feelings.

Still, she peeled each word from her psyche like she was picking at a scab. "I want to be enough for you."

"What?"

"Oh God, don't make me repeat it."

He stepped forward and took one of her hands. "Josie, you are enough for me."

"How do you know?"

He laughed and placed her hand over his heart. "Because I know," he said simply.

"But you spent every spare second at the hospital with that baby. What if you want a baby? What if I don't want a baby? What if it's not something we can resolve or agree on? Kids? That's not something you agree to disagree on. You either want them or you don't, and I don't know if I want them. What if I don't and you do? Then what?"

He patted her hand. "Josie."

"I just—how do we know this is going to work? You couldn't tear yourself away from that baby. Every time I turned around you were gone, and I'd say, 'Where did Noah go?' and someone would say you went to the hospital to check on Baby Bestler."

"Josie."

"I don't know—"

"Josie!"

She looked at him, silenced.

He pulled her toward the living room. "I have something I need you to see."

Puzzled, she let him guide her through the foyer and into the living room where a large brown, lidless box sat on the coffee table. "I wasn't with Baby Bestler. I mean, not all of those times. Most of the times I took off, I said I was going to check on the baby, but I was really on the phone or meeting with this woman, Phyllis."

Josie snatched her hand from his. "Are you trying to tell me you're having an affair?"

He laughed again. "No." He reached into the box. "Phyllis is with the Northeast Boston Terrier Rescue." He lifted out a small ball of black and white fur with the most soulful brown eyes that Josie had ever seen. The dog had a handsome, slightly smooshy face, and ears that made perfect triangles. Noah looked from the dog to Josie. "This is Trout," he said.

Josie smiled. "Trout?"

"Yes, a dog named after a fish." Noah set him down on the floor. "He's three years old. He had to be rehomed because his owners fell on hard financial times and had to move to a place where they couldn't have dogs. He's already house-trained."

Trout looked up at Josie and sat down, staring up at her as if waiting for her to tell him what to do. She dropped to the floor and scratched beneath his chin. "Hi buddy," she whispered.

She crossed her legs and scratched between his ears. Tentatively, he moved closer to her. Then he climbed into her lap, circled and lay down, giving a contented sigh. Josie stroked his soft back. Noah got down on the floor, crossing his own legs and sitting directly across from her. He leaned in to her until their foreheads touched. Josie looked down at the warm bundle between them. "You're home, little buddy," she said. "You're home."

EPILOGUE

Trout ran through the woods, his nose twitching at the myriad of smells. Every few feet he would stop to sniff the base of a tree or the leaves of a plant, but he couldn't stay still for long. His little behind shook with excitement. Occasionally, he would stop and look back at Josie, his ears raised to perfect points, his eyes wide and bright.

"It's okay, boy," she would tell him and off he would race once more. She had outfitted him with a red bandana so that he was easy to spot in the forest. But he never went too far from her. In the short time they'd been owner and dog, Josie had learned that Trout was extremely smart and that his previous owner had trained him very well. She used a leash when they were in the city limits, but out in the woods, she let him run free.

She caught up to him as he sniffed a thatch of foxtail, huffing and shifting Lila's urn from her left hip to her right. Overhead, clouds turned the sky a slate gray. The cool morning air had given way to warmer temperatures, but Josie was relieved that the cloying humidity of August was finally gone. Soon, fall would be in full swing, and the lush green trees around them would turn to a panorama of golds, oranges, and reds.

Trout looked up from the foxtail and stared at her, as if waiting for instruction or permission to keep running. "We're almost there," she told him. His head tilted as he listened to her words. Then he trotted off, deeper into the forest.

Josie heard the rush of water before the creek appeared. Her boots squished in the mud as she stepped up to the bank. Trout stepped up onto a nearby stone and watched her. She watched the water rush along. "This is it," she told the dog.

She twisted the cap of the urn until it came free. Slowly, she tipped the contents into the waters of Cold Heart Creek. Trout lifted his snout and scented the air. When she finished, Josie put the cap back on the urn and tucked it beneath her arm. Trout sidled up beside her leg and gave a low, mournful whine. Josie smiled and squatted next to him, scratching the top of his head. He extended his neck and licked her cheek. "I'm okay, Trout. Everything's going to be okay."

She stood and turned back the way they had come. Shafts of sunlight burst through the canopy of trees, dappling the forest with light. A big orange monarch butterfly fluttered past, weaving in and out of the sun's rays. Trout raced after it and Josie followed.

A LETTER FROM LISA

Thank you so much for choosing to read *Cold Heart Creek*. It was such a pleasure to bring you another adventure featuring Josie Quinn. If you enjoyed it and want to keep up to date with all my latest releases, just sign up at the following link. Your email address will never be shared, and you can unsubscribe at any time.

www.bookouture.com/lisa-regan

While I have to take creative liberties with many things for purposes of plot and pacing, you should know that Northeast Boston Terrier Rescue and Search and Rescue Dogs of Pennsylvania are real organizations doing vitally important work. I hope you'll look them up and find ways to support them. Also, there is no Route 9227 in Pennsylvania. Like Denton, as well as Alcott and Lenore Counties, I made that up.

I love hearing from readers. You can get in touch with me through any of the social media outlets below, including my website and Goodreads page. Also, if you are up for it, I'd really appreciate it if you'd leave a review and perhaps recommend *Cold Heart Creek* to other readers. Reviews and word-of-mouth recommendations go a long way in helping readers discover my books for the first time. As always, thank you so much for your support. It means the world to me. I can't wait to hear from you, and I hope to see you next time!

Thanks,
Lisa Regan

LisaReganCrimeAuthor

@LisalRegan

www.lisaregan.com

ACKNOWLEDGEMENTS

Fabulous readers and devoted fans, I cannot thank you enough! Your relentless passion for this series is a precious gift. I can't believe we're on Book 7! Thank you so much for taking this journey with me. You are truly the best readers in the world!

Thank you, as always, to my husband, Fred, and my daughter, Morgan, for all your patience and support. Thank you to my first readers: Dana Mason, Katie Mettner, Nancy S. Thompson, Maureen Downey, Torese Hummel, Ann Bresnan, and Karen Powell. Thank you to my Entrada readers. Thank you to the usual suspects for all your support and love: Donna House, William and Joyce Regan, Rusty and Julie House, Carrie Butler, Ava McKittrick, Melissia McKittrick, Andrew Brock, Christine and Kevin Brock, Laura Aiello, Helen Conlen, Jean and Dennis Regan, Debbie Tralies, Sean and Cassie House, Marilyn House, Tracy Dauphin, Dee Kay, Stacy Stanley, Jeanne Cassidy, Michael Infinito Jr., Jeff O'Handley, Fred and Debbie Bowman, Susan Sole, Claire Pacell, Tanya Veitch, Tanya Anderson, Rebecca Squires, the Funk family, the Tralies family, the Conlen family, the Regan family, the House family, the McDowells, the Bottingers, and the Kays. Thank you to Jaime Kelly and Renee Crabill for sacrificing themselves! Thank you to the lovely people at Table 25 for your wisdom, support, and good humor. Thank you to Cindy Doty. I'd also like to thank all the lovely bloggers and reviewers who read the first six Josie Quinn books for continuing to read the series and to enthusiastically recommend it to your readers!

Thank you so very much to Sgt. Jason Jay for your unwavering patience in answering all my law-enforcement questions at every hour of the day and night. I am so incredibly grateful to you!

Thank you to Vicki and Chuck Wooters, as well as Rini and Quake, of Search and Rescue Dogs of Pennsylvania for your incredible instruction and for letting us come out and watch you work your magic with your amazing dogs.

Thank you to David Alford, Paul Bishop, and Andy Parker, instructors at the Writers' Police Academy's Murdercon 2019 whose classes helped me with vital pieces of this book. It was humbling to learn from you!

Thank you to Oliver Rhodes, Noelle Holten, Kim Nash, Jennie and the entire team at Bookouture for making this fantastic journey both possible and the most fun I've ever had in my life. Thank you to Caolinn Douglas for your spot-on insight. Last but certainly not least, thank you to the incomparable Jessie Botterill for your amazing work and input on this book. I've said it before but it's still true: I could not and would not want to do this without you.

Made in the USA
Coppell, TX
07 August 2021